IN THE
BLEAK
MIDWINTER

Carol Rivers, whose family comes from the Isle of Dogs, East London, now lives in Dorset. Visit her website at www.carolrivers.com

Also by Carol Rivers

Lizzie of Langley Street
Rose of Ruby Street
Connie of Kettle Street
Bella of Bow Street
Lily of Love Lane
Eve of the Isle
East End Angel

IN THE
BLEAK
MIDWINTER

CAROL
RIVERS

**SIMON &
SCHUSTER**

London · New York · Sydney · Toronto · New Delhi

A CBS COMPANY

This is for you, Stan, and
the Buffs

First published in Great Britain by Simon & Schuster, 2011
An imprint of Simon & Schuster UK
A CBS COMPANY

5 7 9 10 8 6

Simon & Schuster UK Ltd
1ˢᵗ Floor
222 Gray's Inn Road
London WC1X 8HB

www.simonandschuster.co.uk

Simon & Schuster Australia, Sydney
Simon & Schuster India, New Delhi

A CIP catalogue record for this book is available from the British Library

ISBN: 978-1-47112-715-1

Typeset in Bembo by Hewer Text UK Ltd
Printed and bound by CPI Group (UK) Ltd, Croydon, CR0 4YY

Acknowledgements

Go to Adrian Bramley, Haras Ullah and Teresa Cann for their help, hard work and enthusiasm in providing a valiant and comprehensive Home Library Service, without which some of us would never enjoy the life-giving world of books. To Connie Rothman and all the staff at Southbourne library – this year celebrating 85 stoic years of opening its door to the public – thank you for your support and encouragement! To Rachel, Barry, Ethan and Samuel, a big hug for always being there.

Thanks to Big C, whose adventurous love of all things digital, I completely rely on. And as always, I am deeply grateful to readers who take the time to write or email me, visit my website, review on Amazon or to post to Facebook and Twitter. You are the tops!

Once again, to Maxine, Emma, and the team of amazing guys at Simon & Schuster and to my great agent Dorothy Lumley, thank you for a wonderful year!

Chapter 1

November 1918

Birdie Connor gazed critically into the rust-speckled mirror nailed to her sewing room wall. Had she arranged her deep brown finger-waves a little too frivolously? Did the cheeky bow on her pale green dress seem a trifle over-done? She'd have to wear a coat, of course, as it was cold, with a cutting wind blowing over the roofs of the East End's dilapidated houses.

There was little about the island on which she lived – a shambles of docks and wharfs, which curved into a horse-shoe of land, sticking out into the great River Thames – to cause a girl much excitement over a stroll. For on a Sunday, even the river was still, the boats and barges and tall goose-necked cranes idle. Only the taverns cheered the men's spirits, but gave little encouragement to their families. A man's wage could be drunk in the space of an hour and, stumbling home, he'd probably not remember his starving children until he fell in the door and gazed into their hungry faces.

But, Birdie was quick to reflect, luckily this was not the case with the Connor family of March Street. Their lives depended not on the docks or the factories huddled around them, but on her skill to sew, and the few extra pennies she earned as a landlady. Nor could the bleak midwinter weather dim her excitement in the least. For today, she and Donald Thorne, the man she hoped soon to marry, planned to spend an entire day together. A perfect miracle, in Birdie's estimation.

Pinching her cheeks to bring out their pinkness, Birdie reflected that a touch of rouge wouldn't go amiss. And it was all the rage to have curved, thin eyebrows to accentuate a powdered face, just like Mary Pickford, the film star. But Don had never approved of make-up, though she had to admit that once or twice she'd given in to temptation and used the lipstick that Lady Hailing, her very best customer, had given her.

'Birdie?' Fourteen-year-old Patrick Connor, her younger brother, cautiously poked his head round the door. 'I'm off to meet Willie.'

'Willie, is it?' Birdie teased as he entered, giving him a curious glance. 'Now would you be telling your sister the truth? Why would you not be walking out some pretty young lady, I wonder? For just look at the height of you – growing taller by the day. And with good, clean looks to set you apart from the average, too.'

'You won't catch me courting!' Pat exclaimed disdainfully. 'Girls don't interest me one bit.'

'That's not what you'll be saying in a few years' time. Just wait till you fancy your first girl. Believe me, she'll take up all your thinking time, as well as what's in your pocket.'

Pat shook his head fiercely, causing a lock of auburn-coloured hair to flop over his eyes. 'Females ain't for me, Birdie. I'm going to travel the world and make me fortune first.'

'The world, is it now? A messenger boy since September and he thinks he's Christopher Columbus.'

'I might join the navy, even.'

'And so you might,' Birdie agreed, folding away her rolls of fabric before Pat could lay a grubby hand on them.

'Or sail up the Nile on a barge,' he mused as he sat down on her sewing chair. 'And see them pyramids.'

'Now that's an idea.'

'Or work a passage to Australia. Shoot a few dingoes.'

'And all you'd need to take with you is a solid pair of boots,' Birdie nodded as she rescued a length of cotton

2

gingham from the table nearby. 'I hear Australia don't call for many warm clothes. Just decent footwear to stop the snakes and spiders from biting.'

'I ain't afraid of spiders and snakes.' This was said with defiance, but Birdie heard a trace of doubt too. 'I'm not afraid of anything. Long as it's not wearing a skirt.'

Birdie laughed. With Patrick's shock of auburn-brown hair – a trait of the Irish Kennedys, their mother's side of the family – and his athletic figure and twinkling brown eyes, he was already beginning to fill out to handsome proportions.

But she didn't tease him today as her mind was on other, more important things. Was this dress really suitable for a brisk walk to Poplar and a tram ride to Aldgate? And what sort of restaurant would they be dining in? Although the shops were closed, Don had said they might stop for a bite to eat under the shadow of St Paul's. And in Birdie's book that meant gloves and a hat, a look to make her tiny five-foot-three-inch figure just a fraction taller. But now she was having her doubts about the dress. Should she have cut the material on the bias? Or created an even lower, more subtle dropped waist? But then, if she didn't wear this one, what would she wear? Navy-blue skirts and white blouses, her neat uniform for seeing her dressmaking and mending clients, simply wouldn't pass muster.

At last, after several turns and twirls, Birdie decided the dress was satisfactory, if not quite perfect. It would have helped, of course, if she'd had decent shoes, not this old pair with a buttoned-strap, and newspaper stuck inside. But, beggars couldn't be choosers. Although, Birdie reminded herself sternly, she wasn't on the steps of the workhouse yet!

'Birdie, are you listening?'

She nodded distractedly.

'You aren't, I know you aren't.'

'I am indeed,' she insisted, her mind still on the doubtful footwear.

'I just saw Don. I was riding me bicycle up East India Dock Road and he was off to church with the two Mrs Ts and little Jamie. Called out that I was to tell you it'd be this afternoon, after his dinner, before he was round.'

'This afternoon?' Birdie gasped. 'But he said he was to call this morning.'

'Seems like he changed his mind.'

'Are you sure?'

'As sure as my name's Pat Connor.'

Birdie shook her head in confusion. Ever since Don's father had died last year from the flu, their plans had been set to one side. Not that she didn't understand Don's predicament. It was only right, she'd told herself a hundred times over, that with the loss of his brother, Stephen, at Passchendaele, and his father a year later, he should attend to his own affairs first. Aggie, his mother, and Lydia, his sister-in-law, both ending up as widows in the space of eighteen months – well, it was a tragedy, to be sure. But life had to go on. And Birdie couldn't help feeling left out.

Why, wasn't it only a few weeks ago – and only through Don's urging – that the two women had put away their widow's weeds? Even Birdie had to admit that Lydia could be a very presentable young woman when she tried, and had every chance of marrying again; an event that Birdie was praying would take place very soon, and relieve Don of the burden of Lydia and little James's care.

'So he was with Mrs Thorne and Lydia, was he?' Birdie pondered again. 'And what would they be wearing? Sunday-best church clothes, was it?'

'And big hats with feathers, all dolled up to the nines,' remarked Pat with a smirk.

Birdie rolled her eyes. 'You know what I mean, you cheeky devil.'

But Pat only shrugged. 'Mrs T was on one arm and the young missus on the other.'

'Oh,' murmured Birdie disappointedly. Not that she minded Lydia being on his arm, not at all. In fact she was glad he'd given the poor girl his company whilst she'd been grieving. But she was missing Don's arm herself now and had expected to be leaning on it today.

Still, she was lucky indeed to have even half a day with Don. Many a man – certainly a hard-working shopkeeper like Don, who put in all the hours God sent, as well as caring for his family – would be taking full advantage of a rest on a Sunday. And she didn't begrudge him his church-going, no, not at all. But Aggie's Sunday dinners were proper performances. They could last an eternity! Not a mutton stew or cold meat and a finger of cheese, like Birdie made, but a real joint, running freely with fat and juices, and vegetables of at least three varieties crammed on the plate, with thick brown gravy to drown the golden potatoes. Birdie knew all this because she had been invited to dinner once or twice when Aggie had been of a mind to entertain. Birdie sighed softly as she considered Aggie and the family she was soon to be part of. She was grateful for Aggie's occasional invitations; the busy routine of the store did not allow for many social events and Birdie felt honoured to be welcomed into the fold.

'Never mind,' Pat said cheerfully, 'a man's got to do the right thing by his own. Them Thornes have got knees hard as pokers from all the praying they do. Can even beat us Catholics, I reckon.'

Birdie smiled. 'S'pose I can't expect miracles.'

'Speaking of miracles, why don't you go over to Flo's? Take those noisy kids of hers to Mass. I'll stay with Dad.'

Birdie shook her head. 'They'll have left for Mass already.'

Flo Sparks was her best friend and lived just round the corner in Ayle Street. Sometimes they went to the early

Mass together, but Birdie had already told her that she was spending today with Don.

'I've plenty to do here,' she shrugged, unwinding a long, red, fox fur from a box. 'There's this poor dead beast to stitch to Lady Hailing's coat and two hems yet to be altered. I had it in mind to finish them this evening, but now the morning is all me own.'

'Fancy wearing that!'

'All the country ladies favour these.'

'Why are them ladies so rich,' Pat demanded, 'and us so poor?'

'It's just a fact of life, love.'

'It's not fair, that's what I think.'

'Pat Connor!' Birdie warned gently. 'We're lucky to have breath in our bodies after the war the world has just been through. Haven't you just landed yourself a grand job? And ain't we got a nice lodger to help out with the rent? And don't I get a few nice cast-offs from the ladies?'

'I know that, Birdie, and I ain't ungrateful. All the same, I don't expect it matters to the ladies of Hailing House that you're always sewing, even on a Sunday, until your eyes nearly pop out your head. Bet they don't even know how to sew a button on.'

'I should hope they don't or else I should have no work. And I'm always mindful that it was at the sewing classes at Hailing House that I learned my skill as a child. And that skill is still serving me well.' Birdie smiled into his big brown Connor eyes, the same shade as her own, though the shine in them was definitely their mother's. Time, however, was beginning to dim even Birdie's memory, for at eleven she had been no more than a child herself when Bernadette Connor had died giving birth to Pat. A kindly neighbour had helped with the baby until Birdie had left school at thirteen and was able to take over his care. But now, more than ever, Birdie wished with all her heart that Bernadette was here to answer Pat's many questions.

'Still don't think it's fair,' he grumbled again. 'Just like putting our Frank behind bars isn't fair.'

At this Birdie was silent, for she agreed wholeheartedly. She couldn't bear to think of their older brother in prison. The army had called him a deserter, but Birdie refused to accept that was so.

'Do you believe our Frank done what they said he did?' persisted Pat, the pink flush of boyhood still on his cheeks.

'No, I don't,' Birdie admitted. 'Frank is no coward.'

'Dad says he let the King down.'

'Dad is a proud man,' Birdie responded carefully, loyal to both her father and brother. 'If things had been different he would have volunteered for the front line, even at his age. And now he is ailing worse, his pride is taking a knock, for all his life he's toiled to keep home and family together. But this is a very grown-up thing to understand, Pat, although the matter may seem clear-cut to you.'

'I'll never believe our Frank ran away,' said Pat stoutly. 'And I ain't far off from being grown up.'

'And proud of you, so I am, Pat.' Birdie's heart clenched with love for her little brother, now almost a head and shoulders taller than she.

'Down the docks, the men say all deserters should be shot.'

'Nonsense!' Birdie exclaimed. 'That's ignorance talking. I reckon our Frank should've got a medal, not a court martial.'

'Even old Charlie Makepiece down the road shouted out a rude name when I cycled by.'

'That's because he's half barmy with drink,' Birdie said, thinking that she'd have something to say herself to Charlie about his cussing and bawling loud enough to wake the dead on his way home from the pub.

Pat drew his cuff across his nose and sniffed. 'So it's not true that our mum turned in her grave for what Frank did?'

'Course not!' exclaimed Birdie furiously. 'Did the buggers say that, an' all?' Pat looked away guiltily, but Birdie caught his arm. 'Now listen to me, Patrick Connor, this is God's truth I'm telling you. For a start, Mum ain't in her grave. She left it a long time ago to watch over us. And you can be sure of this: our mum would have been the first to stand up for our Frank.'

'Do you think so?'

'Indeed I do.'

Pat scratched his head. 'But our dad says he's never speaking to Frank again.'

'Time is a great healer,' answered Birdie, although privately she was a little fed up herself of waiting for their father to relent. 'Meanwhile, as there's nothing we can say just yet to change Dad's mind, you must remember that it was Mum who said to be proud of our family, and the Kennedy pride is what I'm passing on to you this very moment.'

Birdie reached out to comfort him; it wasn't often that Pat spoke as he had today. He had always been a happy child, despite being motherless.

'I've got to oil me bicycle and polish me boots for tomorrow's rounds,' he muttered, pulling away and banging the door after him so that even the walls seemed to shudder.

Birdie sat quietly, lost in thought. Both Pat and Don were of equal importance in her heart, though selfishly, it was Don's reluctance to name the day that concerned her the most. And how would she, Birdie, fit in with the Thornes when they were married? She was a cradle-born Catholic and Don a regular-as-clockwork churchgoer. And although Don had not contested a Roman wedding, Birdie knew of Aggie's disapproval.

Also the question of where they would live had not yet been settled. The Thornes kept a general store in Poplar. Don had suggested that, after they were married, Birdie give up her dressmaking and assist Lydia and Aggie in the shop. But try as she may, Birdie couldn't fancy serving customers with such unromantic things as strong-smelling cheese and bacon and Lifebuoy soap and pickles. Neither could she warm much to Lydia, who counted every penny taken, twice over. Little James was a darling boy, the very image of his dead father, Stephen. But Lydia and Aggie watched over him like hawks.

Birdie sighed again. She would much rather they lived here, in March Street, so she could continue with her business and keep an eye on her father and brother. Besides, there was far more space in the tall Victorian building she had grown up in. Granted, the place was considerably dilapidated and smoke-blackened, but a few repairs here and there would soon put things right.

Her mind preoccupied with the problem, Birdie hurried downstairs. In the parlour, she cast a critical eye over the high, plaster-peeling ceilings and shabby walls. If only she could make it a little more enticing, then surely Don would see her point of view? Since Frank had been conscripted in 1916, the house had gone slowly downhill.

New curtains were badly needed for the sash windows. The big dresser required more than one coat of polish, and was that a crack just beginning over the upright piano? And what more mending could she do to the carpet that was so threadbare you could see the lines of the bare boards beneath? But money was scarce, and she began to consider how she would stretch her income this week. A full two-and-sixpence was coming her way tomorrow, when the ladies of Hailing House were to collect the coat and two dresses. Then there was the four-and-six due from their lodger, Harry Chambers. All in all, with the three shillings

Pat would provide from his wage, she would have enough for the rent and a shilling spare for the gas. This still left the larder, but somehow she would make ends meet.

Just then, Wilfred Connor walked in. Dressed in his crumpled Sunday suit and best shirt, he closed the door quietly behind him. 'What's up with the young 'un, lass? Run past me as though he had a match under his arse.' Heavy brows creased into a bushy grey curve as he stood warming his hands over the fire.

'He's got an oiling job to do,' Birdie explained, although through the window she had just seen Pat scoot off on his bicycle to see Willie Mason. 'For his rounds tomorrow.'

'Let's hope that job don't go to his head,' muttered Wilfred as the wheeze from his chest erupted and the rough rasp followed.

'Sit down, Dad. I'll bring your medicine.'

'Fat lot of good it'll do an' all,' coughed Wilfred, collapsing in the chair. 'I'd be better off going down the Quarry for me pint.'

Birdie didn't bother to reply but went to the scullery, where a strong smell of disinfectant clung to the walls, the only deterrent to the scuttling roaches.

Birdie took the bottle of J Collis Browne's Mixture from the shelf and Wilfred frowned in distaste as he swallowed the unpleasant dose. At fifty-two years of age, too old to serve in the forces and now suffering with his health, her father was nevertheless a proud man. So she was not in the least surprised at his reply.

'Thanks, ducks. Climbed out of bed the wrong side this morning. When I get me breath back, I'll go out and give the backyard a sweep.'

Birdie knew that climbing out of bed the wrong side had nothing to do with the coughing fit. And despite him being determined to keep active, he was often thwarted in his efforts, for the cold winter months had brought him very low. After years of inhaling the gases from the chemical factory where he'd worked, he was now retired, the poisonous fumes having taken their toll.

'So when is Donald calling?' he managed to ask.

'Pat saw him walking Aggie and Lydia to church. So it'll not be till this afternoon.'

'A good man to do his best by them women. You'll do well as his wife, Brigid. Just as long as you settle the matter of your children being raised as regular Catholics.'

Birdie was tempted to say that she'd never be married at all if children were to be taken into consideration. She knew it would not please Aggie one bit to see her grandchildren on their knees to the Virgin Mary.

'A sad pity that Don's father had to die last year,' Wilfred continued, coughing slightly. 'And Don then having to leave a good job like he had on the railways and go into the business. Had he lived, Ted Thorne would have been proud of his two sons. Both the one that lived and the other that died.' Wilfred shook his head gloomily. 'I only wish I could boast pride of me own elder son.'

Birdie's cheeks flushed. She hated it when their father spoke about Frank in this way. 'We don't know exactly what happened,' she protested. 'The Army never gave us a chance to see Frank.'

'What are you saying, Brigid?' Wilfred's mouth tightened as he looked up.

'It's just that we ain't heard his side of—'

'I'd have any man abide by the laws of his country,' Wilfred cut in angrily. 'There is no excuse for disappearing from the battlefield and turning up after the action is over!'

'But, Dad, our Frank—'

'Not another word, girl!' shouted her father, beginning to cough and going red in the face.

Birdie patted his back, demanding of herself why she couldn't keep a still tongue in her head for once. Hadn't

11

she only just a minute ago warned Pat to do the same? Sure, she had her own fierce opinion on men being needlessly slaughtered in their thousands, but this wasn't the time to voice it.

'Don't fuss, leave me be.' Breathless and gasping, Wilfred turned away.

Silently Birdie sank to her knees and shovelled the last of the coal on the fire. The scuttle was empty and very little coal was left. Just as she picked up the bellows to encourage them to light, her father sat forward, his body and face contorting as he coughed.

'Dad, are you all right?'

Wilfred didn't seem to hear her as he coughed and gasped for breath, his eyes staring blindly into space. She dropped the bellows and went to him. A trail of spit rolled out from his mouth and Birdie gasped as he twisted this way and that, wrestling himself from her grasp. She ran outside in the hope that Pat was within calling distance, but neither her brother nor his bicycle were to be seen. Her heart pounding in fright, she rushed back, only to find that her father had collapsed on the floor.

Chapter 2

Birdie had never seen her father so ill. He lay shaking and jerking, with his eyes rolling upward.

'Dad, what's wrong?' she cried, trying to make him hear her. But there was no response as he continued to choke and splutter, his face deathly pale. What was she to do? If she ran for the doctor, she would have to leave him alone. Birdie knew she must stay close, yet she had no power to help him.

'Birdie? What's going on?'

She looked up to see the tall lean figure of Harry Chambers, their lodger. 'Oh, thank God you've come home, Harry!' she blurted as he hurried from the passage and kneeled beside her. 'Dad's taken a turn and I can't rouse him . . . oh, Harry, what shall I do?'

Harry swept off his cloth cap and threw it aside, then unslung his work-bag from his shoulder. 'When did this happen?' he asked, his weather-beaten brow furrowed in concern.

'A few moments ago . . . he began coughing and choking and looking all queer. So I called for Pat outside but he'd gone. And when I came back Dad was—'

'Steady now, girl, let's have a look at him.'

Gently, he lifted Wilfred's head and slipped a cushion beneath. For a moment Wilfred's eyes opened wide, as if in recognition, and Birdie called his name, hoping he might speak. But very soon he began to twist and turn again despite Harry's firm restraint.

'What's wrong with him, Harry? Why is he acting like this? I'd only just given him his medicine and he started to cough, but not normal like. I tried to help him but it was as though he didn't hear or see me.'

'It looks like a seizure,' Harry muttered as he held Wilfred's arms. 'I've seen them before, in the army.'

'A seizure? But why?' Birdie asked in distress.

'I can't say; I'm no medical man,' Harry shrugged. 'But one thing I do know is we must stop him from harming himself.' He looked around. 'Give me the spoon from the mantel there.'

Birdie grasped the spoon, still sticky with linctus. 'Do you want the linctus too?'

'No, just the spoon. It will stop him from biting his tongue.'

Birdie turned away, unable to witness her father's distress

13

as Harry gently slid the spoon between Wilfred's agitated lips.

Birdie sat in the chair beside her father's bed. She watched Harry loosen the laces of her father's boots, relief filling her as Wilfred seemed calm again. If it had not been for Harry, she dreaded to think what might have happened. But the spoon had prevented an accident and the seizure had gradually left his thin body. Then, taking Wilfred's light weight, Harry had assisted him upstairs to the safety of the bedroom.

'How are you feeling Dad?' Birdie asked as Harry placed the boots under the bed and folded the counterpane over him.

Her father nodded slowly as he rested his head on the pillow. 'Not bad, girl.'

'I think the worst is over, Mr Connor, but you should see a doctor.'

At this, Wilfred stirred sharply. 'No, lad. No!'

'But it would be for the best.'

'It won't happen again,' insisted Wilfred, coughing. 'I just need a bit of shut-eye.'

Birdie took her father's cold hand and, seeing the fear in his eyes, said softly, 'I'll do as you ask and not call the doctor this time, Dad.'

Wilfred smiled weakly. 'It was just a touch of the ague, lass. I'll have forty winks and be up on me feet in no time at all. Now draw them curtains and leave me be.'

Birdie's knees were still trembling as she drew the heavy drapes and followed Harry downstairs.

'I've never seen him so bad, nor ever want to again,' she admitted as they stood in the kitchen. 'Goodness knows what I would have done if you hadn't come home, Harry.' She nodded to the table. 'Sit down for a moment, won't you, and I'll make us a brew?'

As Birdie boiled the water, she couldn't help wondering if it was the talk of Frank that had brought Wilfred's seizure on. In trying to defend Frank, had she made things worse? With Wilfred believing that his son's cowardice had caused him to desert his post on the front line, there seemed nothing she could say to change his mind. The court had given its verdict and Frank had been pronounced a deserter. He had been sentenced to prison, bringing shame on himself and his family. Had their father forgotten that when their mother had died, Frank had been the strong shoulder to lean on? At sixteen, with baby Pat to care for, he'd done all he could to help her when his work in the docks allowed. He had been their breadwinner and protector, whilst Wilfred had been grieving, too wrapped up in his sorrow to care. It was Frank who had taken responsibility for the family and raised Pat. Birdie had never believed that her brother was capable of any crime, let alone desertion.

'That tea you're stirring will be getting too giddy to flow from the spout,' Harry chuckled, sliding his hand through his wild black hair.

'Oh!' Birdie blushed as she came back to the present. 'What am I doing?'

'Here, let me help. Sit down and rest awhile.'

Birdie sank gratefully to the chair as Harry set out the mugs, poured the tea and placed the cosy over the pot. Birdie saw how burned brown his skin was, even in winter. No doubt this was from his service in the Middle East during the war. Even now he was out in all weathers, doing back-breaking work on the roads. The whites of his eyes were very bright and seemed to gleam like his straight, even teeth. He was a pleasant young man but without much desire to smarten his appearance. Unlike Don, she found herself comparing proudly. Don, her beau, who was the neatest and most dapper man she had ever known! Yet Harry seemed unconcerned about his looks. Perhaps it was because he seemed to have no girl in his life? He was barely thirty years old and had been eager to rejoin his regiment earlier in the year, but the bout of the jaundice that had interrupted his service lingered until the end of the war. Birdie always felt it was to the Connors' good fortune that the armistice had been called and Harry had remained with them instead as a well-paying and trustworthy lodger.

'I owe you me thanks, Harry,' Birdie said quietly as he took the chair beside her. 'Are you certain it was a seizure?'

Harry nodded. 'A pal of mine in the Buffs went this way as a result of the shock and upset of the shelling.'

'Shock and upset? Oh, so it might have been the words we had over Frank that set him off!' she exclaimed helplessly.

Harry looked at her for some while before speaking. 'Your father spoke only once to me of your brother. It was on the day I came to enquire after lodgings. He told me his son had been sentenced as a deserter. Said it might change my feelings towards lodging here, and he'd understand if I looked elsewhere.'

'Harry, that's the first I've heard of it.'

'Your father is a fair man, Birdie. He made the case plain, so there should be no misunderstanding. But I told him it was no business of mine. I was grateful for a roof over my head in a decent house and with a decent family. In my opinion the war is past and should be set to rest.'

'A grand way of thinking,' said Birdie admiringly, wondering what Don would have to say about such a rare sentiment. Although Don hadn't served in the war as he had done essential work on the underground railways, he was of the same mind as her father. She felt resigned to the fact now that Don went along with the general view of deserting, yet it was still a bone of contention between them. The Thornes were a proud family. Birdie knew that they had lost Stephen in battle, and both Aggie and Lydia stood taller for his sacrifice, making Frank's desertion look even more disgraceful.

'Where is Frank now?' Harry asked after a moment.

Birdie found it a strange thing indeed to be talking about her brother so freely. It was only between her and Pat he was mentioned and then in whispers.

'He wrote once or twice from Wandsworth. But his letters stopped when our dad wouldn't hear of me visiting him.'

'So you don't share your father's opinion?' Harry asked.

'Frank was my guardian angel when our mum died. Though he was only sixteen, barely five years older than me, I reckon he saved us from destitution,' Birdie explained, a pain across her heart as she remembered. 'He brought in a good wage from the docks, and paid a neighbour to look after Pat till I left school. Me dad didn't have much left in him after he came home from the chemicals factory, stinking of their gases and still grieving for Mum.'

'Then Frank has my greatest respect,' answered Harry sincerely.

Birdie smiled sadly. 'You'll be the only living soul who's ever said a kind word about my brother.'

'What evidence did the Army have that he deserted?' asked Harry.

Birdie could only shrug. 'He was tried and found guilty. We was told he was lucky to have escaped the firing squad.'

'It's a true and shameful fact,' nodded Harry with a hitch to his soft voice, 'that many young men were mistaken for deserters and met their ends unjustly.'

Birdie had never shared such things with anyone before. It felt like a weight falling from her shoulders. 'I don't blame me dad for feeling the way he does,' she conceded. 'He went through a lot when Frank was put away. Ma Jenkins from number thirty-two was the first to say her four-penn'orth, going on about bad blood being in some families. And then there were the Carter sisters, gasbags both of them, who crossed the road to avoid him, their noses in the air. Though I've not let them get away with such bad behaviour and have stood in their way deliberate, like, with my arms across me chest and a fire in my eyes that lets 'em know Birdie Connor won't be ignored!'

Harry smiled. 'Good for you, Birdie.'

'And I'd have something to say to all the gossips that make young Pat's life a misery,' Birdie continued. 'But I can't fight his battles, much as I'm tempted.' Birdie looked up and nodded at the faded photograph on the mantel. It stood beside a small statue of the Virgin Mary, a wooden rosary draped round it. 'Our mum wouldn't want that. Pat has to prove himself as a man now.'

Harry followed her stare. 'A handsome woman, indeed.'

Birdie's eyes glowed with pride. 'It was taken in County Cork, Ireland where she was born. But there was no work there and so she came to London and met our dad. It was soon after they married that he got work at the chemical factory down by the docks. It was known to be a rotten job, and is what gave Dad his bad chest. But he kept at it, as there was nothing else better and he had a family to raise. Mum did sewing and cleaning, but it was barely enough to keep body and soul together. And when Mum died giving birth to Pat . . . well, our dad just gave up. He went in on himself like, and it was Frank who took over. Frank who kept us going and made more of a father to Pat than . . .' she sighed again, glancing up into Harry's thoughtful stare. 'And what about you, Harry?' she asked, regretting that she hadn't done so before. 'Your family?'

Harry's face clouded. 'Sadly, I have none.'

'What, none at all?'

'None that I know of.' He smiled too quickly. 'I'm the screaming scrap who was left on the orphanage doorstep, that's me. Newborn they said, and took me age from that day.'

'Oh, what a crime!' Birdie's voice softened with sadness. 'How could a mother do such a thing?'

'I've often wondered,' Harry said quietly. 'But over the years I've come to believe she may have been ill, or too young or poor to care for me. But she saw I was found, not left to the elements, and for that I'm thankful. And for the roof over me head that I was given at the orphanage, and turned me out with a thirst for freedom so fierce that I joined the navy at fourteen, a baker's scullion and saw places and people that many have never seen in a lifetime.'

'Oh, you are a decent man to think like that, Harry Chambers.'

He smiled cheerfully at her, the twist of his lips and twinkling eyes showing not a glimmer of self-pity. 'Well, now that you've heard me life's story I'd best be on me way,' he chuckled.

At the front door, he paused. 'You know where I am if you need me. Don't hesitate to knock.'

'Indeed, I won't,' Birdie assured him as he returned his cap to his head and left for his rooms below. When Birdie heard the airey door close, she glanced left and right in the hope that Pat would appear. But the street was empty, save for the children playing after Sunday school.

She shivered, gazing along March Street at the many tall, terraced, three-storeyed houses that were so blackened with soot and grime that even the dullest of lace curtains strung at the windows looked white. How lucky she and Frank had been to grow up as a family in this house, to know what it was like to have a mother and father, even though Bernadette's life had been cut short. Harry had never had a family or a home. Not even a slum tenement over at Blackwall, or a derelict cottage on one of the foreshores. Yet, not a word of complaint had ever dropped from his lips. And what would she have done without his help today?

Hugging herself, she went back in. All was silent and still. Could Harry be mistaken about these seizures? The only way to find out was to consult the doctor. But she knew Wilfred would not agree. After the shame brought on them by Frank, her father believed that people were eager to brand Wilfred Connor a malingerer, a pariah on society. Even though his poor health had been caused by the chemicals at the factory, he knew the sight of the doctor would give rise to gossip. Anything to confirm the fact that the Connors were cast in the same mould as their cowardly son.

Birdie went in to the parlour. A chill was setting in. She gazed from the window through the carefully darned curtains to the street and wondered if she might just have time to finish stitching a seam or two before Don arrived. At the thought of him, her heart leaped; a great comfort after what had happened to Wilfred.

It was late in the afternoon when Don finally arrived. Dressed in his dark blue Sunday-best suit, starched white shirt and neatly knotted tie, he was, as always, immaculately turned out. Not a hair on his head seemed out of place, the middle parting as straight as an arrow and his brown hair combed sleekly in a wave either side of the parting. He was an upright man and stood with his chest out and his shoulders back.

Birdie never tired of admiring his clean-shaven chin, and though he was not a great height, perhaps five foot nine or so, he had elegant shoulders and a straight back that took a good-quality cloth very well. It was his smart appearance that had caught her eye one day early in 1914, a few months before war broke out. Dressed in his guard's uniform, he had offered to carry her bags and Flo's to the train that was to take them to Finsbury Park, where Flo's aunt and uncle lived. They were to stay for a weekend, and had packed an enormous amount. He had smiled at her and talked in such a way that she had looked for him on their return journey. Fate had brought them together again, and when he told her that his family owned a store in Poplar, she had promised to shop there one day. And so their friendship had begun, to be interrupted by the war and its repercussions on their families, sometimes causing Birdie to doubt they would ever tie the knot.

He bent to peck Birdie's cheek. 'I thought we might walk to the park,' he said as Birdie led him into the parlour. 'And then to Greenwich, if there's time. It's a pity we don't have the day, but—'

'It was heaven-sent that we didn't go out this morning,' interrupted Birdie, her words spilling out in a rush. 'Sit down and I'll tell you what happened.'

Birdie saw a frown appear on Don's smooth, high forehead as he sat on the couch. She thought how handsome he was. His wide-set hazel eyes, more green today than brown, were filled with a pinch of surprise. How flattered she felt that he had made every effort to disengage himself from his own family in order to make time for her.

He looked critically at the hearth. 'Brigid, the fire has gone out.'

'We're rationed a little on the coal.'

'But the room is freezing.'

'My customer doesn't pay for the alterations until tomorrow. I'll see the coalman then.'

'But how is it you're always running short?'

Don shifted his position slightly in order to avoid the horsehair that leaked through a hole in the leather. They had had this conversation many times before. For some reason, Don's opinion of her management of the household expenses was not very high. He'd hinted that when they were married, he would expect a sharper degree of accounting. But Birdie knew she didn't overspend in the least. It was often a case of robbing Peter to pay Paul, as no two weeks ever tallied.

'Shall I make us a cup of tea?'

Don held out his hand. 'Brigid, come and join me.'

Eagerly she sat beside him. He bent and kissed her, his lips warm and inviting. 'I like your waves,' he murmured, 'though I can't imagine how long you spent in arranging them. Now, tell me all your news.'

'Well,' said Birdie slowly, blinking her long lashes in an effort not to try his patience, 'it happened so quickly and I've no idea why – no idea at all.' She placed her hand on her chest to calm herself and was glad to see that Don was still smiling. 'This morning, Dad dressed and came to sit by the fire.' She added quickly as she glanced at the lifeless embers, 'Almost a bonfire it was, an' all. Then suddenly he was coughing – no, not coughing, but heaving up his lungs. And his face was a dreadful colour, the shade of a sky full of thunder, and me heart started a dance in me chest as he was twisting and turning, sort of jerking, with his eyes rolling at the back of his head—'

Don put up his hand and laughed. 'Brigid, slow down. I can't keep up with you.'

At this little interruption, Birdie obediently took time to gulp a deep breath and clear her throat. 'Well, it was like this,' she faltered. 'I ran for Pat, so I did. But he was not to be seen. And then I saw Harry. And Harry came in and said it was a seizure. So we put a spoon in his mouth—'

'A spoon?' Don repeated with a frown.

'Yes, I didn't think of it meself. But it stops the tongue from being harmed, you see.'

'I think I see,' said Don, bending to kiss her brow. 'But how was your lodger to know this event was a seizure?'

Birdie tried to concentrate, as the little spot where Don

had kissed seemed to be tingling. 'It was dead lucky really. Harry had a friend in the services, a soldier who suffered the shell shock. He took on in just the same way, though don't ask me where they found the spoon in all the fighting.'

Don drew back his shoulders and smiled. 'You do have an imagination.'

'It's all true, I swear it.'

'What was the doctor's verdict when you called him?'

Guiltily Birdie twisted the bow on her dress. 'I'm afraid our dad refused to be seen.'

'Refused?' Don repeated, his eyes wide in disbelief. 'But why should he do that?'

'You know me dad don't like a fuss.'

He stared at her. 'But in this instance surely?'

Birdie had run out of breath and excuses, and for the first time was silent as Don studied her.

'I think I should speak to your father.'

She gripped his arm. 'No, Don, he's dozed off. And it's the rest that'll do him good.'

'In that case,' he murmured, drawing her close, 'I see no reason why we shouldn't take our walk.'

Birdie's heart sank. As much as she wanted to be with her sweetheart, she couldn't leave her father alone. 'A walk would be a fine thing, but not right this minute—'

'Brigid,' Don interrupted, holding her away, 'this wouldn't be a sulk, would it? Because of my postponement of our day together?'

'A sulk?' she repeated, eyes very wide. 'Would you accuse me of such a thing, Don?'

'Listen, my sweet, you must understand that I had no choice this morning. Mother reminded me I'd promised to take her to the morning service. Prayers were said today for Father and Stephen. So of course, Lydia and James joined us.'

'Of course,' agreed Birdie, lifting her face and particularly her lips, hoping he would kiss her again.

'I would have liked you to join us,' Don continued regretfully. 'And when we're married, I hope that you might.'

'Oh, I don't know, Don. I'm a Catholic. Me dad would have something to say on the matter, so he would.'

'But he's not even a Catholic himself,' Don said dismissively.

'No, but our mum was. She brought us all up as Romans and Dad expects us to follow.'

'We shall see,' Don smiled as he kissed her.

Birdie thought how much she loved him and wanted to be his wife. What did it really matter in what building a person worshipped? It was people that counted.

Don kissed her so passionately that her body filled with delight. She was aching for love and for motherhood, for a family of her very own. And by Don's eager embraces, she felt certain that he too, felt the same.

At the loud shouts from the passage, Don let her go and she jumped to her feet, smoothing down her rumpled dress and adjusting her little bow with shaking fingers.

'Pat, where have you been?' she stammered as her brother flew in.

'I called for Willie. We went up Poplar for a ha'penny of winkles and then I saw Harry. Is it true Dad took a turn?'

'Good afternoon, young man,' interrupted Don, standing up and straightening his tie.

Pat returned a disagreeable mumble, and Birdie was about to check him when Don gave a sharp cough. 'Whatever you've been told, Pat, none of us will know the truth until your father consults with the doctor.'

Pat's cheeks crimsoned. 'Harry knows what he's talking about. He's been in the war.'

'Pat!' Birdie exclaimed. 'Where are your manners?'

'Can I see Dad?'

'Not till you've washed that dirty face and combed your hair.'

'Brigid, your brother's behaviour has in no way improved,' Don complained gently when they were alone, although his cheeks had gone a bright pink.

'And I'll be telling him so, never fear,' Birdie agreed with a swift nod.

'I don't want that sort of talk rubbing off on James. Lydia would disapprove most strongly.'

This remark set Birdie back for a moment. What had Lydia to do with the matter? There had been no agreement – yet – on living at the store with the Thornes.

'Don, there's something we should—'

'My dear,' Don interrupted, seeming to recover his good humour, 'I think we should adjourn our day's meeting, don't you? After all, you have your brother and father to attend to.' Swiftly he kissed her.

'I wish you would stay.'

'Go along now, and we'll see each other next Sunday.'

'Could you call in the week?' she begged.

'You know the answer to that as well as I do. My day doesn't end when I close the shop doors. Not like it did when I worked for the railways when I came home and the evening was my own.'

'I wish you were still on the railways,' Birdie sighed, immediately regretting what she'd said as Don's face clouded.

'I had no choice but to leave,' he reminded her. 'Father built the business from nothing. And Stephen was his right arm. Whilst they were alive, I pursued my own career with a freedom that is denied me now. It was only fair to Lydia and Mother that I took over last year. It wasn't my wish, but the store is a good livelihood, at least as good as any other.'

Birdie felt very selfish for having voiced her true feelings. 'Yes, I know, Don. A very good livelihood indeed.'

'Goodbye, dear.' He kissed her once more, then left.

Birdie watched him stride down March Street, his upright figure soon disappearing as he turned into the alley towards Poplar.

As Birdie's eyes lingered she reflected on the terrible shame it was that they hadn't been able to marry on her twenty-second birthday, as she'd hoped. She had met Don when she was twenty-one and he had been her only true beau. Had not the war been declared, perhaps she would have been Mrs Donald Thorne by now. Everyone had thought the conflict would be over by the Christmas and so Don had suggested a summer wedding. But as time wore on and more men were called to the front, Don had hesitated. He'd speculated that even though he worked for the railways, if Germany really put Britain to the test, every man in the nation would be needed.

Thank God, Don had never been called up, thought Birdie gratefully. But just as her hopes reignited for marriage, along came the death of his brother and father, and once more their plans had taken a back seat.

Birdie closed the door and gave a deep sigh. How sensible Flo had been to have persuaded Reg to marry her before he went to the front. And despite being wounded twice, Reg had survived the war. Not that Flo and Reg had two pennies to rub together, but they were still a family. She had a husband and children of her own, whilst she, Birdie, had a father and young brother who sometimes felt like her children. How long would it be before Don decided to slip a wedding band on her finger?

Chapter 3

'Now, didn't that mutton stew slip down a treat?' Birdie eagerly studied her father's face, which, although gaunt and tired, looked a little more lively than it had this time a week ago. Since the seizure, she'd fed him up and watched him with an eagle eye, and had seen no signs of the shaking and jerking. All the same, she'd kept a spoon in her pinny pocket, just in case.

Wilfred made no reply but gave a grunt of approval and sipped from the enamel mug that brimmed with water.

'And I've baked a nice rice pudding for afters,' Birdie continued encouragingly, 'with a sprinkling of sugar on the top and browned to a crust, just as you like it.' Removing his plate, which still held a knuckle, reluctant to waste the meat, she discreetly set it aside.

'I'm finished now, Brigid.' Wilfred stood up. 'But I'm sure there are two stomachs at this table that still need filling.'

'But, Dad, the rice pudding—'

'I'll sit meself down by the fire for a while.'

Birdie watched him walk slowly out, the sound of his barking cough echoing in the passage.

'I'll eat Dad's leftovers,' offered Pat as he pushed forward his empty plate.

In the warmth of the big kitchen, where the smell of the stew had risen up into the drying clothes overhead, two healthy faces stared at her. Both her brother and Harry had finished every scrap.

'Ah, well, at least nothing is wasted with you, Pat,' smiled Birdie, placing the knuckle on his plate and returning it with a spoonful of gravy. 'Harry, will you have a little more broth?'

'I'd rather see you eat it,' Harry replied, a smudge of dirt still on his nose from his day of labouring. His black hair curled over his ears and crawled down to his open collar, which was also less than clean. But the poor man had been working all day, despite it being Sunday. Birdie noticed, that, although on the lean side, his arms were strong and muscular under his rolled-up shirtsleeves. And now that her eyes were in this area, she could see a button missing on his shirt. She said nothing, but made a mental note to repair it.

'I can't fit a spoonful more inside me,' Birdie shrugged as she ladled a good helping over Harry's spotless plate. It was decent manners of him to consider her, though. But having enjoyed one modest portion of stew, she had deliberately saved the lion's share for the men. If there was any pudding left, she might have a thimbleful. After all, there was more than enough to go round tonight; Pat had paid his three bob and Harry had insisted she take two shillings more for his laundry. He was generous indeed, but it was never going to be said of Brigid Connor that she didn't give her lodger a good innings for his board and keep.

When the meal was over, Pat joined his father in the parlour, but Harry lingered. 'That was a grand dinner, Birdie,' he said as he took his empty dish to the draining board and placed it with the others. 'Can I help with the dishes?'

'No, but thank you for the offer,' smiled Birdie.

'In that case, I'll bid you good night and look in on your father before I go.'

'Good night, Harry.'

As Birdie washed the dishes, she thought how their lodger had never been one to wear out his welcome, nor had he forgotten his manners. Why a healthy young man such as Harry wasn't walking out a nice girl, she couldn't fathom. He was a hard worker and decent-looking, and his money wasn't wasted in the pub, nor was he daft in the head.

Perhaps he relished his freedom after the years he had spent at war? Pensively smoothing the bar of Sunlight soap over the dirty dishes, she caught her reflection in the window and was happy to see that despite the hours she had spent in the steamy kitchen, her finger-waves were still in place – thanks to the Vaseline that Lady Hailing's money had bought. Her frilled white blouse peeped above the cross of her pinny, looking as fresh as a daisy; a blouse she'd starched and ironed with such care for her outing with Don this afternoon. If only he could have spent longer in her company! But they'd hardly had time to walk to the park before having to turn back. The shop needed a good turn-out before tomorrow, he'd said, a duty, he'd impressed on Birdie, that was to be hers one day.

At the memory of Don's gentle hint, Birdie decided the very next time she saw him, she must speak her mind. If she was to be part of the business, then she would insist on a Saturday boy. Why, imagine her having to scrub that dirty floor where the Thornes stored the bundles of firewood tied with tarry string, placed almost on top of the creosote and the paraffin dispenser! In Birdie's opinion, the perishables should be kept separate, for even Flo, who was not really that particular, had commented that she could taste tar on the Thornes' butter!

Birdie was staring into space when suddenly her heart gave a lurch. Looking directly into her gaze there seemed to be another face, one on the other side of the glass. Birdie closed her eyes and opened them, very firmly, only to find her own reflection staring back again. Leaning closer to the glass, she searched the inky blackness outside. The silhouette of the closet became clear under the moonlight and she could just discern the outline of the broken gate that led to the back alley. But other than this, there was nothing. Not a single movement.

Birdie dried her hands and went to the back door. Cautiously opening it, she felt the cold air blow in with a rush. There was only the echo of the Kirby kids, three doors up, knocking seven bells out of one another. This was a reassuring sound and gave Birdie the courage to step out. Nothing moved but the breeze. Braving a step or two more, she jumped when next-door's cat scooted across her path, but as the sounds of the river and the great city beyond filled the dark night, there was no movement, not even from the alley beyond.

It was a while before she turned back, telling herself how daft she was. Then a hand went over her mouth. Silently he carried her, with no effort at all, it seemed. As much as she wriggled, it was no use, her heart trying to fight its way out of her chest as she smelled the oil and tar on the palm of the man's rough hand.

Though it was darker than an inkwell, Birdie knew she hadn't been taken far. If she was to have her throat slit, it would be in her own back yard. The thought was of little comfort, but her panic eased at the sound of the soft Irish curse amongst the harsh cockney.

'Quiet, gel. Bejesus, you're kickin' me shins black and blue.'

'F . . . Frank?' she stammered as the fingers slipped away from her mouth. 'Is that you?'

'It's me. Now speak in a whisper.'

She felt her feet touch the ground as he lowered her. Then, in the moonlight she saw the face clearly. It was not Frank as she remembered him, but an older, more haggard version, with staring eyes, white-rimmed with fear.

'Oh, Frank! Frank! Is it really you?'

'I've made a bolt from the nick.'

Birdie gasped. 'You've run away? But how? When?'

'The guards from Wandsworth was taking me to the 'ospital.'

'Are you ill?'

'Nah, I got these spots.' He pulled open his coat and scratched at his chest. 'I reckon it's the bloody lice and nits. They're all over me, eating me alive. See?' Birdie strained her eyes and got a strong whiff of unwashed body. 'Last night I swelled up like a balloon and none of the screws would get near me in case it was the pox. So they shoved me in an 'ospital wagon and it was on me way there I hopped it.' He raked his dirty fingernails over the sores on his face. 'I still got these buggers but they ain't nothin' catching. If it was the pox, I'd surely be dead by now.'

'Oh, Frank, won't they punish you when they catch you?'

'Yeah, but they haven't yet.'

Birdie stared at the dishevelled bent figure that only vaguely resembled the good-looking, blue-eyed young man who had gone to war.

'Don't suppose Dad has changed his mind about me?' Frank asked hopefully.

'I wish I could say he had,' confessed Birdie, her teeth chattering with cold. 'But me and Pat don't believe what they said. I told you so in me letters.'

'Thanks for them, gel.'

'What happened, Frank? Why did they judge you a deserter?'

'They didn't give me no chance to prove I wasn't. One minute I was on the battlefield walking towards this Hun and then it all went black. Came round in this farmhouse, with a foreign lingo in me King Lears. This old geezer looked after me and eventually took me back to me unit.'

Suddenly the back door opened. A figure emerged and blocked the light of the window.

'It's Dad,' croaked Birdie, and once more Frank's big hand squeezed her shoulder as the silhouette was briefly illuminated by the light of a match. They remained still, until a few minutes later when, coughing softly, their father returned inside.

'I been watching you all through the window,' whispered Frank, scratching himself violently. 'Who was that geezer sitting next to our Pat?'

'That's Harry Chambers, our lodger.'

'Lodger? Is he kosher?'

'He's a very nice man, is Harry. Pays a good rent and never oversteps the mark.'

'Does he know about me?'

'Course he does. Oh, Frank, I've missed you. The house ain't the same without you.'

'Birdie, the coppers might come round.'

'Dad won't like that.'

'I know, but I didn't know where else to go. I 'oped the old man might've had a change of heart but I ain't got a chance wiv him, have I?'

Birdie said nothing and Frank shook his head sadly. 'Wouldn't visit me in gaol, just wrote that he couldn't forgive any man for deserting his post. Christ Almighty, Birdie, I'm his kin!'

'I know, I know,' Birdie nodded, 'but you running away again isn't going to help.'

'I've got to prove I ain't no deserter.'

'But how will you do that?'

Frank shrugged. 'Dunno, I got to think of a plan.'

'Oh, Frank, I don't know what to say. I'm worried about you.' He smelled so unpleasant that she stepped back. 'Where did you get this old coat?'

'I found it in a bin.'

Birdie's mind was racing. Should she try to persuade him to return to prison, where perhaps the authorities

32

might lessen his punishment if he went back of his own accord? But if he was innocent, was this the only chance he'd ever have to prove that he was no deserter? If only she knew what to do for the best.

'Listen, you can't stay here, Frank. But there's those old broken-up barges down on the silt. You could kip there and I could meet you tomorrow, bring clean clothes and food. I've got a couple of bob put by.' She would take it from the rent, and think how to replace it later.

'Would you do that for me, gel?'

'Course I would. You're me brother.'

'Now I'm out, I don't wanna go back to that hellhole.'

Birdie was doubtful that Frank would stay free for long; they would be looking for him, searching first south of the river and then the East End.

'Where will we meet?' she asked hurriedly.

'The park, under the arches.'

'All right. I'll come about ten.'

'Thanks, Birdie.' He gave her a big hug and Birdie held her breath as the bad smell enveloped them.

'Be careful, Frank.'

She watched him creep across the yard and lift the back gate. It had been missing a hinge, though Wilfred had tied string round the top and it creaked noisily.

Quietly she opened the back door and stepped in; perhaps no one had missed her. But then she heard her father calling.

'Where have you been, gel?' demanded Wilfred when she entered the warm parlour.

'Thought you was making the cocoa,' said Pat with a frown.

'And so I was,' Birdie retorted, hoping the flush on her cheeks didn't show. 'What's wrong with a girl taking a breath of air, first?'

'I had a smoke,' said Wilfred with a frown. 'Didn't see you outside.'

'I was in the alley, minding my own business, gazing up at the stars and hoping for five minutes' peace.' Birdie lifted her chin. 'But seeing it's doubtful I should have even that, I suppose I'd better be making those drinks!'

With that, Birdie hurried back to the kitchen, feeling guilty, as though she herself had committed a crime and lied into the bargain.

Frank was a wanted man, on the run from the law. How could she help him? Would the authorities come here? And would he turn up tomorrow as they'd arranged?

Chapter 4

It was nine o'clock the next morning when Birdie set off after telling Wilfred a half-truth: that she was postponing the wash for a much-needed shop at the market. So, having gone via Cox Street, it was past ten by the time she got to the park.

The grass was the only stretch of green for miles around, save for the Fields, as everyone called the undeveloped piece of wasteland on the very southern tip of the island. Birdie cautiously glanced behind her; she'd had a curious feeling at Cox Street as she was badgering the old girl who ran the second-hand clothes stall, like someone was watching them. But when she'd paid for her purchases, then bought bread, cheese and a lump of ginger cake, stuffing them deep in her shopping bag, she was sure no one had followed her out of the market.

All the same, she was careful. She'd taken short cuts through the back alleys, and walked a big circle, waiting on the corner of the East India Dock Road to make certain she wasn't followed. Now, as Birdie trod over the brittle grass, scuffed and holed by the kids' boots, she gave a last glimpse over her shoulder. Save for two old men, smoking and stamping their feet to encourage warmth, the park was empty. Making her way towards the arches, she stopped by a plane tree. Leaning against its barren trunk, she waited as her eyes adjusted to the gloom under the railway line. No Frank. A mongrel dog lifted its leg and nosed for scraps. A sheet of old newspaper wrapped its way around the brick walls. In the far back yards, boarded up with broken bits, a woman in a headscarf, with an ancient perambulator, bounced it across the uneven ground.

Birdie left the tree, once more glancing over her shoulder. Could Frank see her? She didn't like going under the arches. Sometimes old men slept there, sometimes the 'parkie' jumped out, boxing the boys' ears for playing truant or warning the girls not to be so flighty. Years ago, she and Flo had made faces at the man who wielded power in the park, and to their cost. He'd found out who they were and reported them. A sin she'd had to confess to Father Flynn, receiving ten Hail Marys and one Our Father as penance.

Birdie smiled as she thought of it. Of Flo and her in church, giggling and not feeling in the least repentant.

Just then, her neck prickled cold. The alert sent her shoulders stiff and she let her eyes linger on the middle arch. She saw a figure, almost melting into the brick. It was still as a petrified rabbit, but it was Frank, she was certain.

Walking slowly, trying to look as though she was taking a stroll, with one hand in her coat pocket and her beret well down over her ears, she bent and tipped off her shoe as though she had a stone in it. But her eyes were raised and there was no one watching, the pram lady having vanished, leaving the two old men a far distance away.

'Over here, Birdie.'

'I'm coming.'

She slipped into the shadowy space. The voice had come from the very back where the thorns and pebbles and grass grew intermixed with the weeds.

'Where are you?'

'I'm sitting on me arse, waiting.'

She saw him then, crouched down, a look on his face of the hunted. His wild eyes had been robbed of their piercing blue but, as he pulled off his cap, his crown of ginger hair, which matched the growth on his chin, had never seemed more prominent.

'Did anyone follow you?' he rasped.

'No,' she replied, not wanting to alarm him with her vague feelings of unrest. She stood beside him, placing her basket on the ground and took out her purchases. A serviceable-looking overcoat, thick working trousers, a frayed but warm grey woollen jumper, a soft cloth cap and elderly but clean long johns. 'I got these from the old girl's stall at the market. And there's cheese and bread and—'

'You done good, Birdie. Real good.'

'There's a couple of bob in the overcoat pocket to see you through.'

'You can't afford that, gel.'

She waved her hand. 'Frank, that ginger beard of yours is a dead giveaway.'

'Don't have no cutthroat, do I?'

'No, but I've brought me scissors.'

'Blimey, what you gonna do with them?' Frank shrank away from the sight of the big dressmaking cutters.

'What do you think? Now come here and let me do

36

what I can. You can hide your hair under the cap, but you can't disguise your beard.'

Positioning her brother behind one of the arches where the light flowed in, Birdie set to work, clipping away the growth, which was running alive with tiny, blood-sucking insects.

'No wonder they thought you had the pox,' she sighed as she cast aside the bits with her fingertips. 'How long is it since you washed?'

'Dunno. I forgot.'

'There's a finger of Lifebuoy in the overcoat pocket. Not much for the size of you, but enough for a strip wash before putting them clean clothes on.'

'I'll scrub up ternight in the river. Reckon the water will freeze me privates off, but the pen-and-ink is upsetting even me.' He scratched the seeping red welts over his face. 'What I wouldn't give for a nice hot soak in the tin bath,' he sighed longingly. 'Remember when we used to drag it indoors in front of the range and fill it from the copper? I ain't been clean since before the war. It was filth in the trenches, up to our eyes in mud and shit. I got a bad case of scurvy, like worms have crawled under my skin, in the nick and give me these blisters.'

Birdie reached into her bag for a small brown bottle. 'A thimbleful of chloride of lime should do the trick.'

'Don't you put that on the walls?'

'You'll only need a drop or two, or maybe three for a big fella like yourself. It'll burn something rotten, but it'll put them off. Don't get it in your eyes, mind.'

Frank stumbled over to the food. 'I'm starvin'. Found meself a few scraps last night at the back of the rubber-dub-dub, but it weren't much.' He crouched amongst the weeds, tearing the bread and cheese with his teeth, plugging his mouth full, more quickly than he could swallow.

Birdie wished she'd brought ale, but she'd spent right to the last halfpenny.

After a while, she kneeled beside him. 'Did you find a barge last night?'

Frank wiped his mouth with the back of his hand. 'Yer. One end of it was dry and I nodded off.'

'No one saw you?'

'Don't fink so.'

Birdie's heart felt as though it was split in two as she watched him eating, his animal grunts and groans and itchings all entwined. Was this her lovely brother, the good Catholic boy who had raised Pat, and worked all hours in the holds of the ships, and missed their mum so much that it was only she, Birdie, who knew that he'd cried out in the closet, stifling his sobs so he still appeared like a grown man when he came in.

'Frank, I can't stay long.'

'You ain't told me nothing about what's been going on while I been away. You ain't hitched yet? Don't see no wedding ring.'

'Don's been . . . well, busy. He lost his dad last year to the flu, his brother the year before at the front.'

Frank stopped eating. 'I'm sorry to hear that.'

'He left the railways and now runs the store with Lydia and Aggie.' Birdie added slowly, 'We've yet to decide where we'll live.'

'You ain't leaving home?' Frank said in surprise.

Birdie straightened her back. 'The store's not such a bad place to live.'

'What about Dad and Pat?'

'Are they not able to look after themselves, and am I to be at their beck and call all me life?' Birdie didn't mean for a moment what she said. But it was an irritant lately that her care was taken for granted. She hadn't spoken to her father or brother about living over the store when she was married. But then, moving was not what she wanted either. And now there was the question of Wilfred's fitting too. Should she confide in Frank, but then didn't the poor soul have enough worries of his own right this minute?

'Does Dad ever talk about me?' he asked, pausing and glancing at her from the corner of his eye.

Birdie was silent and wished she could think of something kind to say. But her hesitation caused Frank to thrust the last of the bread in his pocket with a despairing sigh.

'But you'd be dead proud of our Pat,' she rushed on. 'Me and him talk of you all the time.'

'It pains me to think of him,' murmured Frank with a hitch to his voice. 'He was no more than eleven when I left.'

'He's just like you, Frank, tall and strong. The PLA gave him a job in September. Got a messenger boy's uniform, an' all. Gives me three bob for his keep and rides a bicycle like the wind.'

Frank smiled. 'Has he got a girl in tow?'

'Says he's going to travel the world first.'

'Birdie, don't let him think the worst of me for escapin'.'

'He won't do that, I promise.'

Birdie saw him turn away and draw his arm across his face. Then quickly he stood up, the wild look returning. 'I'm goin' now. I gotta stay ahead of the law.'

She stood too as he scooped the bundle of clothes under his arm. 'Where will you go?'

'I got somewhere in mind.' He grinned.

'A female is it, Francis Connor? Oh, I hope you know what you're doing. For you might have been Jack-the-lad once, but in your current state, very few will want anything to do with you.' She knew that Frank had always been a lovable rascal, and liked nothing more than to take a pretty girl for a stroll of a Friday night. He had very little money to spend from his casual work in the docks. And he'd always given Birdie first claim for the housekeeping. But he once knew how to enjoy himself, and perhaps there was still someone – someone special and who he trusted from the old days – who would risk helping an old friend?

'You're not to fret over me, gel. I've got me next move sussed.'

'But how will I know where you are?' she asked worriedly.

'Listen, what you don't know can't hurt you.'

'I'll be worrying meself half to death not knowing.'

'I'll find a way to let you know, but don't tell our dad or even Pat. Don't tell no one, see?'

'Just take care of yourself.'

He took her in his arms and hugged her. 'Come on now, chin up, gel.' She nearly fainted from the foul smell but she hugged him tight, not knowing how long it would be before she saw him again.

Chapter 5

It was the following evening when a heavy knock came at the front door. Pat had just wheeled his bicycle into the yard and was standing in the kitchen, looking over Birdie's shoulder as she mashed the potatoes.

'I'm starving,' he informed her, sticking his finger in the pan and thieving a blob of mash.

But it was only just in his mouth before the heavy thumps came and Birdie jumped, dropping the big fork on the table. She left Pat licking his lips as she hurried along the passage. Smoothing her hands over her pinny and lifting the lock of brown hair from her eyes, she felt her legs turn to jelly as she opened the door.

A policeman stood there, his eyes flying over her shoulder to the inside of the house before she had time to draw breath. No one on the island trusted a blue uniform, and Birdie noted the noisy protests of the kids who were being called in from the street. Doors closed and lace curtains twitched, and Birdie squared her shoulders.

'What do you want, banging like that?'

The policeman studied her carefully. 'I'm Police Constable Rudge,' he boomed. 'Is this the home of Francis Declan Connor?'

Birdie's heart almost lifted out of her chest. 'You know very well it is. Or else you'd be bothering some other poor soul.'

'Is he here?'

'And you know the answer to that, an' all. He's behind bars, where you put him a year ago.'

'If that was the case,' said the young constable shortly, 'this conversation wouldn't be taking place.'

'What do you mean?' Birdie hoped her flush was considered annoyance, not guilt.

'Francis Declan Connor—'

'I'm fully conversant with me brother's name,' interrupted Birdie haughtily. 'I'm his sister, Brigid Connor, and I'll thank you to spit out what you've come here to say instead of asking daft questions.'

The colour of the constable's face below his tall helmet began to darken as he eyed Birdie with suspicion. 'On Saturday night, your, er – the prisoner escaped from His Majesty's custody and, as yet, is still at large.'

Birdie kept her gaze straight, as straight as it could possibly be, when having the fear of God put inside her. 'So me brother made a run for it, did he? And sure, if he did, do you expect him to be here, waiting for you, like only a halfwit would?'

Birdie was deciding whether to continue in the same

vein, or try to still her tongue, which would be a great effort indeed, when she saw Harry coming up the road.

'You all right, Birdie?' he called, swinging his bag from his shoulder and pausing at the railings.

'Good evening to you, Harry,' she called, speaking as though the rigid body dressed in blue was not standing there. 'Our Frank's done a bunk and they've come here to arrest him. A pity really, since he was just enjoying a good supper and had his feet up on the kitchen table. He was hoping they'd give him another night or two's grace, so's he could nip to the pub and slake his prison thirst.'

Since the door was wide open there was a clear view along the passage to the kitchen and scullery, and only Pat staring back, his eyes wide as Birdie enjoyed the copper's discomfort. But she wasn't ready for Harry's response, as, with a twinkle in his eye, he strolled lazily to the door and leaned his shoulder against the jamb, an inch or two away from the bobby.

'A pity indeed,' he grinned, 'as I should have liked to join him.'

Birdie couldn't help but smile, but the grin was soon wiped from her face when she heard her father's voice a flight up, followed by the sight and sound of his boots on the staircase.

'What's this?' he demanded as he confronted the policeman. 'What's your business here?' He frowned, raising his braces over his shoulders, let loose half an hour ago for his nap.

'Who might you be?' the bobby returned as Pat joined them too, his young face full of apprehension.

'I'm Wilfred Connor, head of this household. Brigid here is my daughter and this is my youngest, Patrick. And Harry beside you is our lodger. Now state what it is you want.'

'We are looking for Francis Declan Connor,' said the

policeman in the same dead tone, 'who has absconded this past Saturday from His Majesty's detention.'

'Frank?' Wilfred's face drained white. 'Absconded?'

'Have you seen him?'

For a moment Wilfred seemed too shocked to speak. Then slowly his expression hardened. 'You'll have no luck with your enquiries here, son. The person you are looking for has no business in this house, nor ever will have.'

'So you'd best be on your way,' Birdie intervened, though she wanted to scream that Frank was an innocent man, falsely accused, and if only someone would listen, they would see the real crime had been committed against Frank himself.

Just then, Pat turned, scuffing his boots on the wooden boards. Going out of the back door, he banged it hard. Wilfred muttered under his breath and began to cough.

'Go inside, Dad, the cold is getting at your chest,' Birdie urged.

He nodded, shifting himself slowly towards the parlour door. Angry and upset, Birdie pointed her finger at the policeman. 'Now see what you've done? You've set me dad off coughing and sent me young brother into a sulk. What more trouble will you cause us?'

Harry lifted himself from the jamb. 'Best be on your way,' he told the constable. 'You're wasting your time here.'

Birdie saw no threat, nor dislike in Harry's face, yet his dark eyes were cooler than she had ever seen.

'Nevertheless, it's your duty to inform us if he turns up,' retorted the policeman, glowering at Harry. 'The law counts aiding and abetting criminals as a serious offence.'

'You've made that plain enough,' nodded Harry, not moving a muscle.

'As if our Frank would come here!' Birdie exclaimed, trying to feign surprise after the policeman had gone. 'That's the law for you, thick as two planks.'

'I'm sure he'd not make that mistake.' Harry tilted his head. 'Your brother would have more sense, of course. But if it was me in such a position, I might be tempted to make me presence known somehow.' He arched a dark eyebrow, keeping his eyes on her face.

Birdie went scarlet under his scrutiny. He was no fool and she felt for a moment that he could read her guilty thoughts. 'It's Pat I'm worried about,' she evaded, her voice rising with the effort of putting a show on. 'He don't understand why Frank was put away and has developed a passionate dislike for the uniform. Now he's gone off and heaven alone knows when he'll be back.'

A smile formed on Harry's lips and quietly he asked, 'Would you like me to go after him and bring him back for supper?'

'It'll be ready and waiting for you both.'

Harry threw his bag over his shoulder and hesitated, his frown returning once more. 'Take care, Birdie. I admire your spirit in fending off that youngster, but he was only a rookie and if they're seriously after Frank, one visit won't be enough.'

Birdie felt another little jerk to her stomach, as though Harry had guessed her secret. 'Then they'll be wasting their time in knocking on this door again,' she replied, tossing her head. 'They won't find any evidence of Frank being here.'

Harry nodded slowly, his dark eyes meeting hers. Then, his breath curling up in the cold air, he set off, whistling his way down the street.

With uneasy thoughts crowding her head, Birdie closed the door and went to the parlour. She found her father sitting by the fire.

'What do you know of all this?' he thrust at her.

'As much as you do, Dad,' she answered, bending to tend the fire in order to cover her guilt.

'If your brother has the gall to come here,' Wilfred continued, 'I don't expect you to welcome him. This is a respectable household and we've had enough thrown at us through what he did.'

Birdie tried to keep her feelings in check, but at this, she jumped to her feet. 'We ain't heard Frank's side of it,' she argued, knowing immediately it was the very worst reply she could give.

Wilfred pointed a shaking finger. 'He was tried and found guilty of desertion,' he began, coughing, 'so let's hear no more of . . .' The effort to speak was too much and Birdie rushed to his side, patting his back. Still the coughing continued and she flew to the kitchen for the Collis Browne. When she returned she too was shaking as she levelled the spoon to her father's lips. The bout of coughing subsided as he pulled a face and flapped his hand. 'Don't fuss, don't fuss!' He turned his eyes slowly on her. 'I don't mean to speak harshly, Brigid,' he said, a rough depth to his voice. 'But you're like your mother, God rest her. She was everything to me, but she had wild ideas that sometimes caused . . .' he shrugged, turning away and gazed into the fire.

Birdie left him to his thoughts, feeling the weight of guilt like a stone in her ribs. It was hard to love a father so much and deceive him.

But she loved Frank too.

A few days later Birdie set off to collect her work from Hailing House, the imposing red-brick manor run by aristocratic ladies for the benefit of the poor. It wasn't often Lady Hailing or her daughters, Felicity and Annabelle, were in residence, for their country seat took up much of their time. But Mrs Belcher, the housekeeper, sat Birdie down in the kitchen beside the big black-leaded range.

'I'll brew you a fresh cup, love,' she told Birdie with

affection. 'Warm your hands by the oven there and I'll find us a nice hot scone and a pat of best butter.' Birdie had known Mrs Belcher from the time that Bernadette had cleaned for the ladies, taking Birdie with her to the sewing classes. Afterwards, the housekeeper would treat them to a scone in the homely kitchen.

Now the elderly lady was close to retirement but Birdie knew the Hailings were reluctant to let her go; she kept the household running like clockwork. Mrs Belcher bustled around the kitchen, her wide hips swinging under her apron and a strand or two of brittle grey hair escaping from her cap as she wiped her sweating forehead with a rag. But it seemed today that the housekeeper was agitated as she related the news of the twice-weekly soup kitchen and refreshments she prepared for the sewing classes.

Birdie listened patiently, whilst making swift work of the hot scone served up from the oven. A rich brown tea poured into a real china cup accompanied it, and when Mrs Belcher had at last run out of steam she sat down with a sigh and glanced uneasily at her guest.

'The misses have gone off yesterday,' she said, bringing down Birdie's hopes of asking for extra work. 'Lord Hailing rides with the hunt at the weekend and wants his family with him. But Lady Annabelle left you a big bag of alterations, some for herself, and another bag for the little 'uns of the nursery, what don't have a clean pair of drawers between them. It's all quality, mind, from the ladies' nieces and nephews. All clean crotches and lace frills, but with the elastic gone or the sides split. Nothin' you can't put right, love.'

Relief filled Birdie as two bags would provide the extra half-crown she was hoping for. The ladies paid very well, knowing they could rely on Birdie's skills and swift return.

'I'll take one bag with me,' Birdie decided, 'and Pat will cycle round for the other as soon as he gets home.'

'I'll be here, ducks.' She once more wiped her sweating brow. 'Look, Birdie, don't think me a nosy cow, but is your Frank still at Wandsworth?'

Birdie put down her cup with a clatter. 'Why? What made you ask that? And why should I know, anyway?'

Mrs Belcher looked uncomfortable. 'You are his sister, love.'

'And what good does that do me? Dad don't let me visit him and Frank ain't exactly a dab hand at letters.'

'Now, now, I was only asking.'

Birdie looked keenly at the housekeeper. 'Yes, but it's a funny thing to ask.'

'There was a couple of lines, see,' Mrs Belcher said, her eyes flicking down to her cup as she twirled it slowly round, 'in last night's *Gazette*. Said a prisoner that came from the island escaped from Wandsworth. It weren't much, didn't give no names, but I must admit, it got me wondering.'

Birdie sat in silence, her heart pounding. She should have expected this, but had been hoping that somehow the news wouldn't get out. 'Did it say much else?'

Mrs Belcher shrugged. 'Nothing as I can recall.'

Birdie wondered why the *Gazette* hadn't written more, that Frank was on his way to the hospital when he escaped. Then she realized what an outcry there might have been. The authorities would have been accused of allowing to escape a prisoner with a possible contagious disease. Now that fact was being deliberately hidden from public knowledge.

'Well, I might as well tell you, Mrs Belcher,' Birdie began, feeling she had no option but to admit to the truth. Being an old friend of her mother's, the housekeeper had known Frank since he was a boy. 'It was Frank who escaped.'

Mrs Belcher put a hand to her mouth. 'Oh, my Lord!'

'The coppers have been round, and said if he turned up, it was a crime to help him.'

'The hard-hearted devils!'

'Mrs Belcher, you won't say anything, will you? If the *Gazette* didn't give any names, it might not get around too quick.'

'Course I won't, Birdie. How has your dad taken it?'

'Not very well, I'm afraid.'

Mrs Belcher nodded. 'Your father is a proud man. But I can tell you this, love, if Frank turned up at my door, I'd give him a good meal and wish him the best of luck. Have you any idea where he'd go?'

Birdie shook her head. Her lips were sealed as far as Frank's movements were concerned.

'Listen, girl, I knew your mother when Frank was just a nipper, and I saw you swell out her belly till she could hardly walk, and then birthed you with a labour that took two days and nights, and there was no finer family on this island, with your father toiling all hours and instilling into you kids a decent way of life. No one was more saddened to see Bernadette Connor go than me. Taking her last breath to save her child was the bravest thing a mother could do. I don't care who knows it, but my belief is that your Frank is no deserter. He came from fine stock. It's the Army that has it all wrong.'

Birdie felt overwhelmed at this declaration. She had always liked Mrs Belcher, with whom she conducted her business when the ladies weren't present. But she had never heard the old housekeeper speak this way before.

'Yours are comforting words, Mrs B,' Birdie said gratefully. 'It's Dad who's suffered the most. People's spite has hurt him. Me, I give them a slice of me mind, and Pat, well, he's young and learning to stick up for himself. But Dad, being a staunch supporter of King and country, he ain't come to terms with what Frank is supposed to have done.'

'My sympathies are with you, dear. It can't be easy, certainly not. But tell me, how is that young man of yours? I hope the gossipmongers ain't spoiled it between you.'

Birdie felt a sinking sensation as she thought of how Don's loyalty to her had been tested over the past months. Though at times his feelings towards Frank had surfaced, causing them minor disputes, he had still walked out with her, for which she loved him all the more.

'He's very well indeed, Mrs Belcher.'

'Have you named the day yet?'

'Not exactly,' said Birdie, 'but to be sure, it ain't far off. It's only last year he left the railways to take over his father's store.'

'Poor lamb,' agreed the housekeeper with a deep sigh, 'he's had a lot on his plate.'

'We'll get through it,' said Birdie.

'Does he know about your brother's escape?'

Birdie hadn't given much thought yet to how she would tell him, but perhaps he too had seen it in the newspaper? And yet she was certain that Don would have called round immediately if he'd suspected the escapee in question was Frank.

'I'll cross that bridge when I come to it,' she told the elderly lady, who nodded understandingly.

'Now, will you have another nice warm scone before you go?' Mrs Belcher asked. 'I've a jar of me own jam in the larder.'

'A real temptation that is,' smiled Birdie, 'but I'd best catch our Pat and get him to cycle over for me parcel.'

Mrs Belcher rose to her feet and crooked her finger. 'Come into the scullery and fetch your work, then. The parcels ain't lightweight, by any means, and you're such a tiny thing, it pains me to think of you carrying it across the island.'

'It's not that far,' claimed Birdie as she lifted the heavy

bundle from the scullery shelf. 'It was nice hearing about Mum,' she added as she lugged the parcel to the back door.

'She was full of spirit, like you, love,' reflected the house-keeper, letting her out into the courtyard, surrounded by a high brick wall where the poor and destitute waited for the free soup. 'With never a bad word to say for no one and always a smile on her pretty face.'

Once again, Birdie felt moved. She walked home feeling better, even though the weight of the parcel caused sweat to form on her brow and dampen her hair. But with the extra work she now had, she could make up the money she had given to Frank.

At the thought of Frank on the run, Birdie said a little prayer, not knowing quite how to word it, as she wanted no harm to come to Frank. And yet, how could that be, when there could be only one end in sight?

When Pat returned from work late that afternoon, hot and breathless from his cycle, he could hardly wait to spit out his words.

'Where's Dad?' he demanded, pulling off his messenger boy's pillbox cap and throwing it on the kitchen table.

'Gone up to buy some baccy.' Birdie knew there was something amiss as Pat launched himself in her path. There was both excitement and anger in his face, and Birdie steeled herself for what she would hear next.

'Frank's escape was in the newspaper,' he blurted to Birdie. 'Everyone knows! Everyone's guessed!'

'And it's only that, just guessing,' Birdie dismissed.

'So you know?'

'Mrs Belcher told me today.'

Pat couldn't wait to go on. 'It's all round the island that the copper called here. The men at the docks said they'd turn a deserter in if they caught one, fully knowing I could hear them talking.' He sank down on the chair and, undoing the top buttons of his uniform, he wrestled open his jacket.

'The girls weren't much better at the offices. Sniggering and nudging each other. They're all a lot of silly cows.'

'Pat! Language!' Birdie reproved, nevertheless in full sympathy with her brother, and immediately set about breaking her golden rule. 'If they open their mouths and something vile comes out, then you just tell them to come and see Birdie Connor, who'll soon put 'em straight.' Birdie couldn't help herself. She would like to get hold of just one of those silly creatures who had nothing better to do than embarrass a young boy, barely into his new job and shy of the opposite sex.

'I'll tell them meself,' said Pat indignantly. 'I'm no sissy, getting my sister to speak for me.'

'Course you're no sissy,' she answered quickly. 'You're a fine young man now, and forgive me if I forget sometimes. Let 'em think what they like, it don't matter to us. You and me know our Frank is innocent. With being wounded—' She stopped, suddenly realizing what she'd said.

Pat looked up, his eyes widening. 'What did you say?'

In an effort to cover her mistake she grabbed hold of the unopened parcel on the table. 'Listen, there's another of these to be collected from the House. I told Mrs Belcher you'd be along before supper.'

But he wouldn't be put off. 'You said our Frank was wounded,' he repeated. 'You couldn't have known that, unless he told you.'

Birdie felt the heat flow over her. Pat was bright as a button and he'd caught her out. But if she told him that she'd seen their brother, her promise to Frank would be broken.

Slowly Pat swivelled round on the chair, his eyes full of reproach. 'I'm right, ain't I?'

Birdie nodded. She couldn't deny it.

'When? Where?' Pat demanded, sitting forward, his knuckles white, as he gripped the table.

'On . . . on Sunday, in the backyard, after supper.'

'The night you was late making our cocoa?

Again Birdie nodded.

'But you told Dad and me—'

'I couldn't say the truth, could I?' Birdie had a lump in her own throat from being discovered. 'I had to think of something and it wasn't a real lie, only a fib.'

'But Frank is my brother too. I wouldn't have let on.'

Suddenly there was a knock at the front door. Not just an ordinary knock, but almost a pounding. Birdie froze, not moving an inch, as though she'd been caught again in the act of something terrible. Was it the bobby back?

She looked quickly at Pat and lifted her finger to her lips. 'Not a word,' she whispered, and suddenly Pat's angry face turned fearful.

When the pounding came again, this time louder, Birdie gave a despairing sigh. 'I'll have to answer it,' she decided. 'Are you all right, love? You're not going to give me away?'

Pat's reaction was to scuff his eyes determinedly with the back of his hand. 'Course I'm not.'

She went with a feeling of powerlessness welling up inside her, though thanking heaven that at least Wilfred wasn't at home to face this encounter. Bracing her shoulders she made her way down the passage, each step keeping time with the thundering beat of her heart.

Chapter 6

'Don!' Birdie exclaimed as she opened the door. 'What are you doing here?' Relief melted over her as she looked into his handsome, familiar face. She had been fully expecting to see Constable Rudge.

Don glanced warily along the passage. 'Are you busy?'

'No. I didn't expect to see you till Sunday.'

Don joined her in the passage and, seeing Pat in the kitchen, he nodded in greeting. 'Hello there, Pat.'

Birdie quickly took Don's arm. 'Come into the parlour. I've a nice fire going.'

'Is your father at home?' Don asked as he followed her in.

'No, he's gone up for some baccy. Sit yourself down for a minute and I'll make us a brew. And I'll just send Pat off to Hailing House, for my work. It'll be nice to have the place to ourselves.'

'I haven't time to stop,' Don told her sharply. 'I've left Mother and Lydia to close the store.'

'Oh! Well, I shan't be a moment.' Birdie hurried out to the kitchen where Pat was waiting. 'Listen now, love,' she coaxed, 'I'll tell you everything tonight. I haven't time now and, anyway, Mrs Belcher is waiting for you. Now don't go pushing the parcel around too roughly in that basket. Last time, the cloth got caught and pulled a thread or two.'

'You promise you'll tell me?' demanded Pat as she pushed him towards the back door.

'I promise,' Birdie nodded, eager to return to Don.

Pat shuffled into the backyard, a chill wind whistling into the kitchen as Birdie waited until she saw him take his bicycle, open the gate with a loud creak and disappear down the alley.

Hurriedly putting the kettle on, Birdie then set out the best china and returned to the parlour.

'Oh, Don, how wonderful it is to see you,' she gushed as she went over to him, feeling anxious that he hadn't seated himself, but instead stood stiffly in the spot she had left him, his back straight as a washboard and his chin lifted, tightening his lips unflatteringly as he ignored her warm greeting.

'Birdie, there's something we must discuss immediately.'

'What is it, my love?'

'Your brother. Is it true he has escaped custody?'

With a feeling of dismay, Birdie searched his eyes for a glimmer of sympathy. But she found only the absence of the soft green flecks that revealed his warm and better nature. 'I'm afraid it is,' she conceded. 'It was only today Mrs Belcher told me it was in the *Gazette*.'

'So you had no inkling of it before?' he asked, causing Birdie to look away from his accusing stare, hardly able to admit it was all of three days ago that the bobby came round.

'It was, er . . . let me see, Tuesday,' she managed in no more than a whisper, 'that a bobby called.'

Don's eyes opened to their fullest extent in astonishment. 'Tuesday,' he repeated and she nodded, praying that he would at least sit down and not collapse.

'I can't believe it of you,' he barked at her, giving Birdie such a jolt that she felt like collapsing herself. 'Tuesday!' he exclaimed again, his face draining of colour.

'It's not such a long while ago,' Birdie reasoned. 'And it wasn't news until yesterday. Even then, Frank wasn't mentioned by name—'

'Clearly it was enough to give rise to speculation,' he interrupted her angrily. 'People are no fools, not at all. I would have thought that you could at least have given us warning.'

Birdie looked repentant. 'I'm sorry.'

'I have a business to run. Remember how it was when Frank's trouble brewed up? It wasn't easy at all. People are quick to draw conclusions and assume you too are tarred with the same brush.'

'Frank's no criminal,' she insisted. 'Why won't you believe me?'

'Because a court of law has pronounced him so,' Don replied, a little less accusingly as he saw her distress.

'Then they're wrong,' Birdie said, squaring her shoulders. 'A criminal is someone that's broken the law.'

'Then what has he done?' Don asked, raising an eyebrow. 'I'd be grateful if you'd tell me, my dear.'

How could she tell Don what Frank had told her? And even if she could, as she'd said to Pat, there was no proof, none at all, only Frank's account of what had happened. 'Don,' she pleaded, catching his arms, 'just suppose . . . just imagine, if there might be an explanation, something that wasn't said at his court martial . . . something of importance that never was given the light of day—'

'Birdie, I thought we had talked this through? Now, stop all this speculation. It's too much, it really is.' Then calming himself visibly, he took her hands and drew her to him. 'Birdie, don't you see, I'm worried for you, about your soft heart and perhaps Frank turning up here, though he would be mad to do so, with every eye on the lookout for him. A man who has deserted his post and left others to do the fighting – well, even you, my dear, must see why people are so against that?'

Birdie laid her head on his chest, feeling the comfort of his arms, which so opposed the ache in her heart. 'It's the gossip, the tongue-wagging, that is so upsetting and bad for business,' he continued. 'We shall be pestered again by the gossipmongers. Can't you see that your brother is putting us through more than we deserve? He should have served his time, finished his sentence with dignity. Not set himself on the run, causing a repeat of all the distress. It really won't do!'

She wanted to defend her brother but just then she heard a key being drawn up from the letter box.

'It's Dad,' she whispered, and Don let her go.

Wilfred came slowly into the room, puffing and drawing short breaths. 'Hello, lad,' he said at the sight of their guest. 'What brings you here of a weekday?'

'Uncomfortable matters, I'm sorry to say, Mr Connor. We've heard today – that is, Mother, Lydia and myself – that there has been an escape from Wandsworth.'

Wilfred nodded. 'Yes, it's true, I'm grieved to admit.'

'This reflects very badly, Mr Connor. Though I am sure you're aware of the discomfort it causes and I have no wish to add to your worries.'

'And I'm grateful for that,' replied Wilfred, struggling out of his coat and going to his chair where he sank down with a worried frown.

'Goodbye, Mr Connor,' Don said abruptly, and left the room. Birdie followed him out.

'You must bolt the doors at night,' Don warned her as they stood alone in the passage. 'Tell Pat to be discreet. He must give no cheek to feed the gossipers until your brother is apprehended. With luck, it will be soon.'

Birdie felt her insides shiver at these words. He kissed her briefly and she felt a sad absence of the deep under-standing that she had thought united them.

'Put a smile on when you go out, my dear, and hold your head high,' he whispered. 'People will forget all this when you become my wife.'

That night, as Birdie was about to climb into bed, the cold of the room making her shiver under her nightgown, there was a soft knock at her door. She guessed it would be Pat, as all through their meal and afterwards in the parlour, his eyes had been darting to hers, their expression reminding her of her promise to tell him about Frank.

'Come in.' she whispered as she opened the door a crack, to allow Pat to steal in over the bare boards. 'Let's sit by the window,' she urged, fearing that Wilfred, in the next room, might overhear their whispers. Bringing a rug from the bed, she sat on the wooden bench under the sash with him and placed the warm cover over their knees. The only light in the room came from Birdie's oil lamp placed on her dresser beside the jug and washbasin.

'Well?' asked Pat expectantly, folding the baggy, darned sleeves of his vest over his cold knuckles. With his shock of dark hair and his freshly scrubbed cheeks, Birdie thought how young he looked. Again Frank's warning went through her mind, not to tell a soul of their meeting. But now that Pat had found her out, she didn't have a choice.

'Pat, you must promise not to tell a soul,' Birdie warned again in the firmest tone she could muster.

'Who would I tell?' Pat asked impatiently. 'There's only me and you on our Frank's side.'

'One word would give us away,' Birdie insisted, 'like my own blunder. You can't take back the spoken word.'

'My lips are sealed.'

'All right. I'll tell you everything, though how we can help our brother I don't know. Frank didn't escape from prison, but on his way to hospital.'

Pat gasped. 'Is he ill?'

'Now, calm yourself, little brother,' Birdie said gently. 'He'd started a fever, then was covered in spots and rashes. His guards were reluctant to go near him, thinking it might be the pox. So they sent him to the hospital and it was this that gave Frank his chance to escape.'

'So the spots wasn't the pox?'

'No, course not. He was filthy and running alive with lice that caused his sores. The authorities got the wind up, that's all.'

'Did he say what happened?' Pat burst out almost before she'd finished. 'Did he say he didn't desert?'

'Now, I'll try to explain in me own way and it ain't easy, as Frank was confused himself. This is what he told me, not word for word, but near enough. One minute he was fighting the enemy, then he found himself lying in this farmhouse.'

'And wounded?' Pat said excitedly.

'I felt it, Pat, a real dent in his skull.'

'So he never ran away. Our brother is innocent, like we thought all along.'

'Yes, but it's Frank's word against the Army's.'

'Can we tell Dad?'

'Even if he believed us, what could he do, except worry?' Birdie reasoned, shaking her head.

'We've got to do something,' Pat said indignantly. 'Where is Frank hiding?'

'I don't know and that's the honest truth,' she admitted. 'The last time I saw him was the next morning, under the arches at the park. I took him some clothes and a bite to eat. He'd slept on a barge and said he was thinking of going to someone he knew. I gave him some chloride to help the bites. And that was all I could do . . . so very little . . . and yet I yearned to . . .' She stopped, her voice breaking with a tiny sob.

Pat sat in silence, his eyes looking deep into hers. There was a glisten of a tear there too as the truth slowly dawned on him that Frank couldn't be helped, not by a sincere wish of theirs to assist him or the plain facts as he presented them, which were in themselves very loose.

'Will he have to go back to prison if they catch him?' Pat sniffed.

'I fear so.'

'That's a real unjust thing,' Pat wailed angrily. 'Turn a good man into a wild dog and hunt him down. I hate the law.'

'Don't say that, love. Hate is a strong word.'

'But I do.'

'Hate won't help our Frank. We've got to keep cool heads.'

'So what shall we do if he comes to the house again like he did on Sunday?' Hope shone from his eyes.

'He wouldn't chance it. We might be watched.'

'I'd spot a copper a mile off,' Pat argued.

'Yes, but they don't all have tall helmets and flat feet.'

'Why is it people hate our Frank?' Pat demanded. 'When Fred Kirby up the road burgled all them posh houses in Poplar, Willie told me they was supposed to have drank a toast to him in the pub.'

'Fred Kirby wasn't accused of desertion,' Birdie explained, feeling the injustice too. 'Desertion is a mortal sin in the Nation's eyes, next to murdering the life out of someone.'

'Yeah, but our Frank's not guilty!' Pat protested again. 'He's an innocent man.'

Birdie nodded slowly. 'I know, I know . . . Now listen, it's late and now you know everything you have a responsibility to Frank to keep a wise tongue. You're in the same boat as me now. I had to act out that little scene in front of the constable and must even keep my secret from Don. You won't even be able to tell Willie.'

They sat quietly and finally Pat stood up, folding the rug over her knees. He looked down at her in the soft light from the oil lamp, then bent and kissed her cheek.

'You don't have to worry about me, Birdie,' he told her. 'But will you tell me if you see him again?'

'I won't hesitate, love. Now, good night. God bless, and sleep well. And don't forget your prayers.'

He smiled briefly and padded off, one leg of his long johns where she had shortened them, stuck up around his calf, his bare feet going silently across the draughty boards.

Birdie sat for some while, shivering in the wind whistling through the cracks of the sash, her concerns multiplying now that Pat possessed a knowledge that might be too heavy a burden to bear. She had longed to share her worries with Don today, her heart persuading her that their love could overcome anything, but she had heard from Don's own lips the wish that Frank would soon be captured, safe in the hands of the law.

Chapter 7

A fortnight later the police arrived to turn the house upside down. Two big, burly constables barged their way in on Friday morning, just as Pat was wolfing his breakfast and Wilfred was coming downstairs. They hammered on the door, giving Birdie a fright that set all her nerves on edge, then burst into the house, waving a paper they said entitled them to search the premises.

It was clear to Birdie she couldn't stop them anyway, as they banged behind doors and in cupboards, tramping up and down the stairs and investigating even the closet. They made as much mess as they could and Pat failed to go to work on time. They left Birdie's sewing room in a state, with her rolls of cloth pulled from their neat piles and her cupboards emptied. And when they made down to the airey, only to find Harry's door locked, one of them remained to wait until he came home.

Birdie flew down the steps at half-past six and found Harry's door open. 'Harry! Are you there?' she called.

He appeared from the dark passage that led down to the scullery and his bedroom. His face bore the traces of dirt from his labours, as did his baggy working trousers and rough cloth shirt. He hadn't even had time to remove his boots, she noticed.

'Come in, Birdie. Don't stand on the doorstep.'

'Did you find a policeman waiting?' she asked, her eyes

flitting around the large room she hadn't seen since Harry had moved here early in the year.

'I did that,' he nodded. 'The fellow is searching the scullery and will be gone soon.'

Birdie heard the bangs and thumps. 'They have the cheek of the devil!' she protested, indignant on Harry's behalf. 'Not content with disturbing us, now they are bothering you. As if Frank would hide here!'

'Calm yourself, Birdie,' he reassured her. 'Sit down and warm yourself by the fire. I've managed to light it despite the interruptions.'

She sat on a small leather chair made comfortable by two plump chintz cushions, a few stitches missing to their seams, but otherwise pretty-looking. The dark oak mantel was polished and uncluttered, while below it, in the hearth, stood a black iron companion set and little bundles of kindling beside a full scuttle of coal.

'Do you make up the fire every night?' she asked, noting the dry duckboards that were once very damp and were now partially covered by a thin carpet, a square that still retained its deep greens and browns.

'In the winter and up until spring,' he nodded. 'And sometimes of a cool summer's evening.'

'You've got it very nice,' Birdie decided in honest surprise as she stared around the big room, admiring the square dining table covered in a heavy green tasselled cloth. Beneath it appeared four round, strong curving legs that matched the shape of the sideboard opposite. The shelves were filled untidily with books and personal things that looked as though Harry took an interest in reading and writing.

'So they called on you today?' Harry asked, sitting on the arm of the chair opposite. He spread out his long legs, leaning one elbow on his knee as he took hold of the poker and encouraged the fire.

'I've only just finished setting our place right,' Birdie burst out, her thoughts redirected back to the reason she'd come. 'They were here at the crack of dawn, turning out every drawer and cupboard needlessly. You'd think we were hiding the devil himself.'

'I suppose it was to be expected if your brother is still free?'

'The conclusion I came to meself,' she whispered eagerly. 'Frank has outwitted them so far. Not that any one of the coppers had the decency to give me any news!'

'Which can only mean they have none to give,' Harry returned in a conspiratorial tone.

'Do you really think Frank might be safe?' she whispered.

'What else would warrant such a search?'

'And Frank has been free for over two weeks,' she agreed. 'So you may be right.'

A loud clatter from the scullery caused Harry to rise to his feet. 'Now, rest easy there, whilst I take stock of the damage, though they won't find nothing to interest them – not unless they're after me treasure, and they'll have to dig to Australia for that.'

A smile touched Birdie's lips as he went, his tall frame and broad shoulders swinging past the table with an easy flow. She liked the way he conducted himself; he put her at ease, finding a light touch to the situation, yet she knew that he must feel invaded.

Soon she heard Harry's deep voice from the scullery as he addressed the constable and after a few minutes the bastion of the law emerged empty-handed. Birdie gave him a fierce stare and toss of her head. But she felt a little sorry for having done so when he bade her good evening politely and quickly left.

She breathed a long sigh of relief. At last they had peace again. And her spirits had lifted after what Harry had said.

The police certainly wouldn't have taken so much trouble if Frank was anywhere near being caught.

Glancing down the passage, she wondered if Harry kept the other two rooms as pleasantly as this. She recollected the tiny scullery at the rear with only one small window, too high to open, but the light it let in from the yard above was vital. The remaining room, though large and high-ceilinged, had been filled to bursting with kids when her mother had been alive. Bernadette had rented the airey to an Irish family that seemed to multiply by the month. The sight of the oil lantern burning on the sideboard brought back to Birdie memories of her mother, as together they had braved a visit to the noisy rabble from County Cork. There had seemed to be children and babies everywhere.

When Bernadette had died, Wilfred, ailing and grief-stricken, had closed up the airey and the family had returned to Ireland. It wasn't until earlier this year, when it had seemed to Birdie that, with a little attention, the airey could again be a means of income, that they had let it to Harry.

'So, the place is to your liking?' Harry asked as he placed a real white china cup and saucer in front of her, the freshly made tea a rich, steaming brown.

'For all the years it was closed, you've done a grand job.'

'I'm relieved it's to your approval.' He took a seat and drank from a mug he had brought for himself. She could see the twinkle in his dark eyes as he gazed over the rim.

'Did the officer make a mess?' she asked, feeling a little shy under his gaze.

'None to concern me, and he was civil enough,' Harry shrugged, adding drily, 'though I can't say we've become lifelong friends.'

Birdie found her mood changing, for she'd bottled herself up all day with anger that her home could be seized and inspected on the authorities' whim. But Harry seemed unruffled and she too saw the better side of things now: Frank still kept his freedom.

'I'm sorry it is because of our problems this has happened,' she apologized.

'There's nothing harmed here,' he told her. 'And you know my feelings on your brother, though staying on the loose will be no easy task for him.'

'Perhaps he's found friends,' she agreed hopefully, beginning to think that Frank might have found a safe harbour with that person he mentioned. But not wanting to be drawn, she went on quickly, 'You make a fine brew, Harry.'

'Aye,' he smiled, with a charming curve to his dark eyebrow. 'I've made many such brews in my life.'

At this, curiosity filled her. 'Was it the orphanage that taught you?'

'Sadly, there were no such luxuries as tea-making,' he returned smilingly. 'I owe my domestic skills to the services. The merchant navy and the army became my family.' He turned the mug slowly between his long fingers. 'I've travelled the world and enjoyed all human nature, and would have continued to do so, had not war broken out.'

Birdie saw a faraway look come into his eye. She knew that he must have endured many unhappy experiences whilst serving his country, as most veterans of that terrible war had suffered. But Harry was not one to complain, nor brag about his time in uniform.

Suddenly a pair of feet came pounding down the stairs outside. Harry jumped up and was at the door ahead of her. When he opened it, Pat stood there, his face ashen.

'It's Dad,' he babbled. 'He's going wild. It's one of them fits, I'm sure it is.'

Birdie almost dropped her cup as she sprang from the table and all three of them ran upstairs.

★

Dr Tapper entered the parlour where Birdie, Pat and Harry were anxiously waiting.

Birdie stood up. 'How is our dad?'

The elderly doctor, dressed in a black frock coat, placed his Gladstone bag on the table and slid the pince-nez spectacles from his nose. 'I've administered a restorative but it's likely the seizures will return. I can't be specific about when, but with having two already, well, a recurrence is likely.' Dr Tapper handed her a small packet. 'Mix this restorative powder with a few drops of castor oil and the yoke of one egg when the fit strikes. But I warn you that sometimes very little helps.'

'But what causes these fits?' asked Pat, his face very pale.

'I can give you no straight answer, lad,' Dr Tapper shrugged. 'Perhaps a deep-seated agitation, that is triggered off by an event such as you told me of today. Your father may be concerned over your brother, although you say he rarely speaks of him. On the other hand, his own health may be troubling him. Perhaps the seizure is nature's way of letting off internal steam?'

'So you mean they could be good for him?' Pat asked doubtfully.

'Who knows? But if you were to regard them in this way, combined with the infusion I've given you, then you have the better aspect of it altogether. Please call me again if you need me.'

Birdie followed him out into the passage and opened her purse.

'Can you afford my fee?' the doctor asked kindly.

'I'm not after charity, Dr Tapper.'

'I knew your mother well enough to know that,' he answered gently. 'And though I've not seen your father in some while, I fear that you may need to call on me again for his chest. There may come a time when the Collis Browne will not be sufficient.'

Birdie paid him the shilling consultation fee, but his words struck fear in her heart. Her dad was ailing and, for all his reluctance to seek help, she knew Dr Tapper was right, as the Collis Browne did now take longer to work.

She thanked him and watched him climb aboard his trap, placing his top hat over his grey head. He shook the reins attached to the harness and the small, black pony trotted off.

'Will that powder cure Dad?' Pat was still ill at ease when she returned to the parlour.

'It'll help, along with the good doctor's idea that these episodes help to ease rather than agitate,' she reassured him, though after what the doctor had said, she was all at twos and threes herself. 'Now come along, sit with Harry for a while whilst I lay the table. I must get meself over to Don's and let him know what happened today. Harry, would you stay and keep Pat company for an hour?'

Harry glanced out of the window, a deep frown on his brow. 'Darkness is falling. Could your visit wait until first light? I'll be happy to stay with your father then and I'm certain the drains I'm digging won't fall in for the sake of an hour,' he assured her, his dark eyes surveying the gloomy street.

At this Pat looked expectant. 'Can I stay home too?'

'Indeed you can't,' Birdie replied, casting him a rueful glance. 'You've only just got yourself a decent job, Patrick Connor, I'll not have you risking it.' Turning to Harry she asked in a softer tone, 'If you're sure that's all right, Harry?'

He gave her a nod for reply and Birdie went to the kitchen, grateful she hadn't had to venture out in the dark. She would now be able to finish her sewing and consider what to wear in advance of her meeting with Aggie and Lydia when she went to visit Don.

Chapter 8

Birdie sat on the bus to Poplar, dressed in her smart blue woollen coat and matching felt cloche hat. She had fingered a few waves to peep out delicately from under its brim and pinched her cheeks half a dozen times to urge a little colour. Temptation had come in the form of Lady Hailing's lipstick, but she'd resisted it, knowing that falsity wouldn't meet with Don's approval. She'd added a pair of elderly, but good-quality gloves to her ensemble, of a fine brown leather, all thanks to the generosity of the aristocratic ladies, and she felt that Don could be proud of her, offsetting somewhat the news of the police visit. Despite the crowded conditions she sat in, with the rattle of coughs and sneezes all around, and the smell of the disinfectant sprayed inside the buses and trams to combat any lingering flu germs, Birdie was not disheartened. She was going to see Don, and she hoped that after the unpleasant facts were out, they could find a few moments alone together. At the thought of his arms around her, she gave a little shiver and a smile formed on her lips.

As the bus travelled through Millwall and Cubitt Town, the sun peeped out from what had been a cloudy sky. Horse-drawn carts from the docks, their Tilley lights extinguished, clattered noisily past, tooted by an occasional motorized vehicle. As they neared Poplar, an army of dustmen hoisted battered bins on their shoulders and tipped them noisily into open-topped dustcarts. Here, long queues formed to the city and the three-wheeled open carts of the road cleaners caused temporary but annoying obstructions. The strong disinfectant of the water carts spraying the streets wafted into the bus. Every drain was an ancient menace, in dire need of unblocking. Pedestrians swerved or jumped to dodge the filth and were jostled by the street traders and barrow boys who had begun their day in the dead of night.

Birdie alighted at the High Street, relieved not to be part of the throng who fought for a seat aboard every bus and tram available. How lucky she was to begin her day in the calm of her dressmaking room, with the view of the river over the tops of the smoke-blackened roofs and yards. Here in Poplar, the mighty workforce surged out to Wanstead and Dagenham, Paddington and Marylebone, Brixton and Blackheath, even as far as Hackney and Stoke Newington in the north.

Making her way past the Hospital for Accidents by the East India Dock gate, she crossed the busy junction, stepping nimbly out of the path of a chocolate-coloured Atlas bus. The surge of pedestrians was suddenly halted by a brightly painted traction engine trundling from its yard. Birdie discreetly held her nose as it belched a cloud of smoke from its boiling furnace. The thick fog caused her to cough, but it soon rumbled off to leave the way free to the store.

A familiar smell of horse dung and over-ripe vegetables, laced with paraffin and coal sulphur rose up, an odour she associated with the Thornes' shop. Each shop boasted a smoke-stained blind rattling in the morning breeze, and guiltily Birdie found herself comparing the pleasant calm of March Street, with its tangy, seafaring aromas, to the conflicting chaos of the shopkeeping heart of Poplar.

What would it be like to live here? she allowed herself to wonder. To wake every morning to the demands of the store. There would be no time for nostalgia, as she was so used to, drawing her bedroom curtains to the sight of the estuary in the distance; to breathe in the wind that shivered around the house in recognition of London's seafaring might. No, life was quite different at the store. Birdie had listened with admiration as Don had rattled off the busy, never-ending routine of a shopkeeper's day. From the crack of dawn to sunset there was never a moment to pause. Was she capable of entering such a world? She had never sliced a shoulder of bacon or halved a mouldy cheese with a wire. Neither had she weighed or served a bagful of dusty, sometimes rotting potatoes, and worn a coarse sack apron, such as Aggie so gallantly endured, for protection. It was no wonder that Don regarded his mother with such respect!

Just then Birdie saw Don's upright figure ahead of her. He was helping a woman to fill her shopping basket. In his smart brown overall, with his parting dead centre in his fine head of hair, he looked as handsome as he did in his Sunday-best suit and tie. Her spirits lifted to such a degree that she wondered why, a few moments ago, she had ever doubted that she could learn to live and work at the store.

When he saw her, he left his customer and strode eagerly to meet her. She wanted to throw her arms around him and tell him how much she loved him. But of course, that wouldn't do in the street.

'Birdie, what a pleasant surprise!'

'Don, have you a moment or two to speak?'

He looked uncertain, then smiled, pulling back his shoulders. 'We are rather busy, but I'm sure Mother would like to see you.'

Without more ado, he guided her into the store. 'Mother, look who has paid us a visit!' he called to the busy figure behind the counter.

Aggie Thorne welcomed Birdie with a curious frown. 'What brings you this way, Brigid?' she asked in her clipped, sharp tone, though Birdie knew it was only Aggie's way. After the loss of her son and husband, grief had carved deep lines around her small, suspicious eyes. Birdie was unable to dismiss the thought that Aggie had no artistry at all, with her thin, light-brown hair scraped back into a plaited bun. The style did her no justice; rather it added a decade to her fifty-three years. Her red, chapped hands were placed on a well-thumbed notebook, resting near a freshly made tray of dripping. Aggie took a cloth from under the counter and wiped the grease from her hands.

Birdie guessed by Aggie's question that the Thornes knew nothing of yesterday's events. She knew she must find the courage to start on it.

'Don, did you know Brigid was coming?' Aggie asked with a sharp glance at her son.

'Not at all, Mother,' Don answered hesitantly. Then added suddenly and with a burst of eagerness, 'But a good thing, don't you think, after what we were discussing this week?'

Birdie forgot her mission completely as a thin and rarely seen smile formed on Aggie's lips. 'Maybe you're right, son – yes, perhaps this is as good a time as any. But I'll warn you, Lydia is upstairs, readying herself to come down for the accounts. So use the office whilst it's free and I'll keep me eye on the shop.'

Birdie wondered what Lydia had to do with anything. And why was Aggie looking at her in that strange way?

'I can't stop long,' Birdie protested, wondering why she felt so uncomfortable under Aggie's scrutiny. 'I've me dad at home to—' She stopped as the shop bell tinkled and several women bustled in, placing their baskets directly in front of Aggie, on the counter.

Don put his hand to the small of Birdie's back and she found herself stepping down the passage, past crates and boxes and big swollen sacks of vegetables, giving out strong whiffs of mould and decay. Above these loomed shelf upon shelf crammed with every conceivable item. Carob beans and liquorice root, tapioca pudding, reels of cotton, laces, dates, pease puddings, locust beans, bars of chocolate, Vaseline and nougats of all shapes. Squat bottles of castor oil propped the boxes of senna pods and the rolls of flocking. There seemed no order to the mixture, but every inch was used.

Further along, the air changed again: a cocktail of mothballs and sickly sweet treacle. Birdie's stomach lurched and she walked on quickly to the office, the heart of the Thornes' empire and Lydia's kingdom. As she pushed open the door, Birdie was met with the spectacle of the huge carved mahogany roll-top desk, standing like a great altar, stacked with papers and books, and seeming to support the shelves above it, laden with dog-eared ledgers. The air turned musty then, like an old museum in which the dust and paper had a taste of its own.

The rest of the room was sparsely furnished. A couch stood under the small window and a wooden highchair, which Birdie guessed had once been James's, hid in the corner beside two elderly dining chairs. Birdie took care to stifle her gasp of relief as Don lifted the sash and let in the breeze.

'So, dearest, we'll have a few moments of quiet together,' Don said in such a sweet voice that Birdie forgot all about Aggie as he took her in his arms and without hesitation kissed her. His hands pressed her close and his lips were so welcoming that Birdie closed her eyes, enjoying the sense of wellbeing.

'You look delightful,' he whispered admiringly, holding her away, 'not that I've ever seen you looking anything other than topnotch.'

Birdie blushed unguardedly, desperate to be kissed again, and praying that neither Aggie nor Lydia would appear.

But with a pat to her cheek, Don darted forward and wrestled one of the chairs free from its clutter. 'Now, my dear, you must sit and listen to what I have to say, for I know when you get going there's hardly a gap for me.' He laughed, brushing aside the stray tendrils of dark brown hair that escaped around her face. Sitting beside her, he took her hand and squeezed it. 'First my confession!'

Birdie's eyes flew wide. 'Your confession?' All thoughts now of the police raid were gone from her mind. She didn't think she had ever heard Don use that word before. It was much more to her Catholic vocabulary than his.

'Indeed, indeed. I have been very remiss in delaying our plans to marry. Very much so.' He looked so crestfallen that Birdie laughed.

'Oh, but Don, I never doubted you. I never thought—'

'Brigid, dear, let me finish.'

She put her hand to her mouth, nodding silently and giggling. He was in such an excited mood that she couldn't help feeling that way too.

Giving her hand a pat, he continued. 'You see, Mother and Lydia and I have been giving a great deal of thought to the future. The store is on its feet again, though our losses have been severe with Father and Stephen going.'

Again Birdie nodded, keeping her lips together with difficulty, as her heart leaped in anticipation.

'And with Mother being bereaved,' he continued, sitting upright, 'and Lydia and James to consider, and indeed, the anxiety of my change of career from the railways, my own desires have taken a back seat. But now, at last, we've decided that before the rush of summer – which will stretch us to the limits – the Thornes will set aside a day for a certain wedding!'

'Oh, Don!' she exclaimed, unable to believe her ears. 'You mean, us? We can be married?'

'With a little conniving, yes.'

'Conniving?' Birdie repeated, her ecstasy briefly tempered by the word.

'In the world of business every day is as important as the next, and selecting the right time to close the shop has been a difficult task. But we are considering early next year, shortly after Christmas.'

'What, so soon?' Birdie gasped.

Don leaned forward. 'What have you to say to that?'

'Oh, Don, I can't believe it, I can't!' she began deliriously. 'But won't it be an awful squeeze to have it booked at church? And there's me dress,' she added, thinking of the white satin she'd have to order in, and the veil, and the expense of quality cloth. 'But I suppose if I went hammer and tongs, it could be made in that time. And there's me bridesmaids' dresses. Enid and Emily—'

'Dearest,' Don interrupted firmly, 'Mother and I have given consideration to a papal service. But we have attended our church for years. Yes, yes . . .' he held up his hand at her protest, 'it will mean compromise, but on reflection, think how painful it will be for me – pews full of your side and none of my own. Now, we can't have the best of both worlds, agreed? So I'm sure you'll see it won't be any sacrifice to be married by licence.'

Birdie's scattered thoughts suddenly stopped flying in all directions. 'By licence?'

'A civil service,' he murmured so soothingly that for a second Birdie felt no pain at all, 'so that both families can be represented fairly. Lydia will take care of the details and Mother has consented to arrange a small reception here, though, of course, in the afternoon the shop must open.'

Birdie felt as if all the wind had been knocked from her sails. She tried to speak, but a mumble came out, so quiet and forlorn, that Don's smile faded into clear irritation.

'Brigid, this isn't like you,' he coaxed. 'Isn't it the fairest, most agreeable decision to be married in the presence of both our families?'

'But . . .' she began, 'it's different for Catholics. It's a sacrament, see? A holy thing. I was to walk down the aisle with me two little bridesmaids, with the priest waiting and the organ playing—'

'I've never agreed fully to that,' Don stated firmly. 'And we've less than two months, remember.'

'But why then?' Birdie asked. 'We could wait until spring or summer even.'

'I thought you were eager to marry.' He let go of her hand.

'I am. But—'

'Come, my dear, I think you're suffering a little shock at the excitement of it all. Think of our future and our life together here at the store. We can build on two generations of Thornes, and our children will inherit a business to be proud of.'

'Me dad won't care for that.'

'Your father isn't getting married,' Don answered sharply. 'It's you and me, Brigid, who count.'

'Oh, Don, I'm all confused.'

'Don't be, my love,' he murmured with an encouraging smile. 'Mother and I have talked this over, seeing it as the very best way. And there is yet more good news. Lydia has consented to move with James to the premises next door. She has generously agreed to give up her rooms here. We can rent the new place very reasonably and, knowing our reliability, the landlord has offered us the lease at a nominal sum. The move, of course, will be a little unsettling, so Mother and I will value your help and friendship to Lydia.'

Birdie saw all her dreams vanishing. What was she to do? The store dictated the Thornes' lives, to the day a person got married. And it wouldn't even be a day, as Don had said the shop would reopen in the afternoon. She'd had her heart set on marrying in church. What would Dad say?

'You'll soon see the sense in it.' Don drew her to her feet and planted a kiss on her cheek. 'I'll call Lydia down now.

Please, my dear, try your best with her. I know she has seemed distant, but becoming a widow has been a great distress. With a little coaxing on your side, you'll find her very good company.'

'Don, don't call Lydia yet.' Birdie caught his sleeve. 'I've something to tell you.'

'What is it?'

'The police came yesterday.'

'What!'

'They searched the house, not leaving an inch unturned.'

'Did anyone see?' His jaw dropped.

'A constable was made to stand outside Harry's too. All day it was, till he came home.'

'You mean the whole neighbourhood saw?' he gasped, as though he hadn't understood what she'd said. 'Everyone knows your brother – the *escapee* – is still at large?'

She lifted her shoulders helplessly. 'I thought you'd want to know immediately. That's why I came to tell you.'

'But this is dreadful!' he exclaimed, startling Birdie, so that she let go of his sleeve. 'Why are the authorities not acting? Why do they allow such a thing?'

Birdie felt desperate. Any brief hope that she'd had that Don might not be upset now disappeared as patches of red fury sprang to his cheeks.

Chapter 9

'Don't you see what this means?' Don demanded, hardly able to speak. 'It will be all round Poplar that the offender – with an undoubted connection to us, and to the business – is still at large.'

'But it's not as if Frank is dangerous—' Birdie began, only to draw a gasp of astonishment from Don.

'Of course your wretched brother is dangerous!' he spluttered. 'He's broken the law and put the authorities to shame! A man on the loose who will go to any lengths to secure his freedom!'

'But Frank wouldn't,' she insisted, knowing how Don hated to hear a word in defence of Frank, and yet how could she keep silent? 'He's a kind man, a gentle soul who wouldn't harm a fly.'

'Then you're clearly deceived,' he returned with a look of disdain on his face. 'That man is a rascal, a ne'er-do-well.'

Birdie was hurt to the quick. 'Don, I won't have you say such things about me brother. You've no reason to make such a judgement, even if he was sent away.'

'You see?' he accused, pointing a finger. 'You're blind to the truth!'

'He's family, Don, that's what he is,' Birdie defended, a terrible sinking sensation inside of her as she struggled to defend Frank from the man who was to be her husband.

'But he's been sentenced as a deserter!' Don exclaimed, intent on having the last word and pronouncing Frank not only guilty, but a danger to all mankind.

'Then they got it wrong,' Birdie answered quietly but resolutely. 'And I'm as certain of his innocence as you are of his guilt.'

This had such an alarming effect that Birdie felt quite threatened. Don stuck his chin out aggressively and with clenched hands, demanded, 'You would put *him* before us? Before our forthcoming marriage? Our future?'

But Birdie stood firm. 'You're twisting my words.'

'Indeed I'm not,' he argued fiercely. 'And if you want us to be married, Brigid, there is only one course of action for you to take. You must disown him. Put him out of your life. Dismiss these fanciful notions from your head.'

To Birdie, these words felt like physical blows. Don was giving her a choice, an impossible one. In her heart of hearts Birdie knew something about all this was wrong, so wrong. But before she could speak, the finger pointed again.

'I've said all there is to be said,' he ended. 'Now you must decide which one of us means the most to you. I thought he would be recaptured in just a few days, and we should have no more of this humiliating affair. It was enough when he was tried and sent to prison. Mother and Lydia had to suffer great embarrassment. But for your sake, we made allowances. To hear you now, defending him, as I've always suspected you might in your heart – well, it just won't do. Give me your word that you're done with him. And should he dare to contact you, you must give him up to the police.'

Birdie felt sick inside. She would never disown Frank, not even if he *had* deserted, which he hadn't. Did Don really mean what he was saying?

'Well?' he demanded. 'Your answer, please.'

'You know I love you, Don,' she answered truthfully. 'I want us to be married. But I can't disown Frank.'

Birdie wasn't certain what she expected next, for she had hoped all along that a quarrel of such bitterness might somehow end in a loving reunion. But as he looked coldly down on her, his mouth as tight as Aggie's had been when they'd walked in the shop, Birdie knew she'd gone too far in defending Frank. In silence they faced one another and though she longed to fling her arms round him, to end this silly dispute, she knew that was impossible.

Just then, a light footstep could be heard on the back stairs. The door opened and Lydia entered. 'I'm sorry to interrupt,' she apologized, her skin very white against her long, dark hair taken up at the back and pinned neatly above her white working collar. 'I thought I heard shouting – is something amiss?'

'Nothing at all, Lydia,' Don snapped, moving towards her tall figure dressed in grey, her head held high, accentuating her handsome cheekbones. 'Come in, we've kept you from your work long enough.'

'Hello, Lydia,' Birdie said in embarrassment as Don made no attempt to disguise their quarrel.

'Good morning, Brigid.' Lydia offered her a curt nod.

'I'll see you out,' Don said briskly, taking Birdie's arm with such force that she knew all hope of resolving their differences was gone.

Propelling her down the passage and into the shop, he called across to Aggie, 'Mother, Brigid is leaving.' The little group of women surrounding Aggie all turned to stare at them. Birdie read their expressions and knew at once that she, or rather the Connors, was the topic of their conversation.

Aggie didn't even have time to call goodbye before Don had hustled Birdie out on the street. 'I'll bid you good morning,' he muttered in a gruff whisper, careful to keep his voice low as people passed them on the pavement. 'Though I can hardly say that anything much good has come out of it.'

'Don, please reconsider,' Birdie responded, hardly able to speak for the lump in her throat. 'You can't really mean to make me chose between you and Frank?'

'Why do you hesitate, Brigid? I have just asked you to marry me.'

'You didn't ask,' Birdie pointed out tearfully. 'You referred me to Lydia to make the arrangements.'

'Now you are being silly.'

Birdie swallowed back her sob. Her pride and feelings hurt beyond measure. 'Silly, is it,' she blustered, 'to make the effort to come over here and neglect me dad in order to put your feelings first? Silly that a minute or two ago, I was ready to give up me standards by not marrying in church?'

His smile was disdainful. 'For what you would gain, your inconvenience amounts to nothing,' he dismissed.

'What!' she gasped, barely able to breathe.

'Security, a fine home,' he intoned, as if he was reading out a list. 'Not many women are given the opportunity of such good fortune.' Before Birdie could splutter out a word he continued, 'And don't expect me to give you a second chance, Brigid, when the scene turns ugly and it becomes clear to you how right I am.'

Bracing his shoulders and leaving her open-mouthed, he turned, paused politely to allow a customer entry to the shop and followed her in without a backward glance.

Birdie stood on the pavement staring at the empty space. So painful was the lump in her throat that she failed to board a bus at the top of East India Road and instead, turned towards Cubitt Town, and the long walk home to March Street.

Chapter 10

Harry stoked the fire, turning the red coals over and adding several large lumps of timber that he'd brought home with him. The blaze gave a burst of heat that caused Wilfred to sigh appreciatively from his chair.

'That's nice, lad. You've got a good flame going there.'

'This old wood from the building site burns well when it's dry,' Harry smiled, easing himself up and stretching his legs. 'Now, what do you say to a bite to eat? I'm a dab hand at the bread and dripping, if I say it meself. A couple of good slices will settle you for the rest of the day.' He nodded encouragingly, but Wilfred looked disinterested.

'Can't work up much of an appetite. But I wouldn't say no to a brew and a fag.'

Harry sighed dejectedly, taking the bottle of Collis Browne from the mantel, not that the medicine had resulted in much. Wilfred's bark had grown noisier through the morning. He'd lit up any number of times, choking on the cigarette and giving himself a struggle to breathe. A fit hadn't come on, but Harry had watched him carefully, though his presence hadn't altogether been welcomed.

'Don't need company,' Wilfred had objected when Birdie had gone. 'You can go off to your work,' he'd muttered as though he'd been insulted, but Harry had made light of it, saying he could do with a breather from his labours, and for an hour he'd managed to interest Wilfred in a round of dominoes. Now, however, Harry was caught in the jaws of a dilemma. He feared Wilfred was restless and intent on making his way to the Quarry and his customary pint, though Harry felt Birdie would have something to say on the matter. But how could he restrain him? He had no authority to do so.

As he put on the kettle, he glanced at the mantel clock and saw it was midday. Birdie's visit to the Thornes must have taken more time than she'd expected. Not that he minded for himself. Although his crew would be wondering where their boss had gone, they were reliable and would know he'd not be absent from the graft himself unless he'd been urgently called upon.

Harry smiled in satisfaction at the thought of his small, but expanding business. He was beginning to see the hard work and long hours he'd put in since last summer might make him a decent living – he'd dared not put it into words – that he might be successful. When, in the conflict, he'd seen men falling like flies around him and gunned down without mercy, the thought that had kept him going was that he hadn't been born a bastard for nothing. He'd come through the loveless, exacting life of the orphanage and years of travel, to experience how other men lived and many were worse off than himself.

The kettle boiled noisily on the range, bringing Harry out of his reveries. Having taken the pot and warmed it, he poured in a spoonful of tea, noticing the caddy was very light. He'd bring a few ounces home and slip the leaves in unnoticed. Birdie was too proud to take it without argument. He smiled again. But this time with affection.

'Ah, so you're making the tea, are you?'

Birdie's voice startled him and he almost dropped the pot. 'Birdie – you're home.'

'That I am, Harry. And sorry I am for the delay.' She picked off her gloves, each finger loosened daintily and then her hat, leaving her pretty waves to fall free, all brown and soft around her face. But he saw something else too: a sadness in her eyes in the quick moment she glanced at him, and the smile she gave didn't fool him for a minute. 'The buses were all late,' she rattled off. 'A fine thing it is when you pay for your ticket and need to be prompt. It would have taken me less time to walk . . .' Her coat went briskly on the peg behind the door as if she couldn't bring herself to stand still for an instant.

Harry stirred the pot, hiding his smile. There was nothing of her, not really, with her quick little movements and straight back and happy disposition that beguilingly made him feel like he was part of their family. Though, he reprimanded himself swiftly, that was not a thought he'd be wise to cultivate. He knew darned well that some day he was going to have to leave the airey. There hadn't been a lodgings he'd ever stayed in that hadn't packed him off for one reason or another. Mostly it was family moving in: a long-lost daughter or son and their expanding family, an aged parent or distant uncle or aunt who had turned up on the doorstep. Households swelled like balloons in the East End, cramming in every available body.

'Is me dad all right?' Birdie asked then, pausing briefly her circuit of the kitchen to glance along the passage.

'As right as ninepence,' he nodded, 'and will be even better when I've made him a brew.'

'Now, you leave that and be off,' she trilled, swiping the teaspoon from his hand and shutting him up with the surprise of it. 'Get yourself to work, and tell your boss it was your landlady who made you late. A man has to earn his living and if he can't be relied upon to turn up on time, then he'll slip right down the pecking order.'

'But I don't have a—' Harry began, intending to tell her he answered to no one but himself, but a small, urgent hand pushed at his shoulder.

'Off you go. And thank you again.' Her voice held a little tremble, her eyes not meeting his as a lock of hair fell across her face.

Harry watched the spoon twirl violently round the teapot, splashing the brown liquid until the lid snapped on. Then the mugs were laid out, one, two, three, and another, which made him wonder how many were going to turn up for a bevy – perhaps the whole street? – followed by the sugar bowl and several spoons. When the cosy went over the pot with such force, Harry saw the accident before it happened. The pot was at such an angle that it went flying across the table as though it had wings. Harry dived for it but the weight of the tea took it over the edge. In the next blink, the brown china was split messily apart on the floor.

'Oh! Whatever made me do such a thing!' cried Birdie, her hands over her mouth. And before he had time to prevent her, she'd pounced on the broken pieces, only to cry out again as she held up a bleeding finger.

Gently he took her, lifting her to her feet and led her to the sink. 'See, it's only one small cut. And fingers bleed a lot so it always looks worse.' He turned on the tap, and they watched the blood disappear down the drain.

'It's me thimble finger too,' she wailed as Harry held her still.

'Where do you keep the bandages?' he asked.

'In the table drawer.'

'Don't move, now.'

Trusting her to stay where she was, he went to the drawer and opened it, finding the tin and the bandage. Then, grabbing the towel, he sat her down and set to work. In comparison to his big, rough hands, Birdie's little fingers felt light as a child's. They were all bendy and weightless, with nails shaped perfectly round and smooth. He'd never touched her before, never even brushed shoulders, but now he could feel her breath on his face and there was a certain smell – was it soap, or was it lemon? – some fragrance that sent the blood flowing straight to his cheeks.

'I won't win a prize for neatness,' he tried lightly, clearing his throat with a manful cough, 'but this will do the job.'

'Thank you.' She sat, as dainty as a flower, as quiet as a mouse, which alarmed him more than anything. She was always on her feet, flying here and there, talking and moving at a rate of knots. He found the pail and the mop and cleared the mess on the floor, and when all was restored to harmony he cautiously took the chair beside her.

'Is it painful?' he asked after a while and received no words as her head lowered and gave a little shake. He could see how thick and rich-looking her brown waves were, all a bit untidy, falling this way and that, and he had the unreasonable urge to reach out and lift the stray wisps aside. But of course, he didn't. He was taking a liberty as it was, parking himself here, waiting for what, he didn't quite know.

Other than this gut feeling inside him, that something was amiss.

'I'm sorry,' she mumbled again, almost too softly to hear.

'It was only a teapot,' he shrugged.

'And now I've made you even later.'

'Birdie, I've been trying to tell you it don't matter. I'm my own boss and can do as I please.' It came out sounding very grand and he could have kicked himself as her head snapped up.

'Your own boss?' she repeated.

'Well, more or less,' he reversed quickly. 'I've just had a bit of luck since last summer . . . me and a few mates working together on the buildings . . .'

She smiled uncertainly. 'All the same, I took advantage of your offer to stay with Dad for an hour,' she insisted. 'There was no need for me to delay, none at all, not if I'd come home straight away, instead of going off to the park and—'

'I thought you said it was the buses,' he frowned. 'Being late, an' all.'

'The truth is I sat on a bench.'

Had something happened at the Thornes'? Not that it was his place to judge, but her being prepared to go over to Poplar at night, just for the benefit of . . . well, he shouldn't think it, as it was none of his business. But that preening peacock she mooned over, the drip who could only fit her company in for two hours of a Sunday afternoon, well, *he* should be the one to come to her.

'Is it something you'd like to talk over?'

'No, I'm too embarrassed.'

'Now, that's certainly not like Birdie Connor,' he teased.

There was a little groan. 'Don't look at me, then. I'm in a state.' She tried to turn way again. 'I've made a fool of meself, Harry.'

'I wouldn't say that.' He grinned, relieved to see the crisis was over.

'What would you say, then? What can you think of me?' Her face was all pink and damp.

'I think you had a good reason to take the long way,' he said, gauging his words carefully. 'And it's not up to me to know why, but all the same, a problem shared is a problem halved.'

'I suppose you're right. The truth is, Don told me he was considering a date for our wedding. It was to be just after Christmas . . .'

To his own great surprise this news gave Harry an uncomfortable turn. Though he knew little about Birdie and her sweetheart, what he did know was mostly from Pat, who had little time for the grand romancer Donald Thorne. What the deuce he was playing at, not engaging himself formally to a girl like Birdie, Harry couldn't guess. From the little he'd had to do with the man – a brief nod here and there, a dismissive greeting at best – Harry had never understood what a warm-hearted creature like Birdie could see in such a cool customer. Or perhaps it was the life of a shopkeeper that appealed to her? Undoubtedly that would present an attraction to many women. But somehow, he just couldn't see it as being right for Birdie.

'. . . according to the shop's hours, naturally, as it will have to open in the afternoon,' he heard her continuing. 'And it will be fairer if we marry by licence at the register office where both families can attend. And even though I wasn't to wear white satin, I'd have something nice, a suit for instance . . .' she stopped, her lips trembling.

Harry tried to assemble all the information, but he'd had no formal training with women; no mother or sisters, only the elderly nurse at the orphanage who had poured a dose of cod liver oil down their throats every week. When he'd joined the merchant navy, he'd fallen headlong for a girl in Malta but she'd ditched him the next time the ship docked. Not that he'd remained in a state of mourning for long.

Life had always tasted good to him, and there had been one or two pretty girls to wave him off from port.

'So you're saying,' he began hesitantly, 'this marrying arrangement – on the whole – is a good thing?'

Birdie nodded slowly, her eyes staring straight into his. 'Oh, yes – on the whole – a good thing. But it was the *other* thing,' she faltered. 'I just couldn't! I just couldn't! I'd give up me white wedding so it would all be fair, but I just couldn't do *that*! It's too cruel, Harry.'

'What couldn't you do?'

'I couldn't – no, *wouldn't* – give up my own brother.'

Harry shook his head in puzzlement. 'But why should you?'

It seemed all too much for her and she sank her head to her hands. 'Don thinks there will be gossip and nastiness, as there was when he went to prison. And the only way to settle it is to cut Frank out.'

'Ah, I see it now,' he consoled as he tried to decipher the explanation that was drowned in her despair. He was listening intently, when the back door burst open.

'Birdie! Birdie!' shouted Pat as he rushed in. With his messenger boy's hat on its elastic strung chokingly to the back of his neck, he pulled open his tunic buttons. 'It's Frank! I've seen him, large as life—' He went red when he saw Harry. 'Oh blimey, didn't know you was home.'

Harry glanced awkwardly at Birdie. 'I think I'd better make myself scarce.'

But she put her hand on his arm. 'Close the door, Pat. Harry is like one of the family. He deserves to know the truth.'

The remark gave Harry a warm glow, for he had never been called family before.

Chapter 11

'I opened me big mouth again, didn't I?' said Pat, as he took a seat at the table.

'It's a Connor trait, love. I'm guilty of it meself,' Birdie admitted with a smile. 'Now I'm dying to know what you have to say, but let's start at the beginning for Harry's benefit.'

Harry gave an awkward shrug. 'Not a word will be breathed by me.'

'You've heard more than enough to wonder what we're up to,' Birdie nodded. Harry had something about him she wanted to trust. It was even a relief, after her outpouring about Don. 'I've seen Frank, Harry. He came here on the night he escaped. He was being taken to the isolation hospital as they thought he might have the pox. But he made a bolt for it and hid in our yard. Fair scared me witless, an' all.' She lifted her shoulders, turning to Pat. 'I never told Pat, or anyone, not then, but the next day I met Frank at the park, under the arches. He'd spent the night on a barge and stank to high heaven, and his chin was covered in that red hair of his. So I cut off what I could with me scissors. He was so hungry that he swallowed what I gave him almost before I'd blinked.' She caught her breath and added, 'He's innocent, Harry. Honest to God. He swears he never deserted. And I believe him.'

Pat nodded too. 'Go on, tell Harry what he said.'

She looked into Harry's dark eyes and told him about the farmhouse and how Frank couldn't remember everything because of his injury. 'But they must have been good people, since they got him back to our side, though only for him to be arrested.'

Harry nodded slowly. 'Did Frank catch any names?'

'Not that he can remember.'

Slowly she turned to Pat. 'Now, love, what's your story?'

Pat couldn't wait to begin. 'Me and Willie was starting off on our rounds,' he rattled off, 'and I was going across the fields, but before I get to Cutler Street warehouses, this figure steps out in front of me bicycle. I don't recognize him at first. Along with a lot of other casuals, he's humping a mutton carcass over his shoulder, wearing one of them aprons they use in the holds, to keep off the mess. His cap is down over his face. There is not an inch of red hair showing. His chin is as hairless as mine, and it's only as we look into each other's eyes that I see who it is. "Frank," I gasp, pulling on me brakes, so I nearly go over the handlebars, "is it you?" But he keeps his head down and mutters that he'll meet me at the back of the warehouses. So I go off as normal, but then I spot a copper, and it dawns on me, a moment earlier and I might have given Frank away.'

Birdie smiled encouragingly. 'Well, you didn't. Go on.'

'So I whistle my way past the Bluebottle,' Pat continued, gulping a breath, 'and cycle twice round the block before I turn into the yards. There's all these lorries being loaded and I couldn't see Frank. Mind you, they all look the same, these casuals humping the meat from the holds. Then this person cuts across, without his apron, and I know it's Frank. He nods to the far side, where there's all these crates piled, ready for loading. I cycle on, making sure no one sees, and there's Frank, waiting. I'm off my bicycle in a jiffy, and well . . .' Pat passed his sleeve cross his damp nose, 'he gives me this great hug, just like he used to when I was a kid. Then he looks around, and I look around—'

'Pat, love, what did our Frank *say*?' Birdie urged, unable to bear the suspense.

'He wanted to know about us. So I told him about the

law's visit and you telling me about him coming round here. He says to tell you he's fetched up all right with some mates, and the law won't get wind of where he is.'

'But where is it?' Birdie asked impatiently. 'And who are these mates?'

'Don't know, not till he finds me again.'

Birdie was beginning to realize how easily this might get out of hand. 'Listen, Pat, I don't want you meeting Frank without me being there. You're not old enough to understand what's going on.'

At this, Pat jumped to his feet. 'I'm not a kid, Birdie. I'm fifteen next year and I earn my wage by fair means, not foul. I don't scrounge off my family or go in late for work. And I put towards the housekeeping, don't I, just the same as Harry? You're treating me as if I don't have a mind of me own,' he cried, his face growing red. 'And anyway, you can't stop me.'

'Pat, mind that tongue of yours—' Birdie began, but he was tearing past her, striding out of the door.

'He's right,' Harry said gently when they were alone. 'He's not a kid any more.'

'He is to me,' Birdie flung back. 'It wasn't a year or two ago that I was helping him with his schoolwork. Or mending the holes in his trouser knees from his playing in the street.'

Harry smiled and lifted his hands. 'That year or two, I suppose, makes the difference.'

Birdie sank back on her chair and sighed. 'Perhaps Don is right about Frank. I never gave it a thought that Pat might be harmed. Who are these people? Why are they taking an interest in Frank?'

'Beats me,' Harry replied quietly. 'But Pat's all for Frank and there's an end to it.'

'I wish I hadn't—' Birdie began, but the door opened and Wilfred stood there, rubbing his eyes.

'Was that Pat I heard?' he demanded.

Birdie took a breath and nodded. 'He just called by for a bite to eat.'

Wilfred glared at Harry. 'And where is that tea, lad? I close my eyes for ten minutes and wake up on me own, with the sound of boots on the stairs. I thought it was the law again.'

'Sorry, Mr Connor,' Harry apologized, standing up. 'But—'

'I'm just about to freshen the pot.' Birdie threw Harry a sharp look. 'And Harry's off back to work, ain't you, Harry?'

'Yes, indeed,' Harry nodded awkwardly. 'I'll be on my way.'

'He needn't have stayed in the first place,' Wilfred complained argumentatively after Harry had gone. 'And don't make a brew for me. I'm off out to see me pals up the Quarry.'

'Dad, I don't think it's wise to—'

'I don't bloody well care what you think, love. I feel like a trussed chicken hanging from a butcher's hook, being kept in and fussed over. Now where's me cap and coat?'

Ten minutes later, Birdie was sitting in front of her sewing machine, gazing into space. She seemed to have little influence with Pat these days, and her father refused to look after himself. What if he was taken ill at the pub or in the street? But he wouldn't be told, and Pat wouldn't either. Should she have taken more notice of Don? Her thoughts went to him and she felt a strong yearning inside. Perhaps he knew best. She hadn't thought so at the time, but what if Frank's escape was to be the cause of many more troubles? She missed Don's arms around her. She wanted to be his wife and he had, in his own way, made it possible. If she had known then, at the store, what she knew now, would she have agreed to his terms?

The door squeaked open and Pat stood there. 'Sorry,' he muttered.

'Oh, come here, you daft 'ap'orth.' She hauled him into her arms. 'Just be careful, won't you? Don't do anything rash.'

'I've got my ear to the ground,' he grinned. 'Just like the 'tec in the *Penny Popular*.'

Birdie smiled tenderly. Pat might think of himself as fully grown but his head was still filled with boyish dreams. 'Pat, if you see Frank again, you will tell me, won't you? You won't do nothing in secret?'

'Course I won't.' Pat's grin spread wide. 'I'd better get back to work now.'

'I'll cook you your favourite tonight, fried bread and bacon.'

'And I'll bring home a penn'orth of Sharp's toffee.' He kissed her cheek.

Birdie listened to his boots on the stairs, which sounded lighter than before. Happily, they had made up from the quarrel. But even so, she would continue to worry. She began her repairs for Lady Hailing, hindered a little by the bandage on her finger.

A smile touched her lips as she thought of Harry's kindness. Could they trust him? There had been no choice but to explain about Frank and he certainly wasn't of the same opinion as Don. But as the day wore on, Birdie still couldn't forget Don's words and his warning.

Frank grabbed hold of the big wooden chest and marvelled at the weight of its contents, heavy as a ton of bricks. But paper it was, all fresh from the machine in the cellar. Hadn't he seen the little booklets for himself, with all that strange writing of squares and squiggles?

Inga, his translator and the woman who seemed to be in charge of the outfit, had explained how important the material was to those poor people in Russia, who were fighting for freedom. She was passionate about them. And though he didn't understand it, he knew all about freedom. And he hoped, if he did them a good turn, then he was owed one back. At least, that was his master plan.

Together with the man called Erik – though not an English word had been said between them – they carried the heavy weight to the wagon that was drawn up in the stable yard. With an effort, the chest was hoisted on and covered by canvas, just like the previous six containers. The wagon was now fully loaded.

Erik signalled Frank to lift the bales of straw on top of the chests, so disguising their cargo. When the canvas was secured and the two dray horses harnessed, Eric climbed over the bales, offering his hand down to help Frank.

At that moment, Inga appeared, her face as usual, dirtied and unrecognizable under the brim of her cloth cap, which hid her wealth of silken black hair.

Frank was both disturbed and excited at the sight of her. Dressed in coarse cloth trousers tucked into the tops of hardy, laced boots, and a navy-blue donkey jacket, she looked at first glance what she hoped to look: like a man. But it was her movement that gave her away, nimble and light, a glimpse of her womanly curves. Not that anyone would know, Frank thought admiringly. But he'd had time to study her over the past weeks. She was the most mysterious woman he had ever met. Also the most dangerous. She kept a small revolver with her at all times, and a blade, about six inches long, suspended from her belt and strapped to the outside of her leg. He knew this because he'd witnessed her almost using it.

'We are late,' she shouted at them. 'Hurry!'

Frank had learned not to argue. Inga had once pulled a knife on Erik. The argument had been over one of these crates, though Frank hadn't understood a word. What he had understood was Inga's authority. She'd flashed her hand to her belt and the knife appeared. In any language it was plain to see who was boss.

Now Frank scrambled under the canvas and over the bales, sliding down into the recess at the back so that he lay top to toe with Eric. They grabbed the rope securing the bales and, together, edged them slowly over their heads.

The sharp slap of the reins meant Inga was hurrying the horses. Her Russian cockney, 'Get on!' rippled back under the canvas and the wagon swayed into motion.

The two men lay in the dusty, choking environment. Frank knew it would be like this all the way from the cellar to the Shadwell house. It was cramped and uncomfortable, but after the first trip he'd taken a cloth to put over his mouth. Now he didn't need it; he was practised in the art of hiding.

The day began cold and unsettled, just as Birdie felt herself. There hadn't been word from Don and she'd said a whole rosary at Mass yesterday for his arrival on the doorstep. But he'd not appeared and Sunday seemed awfully long without him. Her pride had forbidden her from going to the store, even passing by it casually, as Flo had suggested when Birdie called for her this morning.

Birdie had replied haughtily that if Don wanted to see her, then he knew where she lived. But secretly, the thought of her wedding day even though it wasn't to be in church, disappearing from the marked spot in Lydia's diary was very depressing. And it wasn't easy to explain that to Flo as they strolled to Hailing House, although they did, for once, have the whole morning to themselves as Flo's two girls had gone to see their grandma.

'It's the store, you see, getting the right moment to close it,' began Birdie again, casting her eye up to the stormy clouds above and praying it wouldn't rain. Her work was being ferried in the girls' old pram, but Flo had lost the cover since Enid's arrival.

'You mean you can't have a whole day to marry in?' Flo questioned, wrinkling her small nose and pursing her lips, which were liberally coated in plum red. Under her short, fashionable bob of fair hair, she had defined two eyebrows in pencil that always made her look surprised. Flo loved make-up, as Birdie did, and had enjoyed the Hailings' generosity, more so even than Birdie, who kept the effects to the minimum to please Don.

'Aggie had offered to put on the food,' Birdie added quickly. 'So it might have run to an hour or so longer.'

'Emily and Enid will be disappointed,' Flo confirmed again, her blue eyes matching her blue coat, hat and scarf, which she wore with style, her hips swinging, her shoulders back. And Birdie noticed, a different pair of shoes had appeared on the scene. Not that they were new, but even second-hand ones without bunion bumps cost a pretty penny.

'Yes, I know,' Birdie agreed. 'I was going to make them lemon dresses with little crowns of flowers. I'd take special care with the lengths, an' all, so they could use them again, but it's to be at the registrar's office, you see. Perhaps I'll make them dresses anyway,' she added quickly at the sight of Flo's disapproving frown.

'It won't be the same,' Flo answered sharply. 'At two and three, being bridesmaids was just up their street. What has your dad to say about all this?'

'I've not told him yet. And maybe I won't have to. Not if it's called off.'

'Did Don say it was off?'

'He don't want me to have anything to do with Frank.'

'What?' Flo gasped.

'Well, I couldn't agree, of course,' Birdie said quickly. 'I'll just have to think of a way round it.'

'He's got a bloody nerve, if you ask me,' snarled Flo, pushing the pram up the kerb with some force.

Birdie wanted to jump to Don's defence and yet she felt loyal to Frank. 'Don only wants the best for us. It wasn't easy before, when Frank went to gaol. Aggie and Lydia had to contend with the gossip. Now Frank is on the loose, Don says it will start up again.'

'Strikes me the Thornes can look after themselves,' Flo replied scathingly. 'Aggie is no shrinking violet, but a businesswoman through and through. I don't know the other one much, though when I've shopped up Poplar and gone in their store, she don't win my vote for being personable. And you know my opinion of their butter. If I didn't know better I'd say it was stored by the paraffin. Can't say much for their bacon either, or their cheese, and there is always a farthing put on if you're not careful. Aggie Thorne has a shrewd eye and don't miss a trick.'

Birdie couldn't say much as she knew Flo was right on all points. 'Aggie and Lydia have both lost their husbands,' she pointed out tactfully. 'A double blow in just a handful of years.'

'Yes, but they've got Don,' Flo rallied. 'He don't shirk in his duty to them, does he? In fact, I'd say he puts their demands first.'

'They *are* family,' Birdie reminded her. She knew Flo didn't have much time for the Thornes, though she would never admit it, not wanting to hurt her friend. But it could be noticed when Don was in their presence that she was always quiet and reserved.

'Anyway, your Frank ain't going out of his way to annoy them in particular!' exclaimed Flo indignantly. 'He's done a bunk, but not to get up the Thornes' noses.'

'No,' agreed Birdie thoughtfully as they passed the park. She recalled the day she had met Frank there and given him the clothes and food. He had been like a hunted animal, and once more she felt angry at those who hunted him.

'There's been no word from your brother?' Flo glanced at her sharply.

'Nothing more from the police,' Birdie evaded. 'Pat and me still don't believe he's deserted. One day his innocence will be proved.'

'I'd feel the same way if it was my Reg,' agreed Flo staunchly. 'You hear all these stories about blokes deserting, but Reg says it's the Army that want to put the fear of God up the troops to keep them in order. The only way to do that is shoot 'em or put them in prison, like Frank.'

Birdie looked at Flo gratefully. 'Thank God Frank didn't get shot.'

Flo wagged a finger. 'Well, in my humble opinion, I think Don trying to make you chose between him and Frank is right out of order. If he loves you, he'll have you on any terms. And sod his old girl and the war widow.'

Again Birdie felt that inner unease again, for half of her agreed with Flo, the other half wanted to defend her true love. 'Anyway,' she reasoned as they turned the corner towards Hailing House, 'Don might come round and we'll make up.'

'He'll lose out if he don't. You're a girl in a million.'

'I'll pay you later,' Birdie giggled, and Flo joined in.

Mrs Belcher had brought a tray of scones and tea to the meeting room at the back of Hailing House. Flo had just tucked into her second scone, whilst Birdie had unwrapped her parcel of alterations and was discussing them with Annabelle, the younger of the two sisters, and about Birdie's own age.

Birdie liked Annabelle very much. Mostly because she enjoyed the fashions of the time, always dressing as Birdie would have dressed if she'd had the chance. Or, more like it, the money, Birdie thought ruefully, as Annabelle brought out a swatch of flowery fabric that must cost a fortune if bought by the yard.

'I've made a sketch.' Annabelle showed Birdie the drawing she had made in a notebook. 'I want something to cheer up Mummy's dreary garden party at Easter. All the old relics will be wearing wool and tweeds. I'd like to give them something to stare at and cause a fuss. At least it will make the time go faster.' Annabelle gave a peal of light laughter, but Birdie was impressed with what she saw. Annabelle had a real flair with her drawing. The hips were bound by a tangerine bow, tied at the base of the spine, and the long, simple bodice with delicate capped sleeves would enhance Annabelle's slim figure. The wide brim of the hat she had drawn, with a matching tangerine band tucked into its weave, would look perfect with the addition of a rose.

'I think it's lovely.' Birdie looked into Annabelle's grey eyes and thought how every man she met must fall under her spell. Her soft brown hair was, like Flo's, cut to the nape of her slender neck. The fine wool suit she wore was matched with an oyster-coloured silk scarf draped across one shoulder. She wasn't as tall as Felicity, but she was small-boned and very elegant.

'So will you make it for me, Birdie? I don't trust anyone else. You know what I like. Mummy's dressmaker is always trying to make me wear such frumpy things. Mummy likes her, of course, but then she would, as her taste hasn't changed in decades!'

Even Flo was laughing at this, and Birdie listened with amusement to Annabelle's description of her last dull encounter with the hostess of a hunting party, prompting Annabelle to sneak away with a handsome beau and really enjoy herself. Annabelle moved in such privileged circles that Birdie was always surprised at her enthusiasm for the charity work on the island. Felicity, too, was dedicated to the cause, and was at this very moment helping Mrs Belcher to organize one of the two open kitchens of the week for the poor and destitute. After which, there would be a housewifery class for the women of the island, such as Birdie had attended as a child with her mother. Felicity and Annabelle had been children then, too. But in those days they had been rather remote figures, accompanying their mother, Lady Hailing, in the chauffeured car, rarely making an appearance in the House.

'I'll take your measurements, Lady Annabelle.' Birdie loosened the string of her work-bag and brought out her tape measure. Annabelle lifted her arms, well acquainted with Birdie's rigorous preliminaries, intent on having her work precise. 'I'll make the pattern from your drawing,' said Birdie, 'and then we can have the first fitting.'

'Wonderful,' Annabelle said as Birdie slipped the tape around her slim hips. 'I'll order the material from my people if you let me know how much you need.'

Birdie was happy with this arrangement. She knew she would be able to work wonders with such quality cloth. She took the chance to nibble her scone and drank her tea whilst Annabelle talked to Flo; they all knew each other well now, and when Flo's girls, Enid and Emily, came along, they were treated to something hot from Mrs Belcher's oven.

Annabelle was always eager to know about their lives, and though she spoke of many male admirers, Birdie knew she was as selective of her men as she was of her fabrics, for Annabelle and Felicity were heirs to a fortune.

'Birdie, I hope you don't mind me mentioning it,' Annabelle said suddenly as she sipped her tea, small finger pointed out on the handle of the bone-china cup, 'but one can't help but be privy to so much . . . well, *talk* . . . here at the House. And my concern is for you . . . and only for you.' She paused, her head tilted to one side, and Birdie blushed to the roots of her hair.

'If you mean is it true about Frank,' Birdie mumbled, 'making an escape from prison, then yes, it is.'

'Oh dear,' sighed Annabelle, 'how worrying for you and your family.'

Birdie was filled with embarrassment although Annabelle looked genuinely upset. Stories of woe and hardship were not unfamiliar to the 'slummers', as the aristocratic ladies, were called.

'Can my sister and I help in any way?' Annabelle enquired softly.

Birdie shook her head resolutely. 'Thank you, but no.'

'Well, you must say immediately if we can.'

Birdie managed a smile and was relieved that Annabelle continued the conversation in a light and cheery tone, returning to the making of her frock and the little touches Birdie suggested.

But by the time they left Hailing House, Birdie's spirits had sunk. She knew she was unusually quiet as she and Flo made their way home with the pram, now bearing a new parcel of work. But Annabelle's comments had only increased her unease rather than helped.

'It was very nice of Annabelle to say about Frank in the way she did,' Flo probed in a quiet voice as they turned past the rope factory. 'S'pose she had to say somethin', didn't she?'

Birdie sunk her head down in her collar against the chill wind. 'She was only trying to be helpful, I reckon,' Birdie nodded.

'Listen, don't feel bad,' Flo said in her loyal way. 'Your Frank is the last person prison should happen to. My Reg thinks so as well.'

Birdie stopped then, putting her hand on the pram to halt it. She looked into Flo's earnest blue eyes. 'Are you just saying that to make me feel better, Flo?'

'Course I'm not,' Flo bellowed in astonishment. 'I'm

your mate and I'd stick by you no matter what, just like you would me. But me and Reg knew Frank before he joined up. And we know what a good bloke he is, no matter what anyone says.'

'The mention of prison makes you feel dirty. You can put on a brave face, pretend you don't care, but there are times, like when Annabelle said that, and yesterday at Mass when I saw people giving you and me stares, people we've been to church with for years. And even them down our street, like old Ma Jenkins and the two drippy sisters, Vi and Annie Carter . . . they still go out of their way to spread gossip—'

'Flippin' 'eck, Birdie!' Flo interrupted, looking shocked. 'This ain't Brigid Connor I hear speaking. It's some timid little kid frightened of her own shadow! I ain't never heard you speak like this before.'

'Frank's never escaped before.'

'And you could have stopped him, I suppose?' demanded Flo archly. 'You was the one who opened the prison gates and drove him out?'

Birdie wanted to say that she might as well have. She could easily have tried to persuade him to return to prison that night in the back yard. He might have listened to her, the state he'd been in. But instead she'd encouraged him, clothed and fed him, cut away his beard, then given him money.

'Come on, gel, buck up,' Flo said then, patting her shoulder. 'Things will work out, they always do.'

But Birdie couldn't see how they could. It was as though, in Annabelle's eyes, she had seen herself for what she was, a poor little seamstress, not quite a charity case, but close enough, bravado and gumption being her second and third names, standing against the forces of law and order, to prove Frank innocent. Yet as the pity was directed towards her, she had seen the danger and hopelessness of their case.

The expression in Annabelle's eyes had put more shame and fear into her heart than an army of Bluebottles battering down the front door.

Chapter 12

Donald Thorne stared with alarm at the order book, running his finger under today's date in early December. He noted that Lydia had crossed out the articles Aggie had written down. Two distinct lines had been drawn through the twelve two-penny and three-penny bars of chocolate and the two dozen wooden clothes pegs. Despite his mother's insistence these were necessary, the bone of contention over stock seemed to be ongoing. Placing his finger inside his spotlessly white collar and loosening its hold, he twisted his neck nervously.

It was too annoying to be beset by both personal and business problems at the same time. His offer to Brigid of marrying soon had been more than generous. A little compliance on her part over that wretched man – the convict – was all he had asked for. Lydia had been aghast to think that Brigid had not agreed, though his mother, surprisingly, had not passed comment. But it was Aggie, rather than Brigid, who was at this very moment his cause for concern.

Don assembled the problem in his thoughts. Aggie and Lydia had developed differing views regarding the stock. It had started in September, when James had begun school. A certain friction seemed to have sprung up between the two women. Not cross words – in fact sometimes he wished there were, if only to relieve him of being referee – but he found notes like this, or was given broad hints.

Now he was in the awkward position of having to tell Aggie that the items in the order book, penned by her, had been struck through. And he knew why. Lydia was trying to exert some authority whilst Aggie was resisting. His mother had a mind for the smallest and rarest article, and cared little what state of freshness it was in, whilst Lydia was more modern and go-ahead. For all the years his mother had been selling, she should know best, Don reflected, though Lydia had spent enough time in the shop to try new ways, and Don was at pains to satisfy them both.

Now he went slowly out to where his mother had already lowered the blinds with the pole. Beneath were set out the boxes of vegetables, fruit and assorted items that had a half-penny, at least, taken off them. One-inch bandages with their blue paper missing. Packets of soda gone rock hard, cauliflowers and cabbages mutilated by fly, and fruit that was so ripe, Don had once or twice shovelled the festering flesh into drains. But someone always seemed to want a bargain. His mother insisted there was a customer for everything if the price was right.

'Mother, about the ordering,' Don greeted breezily, as Aggie swung round from the shelves she was scrubbing. Her sleeves were rolled up, she wore her coarse grey apron and her hair was hidden under a scarf. Her lined, but smiling face gave him hope. 'Before we open, may we discuss one or two things?'

'Talk away, son. This has to be done before we get busy.' Aggie returned her attention to the thick brown liquid dripping from the shelf. In one mighty sweep the mess was removed, the cloth plunged into a bucket and a dry cloth whisked over the empty space. With practised dexterity she refilled the shelf with packets of Ex-Lax chocolate, stone jars of strawberry jam, quarter-pound bags of Mazawattee tea, thick rolls of hairpins, and packets of slides. Don's anxiety increased as he saw her reach down for the bundles of firewood that Lydia always kept at the back of the shop. Aggie lifted the basket to knee level, squeezing them on a shelf by the packets of dried prunes, her hand going to the small of her back as she straightened up.

'Mother, shall I carry the firewood to the other end for you?' he tried, sniffing the strong tarry string tying the bundles. There had been a few complaints lately that the perishables had not lasted long in the larder, tasting a little 'sour'.

'I keep telling you I don't like 'em over there,' Aggie snapped. 'They're a regular seller and I want 'em where I can reach them. When I've a queue at the counter I can't go charging all over the place. And don't go moving that nutty slack. It's there for all who want to collect it.'

'I thought the council warned us off selling inferior coal?' Don glanced towards the sacks that he had removed to the yard last week. His mother had returned them, placing them beside the kindling, with discounted prices advertised. 'It's dangerous, Mother, and can spit red-hot stones.'

'Me customers like it,' Aggie retorted. 'Would you have me disappoint them?'

'Well, no, but—'

'Now what is it you want?' she demanded impatiently.

Don gave a little cough and stepped towards the counter. 'Those trifles you've written in the order book, are they necessary?' he ventured uncertainly. 'The pegs and chocolate, for instance? And perhaps the Carbosil, when we already have Sunlight—'

'Trifles! She ain't struck them through again, has she?' exclaimed Aggie angrily, dropping her brush. Don watched fearfully as her red knuckles went crossly to her hips, instantly reminding him of the painful clip on his ear that had struck like lightning when he was a child. 'Go and tell

103

her to write them back,' Aggie barked, a sound that dried the saliva in his mouth.

'But, Mother, they will go off and perish.'

'Are you out to disobey me, son?'

'No, Mother, but times have changed and—'

'Your father would turn in his grave to hear you challenge me,' Aggie shouted. 'I never had a word of complaint from Stephen, God rest his soul, and I'll not have any nonsense from you. Now bugger off and do as I tell you. And while you're out the back, you might as well bring through them crates of brown cauliflowers and sprouting spuds. It's Christmas coming up and the kids will be on holiday. Their mothers will have them doing their errands and where are they likely to go? They'll come to Aggie Thorne because she's got the two-penny and three-penny bars of chocolate up front on the counter. And along with the chocolate they'll buy the cheap veg for their mothers instead of going up to the markets. Now, if you or *she* has got any argument with that, spit it out right now.'

Don resigned himself to being defeated. No one knew better than he the mantra of his and Stephen's childhood: look after the customers' small needs and the big orders will come pouring shortly after. It was his father's first rule of shopkeeping and had rung loudly in his brain right up to the day he had announced his intention to work for the railways.

Sighing, he beat a retreat to the office. Here he tried to experience a few moments of peace but the door opened and Lydia walked in with James. Her smile, a little shy and quite beguiling, caught him off guard.

'Good morning, Donald.'

'Good morning, Lydia. And how are you, young James?' The tiny, delicate-looking, pale-faced child grinned, guiltily reminding Don of his dead brother as he bent and patted the dark curls fondly, warmed by the youthful innocence in the child's eyes.

'We're just off to school. I shan't be long,' Lydia said pleasantly.

'Right you are.' Don stepped back to allow them to pass, meeting Lydia's gaze as he did so. The bloom had returned to her cheeks lately and as always he felt protective, but there was another urge now, a powerful one that tightened the muscles of his stomach in an exciting yet dreadful way.

'Oh, Donald,' she murmured softly, glancing up at him and laying her hand softly on his sleeve, 'did you see my alterations in the book?'

'Yes, yes,' he faltered, not wanting to disappoint her after these few moments of intimacy, 'but Mother feels . . .' he searched his vocabulary unsuccessfully for an inoffensive phrase.

'I understand.' She cut him short, almost conspiratorially, her dark eyes so wide and innocent that he felt himself sink into them. 'But we are managing on a very narrow margin. Business is not at all like it was in your father's time. So why buy in expensive pegs when the hawkers and gypsies sell so cheaply on the doorstep? And the Sunlight and Lifebuoy are quite sufficient. As for the chocolate, we have more than enough left on the shelves.'

Don found himself nodding his agreement and languishing in her dark gaze. He was met with an encouraging smile that made him feel a great deal more in command of things than his mother ever did.

'I knew you'd see it my way,' she said sweetly, then went on tiptoe to kiss his cheek. Don felt her lips so warm and comforting, that his arm slid around her waist. For a moment they stared at one another, just like they had last week in the storeroom. She'd come in unexpectedly and tripped over an orange box. He'd caught her, bearing her weight, reluctant to let her go. And there was the incident before, when he'd taken her and James to Victoria Park. James had perched on his lap by the pond, as they sat watching the ducks, and had called him Daddy by mistake, and Lydia had smiled at the small error, let her gaze linger, a gaze that said so much. He couldn't have been wrong, and he'd felt so enraptured in that instant.

'We must go,' she said, giving the boy a gentle nudge. 'Run out through the yard, James.'

Don watched him dart off and Lydia dallied, her eyes acknowledging the complicity between them with a flutter of dark lashes. For a moment, he felt as though he was a young man again, just starting at the railways in those precious years when he had broken away to find freedom. This thought alone gave him a feeling of being taller, stronger, a law only unto himself.

'Lydia, I—' he whispered, moving towards her.

But she shook her head quickly and placed her finger to her lips. 'Later,' she whispered, her eyes growing wide.

Then he took in a deep breath and nodded, watching her leave by the yard entrance after James. All too soon she had gone and, somewhat detached from his concentration, he tried to prepare himself for the rest of the day.

Chapter 13

Pat Connor was cycling fast through the quiet Sunday streets of the island, finally on his way to meet Willie Mason. He had already seen Willie at Mass and they'd arranged to meet that afternoon at Chalk Wharf, their usual Sunday destination. Willie was providing the ginger beer and no doubt some other goodies, and Pat had bought a sugared doughnut, Willie's favourite, from the Carmen Café by the docks. He'd also sported out three pence for two packets of Woodbines and the *Magnet*. They could enjoy a smoke, whilst reading the comic, and have a few laughs.

Pat had gulped down the meal that Birdie had cooked, eager to get out of the house. But his dad and Birdie and even Harry had been talking about the rise in numbers people of suffering from the flu. There hadn't been a case in March Street for twelve months, and the disease was thought to be on the wane. But last week one of the Kirby boys went down with what was said to be the ague, bringing worries to the fore again. When this depressing subject had been exhausted, the conversation had veered to the national industrial crisis. After which Birdie had commented on the price of spuds. It was then that Pat had asked to be excused. He'd had more than enough of his Sunday observances.

Mass had seemed endless, with the incense making his eyes and nose smart. But at least he and Willie had had a bit of a giggle. They were head altar boys now, and Willie had brought a piece of cordite with him to the vestry and let it off. The stink had filled the vestry and put the younger ones in fits of laughter during the Latin responses.

Now there was a broad smile on Pat's face as the wind whipped through his hair and into the open collar of his shirt. He stopped by the East India Dock, detached the studs from his stiff collar and removed the vest that Birdie said he must still wear, bundling them along with his other goodies into the message pouch attached to his bicycle. He felt free and excited. Today they'd just muck about on the wharf, but tomorrow after work they might cycle to the Hippodrome and look at the old posters of Lockhart's Elephants, the famous touring group. Or even go as far as Mile End and the markets to buy monkey nuts on the stall outside the pie and mash shop.

Ten minutes later Pat came to a screeching halt. Willie

was already sitting on the edge of the mossy wharf, his bicycle on the ground beside him. He held a long stick with a length of string dangling from it, hoping to catch some tiddlers. The most noticeable thing about Willie, Pat reflected, was that despite being a messenger boy, and riding miles for the PLA, Willie's plump thighs rubbed together noisily in his leggings. But today they were free of uniform and Willie sat with an open collar and a smile on his round face.

'How many have you caught today?' Pat asked breathlessly as he took up his position next to Willie.

'You're the fifth!' exclaimed Willie, laughing raucously at his own joke. He scratched his head, which was covered by only in a thin layer of pale hair; since he'd had a bad case of nits, his mother had shaven it close. 'I ain't got nothing on the end of the line. See, it don't even touch the water.'

'You want to find yourself a few new jokes,' shrugged Pat as he dangled his legs over the green, slimy stones, nudging Willie fiercely in the ribs.

Willie dropped his improvised rod in the river. 'Now see what you've made me do,' he protested.

'It was only a stick,' laughed Pat, nudging his elbow. 'And you weren't likely to have a bite. Any fish in that lot would die before it was caught.' Pat nodded to the dirty water below them.

'It was the *Belle* that left that mess from her bilge pumps,' said Willie knowledgeably. 'She docked last week and has gone off again. P'raps to Southend or Clacton.'

'How do you know that?' asked Pat. 'You never said before.' He felt a little indignant he hadn't been told, for both him and Willie had applied to the purser of the paddle-steamer for jobs. The purser had said he would have taken them both on, had not the Woolwich & Clacton Steamship Company sold out to another operator, who had cut the budget. But Pat still lived in hope. Each time the *Belle* came in, he and Willie made their presence known.

'Me brother saw her docked,' said Willie, lifting the cloth package beside him and untying the knotted ends.

'He's not asked for a job too, has he?' demanded Pat in alarm. Willie had six brothers and the *Belle* couldn't take them all.

'Course not. He can't even swim.'

'Nor can you,' pointed out Pat, cunningly. If there was a job going, he hoped he'd be at the top of the list as he was a strong swimmer. And that might count for something if he had to save a passenger's life.

'No, but I can float.'

Pat smothered his laughter at the mental picture of Willie floating, his ample stomach bobbing above the waves. Though they'd been to the open baths many times, and even down in the river, Willie had never tried to learn to swim. He wasn't afraid of the water, though, but laid on his back, bobbing.

'What have you got there?' Pat peered hopefully into the open parcel that Willie had balanced on his knees. Willie's mum always made up delicious snacks, though they were as big and succulent as a meal. Willie's dad was a cook in the city and brought home lots of perks.

'Two sausage rolls,' Willie explained unnecessarily as he fingered the well-baked brown pastry with dirty nails; 'a pancake that ain't hot, but I had a bit of the corner anyway whilst I was waiting for you; this fruit pie, and four buns that have got spice in. And there's a bottle of ginger beer in me saddle bag.'

'Get it out then,' said Pat eagerly.

'Don't eat nothing till I come back,' Willie insisted, his movement clumsy as he climbed to his feet and leaned over his bicycle.

Pat lifted the cloth and inhaled the delicious aroma of

spiced buns. His mouth watered. He fancied most, though, the sausage rolls and the pancake, at least the end that Willie hadn't nibbled.

'We'll go halfsy-halfsy,' bargained Pat, when Willie had sat down again and the ginger beer was fastened between them. He unwrapped his doughnut and watched Willie's eyes narrow to greedy slits. 'And I've got some fags and the *Magnet*. We can read about what Tom Redwing and the Bounder done at Greyfriars. After, we'll jump over them barges and I'll be Tom Redwing and you can be the Bounder.'

'Why do I always have to be him?'

'We can change over next week.'

'In that case you can have an extra bun,' said Willie generously, his tongue going round his podgy lips as Pat exhibited the sugar on his hands from the doughnut.

They began to eat hungrily although it wasn't yet teatime. When they'd finished, except for two buns they were going to keep for later, Pat took out the cigarettes. He had matches too, but they'd got a bit damp on his bicycle in the rainstorm last week.

After looking around to make certain they weren't being watched, Pat leaned close. 'We'll light just one, and swig from the bottle,' he said, happy that a grey day was settling over the river, shadowing the few tugs sailing past and shielding the wharf behind them. There was a pub at the end, but apart from the noise of the singing and a few yells, no one was stumbling out.

'Me mum'd kill me if she saw me smoking and getting drunk,' said Willie with bravado.

'It won't make us really tipsy, not ginger beer.'

'Anyway, I don't care, she's not likely to come here.'

'She might,' Pat teased, looking over his friend's shoulder.

Willie almost fell into the water as he turned, but relaxed

as Pat's laughter rang out. The two boys pushed each other, wrestling gently, managing to keep their balance and the bottle upright.

'You first,' Pat said generously, handing his friend the Woodbine and striking the match several times before the tip caught.

Willie took a puff and coughed until his face turned purple, then handed the cigarette to Pat. A hoot from a boat made the boys jump and the cigarette fell into the water.

'Oh, bugger,' said Pat, drawing a guffaw from Willie. They began to laugh loudly.

'Light another,' urged Willie daringly, 'or shall we have one each?'

Pat glanced along the cobbles. There were a few people sauntering in the distance and there were crates for loading piled high, affording a place to smoke in secrecy. 'Over there,' he nodded and the boys scrambled with their bicycles to cover.

When they were hidden, Pat lit up, passing the Woodbine and bottle to Willie. He lit one for himself, then took a long gulp of the ginger beer and sneezed as the bubbles tickled his nose. He puffed gamely, disliking the taste, but all the same he said, 'Better than roll-ups.' To which Willie nodded, unable to reply, belching smoke from his mouth and clapping himself on the chest as he burped loudly. Pat had smoked one or two roll-ups before, but had never enjoyed them, and Willie had once been violently sick. But he forgot all that now, as they gulped the fizzy liquid and went into hysterics.

Pat fell on his side, his chin coming hard down on the ground, imagining himself tipsy. The impact caused the Woodbine to fly from his lips and lie a few inches in front of him. The ash spilled on the grime-ridden wharf, and Pat was still giggling when the curve of a boot lifted above the cigarette. Pat watched transfixed, as the toe snapped down, crushing what life there was out of it.

As his gaze lifted, attached to the scuffed but serviceable black leather boot with laces tied tightly around a slim ankle, he found a slender leg covered in brown breeches. His gaze raised higher, to the neat, dainty waist strapped by a belt and the upright, slender stance of a woman. He was in no doubt as to the true gender of this person dressed as a man, for the face under the boy's cloth cap, was perfectly and delicately formed. A pair of dark, mysterious eyes with black lashes as thick as fans, gazed down on him. Lips as soft and smooth as silk, but with an indefinable menacing quality, slowly parted.

The days of early December were shorter now, but it seemed a crime to Birdie to stop in when the sun's weak rays faintly lit the island. It had been such a long day. She missed Don more than ever. She'd been to Mass with Flo, and Father Flynn had taken an age to read from the Gospel and incorporate the christening of a new-born child into the service. Pat and Willie, in their black gowns and surplices, had organized the younger boys. And Flo's girls, Enid and Emily, had gone all bashful as they'd gone up with Flo for their blessing, going red as beetroots as Pat had grinned from the altar.

But after arriving home and cooking the midday meal, a beef stew that she had prepared last night, she felt restless. There was no longer the anticipation of waiting for Don's arrival. Even Pat had been anxious to leave after his meal. Not surprising, as the talk between Harry and her father had been about the troubles in Ireland and the state of the British unions. Her own heart hadn't been in the conversation either. She missed her habit of going up to her room and dressing for Don. Not that an outing of two hours was much to write home about, but it had been very precious to her.

Was he missing her as much as she was missing him? Dare she hope that at two or three o'clock there would be a knock on the door? But the hours passed and now the sun was going down, peeping through a cloudy sky that had threatened rain all day.

As Pat still wasn't home and her father was asleep in his chair, and she had already cleared her bench in her sewing room, Birdie lifted her hat from the hallstand and set it gently over her waves. Taking her coat, she wrapped herself up, not quite knowing where she was going. At the last moment, she scribbled a note to leave on the table, explaining her absence. Pat was sure to come in wanting his supper, but he would have to wait.

Outside a breeze was still busy across the pavements, drifting down the sounds of the children at play. The Kirby twins were as riotous as ever, the other children either taking their lead or defying it. A ball came tumbling across Birdie's path, to be scooped up by little Amy Popeldos. Birdie liked the Popeldos family. Mr Popeldos was Greek and worked in the docks as a casual. His wife worked at the markets, often taking the kids with her. Little Amy was no more than four, and the youngest of seven children. Her brothers and sisters were playing outside too, bellowing back at the Kirbys in their own strange language, half-Greek, half-English.

Giving Birdie a sticky grin from under her heavy dark, straight fringe, Amy wiped her runny nose with the back of her hand. Her coat was a size too large for her and her boots were heavy with Blakey's. 'T'ra,' she called to Birdie, and Birdie grinned back.

A little further on, Birdie saw Vi and Annie Carter, standing together on their doorstep, arms folded across their chests. As soon as the two spinster sisters saw her coming, they disappeared inside.

Birdie felt the slam of the door as if it was an insult. She paused for a moment, knowing they would be scrutinizing her from behind the lace curtain. Just as Ma Jenkins, no doubt, would be next door, thought Birdie, the blood rushing heatedly to her cheeks.

She was annoyed and angry, but what use was there in causing a scene? Then to her surprise, the portly figure of Ma Jenkins appeared, as her front door flew open. Dressed in a shapeless brown coat that made her look as wide as she was tall, she gave a little start when she saw Birdie. Her narrowed gaze under a basin-shaped hat gave Birdie only the slightest hint of recognition.

'Afternoon,' Birdie said politely as the older woman stepped out and folded her arms challenging.

'Don't try putting on that sweet smile for my benefit,' shouted Ma Jenkins. 'It don't wash around here no more.'

Birdie felt her anger rise as she stepped slowly forward. 'What exactly do you mean by that?'

'Do I have to spell it out? Bad blood, that's what I'm saying. It runs in the family. You should be ashamed of yerself. First it's that high-and-mighty shopkeeper calling at all hours, then 'im from downstairs always in and out, and Gawd knows how many more you let in by the alley. What sort of house are you keeping, or have I just answered me own question?'

'You suspicious, foul-mouthed old crone,' Birdie gasped as she drew her shoulders back and confronted the bristling woman. 'You sit at the window all day and fester on the lies you're telling. How dare you talk about innocent people in that way? I keep a decent home and make an honest living. It ain't none of your business who comes in or goes out of my door.'

'You'd have to be bleedin' blind not see 'em,' Ma Jenkins retaliated. 'What with the law disturbing everyone's peace, and bringing down the reputation of a good decent neighbourhood. Who knows who you're keeping hidden there, and, mark my words, if I ever get a glimpse of that no-good brother of yours—'

Before Ma Jenkins could finish, Birdie fell on her. She knew that she was close to losing her temper, but this time her neighbour had gone too far. 'Don't ever – *ever* – talk about Frank in that way again.' Pinning the terrified woman against the door jamb, Birdie pulled herself up to her full height and, poking her finger hard in the gossip's trembling shoulder, she threatened, 'Birdie Connor might be half your size, and seeming to be a pushover because she has the manners to bid her so-called neighbour good morning. But go against her kith and kin, and she'll make you'll wish you'd never spoken such filth aloud.'

Birdie swirled round and, without a glance back, flung herself in through her own front door, slamming it fiercely behind her. She stood there, shaking. Her skin pricked with rage. Even her hair felt as though it was standing on end. It was a few moment before she managed to breathe normally, but she was still left seething. How dare that old prune call her a loose woman! And to accuse the family of being bad blood!

As Birdie stood there she knew the street must have witnessed the argument. Ma Jenkins' lies would already have circulated and spread their poison. But no one was going to speak of the Connors in such a way!

For once, Birdie didn't have the heart to put the kettle on. Her anger subsiding, she walked dejectedly to the kitchen. Was she so angry because there was truth in what Ma Jenkins had said? Frank's conviction and escape must seem proof to others that the Connors were disreputable. Had welcoming Harry into the fold as one of the family given the wrong impression whilst she was seeing Don? But it must be known by now that Donald Thorne no longer appeared at the Connors' front door of a Sunday afternoon. Yet Harry's innocent visits were used by Ma Jenkins to fan the flames of idle gossip.

Birdie felt a familiar sinking sensation inside her. It was a feeling that had lived at the pit of her stomach every day since Frank's arrest. She woke up with it each morning, forcing it from her mind, pretending nothing was amiss until her visit to Hailing House. Was Don justified in his comments about Frank?

A desire to see Don suddenly filled her. Why had she refused his proposal? Why hadn't she done as he asked? Instead, she'd allowed her pride to get in the way, believing that Don was behaving unjustly towards Frank. Yet, could she now see it from his side?

On the spur of the moment she left the house again, holding her chin high as she passed Ma Jenkins' closed door. Soon she had skirted the docks and was heading to Poplar. Suddenly she couldn't wait a moment longer. She just had to see Don.

As Birdie walked along the High Street, her heart beat rapidly at the thought of what she was about to do. What would she say to Don? There was a hunger inside her that had to be satisfied. Dear Don, her sweetheart, who was probably missing her just as much as she was him. Had their pride kept them apart? Perhaps she could suggest they begin afresh, forget their quarrel for now?

Birdie crossed the road, in between the carts and lorries, and though the streets were not half as busy as they were on a weekday, the unofficial traders were out, dodging the law: the young posy-sellers with their roses wrapped in silver paper and smelling of perfume; the pub-buskers mingling with the dark blue uniforms of the Salvation Army; the salt-seller with his barrow and block of salt carved by a rusty saw. A lamplighter was dismounting from his bicycle, the long ignition pole balanced on his shoulder.

The hot-chestnut barrow by the dock wall had little paper twists of blackened chestnuts, smelling of charcoal. At the crossroads by the hospital, a woman was standing at her barrow, scooping winkles into newspaper cones.

Now Birdie was so close to the store, a fine sweat beaded her forehead. In just a few moments . . .

She stopped beside the alley that led down to the traction engine yard. There were no smoke-stained blinds ahead, their frills waving in the breeze, and the smell of horse dung and over-ripe vegetables, laced with the tang of paraffin, was nowhere near as pungent as it was on a weekday. The pedestrians strolled slowly along, in no great hurry to get anywhere and in the growing dusk, the lamplighter began his work.

In the distance, quite a way up, were three figures she recognized. A straight-backed man with proud shoulders under his smart Sunday overcoat, a woman in an elegant camel-coloured suit and matching cloche hat, a young boy, dressed in his Sunday tunic and short trousers. James held tightly to Don's hand and Lydia slipped her fingers over his arm. The three of them sauntered slowly to the door that led off from the street.

A pain went though Birdie's chest, as sharp as a knife. She watched them leave the street, saw their casual ease and smiles, noted how James was hoisted easily up into Don's arms and heard the drift of laughter from Lydia as they disappeared inside.

Birdie leaned back against the wooden joist of the yard gate. Closing her eyes, she wiped her brow with her handkerchief. It was only the sound of a vehicle horn that roused her and sent her awkwardly back in the vague direction of March Street.

Chapter 14

When Birdie arrived home it was dusk. She went straight to the parlour and found it empty. The fire needed attention and so she added a few more coals. Then she hung up her coat and hat and went to the kitchen. What was left of a meal remained in a bowl, and the dirty plates were piled on the draining board. She went upstairs and knocked on her father's door but, as she expected, he wasn't there. Pat's room also was empty and she went downstairs again, more than ever aware of the emptiness around her. Wilfred had most likely gone to join his friends at the Quarry and Pat was not yet back from meeting up with Willie.

She tied on her apron to tackle the dishes. She tried to hum and even sing, though something seemed to prevent a melody coming out. As she furiously scrubbed the dishes, a pin fell from her hair, allowing a lock to fall over her eyes. She brushed it back with wet hands, and the scraping of Sunlight that she'd added to the water mysteriously touched her eyes.

'Ouch!' she cried aloud, but there was no one to hear her. Screwing up her eyes, she made it all the worse by running her hands over her face. Half blinded, she felt for the drawer and a clean cloth, but it escaped her grasp. So she tore her apron from her waist and plunged her face into it. Dropping down on a chair, she allowed the sobs to come up from her chest, one after another.

'You daft thing, Brigid Connor.' The apron smelled of the beef stew and other homely aromas, but the faint whiff of paraffin from the kindling made her start all over again. It reminded her of the store and of Don and everything that seemed so far removed from her grasp. 'If only you'd just said you'd do what he wanted,' she told herself

118

miserably. Was his one request too much to ask? 'Oh, Birdie Connor, you are the most—'

'Birdie?' a voice interrupted, and she twisted so fast that she dropped the apron, her fingers going out to follow it, but the soap in her eyes smarted all over again. 'Is that you, Pat?'

'No, it's me.' Harry pressed the apron back in her palms, guiding her hands to her eyes. 'Now you just have a good cry. And don't let me stop you. I only looked in to see you were all right.'

'Well, of course I am,' she said, embarrassed. 'The soap went in my eyes.'

'A great hazard,' he agreed, 'when washing the dishes.'

'Are you laughing at me, Harry Chambers?'

'I should never do that. Unless I had your permission of course.'

'Well, I'll give you permission now.'

He sat down beside her. 'Is it more than soap that's making those pretty eyes red, I wonder.'

'I was giving meself a good talking to.' She heaved a big sigh. 'I suppose me dad's gone down to his pals?'

'He's in good spirits,' Harry assured her. 'Certainly a shade or two up on his daughter.'

Birdie dropped the apron in her lap. 'I've had . . . I've had . . .' she began, refusing to give way to the tremble on her lips, 'what Mum would have called the devil of an afternoon.'

Then, without a word of prompting, she found herself telling him about the Carter sisters and Ma Jenkins and their downright rudeness, and her sudden desire to see her sweetheart, followed by her unexpected march to Poplar. And though she didn't quite know how to put it, how the sight of Don with Lydia and James had so disturbed her. She listened to herself, thinking she sounded so peevish, so small-minded. But she knew very well as she spoke – but couldn't admit to Harry – that she'd been guilty of the worst of all sins: a case of the severest and greenest jealousy.

'I'm sure I wouldn't have liked to be in your shoes,' murmured Harry, listening with quiet attention.

Birdie sat forward hopefully. 'Do you see what I mean?'

'Oh, yes, yes, I do.'

'It just seemed rude to interrupt,' Birdie explained, 'with them looking so . . . so well, *together*,' she settled for. Then added guiltily, 'And why shouldn't they be? There's no harm in a walk out on a Sunday afternoon, no harm at all!'

Harry nodded slowly. 'No, none that I can imagine.'

'She *is* his sister-in-law,' Birdie continued. 'Not as if she wasn't family.'

'So maybe it was all above board?' he ventured, a dark eyebrow shooting up to his hairline.

'Indeed,' nodded Birdie, her attention caught by the expressive gentleness of his face.

'There was your beau,' he confirmed, 'and his sister-in-law, Lydia, and her boy, James, simply out for a stroll. And isn't it the way of nature for James to be close to his uncle? With no grandfather or pa, your man is likely to take their place.' The eyebrow fell back into place. 'Certainly this is not fresh news to you, Birdie. You must have known it for some time?'

Birdie sat in disappointed silence. All at once, the gravity hit her of what she must accept in marriage to Don. 'I suppose I've known it,' she admitted. 'But I didn't quite see it, until today. I've been thinking of our own children and Don loving *our* babies.' She blushed.

'But then again, he couldn't let the little lad down, now, could he?'

Birdie sat clutching her apron. It wasn't as if she hadn't acknowledged the presence of Lydia and James in Don's life. She had, but in a way that was removed from herself and Don. For a moment she thought she might have imagined it all, but then the memory of Lydia's smile and the happy look on James's face returned, his small hand grasped tenderly in Don's larger one.

'Now, how is that finger of yours?' Harry asked, standing up, indicating he was about to leave.

'Oh, it's healed perfectly, thank you.'

'Most wounds do, if left to nature,' he smiled, standing and sliding his work-bag over his shoulder.

'Goodbye, Harry. You can forget all me complaints now. It was just a passing moment.'

'Ah, think nothing of it,' he grinned. 'The world seems an unkindly place sometimes.'

She caught the last of his words as he turned, striding his way up the passage. She heard the front door close behind him and Birdie sat in the silence, a less lonely silence now, where the house didn't seem quite so empty, nor the shadows so gloomy.

Pat's hands gripped the handlebars of his bicycle tightly as he raced towards Stepney. He was excited by the thought of seeing Frank again. The woman who'd been dressed in men's clothing and had approached them at Chalk Wharf had drawn him aside from Willie.

He'd listened in awe to her strange accent as she had said she would take him to Frank that evening. He was to meet her by Stepney Green, but he wished now that he'd insisted on knowing more. Instead, he'd stared, quite beguiled by her big, dark eyes, shielded by the brim of her cap. She had warned him that no one must know of the arrangement, only him. Then, as quickly as she'd appeared, she'd vanished.

As Pat cycled along the Commercial Road, he heard the clock of a church strike seven. He was in plenty of time and wished he hadn't bolted his stew. But he'd been keen to get out of the house after his supper. Birdie had gone to her sewing room and as his dad had taken himself off to the Quarry again, Pat had made a dash for it. Luckily, he'd bumped into Harry and, as an afterthought, left a message for his sister that he'd be home by nine.

Pat gulped the air to the back of his throat, knowing he was entering Stepney, an area jam-packed full of all national-alities. There was a muddle of two-and three-storey houses with narrow streets and dark alleys. He'd cycled through here a few times on his rounds, trying to avoid the dozens of kids playing in the street. Some were the children of gypsies, others costermongers, and this evening a group of men were carrying banners, demonstrating for workers' rights.

As he made his way towards Stepney Green, he thought guiltily of Willie, who had been annoyed that their after-noon had been spoiled.

'Who was that?' Willie had demanded as the woman had left.

'A friend of my sister's,' Pat had improvised, eager to leave Chalk Wharf to solve the mystery.

'Funny friends your sister has, dressed up like a man. How did she know you was here?'

'Birdie must've said. I've got to go and help with Dad.'

'What *now*?' Willie had questioned suspiciously.

'I told you, he has funny turns.'

Willie had given him a doubtful look but had duti-fully picked up his bicycle and the remnants of their food, and Pat had given him two Woodbines to keep him happy. 'See you tomorrow,' Pat had shouted as they parted, though Willie cycled off calling he might not make it. Pat knew he would. Willie was just disappointed their smoking and drinking had been brought abruptly to an end.

Suddenly Pat put on his brakes. There was a commotion going on in the middle of the narrow street. A Salvation

Army band and choir, singing their Sunday hymns, was being heckled. One man, in rough cord trousers and a cap, was shouting at the bandsmen to clear off. A few yards up two men were arguing. One of them waved a board announcing the railway union strike.

'Jesus ain't saved us from Whitehall,' one man roared, trying to silence the drum player. 'So shove off and let us march.'

Pat was horrified to see the drum go rolling down the street and the members of the Salvation Army run off to chase it. Pat knew of the unrest amongst the unions from his rounds. The marchers weren't bad sorts, but their mood was ugly.

He tried to squeeze through with his bicycle. But the crowd was agitated. He began to feel nervous. Suddenly a big, burly man blocked his path, muscles bulging under his dirty vest. The hairs on the back of Pat's neck stood up. He didn't seem to be part of the demonstration but had come out from one of the houses.

'Who're you then?' demanded the bruiser, lifting a beer-jug to his lips and swallowed noisily. Some of the beer escaped down his chin and stained the top of his vest. 'Are you with this lot?'

Pat shook his head. He seemed to be hemmed in on all sides.

It was the wrong answer, he realized as the man's lips curled into an ugly smile. 'That's a nice bit o' machinery you got there.' He reached out and grabbed the handlebars. 'I'll bet it goes at a speed, don't it?'

Pat swallowed hard. He had a sick feeling in his stomach. He knew he couldn't stop the man from taking his bicycle if he wanted. Even if he yelled and screamed no one would be interested in all the confusion.

He searched the crowd for a familiar face, but of course found none. The disruption seemed to have spread. A man wearing a red-spotted neckerchief and an eye patch pushed another man with such force that he fell over.

'So, let's be havin' it then, lad,' said the muscle-man, pulling Pat's bicycle towards him. Though he was terrified, Pat refused to let go. In the next moment, his arm was nearly pulled out of its socket. The pain made him cry out and yet he hung on. The bicycle was the property of the PLA, and if it was stolen, he would lose his job.

Gritting his teeth, Pat yanked back. The pedal hit his shin and once again, he let out a yelp. The man laughed, his beery face and smoke-fouled breath making Pat vow never to want to smoke or drink with Willie again. Then suddenly he was pushed right off his feet. The man had his bicycle, wheeling it off triumphantly. Pat tried to get up but was bowled over by one of the demonstrators. Pat knew he was really in trouble now. The blow of landing on his bottom had sent the wind from him, but he managed to crawl away from the jeering crowd, struggling to his feet, determined to follow his bicycle. He could see it disappearing round the corner and he yelled at the top of his voice.

'Hey, stop, thief! If you don't, I'll set the law on you!' Pat surprised even himself at what he'd threatened. It wasn't as if he'd really go to the police. No one in the East End liked the law or ever called for their assistance.

'What did you say, you little pip-squeak?' The hulk turned, staring menacingly at him. Pat stood shaking as he saw his bicycle was shoved against the wall. Dropping the beer-jug, the man lurched towards him and grabbed his collar.

'Call the law on me, would you, you damned perisher?'

In his last gasping moments of his life, as Pat decided they must be, he wondered why he had been so foolish as to make the one threat that would act against him. Only a dimwit would call out such a thing. But he'd been angry and frightened, and at a loss as to how he could stop his bicycle being stolen.

'Arggh . . .' Pat choked, as he struggled to breathe. 'I didn't . . . didn't—'

'Didn't what?' spat the ale-foamed lips in his face. 'Don't try wheedling your way out of this, you little blighter. I'm gonna show you what happens to lippy kids like you that have got gobs bigger than—'

Pat felt the hold on his neck loosen instead of tighten. The big man in front of him stood still, swaying slightly, his eyes slowly glazing over. Releasing Pat's shirt, he folded at the knees and fell flat on his face. Pat scrambled away, hauling himself up to peer at his rescuer. It was none other than the woman in breeches, wearing a young boy's cap. The coarse breeches did very little to hide the slenderness of her thighs and hips. Her top half was covered by a thin brown tunic, belted as before, narrowing her small waist. In her hand was the remains of the drunk's own jug, which she had just flattened him with. Pat stood in awe, never having seen such an athletic female before, and it was all he could do to rouse himself from the shock.

'Take your bicycle and follow me,' the woman commanded forcefully, throwing aside the broken china. 'And be quick! The police are here.'

At this warning, Pat shook himself out of his trance. He grasped his bicycle, though his hands were still shaking, and flung himself on the saddle. Ignoring the pain of his very sore neck, he pedalled fast after the running figure that sprinted like the wind over the cobbles. She seemed to know the path ahead and Pat fixed his eyes on the flying breeches, bracing himself for – God help him – whatever might lie ahead. One glance behind him told him he had no choice. For they were being followed closely by every other man at the demonstration who had spotted the advance of the law.

Chapter 15

Pat stood still, his heart almost stopping with fright. He didn't have a clue where he was. A tall man with a black beard and hat addressed the woman in a foreign language. She seemed to agree and he reached out for Pat's bicycle. But Pat refused to let it go.

'I'll not be robbed twice,' he argued.

'This man is my friend and won't harm you,' the woman told him. 'If you want to see your brother, it is best you don't know where he is. Tie this around your eyes.' She drew a scarf from her pocket.

'Not on your nelly!' Pat exclaimed, and when he recoiled, clutching his bicycle firmly, she smiled.

'It is for your own safety. Should ever you be questioned, the truth won't spill from your lips.'

Pat didn't like the sound of this at all. Why should he be questioned? Who were these people? But he wanted to see Frank.

'Quickly,' she ordered him. 'There is no time to waste.'

Pat didn't know what to do. Tom Redwing, his hero, brave son of a sailorman and student at Greyfriars, wouldn't hesitate. If it was the Bounder who was in trouble, he'd not be shrinking away from danger, but facing it.

Reluctantly he nodded. The man took his bicycle, and the woman tied the cloth round his eyes. A firm hand attached to his shoulder and pushed him forward. He'd never been blindfolded before. Where did they intend to take him? Would he be parted from his bicycle?

His fear deepened as he was eventually halted by his guard. There was the sound of a lock being drawn and a door squeaking open. He could tell it was a heavy door because it scraped on the ground. Then he was being pushed inside and he smelled the stink of horses and straw.

'Where am I? And what about me bicycle?' he shouted, wanting his sight back.

'Soon you will meet your brother,' the woman told him.

Pat felt himself lifted and placed on a floor. Someone gripped his arms and pushed him down. There were whispers and the sound of boots shuffling close. Next, the noise of a tailgate being latched up. Was his bicycle with him? He reached out, sliding his hand along the bench. He felt the softness of canvas, the tethered strings tied to the covered wagon. The jogging movement began, the sound of hoofs rang out over the cobbles.

Pat listened to all that went on. His ears were pricked, though he was deafened at times by the thunder of his frightened heart. Well, he wasn't dead yet. And the woman had talked about Frank in the way a friend would, though he couldn't quite think how.

The same clock chimed eight that had chimed seven an hour ago. He heard hoots from the river and then another clear sound that he recognized: a busker, singing, 'It's a A Long Way to Tipperary', so out of tune that people would give old Tickle Mary, as he was known, money to send him away. The Mutt 'n' Jeff drunk regularly staggered the fifty feet of pavement outside the Roxy in Commercial Road. Pat sat up, listening even more attentively now he knew they were leaving Stepney.

Pat began to count. He would stop counting when the cart turned and begin again, then try to keep the numbers in his head . . .

'I'll leave you to wait up for Pat,' yawned Wilfred that night. 'I can't keep me eyes open a moment longer.' He gave a bark of a cough and folded his newspaper away.

'I'll give him a chewing off when he comes in,' Birdie

vowed as she peered through the lace curtain. It was too dark to see anything, but still she looked.

'Boys will be boys,' Wilfred said reasonably. 'And Pat is a good lad. If you ask me, he's started his courting. And the last thing he'll want is for his sister to know his business.'

But Birdie had her own opinion on the matter. She didn't think Pat's poor timekeeping was at all to do with a romance. Pat had told her as much himself; that he was more interested in adventuring with Willie than going out with girls. Though of course, a pretty lass could have taken his eye and she dearly hoped this was the reason for his unusual lateness.

Birdie tried not to feel so anxious, but she was. Fifteen . . . nearly twenty minutes past the hour of nine and it was much later than he'd ever stayed out before. If Harry hadn't told her that Pat had said he'd be home by nine, she wouldn't have known even that.

'Good night, girl and God bless,' her father said, patting her shoulder. 'And don't give the boy too hard a time.'

Birdie nodded and once he was gone, making his way slowly up the stairs after visiting the closet, she tried to turn her attention to the events of the day. Had she been too hard on Don, as Harry had suggested? Yet, if his theory was correct, and Lydia and James were so much a part of Don's life, then if she loved Don, she must love who he loved too. Well, she did already! Almost. James was a dear little boy, and must miss his father dreadfully. Birdie had the deepest sympathy for him. But all along, she had supposed a different outcome to the one she had seen today. Lydia was meant to be looking for husband number two. Had she not put away her mourning clothes? And wasn't James the right age to take to a new man? Don, his uncle, should remain his uncle. But a man of good conduct and back-ground — and wasn't there a sprinkling of these at church? — would make Lydia a perfect husband.

Birdie stood up and paced the floor. For a while, she was lost in the game of matching up Lydia to a new husband. A new life awaited Lydia, but would she grasp it if Don's shoulder was there to lean on?

Giving the fire a fierce poke and folding her arms across her chest, she collapsed into Wilfred's chair. She could see Lydia now, sitting at the desk in the office. Was it too comfortable a chair to leave?

Birdie jumped up as the clock struck a quarter to ten. Lydia was immediately forgotten as she came back to the present. Where was Pat? She flew to the window and lifted the curtain. The gaslights gave a dull yellowy glow in the mist that was settling on the street.

She drew in a sharp breath, the feeling of dread coming over her. Pat had never been out this late. She knew something was wrong. She had known it ever since the minute hand of the clock had passed nine.

What should she do? Wilfred must be asleep by now. Should she go out to search for Pat, even though the night was threatening fog?

Harry was whistling his way along the dark street, having enjoyed a pint at the White Horse in Poplar. In the company of his crew he had been making plans for the next day. Ned Shorter was an old hand, experienced enough to take over in his absence. The section of drains they were about to repair in the East India Dock Road was tough going. The earth was as solid as concrete and there were rats in the drains as big as the terriers that were sent to chase them. But the latrine waste was the worst. There was enough to sink a battleship. Their eyes watered and the stench was vile. He needed someone he could rely on, like Ned. If this job worked well, he'd talk to Ned about buying a wagon.

The challenge of the work was what Harry liked.

Identifying the sewerage tunnels and their problems wasn't everyone's cup of tea, and that left the way open for him. The broken shafts and ancient soakaways of London city were held together often by luck, and carrying out repairs to the network was inexhaustible. He'd spent half the war digging trenches for the army. Now he was building a reputation in civvy street. He didn't want drunkards working for him. He needed muscle and a willingness to graft hard. He'd found this in his crew and paid them a fair wage. He kept them happy and they, in return, were to be relied upon.

The night was gathering around him as he strolled towards home. A fine, wet mist hung around the eaves and skittered over the cobbles. The houses looked homely on either side: little nests that were warm and cared for, though he had to smile as a loud cursing came from one front door.

'Bugger off, Jack!' exclaimed the woman, a chink of light exposing her muscular arm directed towards the man. 'When you're sober, you can step over this doorstep and not a moment before.' The door slammed, the man fell back and limped miserably along the road. A couple passed him, arms linked, laughing pitilessly as he heaved his stomach contents into the gutter.

The mist enclosed Harry, and the scent of the docks, the tar and weed that clotted the grimy water and discoloured the surface, filled his lungs. The brisk walk had got rid of the effects of the glass of ale and he was eager to open his own door and be warm and snug inside. As he came to the alley he always cut through, he saw a figure in front of him, bent down. The mist was creeping over the silhouette, but there was something about it he recognized.

In startled recognition, he came to a halt. 'Pat – Pat Connor, is that you?' The head came up and the gaslight showed he was right. But to his dismay Pat looked as though he'd been through a hedge and backwards. His hair was almost standing on end and his boot laces were hanging loose. His shirttails were out and he wore no collar and there was a streak of dirt across his cheek. 'What's happened, Pat?'

'I had a puncture.'

Harry bent down and looked at the bicycle wheel. 'It's too dark to mend here. And anyway, what are you doing out at this time of night?'

'I'm in a jam, Harry. I can't wheel it, else I'll ruin the tyre. But I can't leave it here, either.'

Harry saw the boy was shivering so he took off his own warm duffel and made him put it on. The jumper he wore beneath was sufficient for his own needs.

'Not to worry, there's two of us and we'll carry it.' Harry lifted the front and indicated the back to Pat. 'We'll have you both home in a trice. Now as we go, you can tell me how you got in such a pickle.'

They began to walk along, with Harry listening over his shoulder.

'I don't know as I can tell you. It's supposed to be secret. Though you know about Frank already,' mumbled Pat, sniffing and trying to catch his breath. 'You'd never believe me anyway. I don't believe it myself. And Birdie will kill me for being out this late. Did you tell her I'd be home by nine?'

'I did indeed,' replied Harry, keeping up a steady march.

'I don't know what she'll say and I'll have to tell her. I couldn't do nothing but what I did, could I?'

Harry stopped, bringing Pat to a halt too. 'Depends on what you did, lad.' There was a shifting uneasily in the street behind them, but Harry saw nothing. He brought his attention back to Pat, who was struggling to keep his conscience to himself. 'You'd better give your explanation a try, lad. Make it word-perfect for your sister,' he replied easily, and set off again.

The story that came next kept Harry quiet to such a degree that, other than it being the truth, the alternative was that Pat had developed a vivid imagination. But when it came to the riot, and the blindfold and the jug-wielding female, Harry put this alternative to one side.

'You're saying,' Harry put in as Pat took a breath, 'that this unknown woman found you at Chalk Wharf with Willie, then met you in Stepney and saved your bacon?'

'A rough encounter it was too,' nodded Pat eagerly, 'with a bruiser three times my size, maybe four, about to steal my bicycle. She clouted him with his own beer-jug and there was us escaping, and then me being blindfolded and carried in this cart with this other big bruiser and my bicycle—'

Harry stopped, looking round. 'Did you hear that?' he whispered.

'No, what was it?'

'Footsteps.'

They both looked this way and that, but the mist was turning to fog. Not a sound came from the silent street.

'Harry, is someone following us?'

'Why should they do that?'

'Don't know,' rasped Pat, sounding choked and frightened. 'But I've got the wind up now. After today I'd even believe in the fairies.'

'I've not seen one of those yet,' Harry dismissed, but his skin was now chilling in the damp night air. 'Let's get a move on.'

He didn't add, as they pressed on, that he'd been listening for a while and had come to the conclusion that the yellow veil of fog could make excellent cover for someone who didn't want to be seen, yet who was watching them.

Chapter 16

Birdie wanted to hug Pat so hard she'd squeeze the life out of him, whilst at the same time she wanted to tear him off a strip. It was only the sight of Harry standing with her brother, the bicycle between them, that stilled the reproach in her throat as she opened the back door.

'Before you lay into him,' Harry warned, lowering the handlebars and then passing his hand across his forehead, 'it was unintentional that Pat kept out late. When I found him, he'd got a puncture and so we walked home.'

Birdie spluttered a few words of reprimand, but they soon died under her heartfelt embrace. She hugged him as if fearing he'd disappear. 'You rascal,' she managed lamely, her joy at the feel of him overcoming her terror. 'I've been thinking all kinds of things.'

'I'm sorry,' he mumbled. 'Didn't mean to worry you.'

'Is that all you can say?'

'If it wasn't for Harry I'd be even later. Might not be here now if it hadn't been for—'

'That's an admission I don't want to hear,' Birdie interrupted, glancing at Harry. It was then she saw Pat was wearing Harry's coat and Harry's jumper was grimy and stained from the oil of the bicycle chain. Before he could continue, she remarked, 'You both look as though you've been caught in a storm. Come in and I'll make a hot drink.'

Birdie watched them leave the bicycle by the wall of the yard and troop into the kitchen. They looked a sight for sore eyes indeed. And she wanted to know so much, but Pat kept giving Harry, then her, strange looks. She tried to read their expressions, but her heart was still pumping so hard behind her ribs that all she could do was push them to the sink. 'Now wash those filthy hands and faces with

133

the Sunlight there, and use this old rag to dry them. I don't want no oil or grease over me nice table, and you had better take off that duffel, Pat and I'll give it a damp clean and press it neat again for Harry.'

'Don't trouble, it's only my work coat,' Harry said, draping it over the back of a chair as Birdie rushed around, boiling the kettle, setting out the pot and mugs, and disappearing into the larder. She brought out the loaf and sliced off two good wedges, adding a layer of dripping to their tops. Then, finding the remains of the ginger cake, she halved it, setting it neatly on the table. When she'd warmed the pot and made the tea and the two of them were sitting eating, she felt calmer, though her head was still buzzing from the worry and hadn't had time to settle.

She had guessed that what Pat had been up to was not just down to a puncture, or else he'd be regaling her with the event, instead of eating in silence, with his ears almost drooping around his head.

When supper had disappeared in the space of five minutes and the tea was replenished, she sat herself down at the table. 'Now, who's going first?' she demanded, raising an eyebrow. 'It's a grand thing that you're home safe and sound, Patrick Connor, and me thanks go to you, Harry, for finding him. But your faces are pictures of guilt and the sooner I know the truth the better.'

Birdie folded her arms across her chest, just to show them she was prepared to wait another two hours for their answers. But as Harry looked at Pat with a resigned air and an imperceptible twinkle in his dark eyes, it was her brother who began the outpouring, and reduced Birdie herself to complete silence.

The mantel clock struck half-past eleven and Birdie had only interrupted once. That was when Pat related how he was attacked by the thief in Stepney. Had it not been for this mystery person, a female in breeches, putting his lights out with a beer-jug, and a tall man with a black beard, Pat might have suffered a beating. She had protested that Pat should have cycled off there and then, abando ning this mysterious female. But hard on the heels of escape, it appeared, the Bluebottles arrived.

Now Pat had come to the part where he'd been blindfolded and put into a cart, along with his bicycle.

'Mind, it was dark,' said Pat, his eyes bright with excitement under his fringe of brown hair. 'But I heard old Tickle Mary, see, so I reckoned we was passing the Roxy, and later we was turning to our right, to the river. I knew that, 'cos the cart jerked and I had to reach out to steady meself. So, I listens again, and then there's this smell. It's a shop, where I turn down Cable Street. They sell ice cream and Weights and Woodbines, and sometimes I get me *Magnet* there. There's this stink of tobacco the lascars use, and these men talkin' all queer.'

'You haven't been smoking the weed yourself?' asked Birdie suspiciously.

'Course not,' replied Pat indignantly. 'Willie and me wouldn't touch it. We might have a Woodbine now and then, but not that.'

'It's a tall story you're telling, Pat,' she murmured doubtfully. 'This ain't one of your imagined adventures?'

'No, God's honour it's not.'

'Don't take the Lord's name in vain. I believe you.'

'And then we rumble on,' Pat resumed quickly. 'I can hear all the traffic and noise and I say to myself, this is the Highway, got to be. And then they turn again, down towards Shadwell. And there's this funny lingo, shouts and talking and all that.'

Birdie shuddered. Everyone kept away from Shadwell, even the law. The reputation it had was second to none.

The waterfront was all seedy slums and dock-side opportunists.

'What happened then?' she asked, feeling sweat roll down her back.

'The cart stopped and I was pulled out. The next thing I know is I'm in this room and the blindfold's off but it's too dark to see. There's just this oil lamp and this big face looking at me. His hair's all black and then he smiles and, stone me, it's Frank!' Pat burst out. 'He gives me another hug like he did before. And, oh, Birdie, I never knew it was him. Not till he gave me that smile,' sniffed Pat, trying to clear his throat, but his eyes were all misty and he pushed his fingers into his eyes and blinked. 'They dyed his hair, see? To cover the red.'

'Who's they?' demanded Birdie at once, trying to dislodge the lump in her throat.

'This woman and that man.'

'What did Frank say?'

'He said he wasn't sure where to go after he'd seen you. But in the end, he went to this address that someone in prison gave him. She said he could stay there, just as long as he did what they said.'

'But why would they do that?' Harry interrupted. 'I mean, what do they want with him?'

'Search me,' Pat shrugged.

'And why did that woman send you to Stepney?'

'To throw anyone following me off the scent, so Frank said. There wasn't meant to be a demonstration, though. That bit went wrong.'

Birdie felt her stomach turn over. What had Frank got himself into?

'He says you're not to worry,' Pat continued importantly. 'That he's in with a good crowd, where innocent people like him can hold up from the coppers.'

'But what do they want in return?' Birdie fretted.

'They're not hiding him out of the goodness of their hearts.'

'They might,' Pat answered truculently. 'Otherwise he'd be back behind bars. Frank trusts them. Isn't that enough?'

'Perhaps,' agreed Harry, 'and I know you're all for Frank – your sister is too – but think a minute. How did this woman find you in the first place?'

'They've been keeping watch,' Pat mumbled, his eyes downcast. 'Frank said they had to make sure we're not in with the law.'

'You mean we've been followed – spied on?' Birdie's voice was a hoarse whisper.

Pat looked uneasy again. 'S'pose so.'

'And are they still watching?' Birdie demanded.

'Don't know,' muttered Pat, shutting his mouth tightly and looking under his fringe at Harry.

'Well, I shall give that brother of ours a piece of me mind,' Birdie protested, 'just as soon as I see him. Watching his own family, indeed! And just when is it, do you mind telling me, that Frank intends to speak to his sister?'

Pat scratched at the table with his dirty fingernails. 'He said he'd get word to you. Said it'll be easier when the coppers stop searching.'

'Well, that's a grand offering, indeed,' Birdie grumbled. 'Am I to be blindfolded and taken in a cart too, like some baggage bound for the docks?' Seeing the bewildered expression on her brother's face, Birdie knew it was no use blaming Pat for what had happened and she asked in a kinder tone, 'So how did you get from this place you believe to be Shadwell to where you had your puncture and met Harry?'

'They had my bike, an' all. Give it to me before they blindfolded me again. I didn't mind this time, as Frank said they'd take me to Poplar.'

'So we know they're all at this hideout,' Harry broke in.

'The woman and the man called Erik – and Frank.'

Pat nodded slowly. 'Didn't see no one else.'

'Were you alone with Frank?'

'No,' said Pat with a shrug. 'She was there. Didn't say anything, only when it was time to go. Frank likes her, I reckon.'

Birdie was about to argue that Frank found no difficulty in liking any pretty face, it was his weakness. But when Pat yawned and his eyelids drooped, she said gently, 'You'd better get yourself off to bed, as you have a puncture to mend before work.'

Pat stood up. 'Sorry I caused you worry.'

'No sorrier than I,' Birdie agreed with regret, 'But I wish we might have gone to see Frank together.'

Pat grinned sheepishly. 'If that bruiser had seen you, he'd have thought twice before taking my bicycle.'

'You cheeky young devil,' she agreed with a smile, and she saw Harry give him a wink as he left. But inside, her stomach was clenched as tight as a wrung sheet with the thought of Pat in such wild company.

'What do you make of it?' she asked Harry afterwards. 'Is it tall stories our Pat is telling?'

'I believe him,' Harry murmured.

'But who can Frank be with?' Birdie asked worriedly. 'What kind of people are they, to take in a convict from prison? Our Frank is easily led.'

'I'll see to it Pat's bicycle is mended,' Harry said as he stood up, but she stopped him.

'Pat risks his freedom if the law finds out.'

'It won't come to that,' Harry assured her as he folded his coat over his arm. 'Pat is no fool. He has his wits about him.'

When at last she lay in bed, Birdie took comfort from Harry's words. Ma Jenkins and the Carter sisters had provoked her today. But what did their opinion matter?

Frank was a decent man. He was, she believed, innocent of being a coward and running from his duty. The disgrace heaped on him and his family was unjust. But being on the run made him look guilty.

As sleep came, she wondered if Don was missing her. He had seemed happy with Lydia and James, but that didn't mean he no longer loved her. Had she let jealousy sweep her away?

Her doubts taunted her, as did her dreams. Images of Frank running in the marshy fields to the south of the island burst through her mind. She was standing next to Don and Lydia, calling out to Frank to stop before he sank into the boggy silt left by the racing tide.

Chapter 17

December was Birdie's favourite time of year. By then the scrubby plane trees had lost the last of their leaves, their branches stiffened by the dawn's silver frost and heralding Christmas. Not that there would be money to spend, she reflected early one Sunday morning as she drew the curtains to a sky threatening rain.

Just before she was to leave for Mass, Wilfred began a coughing fit that turned into all the signs of something worse.

Pat called Harry, who had not yet left for work, and between the three of them, they managed to contain the episode. Whilst Harry and Pat restrained him in the chair, Birdie administered the restorative.

'Leave me alone,' protested Wilfred, as he began to recover. Pushing Pat and Harry away, he stood up.

'Please rest,' Birdie pleaded, but her father shook his head, wiping his mouth with the rag that Birdie held out to him.

'You've all but poisoned me with that foul stuff. A man needs nothing but his own strength to get his bearings.' Taking his outdoor coat from the back of the chair he buttoned it up. 'I'm not intending to be home for dinner,' he shouted.

Birdie ran after him. 'Where are you going?'

'Somewhere I can feel normal and not be looked on as an invalid.' He pointed a shaky finger to the small bowl and spoon she was holding. 'And while I'm gone you can give that concoction to the pigs.'

After he'd argued his way out of the house, Birdie's nerves were fraught. This was made worse by Pat, eager to go out with Willie.

'No good going to Mass,' he reasoned. 'It will almost be over by now.'

'Promise me you'll not go to the wharf,' Birdie insisted. 'Or do any daft thing, like searching for Frank.'

'I already promised you that,' answered Pat truculently.

'Promise me again. And if that woman turns up, tell her Birdie Connor wants to speak to her.' Birdie distrusted these people who had befriended Frank, though she could see Pat was taken in.

'If Dad doesn't want dinner, then neither do I,' announced her young brother, squaring his shoulders. 'I'll buy meself a bun from the muffin man.'

'So that just leaves me,' said Harry, after Pat had gone. 'And to be honest, I'd be happy to enjoy an ale and a pie at the tavern. Why don't you take an hour or two for yourself, Birdie, perhaps have a stroll?'

'And what would I be doing strolling all by meself?' Birdie answered shortly. 'Flo will be busy cooking Reg's dinner, and if I was to go out with anyone it'd be her and the kids. No, if I'm to be left to me own devices, I'll get on with me alterations for the ladies. Father Flynn would call it a sin to work on the Sabbath day, but it'd be a greater sin even, to waste it.' She had planned to return the Hailings' bundle on Tuesday, along with a rough pattern for Annabelle's dress, though she had all Monday to finish the work.

'The sin is not religious,' said Harry with a wry smile as he stepped out, 'but that a pretty girl has to work when the rest of the world is at play. Christmas is not far off, after all.'

Birdie's cheeks went pink. 'Now that is a touch of the Irish blarney, Harry.'

'It's the absolute English truth.'

She laughed, shaking her head. 'You always bring a smile to me face. And after the morning I've had, I can tell you it's welcome.' She didn't say that the one thing that would cheer her up was to see her sweetheart, and that Sunday afternoons were the longest of the week in his absence.

Harry gazed at her, seeming reluctant to leave as he swung his work-bag over his shoulder. His dark eyes shone brightly under the lock of black hair that had fallen over his eyes. As he thrust it from his face, she saw his smile widen, showing his white, even teeth. 'Listen, it seems a crime for us to be working, when that stroll I described would do us both the power of good. The weather is fine and mild for this time of year. If I called back at two o'clock, even half-past, do you think we might enjoy the rest of the afternoon together? Perhaps not to its fullest advantage . . . no . . . as there were things we should be doing like wielding a spade and darning a cloth,' he added, going from one foot to the other, 'but wouldn't the air be a good reviver?'

'Well, I suppose it would,' agreed Birdie uncertainly. 'But what would we do? Where would we go?'

Harry put a hand to his head. 'Well, you've got me there.

I just said it off the top of me head, like, without thinking. And being Sunday, the shops are all closed up. It was only the fresh air I was thinking of, on such a fine day as this.'

Birdie saw how uncomfortable he looked and guessed he had only made the suggestion for her benefit. Her hesitation had quite put him off. It was a nice offer too, fresh air being exactly what she needed. 'We might take a walk to the East India Dock Road?' she said brightly. 'You can be sure there is always something going on up there. It would be nice to see the shop windows, perhaps with a few decorations.'

'Now why didn't I think of that?' Harry looked relieved. 'And if we fancy a tram ride, why, there will be plenty of those.'

'A tram ride, yes, perhaps,' she nodded, inspired by her own suggestion. 'Now, are you certain you'll be free?'

'I'll dig half a ditch instead of a whole,' he assured her with a grin.

'I'll be ready for half-past two.'

Nodding his approval, he turned and, with his customary whistle, departed.

Birdie closed the front door and stood in the silent house. Should she start a little work on Lady Annabelle's dress or the two darns in the bag of alterations? But she felt inclined to do neither. Instead she felt another emotion altogether, one she hadn't felt for some while. It had been so long, in fact, since she'd felt it that it was difficult to give it a name. It was the anticipation of an event, rather than the dreading of it, and it gave her quite a thrill.

But it was only a stroll she was going on! A good reviver, Harry had described it. She quickly put aside the thought of her work and glanced through the kitchen window to the back yard. A corner of it was lit up by sunlight, illuminating the dusty earth and the tangle of weeds climbing the alley wall.

Then a sudden panic gripped her, as the sun peeped out even brighter from behind a cloud. Why, she hadn't a thing to wear. And she couldn't even think of stepping out if she didn't have just the right outfit to show off!

By two o'clock, Birdie was dressed, her combination of clothes having undergone several changes. The sun had not only come out, but was shining solidly. She had searched for two or three articles from her wardrobe, including her lovely blue coat, a hat and gloves. To accompany this, she had settled on a wool frock in a shade of red. She had made the dress last autumn from a remnant discarded by the ladies. The sleeves were long and fitted, with little black velvet cuffs, and a velvet collar to match, which lay open just below her throat. Very carefully she had sewn a belted effect to the low waist, of the same material, so that when she walked a little flare went out above her knees. She had added an oval brooch with a gilt surround to her coat, bought at market for just a few pence, clipping it discreetly under the collar.

She had worn it once before, on Aggie's birthday close to the Armistice. It had been more like a wake than a celebration, as Aggie was then still in her widow's weeds. Tea had been taken upstairs, with James made to sit quietly at the daunting brown wood table, amidst the room full of other pieces of gloomy brown wood. Lydia had also worn very dull clothes and had had little to say.

Birdie had felt sad when Don had whispered to her that Aggie was still in mourning – along with the entire country – for the Unknown Soldier; that a page from the newspaper, with a photograph of the ceremony in Whitehall, was now hung in the shop. The very best part of the day was when Don had walked her home. She had held his arm tightly, proud to be leaning on it. Nothing more had been said about the colour of her dress. Instead they'd discussed their plans to see one another, which in the end, had to be postponed since James and Lydia had caught colds.

Birdie examined her reflection in the mirror. Her heart gave a sharp twist. To think, this red sleeve had rested on Don's strong arm. She could almost feel him now, his strength, his uprightness as he stood by her. She closed her eyes and sighed. A pang of deep longing went through her. Was there still hope they could be married? If only she could speak to him alone . . .

A knock came at the front door. Birdie's eyes flew open. She was back to the present in her bedroom, preparing to go out, the imaginary figure of Don beside her having quickly disappeared. The excitement she had felt slowly faded, for she knew the man waiting for her on the door-step was only Harry.

Harry felt about ten years old again. He was back at the orphanage, wearing a collar that nearly choked him, starched to unbearable stiffness, studded to a shirt that constricted his movement under a too-small jacket. At the orphanage, their jackets had all been one size, fitting all and none, made of rough serge, smelling rankly of cabbage, boiled potatoes, disinfectant and the unmistakable aroma of fearful sweat.

Not that this suit smelled. It was his best suit, clean and sponged down, pressed carefully. He thought of himself as domesticated and he could launder, though Birdie insisted she wash his shirts. He could cook too, having served an apprenticeship in the orphanage kitchens, though a daily meal was included now with the price of his rent. Both the orphanage and army instilled discipline; he'd had no trouble in barracks.

But he was a free man now. The shackles of the past

were thrown off. Both his early years and the war were paler in memory.

Still, he couldn't escape the feeling he had today: butter-flies in the pit of his stomach. The suit had merely reminded him. But now he was a grown man, not a boy, he assured himself as he stood waiting. His white cuffs, just showing beneath the navy blue of his sleeve, were not grubby or frayed. His waistcoat held a pocket watch and was drawn tight across his chest. A handkerchief, or at least the corner of it, sat upright in his breast pocket. He'd had no oil to let loose on his hair, which needed a decent cut. So he'd glued back its wildness with sugar-water, combed it from around his ears and clucked his tongue at the dark, loose ends that tickled his collar. His hands were scrubbed and nails trimmed, all done in the half an hour he'd had when he'd come home from work. His crew had mocked him for dashing away, but he'd told them to mind their own damn business – good-naturedly, of course – leaving his end of the drain neatly covered by a yard of wet concrete.

And now he was waiting for Birdie, an army of wings inside him, knowing that at any minute the door would open and she'd be there. And he'd have to think of some-thing daft to say to ease his discomfort. And hers, more like.

Just then, a second before the door opened, the worst thing possible happened. A voice, an unpleasant one, with a crowing, spiteful tone, was raised coarsely in conversation behind him. He heard, 'Now the loose bitch has got in with her lodger, see. It's bad blood that runs in the Connors. Even the old man shoves off every day to drown his sorrows in drink.'

He knew whose voice it was and to whom the poison was directed. The old witch of a troublemaker, Ma Jenkins, opposite, and the two ugly sisters next door, had spotted him no doubt, from behind their twitching curtains.

He'd give them one chance. But one chance only. After

their atrocious behaviour toward Birdie, they deserved not even that. But he had no more time to think on this, for as the door opened, he had to take a deep breath and compose himself. Birdie stood before him, a wistful smile on her heart-shaped face, her full lips open a fraction and her eyes like big brown marbles staring at him under her crown of mahogany hair. He was used to seeing it in neat waves, rolling down the sides of her head and tidied under her ears, as though she'd taken the trouble to mould every wave into place. But something was different today and he didn't quite know what. On top of all this, she had on, beneath her pretty blue coat, a dress that was the colour of a summer red rose, not that he'd seen one round here. But he had abroad, somewhere, and it took him back to the heat and lushness, and he felt strangely transported. There was a splash of ebony at her wrists and beneath her throat. The sun sparkled off a small brooch and he blinked, gazing again into her eyes.

'I . . . er . . .' he began and all his wits left him. He'd not expected to be so tongue-tied, and the effort of rallying himself was extraordinary. But finally he managed it, encouraged by the questioning look in those amazing luminous eyes. 'I think I've arrived at the wrong address,' he teased, self-consciously sliding up his hand to his collar. 'There's a princess standing before me, looking so royal, that I'm wondering what time the coach will turn up.'

He was relieved to see the questioning expression disappear and a smile of delight replace it. 'You daft thing, Harry Chambers,' Birdie bubbled, 'are you coming in, or do you want to stand on the doorstep and make fun of me.'

'I'd never do that,' Harry replied, stepping in. The house was cool and quiet, and Harry glanced along to the kitchen. 'All troops still out?' he asked, hopeful the answer would be in the affirmative.

'I've left a note,' Birdie explained to the mirror beside

the coat stand. 'And a bite to eat on the table,' she continued. 'If Dad comes in, or Pat, they won't starve.' She turned and faced him. 'You look very nice,' she said, and he was glad to see a blush on her cheeks. 'I'll just get me bag.'

When she returned, he held out his elbow. 'Will you take my arm? It's clean as a whistle.'

She laughed then and, looping her fingers over his arm she let him lead her outside. When the door closed behind them, Harry hoped the coast would be clear. But his heart sank as the three gorgons opposite stepped towards them.

Chapter 18

Birdie held her head high, determined to ignore the malevolent stares and loud whispers of Ma Jenkins and Vi and Annie Carter. But she was dismayed to see that further down March Street, Edna Legg and Marjorie Coombs, who had been talking on their doorsteps, glanced her way and quickly went inside. Even Amelia Popeldos, who usually waved, went walking on fast, as though wanting to mind her own business.

Birdie had always received a nod, if not a 'good day' from the two women. A few of the older residents of March Street, like Edna and Marjorie, had known her mother too, though in recent years, new tenants had filled some of the other houses. But there had always been a friendliness in the small community, that was, until Frank's arrest.

'Best foot forward,' said Harry, beside her. But she knew from the looks on her neighbours' faces, pinched tight under their turbans with ill feeling and malice, that Frank being at large had changed things.

She fixed her eyes determinedly on the end of the street, where a group of children were playing. They were outside the Kirbys' house and, as usual, there was a disagreement going on. Two of the Kirby brothers, thin, stringy youngsters, with milky brown skins and curling black heads of hair, were arguing with two other boys. Birdie hoped this disruption would prove of greater interest, but as soon as Ma Jenkins placed her hands on her bulky hips and hitched up the loose stockings that hung around her ankles, staring pointedly as they passed by, Birdie knew they wouldn't escape the barbs dripping from her vicious tongue.

Seeming to sense this, Harry added a little pressure with his arm to her hand. A smile of reassurance touched his lips as he glanced down. In his navy-blue suit, with his weathered tan and the whites of his eyes brighter than ever under his crop of black hair slicked away from his face, he looked quite different from the Harry she knew. For a moment, this unnerved her, and something about the authority that he seemed to command tempered her natural instinct to go on the offensive.

'And now she's proving it . . . proving the bad blood,' Birdie heard. A chill went through her. 'One man after another, silly buggers, 'elping to kit her out in all them fancy clothes.'

Birdie felt her blood boil. She knew Ma Jenkins meant her to hear every festering word. The loud buzzing in her ears made her fear losing her temper again, as she had before. And what good had that last ugly scene done? Ma Jenkins' remarks, however, were simply too much and she detached herself from Harry's arm, her cheeks aflame.

Before she managed a sound, two strong hands gripped her shoulders and drew her gently, but firmly to one side, and Harry replaced his slender but powerfully built figure in the space where she'd stood. She had never measured him up against Don before – hadn't ever thought to – but now she studied him, admiring the length of his straight back, like a protective wall, his shoulders wide and swinging, his long legs eating up the ground in confident, relaxed strides, compared to the shorter, abrupt paces that Don took.

It was Vi who stepped back first, then her sister, Annie. They seemed to shrivel under Harry's gaze. Ma Jenkins bristled and pushed out her cheeks and four chins in a display of defiance. Not that this appeared to concern Harry, as he challenged her.

His voice was not its usual soft tone as he spoke, but it had a kind of low sternness. Birdie realized she had never seen Harry angry before, nor even a little put out. His good nature had never been ruffled and, as he spoke, his head bent slightly from his tall height, Birdie stared at his profile, with his gaze cast down on Ma Jenkins in the manner of a bird of prey.

'Since I'm a little lacking in the hearing department, Mrs Jenkins,' he said so scathingly that even the kids at the end of the road paused in their quarrel, 'and it seems unfair that the rest of March Street, or the entire island, come to that, might be deprived of your wisdom, would you care to repeat – louder this time – that last sentence you just spoke?'

Birdie could hardly believe her ears. Harry's tone and presence seemed so commanding. She almost felt sorry for the mischief-maker, who now found herself alone facing Harry. Her fair-weather friends had disappeared quickly inside, the noise of the bolt on their door ringing out.

'What I 'ave to say ain't for your ears,' began Ma Jenkins, still left with a breath of bravado, though Birdie noticed with amusement that her face had turned as red as a cockscomb.

'All the same, didn't it go a bit like this?' Harry took a step back and, raising his chin theatrically and taking a deep breath, expanded his chest in the manner of a town crier. 'And now she's proving it . . . proving the bad blood,' he boomed, so forcefully, that it seemed each word echoed off the houses. 'One man after another . . . was that it, Mrs Jenkins, *one man after another*?'

Birdie watched the effect on her neighbour, a kind of shrinking down that made Ma Jenkins look as though she was shrivelling into the many folds of her stockings. But Harry was not done with her yet. Calmly he waited for a reply and when none was forthcoming, he continued mercilessly. 'Have you heard the old saying, Mrs Jenkins, that there is a measure of good in the worst of us and a deal of bad in the best? And it's only a fool who finds fault with his neighbour.' Harry stared stonily at Ma Jenkins, whom Birdie thought, was struggling to understand Harry's eloquent warning. But her eyes filled with an expression of fear when he added resolutely, 'As your friend Charlie Makepiece can confirm. For when we were in each other's company at the White Horse recently, he had much to say on the subject of women enjoying a man's company.'

Birdie had no idea what Harry meant, but she could see that Ma Jenkins did. Fighting to push open her door and escape Harry's onslaught, she glanced fearfully back before she fell into her open front door.

Harry held out his arm. 'Shall we continue our walk?' he asked serenely, as the bang of Ma Jenkins' door rang out.

Birdie wanted to giggle. 'What was that about?'

'I'll explain as we go.'

Birdie noted with amusement that the lace curtain of the houses along the road seemed to have a attracted a sudden breeze.

The East India Dock Road was bustling with life. They had walked at least half a mile, along with the tide of the crowd enjoying, in the unseasonably mild weather, the sight of Christmas decorations and spruce trees. From the post office to Brunswick Road, there seemed to be a continual stream of strollers. They glanced in at the fine gems of the jewellers interlaced with tinsel, passed under the three shiny globes of the pawnbrokers, and inhaled the strong alcoholic aromas from the wine company and brewery. They had stopped for the traffic at the bank on the corner of Chrisp Street and passed Poplar Station, where a queue of buses and trams waited for passengers. All the way, Birdie had listened in silence, save a few oohs and ahhs, to the story of Harry's meeting at the White Horse with Charlie Makepiece.

'It was on the night I met Pat,' he explained as they walked. 'Charlie Makepiece rolls in, several sheets to the wind and obviously brassic as he tries it on with the locals. He gets short shrift from everyone and finally staggers over to me and the boys. We were chatting over what's got to be done at work and the cheeky bugger barges in saying he's been robbed. Someone's bashed him over the head and gone through his pockets.'

'Did he recognize you?' Birdie asked.

'Not in that state, he didn't. Anyway, one of my lads demands to see his injury, but it's as plain as the nose on Charlie's face the only injury to him is his empty pockets. He starts to get a bit leery and spots this female, a working girl, to put it politely. He makes an advance on her and for his trouble, she slaps him, good and hard. I tell you, Birdie, the crowd was in uproar.'

'But what did this have to do with Ma Jenkins?' Birdie was eager to know.

'It was what she roared at him. She tells him, if he's that desperate, to bugger off to the ugly old battleaxe down March Street and her three shifting chins. Not that she gives a rat's tail where he gets his oats, 'scuse my language, but you get my meaning?'

'I do, but she couldn't mean Ma Jenkins, surely?' Birdie quickly shut her mouth as Harry guided her past the six stone steps of the police station and guarding constable outside.

When they had reached the more pleasant environment of the bookshop, Harry continued, 'Charlie gave it away entirely and shouted back that at least Ma Jenkins fed him after his efforts. Whereas this fragile beauty only cared for the colour of his money.'

'I can't believe it.' Birdie spluttered.

'Every word is gospel. And as we both witnessed, the old dragon went to no lengths to deny it just now, did she?'

'No, she didn't.' Birdie felt perplexed. 'But how can we be certain this is true?'

Harry smiled. 'You've got a fair way of thinking, after what you've gone through, that should put her to shame. But I confess, I couldn't see it like that and I bought Charlie an ale, to satisfy meself. And with his whistle wet, he expounded to some great length.'

Birdie blushed red. 'He never did!'

'Takes an imagination to see the vision, but it's all true.'

Birdie stopped quite still, shaking her head slowly. 'It's none of me business of course, what she does.'

'It is if she makes your business hers,' corrected Harry. 'But I think she will be less trouble to you now. And if she tries her luck again—'

'Then I've only to mention Charlie and the White Horse?' Birdie asked mischievously.

'Or allow me to mention it.' He was smiling ruefully, his dark head bent to one side, and yet the full meaning of it was that Ma Jenkins had been well and truly put in her place, and the abuse she had let go on the Connors was now in danger of being returned.

'And to think,' Birdie breathed softly, her hands clutching his arm, 'of what she called me!'

Harry's fingers, almost without her noticing and quite naturally, slid over hers and tightened. His dark eyes were so full and deep that she felt a sudden catch of her breath in her throat. She knew that people were passing them, that voices drifted in and out of her hearing, the swish of clothes, the heavy breaths, the laughter, the sneezes, the coughing, the slap of a rein on a horse's back, the chug-chug of a vehicle, the call of a street vendor. The East End was alive and bubbling, but she seemed to be trapped in a quiet bubble where she and Harry were caught alone, a shared satisfaction and small success joining them pleasantly.

But there was something more, something she couldn't quite establish. There was no reason for Harry to have done any of this, or stood up for her, or become her guardian, or even walked her out when she had been all alone today and feeling blue. And there was no reason either why she was feeling this strange elation and eagerness for life, which had all but deserted her over recent times.

'Harry, I—' she began, as he gazed down at her, but a voice broke into their world.

'Brigid? Brigid Connor?'

Her name being called in such a way made her jump. She let go of Harry and turned so sharply that she almost went dizzy. Or was it, she asked herself silently, as her gaze fell on the caller not two feet away, the shock of seeing Don standing there, his mouth open wide, or – as Bernadette used to say – like a mouth hoping to catch flies. On one side of him stood Lydia, the other, James, just as Birdie had seen them that Sunday afternoon outside the store.

Chapter 19

'Hello, Don.'

Don nodded in acknowledgement, but made no effort to raise his jaw and close his mouth, which Birdie found rather comical. Nevertheless, she smiled at his companions, and said politely, 'Lydia . . . James. How are you?'

The little boy trotted round to his mother, sliding his fingers through Lydia's gloved hand.

'Very well, Brigid,' said Lydia without emotion. 'And you?'

'I'm very well too,' Birdie said, her embarrassment overridden as the more unpleasant emotion of jealousy filled her. Lydia's hand remained firmly tucked over Don's arm. So tight was it that Don seemed restrained on the spot where he stood.

In surprise Birdie found her thoughts wandering to how fashionably Lydia was dressed. Not like the Lydia of old, muffled up to the chin in blacks and browns. No, the Lydia of this Sunday wore a fine-quality camel-coloured coat, with matching accessories. Her dark hair was hidden under a close-fitting hat, a small, jaunty brim masking her left ear and a brown velvet band around it, the very same brown as the collar of the coat. James was wearing a quality-cloth coat of dark green. His collar and cuffs were green velvet, and his socks were drawn up neatly to his knees. He wore a fine pair of brogue shoes, too, as highly polished as his mother's. Though in all, Birdie felt the little chap would be more comfortable looking less formal.

'Brigid,' Don said eventually, as if just waking from a dream, 'what are you doing here?'

'The same as you, I should imagine,' replied Birdie tightly, and suddenly felt anything but carefree. Here was her betrothed, or very nearly – once anyway, in the not too distant past, her sweetheart, her adored, now her very-much-missed – here he was in the company of Lydia again, a repeat performance, obviously! And hard on the heels of this deduction, Birdie recalled all the Sunday afternoons that had passed, and many cancelled too, when she had been made to hurry her walks out with him. She'd been fearful that his time was so precious, but here – *here he was* – sauntering along the East India Dock Road, which had been quite off-limits to her, as it would take another half-hour to arrive from March Street. Here was the man she worshipped, another female hand clamped possessively to his arm.

It all but took the wind out of her sails, but she managed somehow to compose herself. 'It's such a fine day,' she blustered, raising her chin and glancing imperiously at Lydia. 'And where else would a person come to while away such a glorious Sunday afternoon?' She turned slightly, hoping that Lydia would notice, beneath her coat, the fine frill of her own rose-red dress, a frill that gave a certain bounce when moved just right. 'In fact,' Birdie continued, hardly knowing what the next word would be that came out of her mouth, 'the tram will be leaving very soon to take us, as an added treat, up West.' Birdie glanced over her shoulder in as graceful a manner as she could. 'Oh, look, Harry, we've only a few moments before its departure.'

Lydia said nothing, but Don gave a kind of suffocated gasp that he soon corrected with a loud clearing of his throat. But Birdie pressed on with her breezy, couldn't-care-less attitude, for what right had he to protest at her, when caught in the act himself?

'Goodbye then,' she said airily, not forgetting to give a sweet and genuine smile to James, who returned hers shyly.

For a few seconds her legs felt about to collapse, but she gripped Harry so keenly, she managed to cross the busy road. She didn't glance back, but walked with what she hoped looked as much grace and dignity as Lydia had possessed in that camel-coloured coat, made of such quality cloth that even the ladies of Hailing House would have admired it.

Harry sat quietly after paying the conductor for their tickets, their exit from East India Dock Road to the tram bound for Aldgate making him almost breathless. Birdie had whisked them aboard the first tram they had come upon, and, pushing past everyone, grabbed a seat by the window. Here she had craned her neck so violently to search for Don and Lydia that he was surprised she was able to turn it back again. She'd given him a full description of the scene she could see from the window, which included the lacklustre trio making their way in the opposite direction.

But now her manner was subdued. The urgency had all but vanished, leaving just a faint frown on her forehead.

Harry decided he would maintain the silence and allow her to gather her thoughts. But after a while, he said softly, 'So, that was a surprise. Meeting them all like that.'

He received a ponderous nod, leaving him none the wiser as the shops passed by: the fried fish shop, the bespoke tailor, a smell of saveloys and faggots wafting from a stall, and the stink of the Charlie Brown's tavern with its upper windows open wide. Then a photographers, and a watch-repairer's, and a big gap until the gas company showroom, next to the eel and pie shop advertising cheap Saturday suppers to take away to the Grand Cinema down the road.

Harry noted that Birdie was not seeing all this busy life. Her eyes were fixed in space and a tiny pulse beat at her temples. Her brown hair haloed her face and hung charmingly to her shoulders. Every now and then her face was softened by a beam of sunshine penetrating the glass.

Harry was amazed to find himself wanting to protect her, to shield her. Yet what right had he to feel like this? He knew nothing about women, well, no more than most unmarried men knew. He'd gone out with a few girls, enjoyed their company but never wanted to marry. But then, he'd entered the world without parentage. He had grown, or tried to grow, a thick skin after the loss of his friends, one by one, at the orphanage. Johnny Smart was the last, who'd not been smart enough to beat the diphtheria. Then Macedonia, 1917. Their trench, overlooked by hidden guns in the mountains, became a grave. Jack Solomon, Josias Newby, Fred Lovell . . . he'd come to know them like brothers. After that, he'd never got close again, not to anyone. Until earlier this year. And the day he'd taken lodgings with the Connors.

Harry glanced at Birdie's profile once more. Pondering on what might be going through her mind, he inclined his head.

'A surprise, indeed, it must have been for you,' he tried again. 'And a surprise you might have avoided, had I not had the bright idea of tempting you out.' For a second or two there was no response, but then she turned, her face an exclamation in itself.

'Oh, but Harry, I wouldn't have missed it for the world!'

'You wouldn't?'

'This afternoon has put me right, so it has,' she said as if he should know it. 'Did you see the way she clung to him? Staring me straight in the eye, she was, with never a blink. Like it was the regular thing to be walking out with my man. Like she was something more to him . . . more than – oh, well, now I've seen it, I'll say it. Like she was his girl!' She caught her breath, almost painfully. 'Did you see it, Harry? Did you?'

Harry opened his mouth to reply – he wasn't quite sure

in what manner – but she rushed on, her lashes blinking fast as she spoke.

'And the Dock Road, of all places! A street so full of interesting things on a Sunday afternoon, and Don always saying to me there was not time enough to go there. And *I* always content to walk to the park instead, thinking how lucky I was to have got even that!'

Harry saw her upset and answered with a touch of diplomacy. 'Yes, but I suppose you could say that Poplar High Street and the Thornes' shop are closer to the East India Dock Road than March Street.'

Birdie's gasp was loud. 'Then why shouldn't we have the whole day together to do such things?' She twisted fully in her seat to face him. 'Can you answer me that?'

Harry shook his head silently.

'Two hours in a week of seven days! How can anyone be expected to do anything of value in two hours?'

Harry mumbled his agreement, taken aback by the colour that had sprung to Birdie's cheeks and the fiery light dancing in her eyes. And when she pulled back her shoulders even tighter, indicating more was to come, Harry braced himself.

'And what about me wedding day?' she asked, her eyes as round as saucers. 'Can I see that now as being real? Can you answer me that?' She shook her head firmly, needing no response. He was intrigued to see brown wisps of hair curling around her pink face, as though electrified. 'Was that date ever really settled? Or has Lydia hoodwinked him, thrown off those widow's weeds in order to set her cap at my man? With Stephen only gone in 'seventeen, as well. But then, in all fairness, if it was another suitor, I'd have congratulated her. But it was my Don she wanted all along. *My* Don! Bejesus, Harry, the cheek of it.'

Harry thought it wise not to comment. His own feelings on the matter anyway, weren't quite those of Birdie.

For though the widow may have hoodwinked Donald Thorne, was he not man enough to ward off her advances? True, it could be said that she might have had him in her sights after her husband's death, but for Donald Thorne, wasn't it a convenient arrangement to have two strings to his bow, until finally he decided just which one he would settle for? And from what Birdie had told him – how he lived for the business and she lived for it too – didn't they have a powerful lot in common? But to express such a feeling at the moment, he gauged, was inappropriate.

Another view he would keep to himself was that Birdie was a deal better off for Lydia's intervention. Marrying into the store, in his humble opinion, was like putting a rope around a throat and winding it slowly tighter.

Suddenly she slumped back, peering up at him with defeated eyes. 'She did look a lady, though. A real lady in that camel coat and all its pretty bits.'

Harry shrugged lightly, again choosing his answer carefully. 'I couldn't tell in a five-minute view.'

She took in a sharp breath. 'Oh, I forgot, you don't know her?'

'No, though I feel some recognition – from your excellent descriptions.'

'I hope I haven't coloured a bad picture.'

'Not at all.'

'If I'd remembered me manners, I would have introduced you.'

He smiled. 'And who should I have been introduced as?'

Without hesitation she answered. 'Me friend, of course.'

Harry thought of the jealous expression he'd seen on the shopkeeper's face. 'I rather think you wouldn't have been much believed,' he ventured, 'for what you're thinking of them, he's no doubt thinking of you.'

He feared he might have gone too far as she clapped her

hand to her mouth. 'You don't think – that he thought – that you and me . . .?'

'I'm afraid I do.'

'But we are only—'

'Good friends,' he nodded, wondering if he should add, 'and I your lodger'.

'Our walking was innocent,' she protested. 'And what does he think I'm to do, whilst he's entertaining another woman? Does he expect me to hide indoors for the rest of my life and become an old maid?'

'You'd never be that.'

'But I might be. If left up to him,' she decided firmly. 'All those hours he's spent with her when he could have been with me. And it was only a small disagreement we'd had. One we could easily have made up . . . if I had agreed to . . .' She fell into a slump again, her lips working in a distressed way, and Harry knew she was thinking of Frank.

'Yes, there's always another way to do a thing,' Harry concurred, much against the grain, for he harboured no liking at all for Donald Thorne, who seemed to be both a fool and a weakling. But he hated to see Birdie so torn. 'It just takes a bit of thinking out. Turning the problem on its head, perhaps.'

'But I've turned it, Harry,' she admitted softly, twisting her fingers in her lap. 'And I don't know as I could put Frank from me life, not even for Don, not even for marriage.' She added with a little rush, 'Unless Don could take back what he said.'

Harry wondered at how Donald Thorne could have said what he did. If you loved someone, you loved them, warts and all. There was a special girl here, deserving a medal for the way she cared for kith and kin. Couldn't that fickle and foolish fellow not see what he was losing?

'Harry?' She squeezed his arm.

He looked down into her face and took a deep swallow as the unexpected softness inside him took over.

'Harry, do you think I'm wrong to stand by me brother? I mean, it could be the devil of a thing in respect of Pat. And if Dad was to find out, he'd probably get a seizure and what would I do then – if it was really bad and it was me who caused it?' She paused, her face full of concern. 'You and I are friends. Tell me what I should do. For despite me protests against the widow, I know it's only meself that's sent her into Don's arms. It's my fault she's there. And I know equally that if I went to Don and told him I'd do as he says, I could win him back – sure I could!'

Harry hadn't expected that. She had seemed so strong for family. And what was it to him? Who was he to decide on another's life? Instead he took a breath and pushed down his strong dislike of the man who was causing this lovely girl so much distress. 'Even the best of friends can't advise the other what to do,' he told her gruffly. 'Ask yourself what you really want, Birdie. Find the answer in your heart, then act on it.'

He saw her think on this, her head sunk down and her fingers returning to their agitation in her lap. But then she looked up and smiled, and when the tram stopped, Harry saw they had arrived at Ludgate Hill. He suggested they find a bus to take them to the Strand and to Piccadilly where they might take yet another stroll. Birdie was eager to agree and he was relieved to find that the cloud that had settled around them on East India Dock Road had disappeared. Though he feared that, in due course, it might very well appear again.

Chapter 20

The days that followed were cold, with showers of freezing rain that chilled through to the bone. Birdie set aside her worries to continue the task of Lady Annabelle's frock. But each time she ran her fingers over the luxurious fabric, she found herself recalling that *other* very fine cloth, moulded to Lydia's elegant figure.

Her resentful thoughts persisted, gurgling away like the gutters outside, drenched from the downpours. All the while Don and Lydia and little James seemed locked in her thoughts, she wrestled with her conscience over Frank. She'd hoped that Harry might have more to say on the matter of her tangled romance as they'd strolled down the Strand that Sunday evening and made their way to the Embankment. But not a word more had been said on the matter, and now she was still in a state of indecision.

All week she worked on Annabelle's dress and before she knew it Christmas had arrived.

At Mass on Christmas morning, she gave Flo and the girls their presents. 'It's just a few sweets and colouring books,' Birdie said apologetically.

'Just what we want,' chorused Emily and Enid.

'Come back and see Reg,' Flo persuaded. 'He wants to give you a Christmas kiss.' Everyone laughed as they stood in the drizzle outside church. 'And you can tell me properly what happened in the Dock Road.'

'I told you it in church,' sighed Birdie as they set off under Flo's umbrella. As they'd sat at the back under the choir gallery, Birdie had whispered her news during the Credo. But Flo always wanted the finer details.

'Strikes me, Don was put out at seeing you with Harry,' Flo smiled happily.

'Harry's me friend and a good one at that,' Birdie protested. 'Anyway, I don't care what Don thinks after seeing him with her.'

'Yes you do. Or else you wouldn't be thinking about him.'

'I want to know about us – one way or the other.'

Flo gave a snort of disgust as they turned into Ayle Street. 'It wasn't only your dreams of a church wedding he ended,' Flo muttered as she pulled up the string from the letter box and opened the door. 'There was two little girls that couldn't wait to be bridesmaids, you know.'

Birdie felt sad about that. Even more so as Enid and Emily gave her their gifts: two drawings of the church, and them in their lemon dresses, with Birdie dressed all in white.

'Oh, they're beautiful,' Birdie said guiltily, promising herself she would make them pretty dresses, anyway.

When big, burly Reg appeared with Flo's apron wrapped round him, or at least half of it, they fell into fits. He ushered them all into the warm, steamy kitchen, which smelled of boiled cabbage and roasting chicken. 'There's a port wine, if you'd like it,' he said, giving Birdie a wink. 'It's Christmas, after all.'

'No, I've got to get home and cook the dinner.'

He poured her a cup of tea instead. 'Come on now, everyone, let's get into the spirit.' Both he and Flo shared an ale.

In the front room they sat round the Christmas tree. The children had made paper decorations and tied little bows on the branches. They didn't have much, Birdie thought, but they were happy. The girls were satisfied with their colouring books, and played in front of the roaring fire. Birdie looked around as she quickly drank her tea. This was a real happy family and she was envious.

Emily and Enid sat on her knee and cuddled up and

asked once again if they were going to have pretty dresses made for them. Birdie and Flo exchanged glances, but Birdie could see the hurt look in Flo's eyes and even though the girls were only young, they had been looking forward so much to being little princesses for one day.

When Birdie arrived home, even Harry hadn't gone to work as it was Christmas Day. Pat was mooning around with a long face and Wilfred was smoking in the parlour, but quickly put out his roll-up when Birdie appeared.

'Is dinner ready?'

'No, but it won't be long.' She had cooked a chicken yesterday, a very small one, and was going to carve it cold to make it look more on the plate. She only had the vegetables to cook.

Birdie hadn't been able to afford a tree, but she had wrapped presents for everyone. They opened them after the meal, sitting round the fire: a scarf for her father, warm woollen socks for Pat and Harry. They were all she had been able to afford. Her father hadn't been able to buy anything, but Pat gave her a new set of needles and a thimble. 'Didn't know what else to get you,' he grinned.

'Just what I want.'

Harry gave her a brooch, a lucky black cat and she was very surprised. She blushed as he helped her to pin it on her dress.

'I hope it brings me good luck,' she smiled into his eyes.

'If it don't, I'll take it back and complain,' Harry grinned.

'It's a miserable day,' said Wilfred dejectedly as they huddled round the fire. 'What are we going to do?'

Harry came up with the idea to play cards first, then dominoes. The afternoon passed pleasantly but Birdie wondered what Don was doing, and found it difficult to concentrate.

'The rain won't last.' Harry's voice broke into her thoughts. He was staring through the window and patting his pockets restlessly after finishing his game of dominoes with Pat. 'Look, the kids are out, even on Christmas Day.'

Birdie stood beside him. The Kirby boys were dragging a wooden box into the road with wheels attached to the front and back. A long string was tied to the front and several of them towed it whilst others sat in the back.

'Look at them!' Pat exclaimed enviously, peering over their shoulders. 'I'll bet Willie's chanced it out on his bike, too.'

'So I suppose you're off as well?' said Birdie, knowing that wild horses wouldn't keep him in now.

'I'll be back for tea.' He pecked her on the cheek and was gone.

'Remember, it's Christmas. Don't get into trouble.'

'Better get a move on, meself,' said Harry, lifting his jacket from the back of the wooden dining chair. 'Thank you for a very pleasant day.'

Birdie didn't want to be left alone with her father, she knew he would go to sleep and she would be driven to sewing, just to keep busy and prevent herself from thinking about Don. She was about to ask Harry if he'd like to stay to tea when a strange noise outside made them all return to the window. A tall, motorized vehicle with two large brass headlamps shuddered violently to a halt.

'What the dickens is that?' said Wilfred, drawing the lace curtain aside.

'Well, well,' murmured Harry in such a way that Birdie edged herself closer to the window to get a better look.

A figure jumped down from the driving seat, positioned under a wavy wooden fringe attached to the top of the van. The man was dressed in a dark, weatherproof overcoat and wore big leather gloves and goggles. Birdie narrowed her eyes as he stood on the pavement and slid the goggles to his forehead. His back was turned to her as he inspected the words painted on the side of the vehicle.

A gasp of astonishment squeezed from her throat. 'Jesus, Mary and Joseph,' she gasped. 'It's Don!'

'Well, I'll be darned,' said Wilfred. 'What's that he's driving?'

'It's . . . it's a . . . oh, well, I can see what it says.' Birdie's heart was racing with excitement. 'It says, "Thorne's General Store, Poplar. No order too small or too large. Every need catered for."' She twisted quickly to look at her father. 'It's one of them newfangled delivery vans,' she burst out, hardly able to contain herself. 'And he's come – my man has come – all the way over here in it to see me! Oh, what a shock! I'm all of a tremble.'

Birdie glanced back at the sight, which was now attract-ing the children. She watched Don brush the rain from the brass headlamp and shoo one of the Kirby boys away. Then, turning towards the house, he saw her and raised his gloved hand in salute.

Donald Thorne shook himself theatrically as he stood on the doorstep, making certain that Birdie noticed the way he tapped the rain from his new gauntlet gloves. He stamped his polished leather driving boots in a very professional manner. He was, after all, now the proud owner of a commercial Daimler that had cost him more than a year's salary, and a few more pounds to boot in fuel and proper sign-writing. Well, the money hadn't exactly come from his wallet, but from, in his mother's case, an old Gladstone bag made of tapestry, a secret he was not meant to know, but one his father had divulged.

'Your mother is a clever woman,' Ted Thorne had told him in a rare moment of intimacy. 'She don't trust the country with our money, not in times of conflict when the nation is hard up. So half our takings goes to the bank, the other half in her Gladstone. It's all nicely tucked away there . . .' his father had stopped to cough. 'I'm telling you this, son, in case . . . well, just *in case.*'

The 'in case', Don understood, had alluded to the possibility that he might long outlive his father. On taking over the store, Don had expected to be enlightened by his mother that funds were close at hand, but he never had been informed, though the Gladstone was never far from her reach.

It was Lydia, though, who made up the accounts and had unfortunately become locked in disagreement with Aggie. 'Your mother removes the takings,' Lydia had complained, 'and replaces a lesser sum.' With cash being siphoned off, Don had kept his guilty secret, but Lydia, in her ignorance, had urged him to stand up for leadership of the business.

It was all very unnecessary, Don felt. And there was he, caught in the middle. Although he secretly took Lydia's side, Aggie stubbornly persisted in keeping him under her thumb. And now he found himself here, prompted by a quarrel with his mother last night over Brigid.

'Happy Christmas!' he said, giving a little flourish of his gloved hand. 'I thought I would pay a seasonal visit and show you our new delivery vehicle. It has made a welcome improvement to our busy schedule over the holiday period. Deliveries and so forth, you see.' He was pleased at the look of surprise on her face. His mother had been right: the new purchase was making a good impression.

'I didn't expect to see you,' she said, and Don shrugged.

'Well, a good man can't be put off,' he replied awkwardly. He was about to step in, when a tall figure emerged and brought him to a halt.

'Afternoon,' said the lodger, who in Don's estimation looked a rough fellow, but was smart enough to have latched on to Brigid in his absence. It was clear, just as

Aggie had shrewdly suggested after hearing of the meeting in the Dock Road, that this fly-by-night was eager to get his feet planted firmly under the Connors' table.

'Son, you'll lose the one woman who is just right for this business,' Aggie had warned him. 'She's not too bright to boss you or ask damn-fool questions, like some I could mention. And she'll not mind turning her hand to the chores even when she's raising a family and caring dutifully for her husband. She ain't spoiled, and other than her religion and idiot brother – problems we can deal with easy once you're wed – she'll be as reliable as clockwork.'

Don had been shocked to hear this. His mother had never made much of an effort towards Brigid Connor, but since the upset with Lydia, he'd noticed a distinct change of attitude. And after that dreadful scene last night when Aggie had made it quite clear she had no intention of moving over for a younger woman and that his inheritance stood in peril, he had come to the conclusion that opposing Aggie would prove a serious mistake.

So, as much as he had argued his doubt on marriage to Brigid, the Dock Road incident had brought Aggie out in the open. She insisted she would have Brigid trained up in no time at all. And after the marriage, they would easily knock the Pope out of her, well before the babies came along.

Don had not argued. If his mother spoke without sentiment, her reasoning was nevertheless sound. Aggie held the purse strings. And those purse strings, half of which was in the bank and the other half in the tapestry Gladstone, were his hard-earned nest egg. They were compensation for the loss of his career at the railways. And he'd see none of it if he made an argument for Lydia and her way of doing things.

'I'll be seeing you later,' said the lodger to Birdie as he left. 'Don't venture out in the rain. I'll fill you a scuttle afore I leave for work in the morning.'

Don scowled into the dark, challenging gaze meeting his. Damn the man! What right had he to be talking to Brigid that way? Their engagement hadn't been called off! She was not a single woman.

Forced to step back, Don felt a shower of rain on his face. 'Confounded weather!'

'You'd better come in then.' She stood back and gave him a cool smile.

Don entered and slid off his gloves and wet goggles. He glanced along the passage. 'And your father and Patrick?' he enquired, hoping the boy was out. There was no love lost between them. He wanted Birdie on her own.

'You've just missed Pat, who's ridden out to call for Willie. Dad's in the parlour. Look in and say hello, but then we'll sit in the kitchen as he'll be wanting his forty winks.'

Don nodded his assent, undid the buckle of his damp driving coat and hung it on the stand. Straightening his tie and collar and the lapels of his best suit, he paid his respects to Wilfred, confident in the knowledge his plan had worked.

Chapter 21

Birdie set out two of the best china cups and saucers, aware of the tremble in her fingers. She could hardly believe Don was here, on Christmas Day, when surely his family were expecting his company? Could it be that he was eager to see her? But no, she mustn't let him see her pleasure, though she wanted just to hold him in her arms. She wasn't to be let down and picked up again, like some plaything!

Birdie sat beside him, pouring tea and adding the sugar as carefully as she could. Feeling his nearness, the warmth of his body, the sight of his dear face with that middle parting of hair, ruffled a bit from the sliding off of those goggles, oh, her heart was hammering!

'Another sugar, perhaps?' She hadn't forgotten he was prone to a sweet tooth.

'On this occasion, why not?' He gave her such a smile as to turn her stomach over in a somersault.

'This occasion?' Birdie glanced under her lashes as she spooned an extra helping. 'You mean, the showing off of that fine vehicle, I suppose?' she asked uninterestedly.

'No, of course not. Though I have to agree it is very fine . . .' He stretched his hand across to cover hers. 'Birdie, we must resolve this silly tiff.'

She could hardly respond for eagerness. The touch of him had goose bumps prickling all over her skin. 'I agree. It's not right, us not being . . . friends.'

'Then why are we apart if we both think the same?'

She swallowed, allowing herself to gaze into his eyes. 'There are one or two points on which we differ,' she answered carefully, hardly able to believe she wasn't flinging herself into his arms and telling him that nothing on earth could ever keep them apart. Not even being caught, twice in a row, with another woman on your arm.

He gave her a thoughtful 'hmm'. Did this mean he agreed but felt disinclined to comment?

'The picture from my side,' she continued briskly, 'is that it seems to me you have . . . other commitments.' She swallowed again, not wanting to say Lydia's name outright. 'Commitments that might veer you away from marriage.'

'Commitments to prevent me marrying?' he protested in a bewildered tone, his eyes now seeming to change from green to hazel brown. 'What made you think that?'

Birdie couldn't help herself. 'I thought it when I saw

you walking out in the Dock Road with those commitments.'

'What nonsense!' He dropped his cup with a loud chink into the saucer. 'You can't be talking of Lydia and little James?' His expression was wounded, astonished. 'I was simply doing a good service for my sister-in-law and nephew. A perfectly innocent service. How can you think otherwise?'

'Because she was on your arm and I wasn't.'

An astonished but endearing smile formed on his lips. 'Oh, my dearest, I am truly flattered! Flattered, by your affectionate but misplaced assumption.' He held up his hand as if she were about to interrupt. 'But I can assure you, walking out with Lydia was of small comfort to me in your absence. And yes, I admit, I would have spoken at length had it not been for that . . . that *fellow*—'

'Harry?' Birdie was overwhelmed at the firm grasp of his fingers around hers. But she managed a small defence. 'We was only doing the same as you, walking out on a fine afternoon.'

He gave a little cough. 'Perhaps. But it was embarrassing, seeing my fiancée in the company of another man.'

The fact that Lydia had been on his arm was forgotten in the mention of the word 'fiancée'. Birdie had heard this exotic word so rarely that it sent her into raptures.

Don forcefully caught hold of her wrists, making her start. 'My darling, I trust you completely, as I hope you trust me. And to show how much I think of you and want to make up, I'm willing to put all this aside. Yes, even the matter of your brother, a subject that unsettles us both. So we shall not touch on it again. Let it be put to rest from this moment and, and . . .' He suddenly reached into his pocket, and, drawing out a small purple box, pressed it firmly into her hands. 'And from this moment on, let's have no other, think of no other – except each other.'

Birdie stared at the box in her palm. It was weathered with age, but it had a small clasp that easily loosened. 'Don! Oh! Don!' she cried when it was open, staring incredulously at the ring inside. 'Is this for me?'

'For no other, my dear.'

She lifted the slim gold band from the faded cloth. It bore a cluster of three white twinkling stones. 'This is beautiful, so it is! Look at the sparkle from such tiny things!'

'They are diamonds, of course.'

'Diamonds!' Birdie had only ever seen diamonds in shop windows.

'The ring is a family heirloom,' Don said proudly. 'Mother was certain you would like it.'

'Oh, Don, your mother would give it away?'

'She approves of you, Brigid.'

'Oh, let me catch my breath!'

'Try it on.' He reached for the ring as she held out her finger. Sadly it was far too large. But it was the thought, the meaning, the word 'fiancée' that was sending her mad with excitement. And the fact that it was Aggie's precious heirloom, denoting to Birdie that Aggie was all in favour.

'No matter about the size,' Don said dismissively, sliding it off again and dropping it in the box. 'I'll have it made smaller.'

'Oh, I don't want to let it go!'

'You'll have it again soon.' He took her in his arms and kissed her, and Birdie felt dizzy with happiness. His kiss was passionate and his hands explored her body, making every inch of her tingle. She kept her eyes closed, praying that this wasn't a dream, that she was really engaged to be married and that, by a miracle, Don had reconsidered on the subject of Frank.

'Brigid,' he whispered insistently, 'kiss me again.'

She gave herself up to his embrace, as he caressed her in

172

bold ways he had never done before. She allowed him to unfasten the top button of her blouse and touch her, adding more desire to the moment for her, so that she would have done anything he'd asked if they had been alone.

With difficulty Birdie fought to keep her senses about her. When a shout came from the parlour, she fell back on her chair, intoxicated with desire.

'It's Dad,' she gasped. 'He's woken up and wants his tea.'

Don rearranged his tie and coughed. 'So we are settled, then, Brigid?'

'Yes, we are settled.'

'I shall return my attention to a specific date.'

Birdie wondered briefly at Lydia's feelings when she heard of this. 'Don, are we still to be married by licence?'

He sat back sharply. 'I have made allowances for your brother. I think it only fair I am to be allowed this.'

She sighed softly and nodded. 'I should still like me bridesmaids, though. Their dresses would be at my expense as Enid and Emily are such good little girls. They'd not be any trouble and it'd be such a delight for Flo and Reg.'

He raised his eyebrows wearily. 'If you must.'

'Oh, thank you, my love!' Even as she said this, a fleeting sadness came over her. She would not be married in a beautiful white dress, nor make her vows in front of Father Flynn. But she couldn't have everything. This morning when she had opened her eyes, her loneliness on Christmas Day had seemed unbearable. Now, only a few hours later, her beloved Don had come to claim her, and the world was almost perfect again.

'Now, I must speak to your father.' He took her hand and, after checking his pocket, the pocket in which her ring – once Aggie's – was gently nestled, they went together to the parlour.

★

'You have my consent, lad,' said Wilfred as Birdie sat with Don. Stroking his salt-and-pepper sideburns, her father added, 'And I wish you both happiness.'

'Thank you, sir.'

'When are you tying the knot?'

Don shifted uneasily beside her. 'We've made no firm arrangement, Mr Connor. But it will be soon.' Birdie knew he was reluctant to break the news that the wedding was not to be in church.

'Her mother, if she were alive,' said Wilfred, 'would want to know all the details. And she'd be putting a fine spread on and getting everything fixed up with the priest. But as I ain't a churchgoer, you'll have to do that yourself, girl.'

Birdie looked guiltily away. 'Show me dad the ring, Don.'

Wilfred took the box and opened it. 'Very fine indeed.'

'Nothing but the best for Brigid,' Don said, smiling.

Wilfred gave a little cough and snapped the lid shut. 'You'll have your mother's wedding ring on the day, Brigid. She'd want you to have it as you walk down the aisle.'

Birdie felt another deep pang. It was to be such a sacrifice to give up a church wedding. Wilfred expected of her what Bernadette would have wanted. What would her mother have to say about this if she had been alive? Birdie knew, as clear as if Bernadette was speaking now. According to Church law, a man and woman weren't wed if not joined together by a priest in the holy sacrament of matrimony.

'Well, girl,' said Wilfred then, 'this is not before time. You've known each other long enough. Am I right to assume you'll be leaving home and living at the store with your husband?'

Before Birdie could answer, Don spoke. 'It will be our home, yes, Mr Connor.'

'Thought as much.'

'But don't worry,' Birdie put in hastily, 'I'll be calling round to help out.'

174

'We'll not be a trouble to you, lass,' her father assured her.

Birdie thought of his loneliness. Who would cook the dinners, sweep the floors and dust the shelves? Who would do the washing? She would have to begin at once with Pat, training him, teaching him a little cooking. It was not impossible. And she could help still, when on her free day from the shop. And she'd put money to the rent, somehow. Only Pat would have to increase his share to meet the outgoings.

All these thoughts were stored in her mind as, abruptly, Don stood up to leave.

'Why didn't you say about the licence?' Birdie asked anxiously when they stood at the front door.

'It wasn't the right time,' Don said as he put on his coat and goggles. 'And, Brigid, I must remind you that in becoming my wife, your life here ends? Remaining nurse and housekeeper to your family is out of the question. I really don't think it wise to make promises to your father you can't keep.'

'But I shall come on one or two days!'

'You can't be in two places at one time. A wife's duty is to her husband. Even your father understands this. Now, stop fretting and let's be glad our differences are resolved.'

'But, Don—'

He drew her to him and kissed her. Then striding out into the damp day, he waved goodbye.

When the vehicle had roared off, Birdie closed the door, her feelings confused. 'Oh, you daft thing,' she muttered crossly. 'Don's right. You can't run two households.' And yet there was an ache deep inside of her. She felt as though she was abandoning her old life without a care, leaving Wilfred and Pat to fend for themselves. Surely she would be able to convince Don that she was needed here too? If only for a few hours in the week . . .

Birdie pulled back her shoulders. Why was she fretting? It had turned out to be a wonderful Christmas Day. She had Don back, the man who meant everything to her. Wasn't she just the luckiest and happiest girl in the whole wide world?

Chapter 22

It came as a shock, after the mild weather at Christmas, that in January the temperatures dipped close to freezing. But to Birdie, everything seemed lighter and brighter from the minute she woke up until the time she fell asleep. At last she was to be married!

It was a cold Tuesday morning later in the month when Flo called round to inspect the girls' dresses that Birdie had begun work on.

'Very nice,' said Flo, somewhat wistfully, drawing a finger across a lemon cotton bodice, which was pinned and tacked to the paper pattern. 'It's just a shame they won't be real bridesmaids, not in the true sense of the word.'

'Well, it's the best I can do,' said Birdie disappointedly, placing the two dresses aside. After all the trouble she had gone to in getting Don to give his approval, Flo didn't seem very appreciative.

'Are you really sure you're doing the right thing, Birdie?' Flo asked after a moment's thought.

'Don't let's go over all that again,' said Birdie irritably. 'I'm lucky Don has decided he'll marry me after all that's gone on.'

'I'd say he was the lucky one,' Flo retorted, her tone

cooling again. 'You're a Roman Candle, ain't you? Doesn't he understand what marriage means to a cradle Catholic?'

'Course he does,' said Birdie, becoming even more agitated that Flo couldn't seem to see her point of view. 'He's got his family to think of too. Their beliefs are just as important as ours. And to keep everyone happy this seemed the best way.'

'It won't make your dad happy,' put in Flo with a grimace. 'I can just see his face when you—'

'Oh, Flo, do let's talk about something else.'

Flo shrugged. 'I was only saying, that's all.'

Birdie was desperate to change the subject. 'Now, do you want to see Lady Annabelle's frock?' she asked quickly.

'Have you finished it, then?'

'Not quite, but I'll have it ready to fit well in time for Lady Hailing's party at Easter.' Birdie took her to the cupboard and at the sight of the frock, Flo gasped.

'Oh, it's lovely!'

'Do you like it?'

'That's a daft question! Just look at the way that tangerine bow sits on the end of the bodice. And the way you've cut the skirt! Oh my!'

'It's cut on the bias,' explained Birdie as she held out the folds. 'And the bow will compliment the one on the hat that Lady Annabelle drew.'

'You've thought of everything. What material is it?'

'Chiffon,' explained Birdie, wondering if Lady Annabelle would like the mischievous sweep of the skirt, which had been very challenging to cut but was all the rage in fashion circles. 'I saw a dress just like it on this woman who was going into the Strand Hotel, that afternoon I was with Harry,' Birdie said thoughtfully. 'She was very pretty, but not as pretty as Lady Annabelle.'

'And what did Harry say about you making it up with Don?' Flo asked flippantly.

'Nothing much,' shrugged Birdie. 'Just said he hoped I'd be happy.'

'What's the matter?' asked Flo as she studied Birdie's forlorn face. 'You look as though you've lost ten bob and found a penny.'

'Nothing's the matter. Not really . . .'

'Spit it out.' Flo was insistent.

'Well, if you must know, it's Harry. I thought we was getting along just fine, but . . .'

'But what?'

Birdie sighed wistfully. 'He doesn't talk so much. And he never stops and plays dominoes or cards these days. Though, to be fair, Pat is always off out with Willie. But Harry used to like my cooking, least he said he did, yet these days it's as though he can't wait to leave, to get out of the house. Says he got a lot of work on, but that shouldn't stop your appetite, should it?'

Flo grinned. 'No, but I know what would.'

'What do you mean?'

'He's a bloke, ain't he?'

'So?'

Flo rolled her eyes. 'He's got his needs.'

'You mean . . .?'

Flo nodded sagely. 'He isn't going to tell you everything. You're not his mum.'

'But he would have said something, I'm sure. Or brought her round. Or something.'

'Listen, Miss Know-it-all,' said Flo, wagging a finger in front of her nose, 'you need your eyes tested, you do. Harry is a good looker, in case you haven't noticed.' She pushed back her hair and tucked a strand behind her ear, adding, 'Me and Reg went to see this film at the fleapit up Stepney. *The Tramp*, it was called, with Charlie Chaplin. It was about this fellow who falls in love with the girl of his dreams and helps her out of a real sticky spot. But she's stuck with this old grumpy guts who is more trouble than he's worth—'

'Flo!' Birdie exclaimed. 'Don ain't grumpy!'

'I didn't mean Don.'

'It sounded like you did.'

Flo only raised her eyes. 'All I've ever heard Don talk about is the store, and that ain't no laughing matter. Anyway, as I said, it wasn't Don I was meaning. All I was saying was there's more to Harry than you think. Like Charlie in *The Tramp*, protecting the heroine, Harry stuck up for you against old Ma Jenkins. From what you told me he put the old cow well and truly in her place. And when has Don ever done that, or taken you up the Dock Road of a Sunday afternoon?'

'He doesn't get time, else he would,' retorted Birdie, annoyed that Flo should point this out, even though it might be true. 'And you can stop going on about Harry, as you've said yourself he's courting.'

Flo gave a strangled cough. 'I only said he might be.'

Birdie hung Lady's Annabelle's dress back in the cupboard. 'If you want to make yourself useful, help me tidy this mess.'

'Yes, madam,' said Flo, making a face and plunging the scissors, cottons and thimble into Birdie's work-bag. But Birdie couldn't stop thinking about what Flo had just said. Her friend must see something in Harry that she didn't. He was just, well, just Harry. The lodger and friend, who never spoke much about himself or boasted – not that Don was a boaster! No – what was she saying? She didn't mean that at all. Don was a proud man, that was all. Why shouldn't he talk of himself and the store in the way he did? And what did Flo mean about Don's sense of humour? Sure, he had a fine appreciation of a joke.

'Come on, let's go out,' suggested Flo, glancing out of the window longingly. 'It's cold, but too nice to stay in.'

'I've got too much to do,' said Birdie, indicating the pile of alterations on her worktop.

'Oh, blow them for a lark,' said Flo rebelliously. 'Let's do our shopping at the market. I made neck of lamb stew yesterday for dinner and there's some left over for tonight. We'll buy a fresh loaf and you can have tea with us, for a change. You could leave something cold for your dad and Pat,' said Flo with a shrug. 'And you don't even know if Harry will show up, do you? It ain't gonna hurt 'em all to look after themselves for once. After all, they'll have to do it when you're married.'

After some persuasion, Birdie gave in. What Flo said was true. One day in the not-too-distant future, her family would have to cater for themselves. The point was made yet again as Flo reminded her that her husband would demand all her attention, as arm in arm, they made their way to market.

After enjoying a tasty meal with Flo and her family, including Flo's mother, Birdie left for March Street. She was well wrapped up in the icy cold and trod carefully over the old iron bridge towards Cubitt Town. Here she paused to watch the boats tied along the jetty. A group of bargemen were gathered, waiting to off-load their cargoes, whilst other groups of other men – casuals in the docks, less fortunate than the bargemen – idled their time on the stones, disappointed at not having been chosen to be hired for a day's labour.

The tugs, with their bright red funnels, let out their hoots as warning, overtaking the Scandinavian timber boats full with their stacked cargo. As a mist threatened, a police launch sped towards some urgent mission and left the smaller boats to bounce in its wake.

Shivering a little in the cold, Birdie paused again by the wall that ran along the foreshore. The smells were all heightened: the river's salt and the seasoned wood, which were so different from the commercial smells of the inner city. For a moment or two she thought about Flo's comments. But there was nothing more in the world that she wanted than to become Don's wife.

Birdie tried to imagine life in the rooms above the shop. The accommodation would be much smaller than March Street. How would they all fit in? Which room would she and Don share?

'Stay where you are.' A sharp command brought her out of her thoughts. 'If you want to see your brother alive, you will do as I say.'

Birdie's heart raced. She turned, only to jump half out of her wits as she saw the woman standing beside her. A pair of dark, fierce eyes were almost hidden under the peak of a cloth cap. Then with another sickening lurch of her heart, she saw the glint at her side and felt the tip of the blade as it pressed into her.

Chapter 23

Birdie sat in the covered wagon, her legs having just managed to carry her from the waterfront to the road, where she had been roughly pushed up into the back of the cart. It was dark under the canvas and she could see very little. As her eyes became accustomed to the gloom, she saw that a man with a long black beard and wearing a dark hat was sitting opposite her.

'Wh . . . who are you?' she stammered, gripping the rough wooden bench she sat on and trying to keep her balance as the cart rumbled along. 'Where are you taking me?'

The man stared at her. Birdie tried again but with no success. She glanced across to the end of the wagon, where two bales of hay were stacked. There was no easy escape and anyway, the woman had barked at her to sit still and soon she would be seeing Frank. Was it true? Were they keeping Frank a prisoner? Where was he? Were they the same people who had captured Pat? Fear was making her panic. A fine sweat ran down between her shoulders blades and over her forehead. Where was she going to end up?

The wagon rolled along and Birdie knew that, by now, it must have left the island. She wondered if she would hear what Pat had heard, a clock or bell somewhere that would give her some indication of where she was. But all she could hear was the loud drumming of her heart. Unlike Pat, she hadn't been blindfolded. As far as she remembered no one had seen her being put into the wagon. The woman had made sure of that, hurrying her along, with the blade of the knife at her back.

When the wagon stopped, Birdie saw it was still daylight. A chink in the canvas let in the pale light. Then suddenly the flap at the back was thrown open. The woman jumped over the tailgate and onto the dusty boards.

She took a rag from her pocket. 'You will be blind-folded,' she said abruptly. 'Nothing will happen to you.'

'Where's our Frank?' Birdie demanded, shrinking back.

'You will see him soon.'

There was nothing for it, Birdie realized, other than to do as she was told. The woman tied the rag round Birdie's head making certain that it came down well over her eyes. She was so frightened that she wasn't sure if she could move. But then a hand gripped her wrist and she was bundled out of the wagon.

'Birdie, it's me, Frank.' He untied the rag and held her

182

shoulders. 'Don't be scared. They had to do it – pick yer up like that. The law have got eyes everywhere.'

Birdie stared into a stranger's face. Frank's hair was dark, not his lovely red colour. He looked much thinner, his high cheekbones thrust out as the skin drew tightly over them. His big blue eyes had a haunted look. 'Oh, Frank, is it really you?'

'Course it's me. Give us a hug.' He drew her close, his arms holding her tight.

'Have they harmed you?'

'No, course not. They're me friends.'

'Where is this?' She looked around and in the light that reflected from a lamp on the table, to her dismay she saw a filthy room. The walls were peeling and mould-ridden. The wooden chairs and table were stained and the floor strewn with rubbish. There was a strong smell of decay.

'I ain't allowed to say. Sit down for a minute, take the weight off yer feet.' He pressed her gently onto a chair. She dreaded to think what muck might cling to her clothes. He pulled up another chair, moving the lamp so he could see her clearly.

'What have you done to your hair?'

'Inga dyed it for me.'

'Is Inga the one who wears breeches?'

He laughed. 'She's quite a looker, an' all.'

'How do you know these people are friends?' Birdie whispered trying not to tremble and shake as she sat there. It had been a shock, being taken off like that, with a knife pointed at her heart.

''Cos, they're kosher,' said Frank nervously. 'They're trying to help their families back home. In Russia they are a lot worse off than us. They got freezing weather and no food—' He stopped as Birdie jumped up from her chair.

'I . . . I just saw something move on the floor,' she cried. 'It had a long tail.'

He laughed. 'It's a rat. There's lots of them round here.' He banged the wall with his boot.

'Frank, this place is dreadful.'

'The peasants in Russia would think it a palace,' he said, taking his seat again. 'Inga told me they kip in the woods and mountains, 'cos they're being done in by these Bolshies. A right lot of cutthroats, according to Inga. They murdered their Royal Family, shot 'em in a cellar. Now they want to take over Russia.'

'But what's that got to do with you?' Birdie was worried about what she was hearing. It didn't sound like her brother.

'Well, nothing, I suppose,' said Frank softly, leaning close, 'but Inga says if I help them against the Reds, they'll help me.'

'Who are the Reds?'

'They're against the Whites.'

'What does that mean?'

'Dunno. But I'm going along with it for now.'

'Frank, you shouldn't be getting involved with something you don't understand.'

'Yes, but Inga's promised to smuggle me on a boat to France. I got to find someone who remembers me.'

'Even if that was possible,' Birdie said doubtfully, 'it would be like looking for a needle in a haystack.'

'It's me only chance,' Frank said earnestly. 'Or else I'm gonna be on the run for ever. I gotta clear my name, so I can look Dad in the face again. Meanwhile, I'll play along with this lot.'

'How did they find me today?' Birdie asked, a shiver going over her as she thought of Frank getting deeper and deeper into trouble.

'It's Erik, see,' Frank said with a wink. 'He nips round everywhere.'

'You mean he's their spy?'

'Well, yes, you could say that.'

'I don't want him spying on me.'

'He won't,' Frank promised. 'It'll be me you see next. Afore I leave for France.'

Birdie looked around at the slum that Frank was living in. What were these people doing in England? He was convinced Inga was trustworthy, but as usual, it sounded as if he had fallen for a pretty face.

Just then the door creaked open. Inga appeared and Frank nodded. 'Inga's gonna take you back now.'

'Frank, be careful.'

'I can take care of meself.'

But as she was blindfolded and returned to the island, Birdie thought about what Frank had told her, and her doubts grew. Frank was naïve, but he was also desperate. He was eager to grasp at any straw to save himself. But what would happen when he was no longer needed for their purpose?

Why, when they had what they wanted, would they take him to France?

Somehow Birdie muddled through the next few days, her thoughts repeatedly going back to Tuesday night. After she had been blindfolded again, the journey home was frightening. She had imagined that her end might be close. She couldn't even hope to defend herself. Why were they doing this? Who were they really? She didn't have the same belief in them that Frank did.

When at last they set her loose in East Ferry Road, her legs had still been shaking. She'd told Wilfred and Pat she'd stayed late at Flo's and felt terrible for the lie. But how could she tell them what she'd been through? And Wilfred wouldn't want to know about Frank, anyway.

The next morning she looked from the window, wondering if Erik was still spying. But there was only the

Popeldos kids and the Kirby tribe causing their usual rumpus.

When Don called for her on Sunday, she looked up and down the street carefully, half expecting to see a shadowy figure.

But when Don stepped in, he was full of his own troubles. 'Lydia isn't well,' he complained. 'She is suffering from . . . oh, well . . . some kind of ague and Mother insists she rests.'

'I'm sorry to hear that.' Birdie didn't want to talk about Lydia. She couldn't of course talk about Frank either, and Don seemed reluctant to talk about their wedding. A definite date still hadn't been proposed and the original idea of their being married shortly after Christmas had never been raised again.

'I can't stay long,' he muttered.

'But I only see you on Sundays.'

'Why don't you come to the shop tomorrow? We shall be hard-pressed without Lydia and your help would be most welcome.'

Birdie's heart sank. She had to finish Lady Annabelle's dress, but how could she refuse him?

'We can be together all day – every day from now on,' he added, squeezing her waist affectionately, 'You will, after all, soon be Mrs Thorne.'

'You mean, start work?' Birdie asked uncertainly. She had so much to do before they were married: a clean sweep of the house right through, putting away her dressmaking things and spending time with Pat in the kitchen, so he'd at least know how to make a meal and be able to keep body and soul together.

'Why not? This is the perfect opportunity. And there is, after all, nothing to keep you here now.'

'But I—'

He waved his hand dismissively. 'It's natural for you to be

nervous but Mother will guide you through every step of the way. Our customers will be delighted to welcome you. Mother already talks with pride of her new daughter-in-law, and though it's a great pity Lydia is absent, there will be no better time than the present. None better at all.' He cupped her chin in his hands and kissed her, a kiss so full of promise that Birdie forgot all her worries, imagining how sweet every moment would be from now on. Her future was assured. With God's blessing, there would be sons and daughters to bring into this world and raise as good Catholics, a point on which she was certain Don would finally agree. He was a hard-working man who could offer her security in uncertain times, and would be considered by many women to be a step up the ladder. What more could she ask for?

Birdie looked around her in awe at the clutter spilling over the shelves of the store. Don had told her that Aggie had trimmed down the stock, at Lydia's request, but from what Birdie could see, every inch of space was filled. On her arrival this morning Aggie had given Birdie orders to clear and restock the shelves at the far end of the shop, above the coal and paraffin.

To Birdie's dismay she had been asked to display the old stock at half price beneath the outside window. But she could see at a glance the dust that covered it announced its age. Dressed in one of the coarse aprons that Aggie insisted she wear, Birdie studied the greasy-looking bottles of Anzora Hair Cream which, through leakage, had faded labels and which stood next to the delicate packets of gas mantles, most of which were already broken and showered their fabric down to the shelves below. Hovering precariously behind these were ancient jars of hairnets and Pears' Brilliantine. These were only distinguishable by the ticket in someone's handwriting that announced a reduced bargain. Crammed side by side on the very bottom shelf were grimy, half-empty bottles of sweets that clung together in unappetizing lumps. Sherbet, liquorice Pontefract cakes, toffee, wine gums, jelly babies, mint imperials, and choco-late squares, hardly distinguishable from one another. A large dog-eared notice strung around the neck of one of the bottles, instructed the opener of the bottle to use – independently for each sweet so there was accuracy to the weighing – a pair of tongs. These were hanging on a rusty nail. The most unpleasant sight of all was a mug of elderly faded pink rock covered in the bodies of dead insects unfortunate enough to have settled on the sticky mess.

Birdie rolled up her sleeves. She had been charged with the duty of clearing and replenishing the shelves before midday and that was what she would do. Aggie wouldn't find her slacking and she would know that her daughter-in-law-to-be, of whom apparently she was so proud, was up to scratch. A list had been written of other jobs, the sweeping, clearing and stacking, and Birdie undertook them all as Aggie was busy with the long queue of customers.

Business was as brisk as Don had warned. Each time Birdie glanced up to draw her arm across her sweating brow, Aggie was flying around like a dervish. Don himself had barely time to acknowledge her. There had been hardly a 'good morning' between them. Since her arrival at seven o'clock, the pace had been relentless.

'You ain't ditching those, love!' Aggie exclaimed that afternoon as Birdie kneeled on the hard tiles, panting with the effort of scrubbing hard with a moulting bristle brush. She had discovered a shelf of flour with burst bags that had spilled down onto the next shelf. A pile of tarred wooden blocks, neglected for years, seemed glued to the shelf. It had taken her the best part of an hour to clean and turf out the rotted stock.

'But they're no use,' Birdie protested as she gazed up into Aggie's frowning face. 'The flour's so old it's going brown, and the blocks have got worm.'

'That don't matter. Someone will buy them at the right price,' returned Aggie, burying her arms in the waste bin and retrieving the soiled goods. 'Bag up the flour in them brown packets over there. No use wasting a profit, no matter how small. As for the blocks, there's a chopper out back. You'll get a nice bit of kindling from them, despite the worm. They split easy enough, just watch you don't get a spark, or you'll set the place alight. Now, get a move on, love, or else you'll be on your knees all day.'

Birdie found herself struggling to obey, for she wouldn't herself eat the flour for fear of being poisoned. Was there really custom for this? By the time she had found the chopper and managed to separate the tough blocks into bundles neatly tied with string, it was well past three o'clock.

When Aggie called across the shop for help in weighing up the potatoes, Birdie hardly dare imagine the sight she must present. Her face and hands were grubby and her apron contaminated by the mould and dirt. Shop work wasn't like dressmaking at all, where everything, including herself, had to be kept clean and presentable.

'Aggie, I'll just go and wash—' Birdie began, but Aggie was already shaking her head.

'You'll do fine as you are. Let's lift in those sacks between us and weigh up a few pounds of potatoes.' Aggie didn't seem to care how Birdie looked. Don's mother worked as though her life depended on it and seemed to expect everyone else to do the same.

By the time Birdie was sent to eat, she had no appetite at all. There was bread set on the table with a large carving knife beside it. A small army of flies had gathered around the gauze on the dripping.

After thoroughly washing the enamel mug left for her, she made herself tea and struggled to ease her back. It was aching from the heavy lifting. Her hands were chapped and rough from the scrubbing, and her hair, over which she was so careful, was lank with dust thrown up by the sacks of vegetables. Her throat was sore, though the tea helped to soothe it.

At six o'clock, Aggie told her to put on her coat, take a lamp with her and sweep the yard. As Birdie found the broom by the closet, the bad smell was overpowering. At least she hadn't been asked to clean in there. But the assortment of rotting cauliflowers, cabbages and carrots that she began to shovel in the pig bin added nauseously to the aromas of the cooked meat shop across the road. Pease pudding, saveloys, faggots and tripe were being cooked in preparation for tomorrow. Over the yard wall, a strong whiff of salted cod and smoked haddock came from the fresh fish shop.

Birdie's stomach heaved. She clamped a hand over her mouth and for a moment, she swayed, leaning against the wall for support.

'Brigid?'

She turned to find Don frowning at her.

'This waste should have been cleared earlier,' he said, his tone a little abrupt, 'but no matter, you'll soon be acquainted with the routine. At least the bitter cold has kept the smell down.'

'Don, I've not had a moment—'

'I am sure of that, my dear,' he acknowledged, side-stepping the mound of vegetables she had swept into a pile. 'Perhaps you realize now I was not exaggerating when I told you how busy the store is.'

Birdie nodded, still fighting off the heave of her stomach. 'I could do more to help in the shop if we had someone to do this. A young lad, perhaps, after school?'

190

'Patience, my sweet,' he smiled, at last moving closer, picking his way carefully across the stones. 'This is only your first day. Once you begin to understand the business, then you'll see that our profit margins are very narrow. And we have just bought the delivery vehicle. Now, it will soon be time for you to catch the bus.'

'But you promised me a ride home.' She was looking forward to being alone with him.

'I have to collect our perishables from the warehouse. I'm sorry but I must go now.'

She tried to hide her disappointment. There would be no kiss or cuddle in the delivery van as she had hoped.

Seeing her face, he drew her towards him. 'There will be other times, my love.'

Birdie leaned her head against his chest. She could feel the strong beat of his heart as they listened to the traders shouting over the wall and the rumbling of the steam engines back to their yards. Was it always to be like this, she wondered. There seemed no romance at the shop, nothing here that could lend itself to affection. Even Don seemed to be another person.

'I'll call for you in the morning. It will be at six o'clock prompt.'

Birdie gazed up at him. 'I'll be waiting.'

Birdie thought of all the things she would have to do before leaving the house in the morning. There was the meal to prepare, the washing and ironing to attend to. And of course, Lady Annabelle's dress. But she would do it all willingly, for Don.

Despite Don's reluctance to hire help, Birdie suggested it to Aggie the next day.

'We might have before your arrival,' Aggie told her tightly, 'but I'm happy to say that you seem to be filling Lydia's place nicely. I told Donald – I said to him, "Despite

191

the slight look of her, Brigid is willing and able." Boys only play about and smoke me cigarettes and pinch the grub. No, dear, we'll manage as we are for now.'

Birdie hadn't time to answer before Aggie was busying herself with the customers. It was a number of heavy chores later, when Birdie met Lydia and James. Her good morning was brief as she made her way from the store to school.

'Is Lydia better?' Birdie enquired as she lifted a box of oranges from the delivery vehicle.

'A little, perhaps,' Don threw over his shoulder. But when Lydia returned she disappeared upstairs and for the rest of the day it was left to Birdie to resume the heavy duties.

By the end of the week, all Birdie's efforts to follow a routine at home had failed. Meals had been missed or were late, the housework had mounted and her back ached from her neck to the base of her spine. She was too tired even to lift a needle.

Chapter 24

Birdie was hopeful that she might deal with the customers on Monday. Don had promised her she would, but Aggie had other ideas. All morning Birdie was kept busy with stacking the boxes of vegetables outside in the bitter cold. According to Aggie's instructions, she had to label the fresh produce. But Birdie saw it was not fresh at all. Aggie told her to trim carefully last week's rejects of their rotting stalks and leaves. It was a dirty – and, Birdie felt – a sly job, lengthened by the disposal of the pig-bin rubbish.

Thankfully this bin had been emptied, but by the time Birdie had finished, it was half full again.

'You had better go easy next time, love,' said Aggie, frowning at the display that Birdie had worked hard to make presentable. 'You've cut too much off the cauliflowers and left them bald.'

'But they were brown,' Birdie protested in her innocence. 'I'd never buy a cauli at the market that was rotten like that.'

'And you won't buy one at Thorne's,' sniffed Aggie crossly. 'There's a knack to tidying up veg and the sooner you learn it the better. Now, Donald's just arrived round the back with the delivery van. He'll have a few sacks of spuds to off-load. Give him a hand, making sure none escape and go rolling about the floor.'

Birdie was eager to help Don, but the van was stacked full. It was back-breaking work. By the time they had finished, there were just a few moments to sit in the store-room. Even Don seemed a little disconcerted by the challenging work.

'It would really pay us to find an apprentice,' Birdie dared to suggest again as they sat in the dusty space beside Lydia's desk. 'A boy for just a few mornings or evenings. Or an older man who needed a few hours' work.'

'Mother doesn't approve of strangers,' Don refused on a final note. 'She doesn't trust anyone except family.'

'And do you agree with her?' Birdie couldn't see the sense in that at all. If the business was to flourish they needed assistance.

'It's not up to me to say,' Don barked back. 'We'll manage somehow.'

Birdie held her tongue. She was no mastermind, but even a fool could see that help was essential. Before, when the wholesalers had delivered by cart and pony, the driver had helped Don to off-load. But now it was clear that in trying to save pennies, Aggie expected Birdie to fill the gap.

Determined to press Don again on the subject when the time was right, Birdie finished her day as before. But there was no time to consult with Don that evening, and she found herself making her way home by bus as before.

On Saturday evening, as she was waiting to step off from the bus, her mind filled with doubts. Would Aggie ever approve of her or allow her to voice an opinion? Aggie's complaints had been relentless throughout the fortnight. Nothing Birdie could do seemed to be right. Her fruit and vegetable pruning was pronounced clumsy. Her hands, which were swollen and chapped, were slow to weigh the dirty, earth-crusted potatoes. Aggie insisted she leave on their heavy clumps of earth. Her motive was clear – to increase the profit – but once more Birdie held her tongue.

Birdie jumped down from the bus, her thoughts on the injustice done to the customer. As her heel turned and she lost her footing, a pair of arms reached out to save her. With considerable relief she looked up to see Harry. And not just relief, she realized, but gratitude at such a friendly face.

'You're sure you can walk?' Harry asked a little while later as he helped her limp along the pavement. What in heaven's name was Donald Thorne thinking of, allowing his bride-to-be to struggle through a day like the one he had just heard about, without the offer of a ride home in that hulking great vehicle he liked to flaunt.

'Look,' Harry suggested, worried by the pain that was etched on her face, 'let's sit down over there in the park. A few minutes' rest will help to ease your foot.'

'All right, but I must get home soon.' Her hand held onto his arm so tightly that he knew she must be suffering. 'There's supper to cook and I've somehow got to deliver Lady Annabelle's dress, which I've just finished.'

'It's swelling slightly,' Harry pointed out, glancing down at her ankle. 'You've given it a nasty twist.'

'Oh, I'm clumsy, I am. My thoughts were miles away,' she agreed, clinging on for dear life as they struggled their way to the bench.

He slid his arm around her waist and, almost lifting her off her feet, set her down on the bench. Harry felt an unexpected shiver go through him. The hairs on the back of his neck rose, as did the ones on his arms. It wasn't even as though he'd been expecting to see her. He'd been sizing up a private job for a chap just off Poplar Lane and was as startled as she when she almost fell into his arms. He'd felt a great pang of protectiveness wash over him, as though heaven had emptied her right into his care. At first he'd listened with amusement to her stream of apologies, but then, as came natural to Birdie, the truth came out and he managed to piece together the events that had brought her crashing down from the bus.

It was those damned Thornes again. They had worked her like a skivvy; he had noticed her sore hands. And it needed no great wisdom to see that her beautiful brown hair was tucked hurriedly away with pins, some of the crushed waves springing out in an unwieldy fashion. There was dirt smudged over her left ear and cheek, though she couldn't have known it, or had time or place to rectify the damage. But worst of all, a nasty red graze glowed on her chin.

'And how did this happen?' Harry indicated the spot and her hand went up to cover it.

'Oh, does it notice?'

'I can see you must have caught yourself on something.'

'It was only a box of apples, that's all.'

'A box of apples?' he repeated. 'What was it doing near your chin?'

She gave an embarrassed shrug. 'It was me own fault. I didn't even know I'd done it. I should've asked Don to lift it down from the van. But you know me, I can't wait for me own breath to come sometimes.' She gave a little laugh, but to Harry it was no laughing matter.

'But what were you doing emptying the van?' he asked, knowing that a heavy box of apples was no easy matter to manipulate. She was so small, so delicate – it just didn't seem right. He'd already been told by Pat that she was up at the crack of dawn, attending to all the chores. And that skinflint Thorne had soon waned in his enthusiasm to collect her, not that Harry had heard one word of complaint. He tried to compose himself as the cold February wind swirled around them.

'It was just a few things I moved,' she told him, not looking him quite in the eye. 'And it will pay me to watch me footing in future.'

Harry's irritation couldn't be contained. He knew he had no right to be angered, but she wasn't cut out for drudgery.

'Ah, well,' Birdie said, putting a bright smile on that he knew was for his benefit, 'it's only a little twist. And tomorrow I'll deliver the dress. Perhaps I'll ask Flo to bring the pram after Mass. Though Lady Annabelle won't be there, I'll ask Mrs Belcher to make certain the dress fits.'

'You can't push a pram all the way over to Hailing House, not in your condition!' Harry was unable to hide his dismay.

'Flo and me have carried things that way before,' she dismissed. 'I'm sure to be as right as rain after a night's rest.' She slid her hand through his arm. 'Now, Harry, I'll lean on you, if you don't mind and we'll make our way home.'

They started off at a slow pace, but by the time they'd gone a few yards, she was struggling. He was in no position to comment or even suggest that the mission tomorrow be delayed, but that ankle would be up like a balloon if she didn't rest.

Then he had an idea. If he said it right, it might even work.

'I'll be going out early meself,' he said casually. 'I've got one or two things on, and perhaps I could be of some help.'

'In what way, Harry?'

'I've the hire of a pony and trap for the day. You see, I'm giving a lift to someone. Just a favour to a friend.'

'A favour?' Her eyes, darker than the brown earth itself, stared into his and uneasily he nodded.

Her face looked suddenly strange, remote, in a way he couldn't puzzle out. But he ploughed on with his imaginative story, knowing he'd have to get to the point of it sharp, before she guessed his intention.

'It will be afternoon – or even teatime, if you see what I mean.'

'Yes, yes,' she nodded, 'I think I do.'

'So with the morning to kick me heels I was going to take meself up to the city. After all, it would be a shame to waste the day's hire.'

'Indeed, a pony and trap must cost a small fortune.'

'Er, no. It's a mate of mine and—' He tapped the side of his nose.

'A very good mate, I would say,' she nodded.

'My point being,' he rushed on, the heat under his collar growing, 'that I can as easy take you to Hailing House as to go wasting me time in the city.' He gave a cough to clear his throat.

'You'd do that for me?' Her glance came up wide and startled.

'It's not out of my way, not by a long shot.'

'Except one way is east and the other west.'

'And neither really matters to me,' said Harry with a genuine shrug. He was beginning to believe his own story!

After all, what better thing had he to do if he was giving himself the day off from work? And tomorrow was such a day. He'd make his way over to a pal who had a nice little pony he used for the races. Grease Jim Pilgrim's palm with a few shillings and Bob's your uncle. 'It's no trouble at all,' he added confidently now.

'As long as you're not late for your friend,' Birdie said with conviction.

'Me? I'm never late. You can set your alarm by Harry Chambers.' He laughed as his arm tightened a little, lifting her gently against him.

'Well, then, I should like to warm up that trap seat for your friend,' she smiled, holding on tightly as she limped along.

'It's as good as settled.' Harry slowed his steps and took the entire burden of her slight weight. He was in no hurry to get home.

No hurry at all.

Lady Annabelle turned on a sixpence, lifting her long-fingered hands above the swirl of her skirt. The tangerine bow that Birdie had taken such care with, lay low on her hips and was tied at the back, matching the colour of the band of her wide-brimmed, floppy hat.

Mrs Belcher, having deposited the best china cups and silver teapot, milk jug and tea strainer on the rectangular coffee table, was all gasps as Lady Annabelle continued to parade over the highly polished boards of the beautiful drawing room.

Birdie glanced over to where Harry was sitting on the gold-braided settee under the long window decorated by heavy brocade curtains and matching golden tassels. His dark looks were silhouetted against the bright sunshine streaming in. He wore a thick jacket, but his collar was open, against the dark grain of his skin. As promised, he had arrived with the little grey pony and trap at half-past ten and, after seeing Birdie was comfortably aboard, had driven them over to Hailing House. It had been such an enjoyable ride that she had quite forgotten her sprained ankle. Sitting beside Harry, she'd enjoyed the fresh morning air and the light breeze, and with Lady Annabelle's dress folded carefully over her lap, she had felt relief wash through her. At last the dress was complete and even if Lady Annabelle wasn't there to try it on, at least the finished article had been delivered on time.

As the trap bounced pleasantly along, Birdie was excited, despite her delicate ankle. Rising early, she'd pressed her waves into order and put on one of her best winter frocks over which she wore her blue coat. She'd given it a good press and pinned the black cat that Harry had given her for Christmas to the collar.

She was surprised when Lady Annabelle greeted them at Hailing House. 'Birdie, how wonderful to see you.'

'I didn't expect to find you here, Lady Annabelle.'

'I decided not to go to the country this weekend. James is driving me into the city this afternoon to meet Felicity, who is just home from the Continent. We are going to have tea at the Savoy. Now, why are you limping?'

'Harry drove me here, since I twisted my ankle.'

'You poor thing!' Lady Annabelle took her arm, calling over her shoulder, 'Come along, Harry! We must be formally introduced.'

Birdie smiled to herself. Harry had told her he would wait outside, but she knew that Lady Annabelle had mischief in her eyes and wouldn't hear of him waiting in the cold.

The joy was evident on Lady Annabelle's face as she twirled again, demanding to know what they thought of the dress.

'It's a dream, Lady Annabelle,' Mrs Belcher sighed. 'Fits you like a glove. Not a stitch to be seen, either.'

'Perhaps just a little tuck here.' Birdie stepped awkwardly forward. Her ankle still hurt, though it was a great deal better than it would have been if she'd walked all the way to Hailing House on it. 'If I am to make this right, then I shall take the frock with me and make one more alteration at home.'

'Do as you please, but I would be quite satisfied with this.' Lady Annabelle pressed her back down in the chair. 'You'll need to rest. Sprained ankles can be such an inconvenience.' She glanced at Harry with a twinkling smile. 'There are some rewards, of course.'

Birdie blushed. Harry sat stiffly on the buttoned golden settee that belonged to an elegant four-piece suite. He too had gone pink as he was introduced to Lady Annabelle.

'Now, do tell me, Harry, what do you think? I must have your opinion,' Lady Annabelle insisted.

Birdie was amused to see Harry's embarrassment. 'I'm not much of a judge when it comes to female attire,' he faltered. 'But a dress made by Birdie Connor is one to be proud of.'

'Oh, well said, Harry.' Lady Annabelle held out her skirt. 'Birdie is such a marvel.'

'It was you who drew the design,' Birdie said modestly. 'All I did was to follow it. And if I am to get it perfectly right, I should like to take in another pleat and see to the finishing of the hem.' Birdie seized a thread that seemed to have escaped and snipped it off expertly with the scissors from her bag.

'How easy you make that sound, Birdie. All Mummy's friends will want to know who made such a garment.' Lady Annabelle paused, frowning thoughtfully. 'Have you ever thought of professional dressmaking? I should be delighted to introduce you to the right people. And with the right premises, you would do famously!'

Birdie thought of Don and his intention that she should give up dressmaking. She was to work at the store. The shop was to be her destiny. For a moment, she felt sad. Bernadette had always told her that she might not have been born with a silver spoon in her mouth, but a needle and thread. And this would see her through life as favourably. Was it possible to do as Lady Annabelle said?

Birdie felt a thrill at the compliment. Yet, she was to become Mrs Thorne soon. Whatever was she thinking?

Harry set down his cup and saucer. 'I must go out to the pony,' he said, nodding towards the window through which the pony and trap could be seen tethered.

Lady Annabelle smiled. 'Thank you, Harry, for bringing Birdie. We should all be in such a state without her. I do believe I have the best dressmaker in all of London.'

Harry smiled at Birdie as he left.

Birdie knew she should tell Lady Annabelle that she would no longer be able to sew for her. But somehow she couldn't find the words.

'What a very nice young man,' Lady Annabelle said when Harry had gone and Mrs Belcher had taken the tray to the kitchen. 'I can see he thinks a great deal of you. Now, how is your father?' Lady Annabelle sat beside her, careful to arrange the folds of her dress neatly.

'He keeps well enough, but his chest can be the devil.'

'And Francis? Is there any news?'

Birdie felt herself go cold. 'None to speak of,' she answered, hiding her face so that Lady Annabelle couldn't see she was lying.

'I want you to come to me if there is anything I can do to help.'

'That's very good of you, Lady Annabelle. But there's nothing.' She added quickly to hide her unease, 'Now, I must insist that I make that alteration and take the dress with me.'

'As you wish.' Lady Annabelle walked over to the writing desk and lifted an envelope. She gave it to Birdie. 'Here is what we settled on, accompanied by a little extra.' The envelope felt heavy in Birdie's hands. 'And remember there is always a friend here at the House, should you need one.'

These kind words went to Birdie's heart as Lady Annabelle went to change. But after saying her goodbyes, and joining Harry, Birdie couldn't help thinking that Frank's plight needed a small miracle if ever he was to prove his innocence and become a free man again.

Chapter 25

Birdie sat beside Harry, her mind far away as she enjoyed the gentle sway of the trap and the rhythmic trot of the pony. Lady Annabelle's delight at receiving the dress had been very rewarding. And now, instead of struggling home with a sprained ankle, Harry was driving her, and even the sun had come out to warm the cold February day.

Lady Annabelle had been kind to offer her friendship, and Birdie knew this was a genuine offer. She also knew that inside the envelope, now tucked safely in her workbag, was a generous payment that would resolve any debts outstanding at home. Whilst she'd been working at the shop, the rent had been left unpaid and she was down to the last of the provisions in the larder. She'd run up ten bob on the slate at the grocery shop along Manchester Road, and there was the gas to put by, but all this could now be addressed. It was just that in the midst of all these things coming right, there was a darker corner of her life, with Frank hidden in it: her brother, her friend, on the run from the law and mixed up with rogues, shunned by their father and reviled by Don.

What was she going to do when she was married? Would she continue in the same way, hiding her feelings for Frank, ignoring his existence? And what if Frank was recaptured? Would she never go and visit him, speak to him, comfort him in his place of capture? For believing what he had told her – that he was completely without guilt – she could never disown him.

'Hey-oop, little fella!' Harry exclaimed beside her, and pulled up the pony as she came back to the present. They weren't in March Street, for Harry had driven them down to the river where the water glistened like a shiny silver ribbon in the sunshine. The big ships were anchored whilst the goose-neck cranes stood like thin, stiff birds, waiting to swoop on their prey. All the cargoes were stacked and silent, before the hive of activity that preceded Monday. Church bells pealed across the city and Harry lay down the reins as the little grey pony chomped quietly on his bit.

'The island is a fine sight,' he mused, leaning forward, his thick dark lashes fanning down on his cheeks. Resting his elbows on his knees he gazed thoughtfully over the river. 'Even in winter, when the water beckons you, tempting you on as far as you wish to go.'

'And where would you be going?' Birdie asked as she heard the note of longing in his voice. 'If you had your chance and all the money in the world, where would you choose?'

He laughed, turning his dark head and smoothing the leather reins absently through his fingers. 'Oh, I don't know. I haven't let meself dwell on travelling for a while now. Not since . . . well, for a bit, anyway.'

Birdie wondered if he was thinking of *her*, the girl who would take her place beside him later in the day, and she asked her next question hoping to draw him out. 'Is there any reason for this?' she enquired with all the nonchalance she could muster. 'I mean, you're still young and healthy, and you've not got a family to think of, a wife and children who might hold you back.'

But she was to be disappointed as he merely shrugged, causing her to notice how his broad shoulders stretched the width of his jacket and how he had a habit of crinkling up his smile as he paused to think.

'I've found me peace,' he said after a while. 'I've fitted into a new life. Oh, don't take no notice of my ramblings. See, any man will tell you he's restless when he studies the horizon. He fancies himself a boy again, with a million adventures enticing him away. But I've had me fair share of travelling. Seen plenty of sights and maybe I'll return to some of them one day. It's said that from Table Mountain you can see all of Africa and smell the perfumes of heaven itself. Some like to think that if you reached high enough, you'd be able to touch the sky.'

'Oh, Harry, that sounds lovely.'

He laughed again, a deep, rich sound that pulled at her senses. 'Like I said, take no notice of me. I'm dreaming – but it's on a day like this that a dream only seems a heartbeat away.'

Again, Birdie wondered if he meant her, the girl without a name, who caused him to sound and look like he did, a man caught up in a desire. Perhaps a man thinking about his true love.

'What about you?' he asked then, quick to turn the tables as he eased back and draped the reins across his long legs. 'Is there a country you'd like to visit, somewhere you've never seen?'

'Oh, I've never been away from the city,' she dismissed. 'But I'd go to the Emerald Isle if I got the chance. Our mother said shamrocks grow in great green fields there. She used to say all the luck in the world was in their four leaves. So, if ever I went, I'd fill me baskets full and bring them all home.' She laughed at the notion. 'But I don't suppose I'll have the chance.'

'And why not? You have all your life before you,' Harry answered sincerely.

'I don't think so,' she hesitated, looking away, 'what with the store an' all. There won't be much time for travelling. Don's never said much about such things.'

'Are you willing to settle for that?' His long, searching stare made her feel as though she might have wings on her heels and could do anything in the world she dreamed of. 'Or have you a thought that lights up the day when you think of it?'

Birdie knew what he meant. Hadn't she felt just such a feeling a short while ago in the presence of Lady Annabelle? When she'd tried to curb that reckless excitement at the thought of making those ladies all their frocks, with herself decked out in a fine wool suit of pearl grey, just like Lady Annabelle's. There, too, was a shimmering silk scarf around her neck and her hair freshly Marcel waved, with a discreet touch of lipstick and a dab of colour on her cheeks. There she was, in the midst of all these ladies, who would so like her to make dresses for them, all clamouring to have her opinion and giving her orders, until she was almost drowned in their requests!

Hadn't she felt it then? Hadn't she felt that lighting up? Hadn't she felt what she had lost, until Harry made it come back again. It was hope she had lost. Hope for the future, for herself and Frank, and for Dad and Pat, hope that life would eventually hold happiness for the Connors and freedom for Frank, and all the other joys that had seemed squeezed out for so long.

'I . . . I don't know,' she lied, looking away. 'Sure, I've got what I wanted. Marriage to a good hard-working man too, in Donald Thorne. Now what girl wouldn't light up at the thought of that?'

Daring then to look at him, she raised her chin and gave a nod, as if to settle the matter completely.

'And what about Frank?' he asked. 'Where will he be in your life when you're married?'

'I . . . I haven't thought much about it.' This time she answered honestly. 'Well, I hadn't, until a couple of weeks ago when I saw him.'

'You saw him?' Harry looked shocked.

'I did, indeed.' Little by little she told him what happened. 'This Inga, the one who wears the breeches, has made our Frank believe she'll help him. Swears she'll get him over to France, but I don't trust her, nor the other one they call Erik.'

Harry was thoughtful for a while. 'They sound a rum lot to me.'

She nodded. 'Frank's always had an eye for the girls and this Inga is no exception, despite the fact she wears a man's clothes. As if he isn't in enough hot water already, he's talking about helping these Whites against the Reds.'

'But these are the two opposing sides in the Russian Civil War. The Red Army and the White Army. Why would they want to involve Frank in their politics?'

'She must have her reasons. Or else she wouldn't have convinced Frank they are his friends.'

Harry gave her a thoughtful frown. He seemed on the point of saying something, but instead shrugged and lifted the reins, clicking his tongue at the little grey pony.

Thanks to Harry's help that day, Birdie's injury soon healed and, on a bright and sunny morning the following week, Don met her as she walked into the shop.

'Good morning, Brigid.' He looked pleased with himself. 'I've settled the day of our wedding.'

'You have?' She could hardly believe it.

'I've made the arrangements for Wednesday, March the twenty-sixth.'

'Next month?'

'Indeed. Here, I have the forms. Wednesday is our least busy day by far. The appointment is for ten o'clock. Mother will have the food ready for midday so that by one, we shall be open again, not missing much trade.'

Birdie took the paper he handed her. It was just a few lines that sounded as though they might be going to the doctor or the dentist, but was to be her wedding day. She tried not to feel as though something romantic and warm and endearing was missing.

'But Dad,' she burst out, 'I've not told him yet. Will you come over this evening so that we can share the news together?'

'I'm certain you don't need me for that.' He drew her close and kissed her on the lips. 'I would just be an encumbrance.'

'Oh, you wouldn't,' she protested. 'Please come.'

'Don't worry, my dear, he'll be very happy for us, just as Mother is. After all, with our respective Churches being so different, this is the only fair way. A middle line drawn down the centre, so to speak.'

Birdie hoped he was right. She'd been telling herself Wilfred would see the sense in a compromise, the quickest and easiest way to be married. But without Don at her side, would Wilfred agree?

'I'm very pleased to say Lydia is feeling better,' he continued. 'She'll be back at her desk today. A word of encouragement as you pass won't go amiss.'

But when Lydia appeared, she held herself quite aloof and buried her head in the books. Birdie made several attempts to speak, but each time Lydia seemed not to hear her.

That night, Birdie resolved to tell Wilfred about the

wedding. But the house was untidy and the ironing was piled high. Just as she sat with Wilfred in the parlour, he began to cough. It was a racking, chesty cough that had him climbing the stairs early to bed. By Saturday, the news still hadn't been aired and on Sunday, there was no time after Mass, as Don took Birdie to tea with Aggie.

Birdie was flattered to think she had been invited, but the first question that Aggie asked as she offered Birdie a slice of fruitcake was one Birdie had dreaded.

'So how is your father?' Aggie asked unexpectedly, drawing her hands over a clean white apron that had been exchanged for the coarse grey one.

'His cough is still troubling him.'

'A good dose of friar's balsam is all he needs,' Aggie decided. 'I've got a bottle somewhere on the shelves. I'll look it out for you. Now come on, help yourself, it's nice fresh fruitcake. None of the old stuff we put out for the customers.' She gave Birdie a wink as though they shared a secret, but it only made Birdie think of all the poor customers who seemed too easily deceived. 'And them's nice sandwiches,' Aggie continued. 'I've spread 'em with plenty of mustard. You too, James, eat up. There's thousands in need of feeding, so I don't want to see a crumb left.' She turned from the silent child back to Birdie. 'Now that the date is set, ducks, we can get down to brass tacks. Lydia and James are to move next door, plenty of space there for a growing lad. That'll leave you and Don two nice big rooms and will serve you both well as it did Lydia and Stephen.' She pulled back her shoulders as she spoke of her dead son. 'My lad done it up nice, before he left for the war and never came back, God rest his soul. A good bit of wallpaper that he found up in the attic and it wasn't too far gone with the moth and don't show the wear and tear.'

Birdie glanced at Lydia, who was sitting, her face ashen and her hands folded tightly in her lap. She tried to put herself in Lydia's place. She and her little boy were to be moved next door, but what say had Lydia in this? The flat over the store had been her home since her marriage and James had grown up here. But Aggie showed no sentiment and seemed to expect no objection.

'So if there's any bits you want to move over before March,' Aggie went on, 'then you'd better move them over on a Sunday. That's the only day the vehicle is free.'

'I'd rather leave moving me things till after – after our wedding, that is.' Birdie didn't want to upset Wilfred and the less upheaval there was, the better.

'As you like,' Aggie agreed, placing the knitted cosy over the china teapot. 'Be assured you'll have a good bed here. There's a fair-sized wardrobe too. In fact you won't need much else, as Lydia has managed all this time with what's in there.'

'Oh, but I'd like a few of me bits and pieces eventually,' Birdie rushed out, 'like my dressing table and treadle. They were Mum's, you see, and I'd like to have them close by.'

'You won't be needing the machine,' Aggie replied, her eyes narrowing. 'I've got an old one in a cupboard somewhere.' Just then there was a rap at the door and Aggie sprang to her feet. 'Now, I wonder who that can be.'

A moment or two later she returned with a short, stout man wearing a dark suit, and a hat, which he removed as he entered. Don got up to offer his hand, saying awkwardly, 'What a surprise! How nice of you to call on us, Mr Howells.'

'Not at all.' The visitor, who wore a white clerical collar around his neck, turned immediately to Birdie. 'Ah, so you must be Donald's intended?'

Birdie nodded as Aggie pulled out a chair.

'Have a seat, Vicar, right here next to me daughter-in-law. Well, she is as good as, ain't she?' Aggie lay a hand on Birdie's shoulder, a powerful grip that squeezed hard into

209

her skin. 'Now, ducks, seeing as you'll soon be part of the family it'd be nice for you to get acquainted with our friends, so I asked the Vicar to drop in. Now, I'll pour us all another cup whilst you and him have a little chat. He needs cheering up as his poor missus went and died only last month.'

'Hello, my dear,' said Mr Howells. 'Aggie has told me all about you.'

'Has she?' Birdie was surprised.

'I'm hoping we might see something of you at church when you're married.'

Birdie looked at Aggie, who seemed preoccupied with pouring the tea. Yet was she? 'I'm a Catholic, Mr Howells,' Birdie explained.

'We welcome all faiths, Brigid.'

'I don't think—' Birdie began, only to be stopped by Aggie, who said sharply, 'A very nice offer, Mr Howells. I'm sure it will be taken up in time.'

Birdie felt colour rush to her cheeks. Aggie had engineered all this, she was certain! But Don was frowning in her direction, his eyes meeting hers severely.

The time passed very slowly for Birdie, and by the time tea was over and the Reverend Mr Howells had warmed her ear on the blessings of his wonderful parish, she was more than relieved when at last Don said it was time to drive her back to March Street.

Chapter 26

For the next day or two Birdie spent every spare moment preparing her bottom drawer. She had collected a modest amount over the years, as most girls did: sheets and pillow-cases, arm and back rests for chairs, which she had personally embroidered, two heavy chenille tablecloths hemmed with looping tassels, although this wasn't really the fashion now. But since she hadn't enough to spend on luxuries, at least she could take what she had. Of course, she'd need new underwear and a new nightdress for her trousseau. What would it be like to lie in Don's arms, to have him touch her, make love to her?

Oh, how she'd ached for him to hold her close, especially in moments at the shop when they found themselves alone. He had been quite ardent once, but recently she felt he was reluctant to show any affection in front of Aggie or Lydia. Despite what he'd promised about enjoying more time together, they seemed to find less and less opportunity to be with each other. But perhaps after they were married this would change.

What was it like to have a man make love to you, she often found herself wondering. She'd asked Flo, who'd giggled a lot and said Reg had been like a bull in a china shop when they'd first married. But Flo, who had three sisters and a wealth of knowledge, had boasted that she'd gradually trained Reg up. But Birdie didn't think that Don would like to be trained. She longed for him so much. Did he long for her in the same way?

On Sunday morning after Mass, Birdie told Flo that the date had been set.

'So you're going through with it?' Flo asked as they sat in the back benches of church whilst the two girls went up to light their candles. 'Have you told your dad?'

'I haven't got round to it yet.'

'That's what you said before.'

'Shush, keep your voice down,' Birdie whispered. 'Father Flynn is giving us black looks.'

'He'll give you more than that when he knows you're

211

marrying out of the Church.' Flo sank back against the polished bench with a protesting sigh. The smell of High Mass incense was heavy in the air and the silence was broken by Enid and Emily running back to them on the polished floor.

'We done it, we lit 'em and didn't get our fingers burned,' said Emily scrambling on to Birdie's lap. 'Is me dress done yet?'

'I was just talking to your mum about that,' said Birdie, taking advantage of the cuddle.

'Is mine?' echoed Enid, squirming onto Flo's knees.

'They soon will be,' promised Birdie, hoping that Flo would eventually manage a supportive smile.

'Are you gonna have a long white dress?' asked Emily, her eyes wide as she looked up at Birdie. 'And a crown on yer 'ed?'

Birdie laughed. 'Don't think I'll wear a crown. But I'll have a nice dress and a hat.'

'Don't know if Reg will be able to come,' Flo said flippantly. 'Not on a Wednesday.'

'But you're my best friends. Can't he get the morning off?'

'He'd lose a day's pay,' Flo shrugged. 'Don't think we can afford it. But it's not as if it's a church wedding, is it? I mean, it'll be ten minutes and then it'll be over.'

Birdie glared at her friend. 'Don't rub it in, Flo.'

'Well, you're the one who agreed to be married by licence,' Flo flung back. 'It ain't my fault, is it?'

'You've never liked Don, have you?' Birdie mumbled.

For a moment Flo was silent. Then, more gently she said, 'It's the way he treats you I don't like. You're me best mate and I want the best for you. Your mum did too, and brought you up with standards – good, old-fashioned values, like going to Mass regular and sticking by your family through thick and thin. But somehow it seems to me that Don don't understand this. Pardon me for speaking me mind, but it's only 'cos I think a lot of you.'

Emily pushed her arms around Birdie's neck. 'Are you and Mummy 'aving a row?'

'Course we're not,' Birdie said, glancing at Flo. But her friend was already taking her daughter's hands and pushing her along the pew and into the aisle, her jaw set tight in the way that Birdie knew meant Flo was upset.

For all Aggie's fussing about stock, Don informed Birdie that, according to Lydia's sums, the profit was down on last year. This seemed to inspire Aggie and Don to even greater efforts of hard work, and Birdie was ordered to fill the shop front each day with as much stock as she could manage to carry. It all went out, the good and the bad, but mostly the bad, with overripe and rotten goods drawing in the flies. Before the shop closed, it was up to her to bring back what was not sold. And there was piles of it. The customers, Birdie saw, were getting wise to Aggie's tricks.

So Aggie insisted the store stayed open even later, though it didn't seem to Birdie to make any difference. By the time she had stowed everything away, it was often past eight. Pat was charged with the duty of preparing supper, if not exactly cooking it. Birdie found his attempts were half-hearted, even though she told him in confidence her wedding day was not far off. He wasn't even very good at the simplest jobs, like mashing potatoes. They turned out lumpy and unsalted, and Wilfred complained of just about everything Pat tried to do.

One Monday evening, Pat broke the news he had been promoted. 'I was given that round I was after,' he announced at the supper table.

'Is it more money?' Birdie was suspicious. This was the first she'd heard of the so-called promotion.

'No, but I won't have the fields to ride over. And no one

wants them, as they're marshy and hard work. This round's nearer to Aldgate, along all the main roads.'

'Aldgate!' Birdie exclaimed as she filled their dishes with mutton stew laced thickly with pearl barley. She pushed a strand of damp hair from her eyes in the warm kitchen, a dozen chores on her mind still left to do. 'But that's miles away. What time will you finish?'

'Dunno. After seven, I expect.'

She wondered if he'd done it to avoid his duties at home. She was about to ask him when Harry walked in the back door. His jacket was slung casually over his shoulder, but his smile disappeared when he saw the look of exasperation on Birdie's face.

'Oh, so you're gracing us with your presence tonight, are you?' Birdie couldn't help her irritation. No one seemed bothered about what was going to happen when she was gone. 'It must be all of two days since we saw you last,' she noted, dropping a hefty portion of stew on his plate so that the gravy splashed over its edge. 'Your appetite must have got the better of you.'

'I've worked late—' Harry began, trying in vain to repair the damage as the gravy dripped on to the table.

'Now eat up, will you, before it gets cold,' she scolded, darting a look across to her brother. 'And what do you find so funny, Pat?'

'You're dropping the stew everywhere,' he informed her, unable to stifle his amusement as he caught Harry's twinkling gaze.

'So you both think it's funny, do you?' she demanded, clattering the pot on the draining board. 'Well, I'm sure I'll be laughing too when I finally sit down and manage to get a fork to my lips.'

'Now, now, girl,' Wilfred reproved gently. Until now he had been sitting without comment and his tone was mild. 'Don't take umbrage, Brigid, for something that wasn't meant. And as for Harry, he's quite entitled to come and go as he pleases.'

'Didn't I just say that meself, Dad?'

'No, you did not. You were more keen to remind us of the day of hard work that you've had.'

Birdie felt her cheeks burn as she stared at the upturned faces. 'Oh, so you're listening at last, the three of you?'

There was silence in the kitchen, until Wilfred placed his hands on the table and with a deep frown, demanded, 'What's happening to this household? A man can't say a thing right these days. And the place is so gloomy it's like a bloody funeral parlour.'

'There's no need to curse, Dad.'

'I will if I feel like it,' Wilfred replied angrily. 'You can give out the orders when you have a roof of your own to live under.'

Birdie's eyes felt moist. 'Well, it'll be a good thing when I marry, won't it? After me wedding you'll be able to do as you please—' She stopped, almost fainting with mortification for what she'd just said.

Wilfred stared at her, the frown so deep on his forehead that it looked carved out of his skin.

'It's something I've been meaning to tell you, Dad.'

'Go on,' Wilfred said quietly. 'I'm listening, girl.'

Birdie felt like a child again, needing approval, yet knowing that she would never be given it. 'It's March the twenty-sixth, to be precise.'

Wilfred gazed at her. 'So it's done, is it?' He took a deep breath. 'Ah, well, it had to come, yes, it did. And you shouldn't be in a fuss about it,' he smiled, 'I've told you before that we'll all manage. So why is it you've that long face on you, lass?'

She fought desperately to think of a way to put it, but in the end there was only the plain truth to tell. 'Dad, we're being married by register. Now I know you won't favour it, but you see, Don's Church means a lot to him—'

'Register?' Wilfred repeated. 'What are talking about, girl?'

Birdie could barely look at him. 'It's the best for both of us, see? Mrs Thorne don't approve of a Roman service. And it's just not fair that Don would have no one on his side whereas there'd be a church full of us—'

'But you're a Catholic, girl,' Wilfred insisted, 'from birth.'

'I know, Dad.'

Wilfred shook his head slowly. 'I want to see you married as your mother wished. I've never converted meself, never felt the need, but you were brought up in the faith. And now you're telling me you're committing yourself, taking vows – promises to last a lifetime – by register?'

'Oh, Dad, don't take it so hard,' Birdie pleaded. 'I'll mean me vows, no matter where I speak them.'

Wilfred sat in silence again, his gaunt frame hunched over the table, until at last he dragged up the strength to reply. 'I never thought I'd see the day when a daughter of mine would give up her faith.'

'I ain't giving it up, Dad,' Birdie insisted, but she was crumbling inside.

'That's for you to decide.'

He stood and stared down at her. For a moment she thought he was going to speak, but all he did was shake his head. Slowly he left the room. Birdie felt distraught.

She had convinced herself he'd see the sense in it, wish her good luck in the life she had chosen even though it wasn't to be started in church. But now she knew it could never happen. And her heart felt torn in two because of it, as if she were disowning her old life, when all she was doing was trying to make a new one.

Chapter 27

'Don't know what you expected,' Pat said unsympatheti-
cally as he picked up his spoon after their father had left
the kitchen. Not a word had been said as they had eaten
half-heartedly and refused an offer of pudding. 'If Mum
was alive—'

'Well, she's not.' Birdie was hurt to the quick, yet feeling
guilty. Why couldn't everyone see that it wasn't her first
choice to marry by register, but that she had to do it? 'It's
me and no one else that's tying the knot, Pat. It's Brigid
Connor who at last is having a wedding ring put on her
finger.'

'You've not had the first one, yet,' Pat returned
spitefully.

'What did you just say?'

'You told us all what a beauty it was, a family heirloom,
an' all, but you've not seen it since.'

Birdie could hardly speak for mortification. How dare
Pat say such a thing especially in front of Harry, who
suddenly seemed entranced by the sight of the gravy marks
on the tablecloth.

'Don is . . . he's . . .' she began in desperate embarrassment, 'he's making sure it'll be a good fit, that's all.'

'I reckon it was a trick,' Pat said boldly. 'To win you over
to the Thornes.'

Birdie laughed in astonishment. 'Whatever are you talking about?'

'Me and Willie heard Willie's mum. Mrs Mason was telling Mr Mason in their kitchen, after she'd bought him
some nails and a hammer up Thorne's. She said there was
a racket going on out the back and Aggie was
shouting—'

'Pat, what's got into you?' Birdie interrupted, shocked at the words that were tumbling out of his mouth. 'It's a sinful thing to talk behind people's backs.'

'It's no sin to tell the truth,' Pat retaliated. 'It was just before you went to work there. Aggie Thorne was in a right strop, accusing the widow of trying to take over the business by getting off with her son. And she would have, an' all, if Aggie hadn't steered him to marry you.'

Birdie's heart rolled over like thunder as a feeling of sickness swamped her. And Pat wasn't finished as he gabbled, 'Then the widow shouted back that Don hadn't put a ring on your finger yet and wasn't likely to, if she got her way.'

Birdie stared at her brother. 'That's . . . that's terrible lies!'

'I'm not lying to you, honest,' Pat insisted, his face red and blotchy. 'I never would do such a thing. You're my sister and always done the best for me. It was you and Frank that I always looked to, and now . . . now . . .' he sucked in breath as he searched for words and couldn't find them. 'Ask Mrs Mason, if you don't believe me,' he choked eventually. 'She was dithering whether to tell you, but me and Willie heard Mr Mason say it was none of their business.'

Birdie stood up, her legs unsteady beneath her. 'I don't believe you,' she whispered, holding tight to the draining board. 'You . . . you're making it up.'

'I'm sorry,' Pat said, scrambling up beside her, tears on his lashes. 'I . . . I never wanted to upset you.'

Even the air around her seemed different, changed, sullied by Pat's cruel words, as if dirt had been thrown over her life.

Loosening the belt of her apron, she folded it and placed it on the table. Then she lifted her coat from the kitchen door and slipped it on. Walking out into the yard, she then made her way through the alley towards the park, breathing in the clean evening air as though she had been starved of it.

★

She didn't know how long she'd been sitting there, on the park bench, in the quiet, as the river mist settled in ghostly pools in the dark. The world continued in its same way, as if nothing had happened to disturb it. The sounds of passing vehicles drifted over from the road along with the hoots of the late river traffic. But it felt to Birdie as though she was part of another world, a place she was looking down on, numbed to the sensations that went with it.

It gradually grew colder and the sky turned black over the arches, where she had played as a child and brought Pat to play after Bernadette had died. And where, this year in the freezing cold of winter, she had met Frank in secret and cut the red hair from his chin.

Gradually, stars emerged and twinkled, and the river noises quietened as the gulls screeched their last hungry cries. From some way off there were voices; dockers most likely, those lucky enough to have been called off the stones and given jobs. Ambling home from a long shift, they would join the straggling queues from the warehouses, shoulders slumped and faces caked in grime. She knew it all so well, the docks were second nature to her, reassuring and familiar. And yet tonight it seemed as though everything was sharp and out of focus.

Why would Pat say such things? Was he angry with her for leaving them? Was he so against being left to manage for himself and look after Dad that he'd think up such a story?

Then she felt someone beside her, a tall frame. It was Harry.

'Take no notice of me,' Harry said as he sat down. 'I'm just going to have a quiet moment.' He stretched out his long legs, rummaging in his pockets for tobacco.

It was not so much the smoke he craved, but something to occupy his hands. He wanted to comfort her, but how could he? There was truth in Pat's words, no doubt, but it had come at a price.

'Why did Pat do it?' she asked. 'How could my own brother say such things?'

'He's just a kid,' Harry replied carefully. 'You said so yourself, that you look on him as a boy. He's too young to be tactful.'

'So you believe him, is that it?'

'I'm not saying one way or the other,' Harry shrugged. 'But Pat's no liar.'

'Then it must be true.'

Harry realized he wasn't questioning the truth of Pat's outburst. He was only wishing it could have been said differently.

'But what if it was gossip? Why should I believe that Lydia is after Don just because Mrs Mason said it?'

'Granted, Pat's done no good to himself or to you tonight,' he tried. 'He only spoke out to save you distress.'

'And what am I in now?' she burst out, and he flinched as though his words had returned to bite him. 'Am I sitting here clapping me hands for joy at the thought of me true love—' She stopped as if the emotion was subsiding enough to let in a bit of calm. 'But I can't put this on no one else. It's me own fault, I know.'

He sat quietly, afraid to move lest he upset her train of thought. He could feel her thinking everything through, as though it was in his own head.

'Harry, do you remember what I told you? When I saw them, that day by the shop, and they hadn't seen me. And Lydia was, well, she just looked happy. But I've never seen her the same again, not until I saw them in the Dock Road that time with you. Oh, a thousand thoughts are whirling through me brain,' she whispered as if to herself. 'The glances between them and, yes, there have been many. But I thought . . . ah, what did I think? And that look on her face when I went to tea, when Aggie said Don and me were to have her rooms. I tried to put meself in her place, so I did – but I was thinking of meself and me own future.'

'That's as it should be,' Harry nodded, 'for a bride.'

'And little James, what of him?' she continued as if not hearing him. 'He was skipping beside Don that day in the Dock Road, as though Don was his father.' Again she stopped and rocked a little.

'The boy is close, I'll admit, but shouldn't an uncle be so loved too?'

'Perhaps James doesn't know the difference? And Lydia herself has been unwell. Could unhappiness be the cause? For surely to goodness, I've not seen her smile since that day in the Dock Road . . .'

She drifted into silence and it was not until a cold wind blew harshly across them that Harry suggested they walk home. She took his arm and they made their way back to March Street, and Harry found himself once again pressed to find any good point in that shopkeeper's nature.

After saying good night to Harry, Birdie found Pat asleep on the couch.

'Oh, you're home,' he yawned, sitting up, blinking the sleep from his eyes.

'I'd only gone to the park.'

'Are you still angry?'

'No, but I don't feel my normal self,' she admitted, sitting beside him.

'I'm sorry. But I had to tell you.'

'And it was all from the lips of Willie's mum?'

'Me and Willie was under the open window,' Pat said quietly. 'Mrs Mason didn't know we was there.'

'So you was eavesdropping?'

'Couldn't help it, could we? We was stuck there till they went in the parlour. Willie and me agreed we'd keep quiet, like Mr Mason told Willie's mum to.'

'But, what you heard was only Mrs Mason's view,' Birdie protested. 'And like you and Willie, she wasn't supposed to have overheard.'

'Yes, but Mrs Mason don't gossip. Not like some do round here.'

Birdie sighed again. 'You're right, Pat. She's not the type to speak out of turn. Now, it's time we went to bed, for both of us have an early morning. I'm off to the store bright and early, for I'll not be satisfied until I know the truth.'

That night in bed, she thought about what she would say to Don. She would demand to know if he was in love with Lydia. And was he only marrying at the insistence of Aggie? What would she do if he told her he *was* in love with Lydia? But that was impossible. There had to be some kind of mistake. But these questions tormented her and she slept only fitfully, before waking up in a cold and clammy sweat.

Chapter 28

The next morning, Tuesday, Birdie made her way to the store as usual. But her heart wasn't in it. Despite the challenging work she had accepted her role and had wanted to please Aggie. But now it was all changed by what Mrs Mason had overheard. She wanted to be resolute, single-minded. But she was thrown back into panic. As she turned the corner of the High Street, her footsteps were slower. She wanted a husband who loved her. She wanted what Flo and Reg had. But was this impossible now?

Lifting her face to the breeze, she swept away a tear.

Then she stopped, gasping for breath. Grey, foul-smelling smoke curled high into the sky above the roofs of the shops and swept into her face. Horses shied restlessly as a thick blanket of smoke filled the road.

'What's happened?' Birdie demanded, clutching hold of the fishmonger's arm as he stood outside his shop.

'It's Aggie Thorne's store,' he coughed, shaking his head doubtfully. 'They had a fire in the early hours. Put out the blaze, the firemen did, but God knows what the old girl had in there. You can't get rid of the stink.'

Birdie moved blindly forward until she couldn't bring herself to move any further. She stared over the people's heads to the canvas awning outside the store, which was now caked in black grime. A steam vehicle with four red wheels and a brass funnel stood in the road and a trail of smoke blew across on the breeze. The long ladder that was held in place on the back of another cart was being lowered by two firemen. The two black horses that pulled a cart further down the street had been led off, out of the reach of the fumes.

'Is anyone . . . was anyone . . .?'

'Dunno,' replied the fishmonger, coming alongside, with a shrug. 'It was a corker, just as dawn was breaking. I could feel the 'eat from my place. Lucky the steam engine yard was next door, as they wheeled out an engine to drive the pump.'

Birdie ran then, trying not to breathe in the fog of fumes as she pushed her way through to the store.

'Don, Aggie?' Birdie stepped warily into the blackened doorway of what once had been the shop. The glass in the door was gone and there was no window at all. She could still feel the heat in contrast to the cold morning and the ash blew up in gusts. A fireman appeared in his dirty tunic, his face and his brass helmet streaked with dirt.

'You can't come in here, miss, it's not safe.'

'Is everyone alright?' Birdie pressed her hand over her mouth. The air was so foul she stepped back. 'My fiancé, Donald Thorne, and his mother, Aggie? And there's Lydia and her son, James. They live above—'

'They're all next door,' he barked at her, dragging a hose pipe after him and stamping his boots in the puddle. 'Lucky for them they'd next door to go to, or else they'd 'ave been down to the Sally Army for a bed ternight.'

'Next door,' Birdie gasped. 'The fire didn't reach there?'

'No, though it's a miracle it didn't spread from the shop. This place was a tinder box,' the fireman grumbled, wrestling the hose through the debris. 'Stuffed to the gunwales, it was.'

Birdie thought of the kindling and coal and the paraffin and the matches crammed together and all the other stock that Aggie insisted on keeping. Aggie had once warned herself of the dangers of causing sparks.

'Nasty business this,' continued the fireman. 'Lucky the steam engine yard is next door and they got the pump going afore we arrived. The fire would have taken down the rooms above too, even the whole block.' He glanced over his shoulder. 'Shop's off limits and you can't go up the apples and pears yet. We've got to inspect the rooms above afore they move back.'

Birdie took a last glance around. Curiously some of the jars and tins on the shelves stood singed but intact. At the other end, where the coal and wood had been kept, there was nothing but debris. The store and all its contents were ruined. And what of upstairs? Would it be safe to return to? All Aggie's plans for the future were in disarray.

What was going to happen now?

'Oh, it's you.' It was Lydia who opened the street-door to Birdie's knock. Her tone was unwelcoming and her clothes smelled strongly of smoke. 'You'd better come up.

I've taken James to school. It's best he is away from all this. Aggie is . . . well, you'll see.' She stared down at Birdie with clear dislike. 'Donald is out in the yard, trying to save some worthless stock at his mother's insistence.'

Without a word more, she turned and made up the staircase. Birdie followed, listening to the sound of Lydia's slight heels on the echoing staircase. Despite the dirty marks over her skirt and blouse, Lydia had lost none of her natural elegance. She was undoubtedly an attractive woman, with a keen appetite for the business and a young son to support, and Pat's words repeated themselves in Birdie's head. *The widow said that Don hadn't put a ring on your finger yet and wasn't likely to, if she got her way.*

Birdie wanted to take hold of Lydia and demand to know the truth. But she found herself at the top of the stairs and standing on the landing, and before she could confront Lydia, Aggie's voice rang out.

'Oh, so you've arrived at last!' Aggie poked her turbaned head around the door. 'Come along in.'

Birdie entered the unfamiliar, musty-smelling room that Aggie had rented for Lydia. A grey haze lingered, banking up thickly in the corners and laying like a blanket over a cheap wooden table and four chairs. 'It'll clean up good as new in here,' Aggie said as she bent down to drag a pail of dirty water across the bare-boarded floor. 'The ash even got up here. 'Spect you saw the damage on your way up. But we ain't done bad, considerin'. Won't be able to go back, though, till they've inspected upstairs. Meanwhile we'll set about business again.'

Birdie was amazed to find Aggie in such determined spirits. Not for her a catalogue of woes, or self-pity. She looked as though she had been fighting the fire single-handedly as two white circles stood out around her eyes as though she'd rubbed away the soot. Her hair was scraped back from her long, thin face and gathered up under the turban. Her coarse apron was already filthy and her laced boots were bound securely by string around her ankles as though to defy any flames.

'But there's no shop now,' Birdie pointed out. 'Everything's in ruins.'

'A bit of a fire won't stop Aggie Thorne,' Aggie answered resolutely. 'I mean to have the insurers cough up and deck me place out proper again. Meanwhile I'm going to make the landlord an offer on the room below. Not that you can see what state it's in as the window is boarded. Has been for donkey's years. But I'll be likely to rent it for a pittance if I promise him we'll do that up, an' all.'

'Do it up?' Lydia said in a shrill voice. 'This place is not fit to occupy, let alone downstairs.'

'If you've a better idea, then spit it out.' Aggie glared challengingly at her daughter-in-law.

'I never agreed to me and James living here,' Lydia retorted, for the first time showing her feelings. 'I've been forced into this and it's all because . . . because . . .' Lydia turned an accusing glare on Birdie, '. . . of her!'

'Shut up, you daft wench,' Aggie interrupted sourly. 'You've been nothing but a misery for weeks. We've suffered a fire, but we're still on our feet, ain't we? You've got a roof over your head and clothes on your back. But what do I hear from you – nothing but complaint! I've allowed you your own way after grieving but now I'll tell you straight to yer face. I always thought my Stephen had wed a spoiled bitch and now I'm proved right.'

Lydia's dark eyes narrowed as she pulled herself up. 'I've always known you've disliked me, Aggie.' Again Lydia glanced at Birdie. 'Indeed, you have my sympathy, Brigid. Your life will be a misery under this woman's thumb.' Lydia turned slowly back to Aggie, her expression bitter. 'Have you forgotten it was me who helped you through the war? You were eager to have me then, but now, having found an opinion of my own, and with your son to support me, you want me out of the way.' Lydia smiled unpleasantly. 'Rest easy, Aggie, for I have no intention of spending the rest of my life at your beck and call. And if Donald has any sense, he'll come with me.'

Birdie stood in shocked silence as Lydia turned and swept out of the room. Her footsteps rang on the boarded stairs and the front door banged.

'Oh, take no notice of her.' Aggie flapped her hand dismissively. 'She won't go nowhere. Got the kiddy to think about, ain't she? Knows when she's well off even though she turns her nose up at this.' Aggie shuffled across and clamped a rough hand on a tired-looking Gladstone bag. 'We was lucky not to have lost anything upstairs. And I might have, if that bloody fire had its way.' Aggie placed the bag on the floor and stood over it, a strange smile on her face. 'Why don't you go and see Donald? Go through the scullery there and down the steps to the back yards. Cheer him up, it will, seeing you.' Aggie gave a twisted grin. 'Then come up and finish this floor off for me. I'm catching the bus up to Aldgate to see the landlord, so we can get crackin' again.'

Birdie stared into Aggie's conniving face and would have laughed if she hadn't been so angry. Did Aggie really think she was so easy to fool? Lydia had confirmed Birdie's suspicions: what Pat had overhead Mrs Mason say was true. But was it possible Don would give up the store for Lydia?

Birdie swept past Aggie without a word. If Aggie thought that nothing had changed, then she was about to discover that Brigid Connor was not the fool Aggie took her for.

Birdie made her way carefully down the slippery green-stained stone steps that overlooked both yards. For all her determination to see this through, she felt sick with dread.

The prospect of confronting Don and hearing words she might not want to hear was almost too much to bear. She wanted to turn round and run away. But this time, there was nothing for it, but to go on.

As she reached the bottom step, she stood still for a moment, asking herself if it could have been her who was in the wrong. Had she somehow made all this happen? Was she scared of growing old alone? Had she been prepared to marry at any cost, any cost at all? Had she spent the last few years running after Don, trying to please him and losing herself into the bargain? But she did love him, she did! If Don admitted to loving Lydia, what would she feel? What if he denied any feelings for Lydia? What if he took Aggie's side?

Suddenly she could hardly breathe for confusion. But then Lydia's words echoed tauntingly. *If Donald has any sense, he'll come with me.* This could mean only that Lydia wanted to be with Don. Did he feel the same about her? Yet if it was Aggie who had forced Don into marriage, then it was already an empty, shallow proposal.

Somehow Birdie managed to pick her way over the piles of rubbish to the broken fence. Soggy, blackened sacks and battered boxes of ruined stock lay everywhere. Don was working tirelessly amongst them, like Aggie, in perpetual movement, as his breath curled white in the cold morning.

'Brigid!' He pushed back his dishevelled hair that no longer had a middle parting or any parting at all. His face was dirt-smeared and his overall covered in stains. 'Have you seen Mother?' he shouted excitedly, as he made his way towards her.

Birdie stood before him, seeing him as she had never seen him before. He seemed a stranger almost, someone she didn't really know.

'Thank goodness you're here,' he panted breathlessly,

waving his arms at the cluttered yard. 'Just look at the state of things, though God only knows how the fire started. We lost everything in the shop, but Mother had the presence of mind to close the passage door. Much of this we can salvage with a little attention. We haven't a moment to spare, not a moment.' Pushing his dirty hands down his overall, he blinked at her. 'Well, my dear, you'll need to change. That coat is most unsuitable for cleaning.' He gave an impatient tut. 'But then, you couldn't have known about the fire, of course.'

Birdie glanced down at her best blue coat. She'd worn it today as she wanted to equal Lydia in appearance. A silly, vain whim, perhaps, but after what Pat had told her, she felt she needed to be at an advantage. Don hadn't even remarked on how she looked but how unsuitably she was dressed for this emergency.

Pulling herself up, she fixed him with a straight gaze. 'No, I didn't know about the fire,' she agreed. 'Neither did I know about a lot of other things, either.'

'Other things?' he repeated vaguely, his attention barely with her as he turned to toss aside an empty sack.

'Is it true you're only marrying me because Aggie wants it?' There it was out! Said!

'What?' He almost jumped round.

'Now Aggie and Lydia have fallen out, is it true that you'd wed me for the sake of the store?' she demanded.

'You're talking in riddles,' he protested, laughing. 'Lydia and Mother may have their differences—'

'Lydia has threatened leaving and hopes you'll go with her.'

'What nonsense!' he scoffed. 'You're overwrought, my dear. Why don't you go home and rest?'

'I'm going, to be sure I am,' she agreed fiercely. 'I would have followed you to the ends of the earth if you'd asked me. All I ever wanted in return was your love. But I was never to have it, was I?' She lifted her chin proudly. 'I thank the Blessed Virgin I never had that pretty ring slid on me finger. Or the gold band that for so long has eluded me.'

'Brigid, this is not like you—'

'It is *quite* like me,' she interrupted, her heart hammering. 'Just why it took so long to dawn on me that I was being shuffled here and there for you and your mother's benefit, and for Lydia's too, I'm sure I don't know. But the penny has dropped at last and I believe there's not a word more to be said.'

She turned and hurried up the mossy steps, past Aggie and down the front stairs to the street. She could hear Don calling after her, his voice ringing out in the ripe morning air. She didn't look back, but pressed on past the steam engine and pump, still hissing and spurting water outside the burned-out interior of Thorne's General Store.

Chapter 29

Birdie walked to the East India Dock Road and caught the first tram she came to. It was headed for Aldgate and quite packed. But she found a seat by a small woman in a battered feathered hat and hoped that conversation wasn't necessary.

'Cold enough for yer, duckie?' said the woman, with a grin. 'These bloody trams are freezing. At least where I work in the laundry they got 'ot water to warm up up yer 'ands.'

Birdie listened to a few more comments that were interspersed with yawns. She was relieved when a gentle snore came from the next seat. She felt weak at the knees and a little sick. Had she really just turned her back on the Thornes? Was her prospect of marriage over once and for all?

Birdie gazed out of the dirt-spattered window, seeing very little. The warmth and the swaying and rumbling of the tram's iron-banded wheels had a soothing effect. She had taken the ride in a kind of daze, replaying each unpleasant memory in her mind as she'd fled the store. Aggie, and the sly, conniving Lydia and her outright resentment, Don and the guilt that was clearly etched on his face. How had she not seen it all before? She had even doubted Pat's word!

A green Parcel Delivery Service van barred the tram's way ahead and just managed to move off the lines, whilst a bus pulled up alongside, slowing down for new passengers. The tram didn't stop. It wouldn't end its journey until Aldgate, when the passengers would file off, having enjoyed an unbroken ride. Birdie wouldn't have cared, this morning, which direction she had gone. She wanted to be alone with her thoughts.

Twenty minutes later, the woman in the feathered hat woke up. 'Did I miss me stop?'

'No, we're nearly there.' Birdie sighed softly. What would she do when she got off? A heaviness had begun inside her, a deep hurt and humiliation. Don had betrayed her. He had been reluctant to name the day, until Aggie had insisted he do so. She had thought his Christmas Day visit had been because he loved and missed her. Now she knew that it was because Aggie had no time for Lydia and believed Birdie Connor enough of a fool to take her place.

'Come on then, gel, move yerself, we're here,' said the woman beside her, almost tipping her out of the seat. She looked at Birdie's smart blue coat and tidy appearance. 'I've got to earn a few bob to keep body and soul together, even if you ain't.'

Birdie found herself pushed off the tram and into the

cold day again. Still muttering, the woman hurried off. Birdie stood there, watching the change-round operation at the terminus, where the careful manipulation of the live overhead conductor pole was in process. The tram would now reverse its forward journey back to Poplar. Should she climb aboard again?

Then suddenly she realized she had used her last sixpence for her fare. She hadn't even recalled paying it over, but she must have. She had been so deep in thought and shock.

As she hesitated she began to pull herself together. The woman in the feather hat had looked at her enviously. But truth be told, she was no better off than the laundry worker. She'd had no wage whilst at the store and had relied on Harry and Pat's money. Lady Annabelle's generous payment had brought them up to date with the rent and stocked the larder. But now, it was up to her to start sewing again.

Birdie pushed back her shoulders. The strength was returning to her legs. It was a long walk home from Aldgate, but it would be good for her. She made her way briskly through the busy thoroughfare. She may not be engaged any more, but what kind of life would she have led with Don? Flo was right: she had been brought up with Bernadette's high standards and had been foolish enough to drop them. If she were ever to fall in love again . . .

For some reason, as she walked, Harry came to mind. He'd been out quite a lot and had stopped leaving his washing. She could guess why. His ladylove must be a very obliging person.

She envied Harry his romance. It was wonderful to be blind with love. Had Don ever felt anything for her? His kisses had always seemed so real. Could a man love two women at once?

Birdie lifted her face to the cold chill. She walked faster and faster, as if trying to leave her hurt behind. Her thoughts turned to Frank. If only he had been here, she could have told him everything. She missed him. Tears sprang to her eyes but she wouldn't let them drop.

It was much later in the afternoon when Birdie reached Westferry Road. The walk had tired her, but settled her mind a little. She found herself passing close to Ayle Street and wondered if she might call in to see Flo. But the sight of a tall figure dressed in a long, dark coat made her pause. She took a few paces more, listening to the cries of the children playing in the street. Some girls and boys had tied a rope to a lamppost and were swinging on it. They almost bumped into him as he passed. Then he seemed to disappear. Birdie walked slowly to where he had stood and looked down the narrow alley into which he must have turned.

'Did you see a tall man go down there?' she asked one of the children, who wiped his dirty mouth with the back of his hand.

'Yer, Old Nick,' laughed the boy, continuing to swing on the rope. 'If you go down there 'e'll 'ave yer, missus.' The giggling became loud laughter as the other children joined in.

Birdie had to see for herself. She walked to the opening and saw a fleeting shadow. The blood in her temples banged so hard it drowned out the children's noise. The man she had just seen was Erik.

If it really was Erik, then could Frank be close? Perhaps she had made a mistake? But she had been certain it was Erik! Should she follow him and would he lead her to Frank? There were hundreds of cuts on the island. One cut ran at the back of March Street – a decent one, where a horse and cart could drive up, or where the kids could play under the gas lamp. But this was no more than a footpath, dark and dingy and full of shadows. The house walls ended and a little light shone over the yard fences. Though it was day it was still very gloomy, the close atmosphere made worse by the smell of urine from the tumble-down closets in the yards. It was a grim area, you could smell the neglect and the hardship. And the noises coming from over the walls and fences only confirmed it: shouting, yelling, cursing and babies crying.

Birdie glanced suspiciously at each hole in a fence or gap in a wall. Could she be mistaken? But she had been certain the figure was Erik. In the shadow of the next block of houses she paused to listen. When she looked behind her, she had the strangest feeling. Was she imagining being watched?

Then a thud came from nearby. A hand went over her mouth. A moment later she was forced into a space in the wall. Big arms were around her, preventing her from struggling and her assailant spoke in a foreign tongue. Eventually, almost unable to breath, she stopped resisting.

Gradually he peeled his hand away. 'Do not scream,' he whispered. 'Be quiet.'

Birdie strained to see his face, covered by the black beard and the rim of the dark hat. 'Wh . . . what have you done with Frank?' she stammered. 'Is he all right? Where's my brother?'

There was an uncertain pause before he snatched his hand away. She was keenly aware of his powerful presence, so close that he could easily grab her again. 'You must come. I take you to him,' he growled in a voice that sounded anything but friendly.

Birdie could just see the long aquiline nose and glinting, close-set eyes. His black beard was cut shorter than she remembered, but it was the menacing aura that came from him that frightened her the most. It was easy to see why the kids in the street had called him 'Old Nick'.

'Have you been spying on me?' she demanded, realizing that he must have planned to trap her.

'Your brother sent me,' he muttered in a thick accent, and Birdie knew he was lying.

She stepped back. 'G . . . go away. Leave me alone.' She glanced right and left down the alley. It was deserted. The Tall Ship wasn't far away. If she ran, could she reach the pub without him catching her? Once she was inside it, he wouldn't dare to follow.

But in the blink of an eye he grabbed her and though she twisted and turned, nothing she did could make him let go. All the while he was muttering in a foreign tongue and she had the feeling he'd expected her to go with him. She wriggled all the more, trying to slide her wrist from his grasp. Then suddenly she heard the rattle of a cart and clip-clop of hoofs. A woman's call rang out and Birdie recognized Inga's voice.

A cruel smile passed over Erik's lips.

Chapter 30

Harry frowned. He'd lost sight of Birdie. She hadn't seen him striding towards her, even though he'd attempted a wave and shouted a greeting. A big bugger had stepped between them and the noise of the kids swinging on the lamppost had drowned out his shout.

He was in good spirits, for after a satisfactory day's labour, he'd sunk a jug or two at the Tall Ship. There had been a bit of a knees-up in the not-so-salubrious ale house and the Sally Army had called by, in the form of a very presentable young female officer. She'd gathered up the generous offerings; him and his mates had doled out a tanner or two, knowing that the bunce went to the homeless and starving. He'd always put his hand in his pocket for the Sally; after all, it was on charity he'd survived as a boy. And with a pretty smile included today, he'd spent a good five minutes almost getting himself converted. But he'd not go down that road. He'd had enough of wearing uniforms for a lifetime. Not that he objected to the blue and red, especially when it was glued so attractively to a female form. But he wasn't a Bible basher, though he had great respect for his Maker. Nor did he have the desire to belt out a hymn or bang a drum. He'd made her laugh, though. And given her one of his best winks. And when he'd walked out into the cold day, he'd felt a good deal better than he had before.

It was then he'd seen Birdie, her small, but unmistakable, figure. But then, quite suddenly, she'd disappeared.

Now, as he stopped a few feet away from the alley where he'd seen her, he was baffled. Perhaps she had called at Ayle Street where Flo lived. It was not far off. He glanced down the alley. It led west, away from her homeward route to March Street and so it was unlikely she'd go that way. But something drew him and he narrowed his eyes against the shadows. He could smell the stench and muck. It was the kind of alley the dock dollies used . . . not a safe place to walk . . . and then, as he was about to turn, two figures appeared.

The sight of Birdie in the big man's grip turned Harry's stomach. At the far end of the alley was a cart and horses, and though the rider wore breeches, the voice calling was a woman's. The moment he gave chase, Birdie was lifted and thrown over the bastard's shoulder.

'You!' Harry yelled, gaining fast on his quarry. 'Put her down, you damned devil!'

She was all screams and defiance, beating his back with

her fists, and Harry effortlessly increased his pace. With a final spurt and a cry of anger, he flung himself forward.

'Run!' he yelled to Birdie, as all three of them crashed down, though no sooner had he gathered breath than a fist as hard as a frying pan flattened his cheek. He aimed one back and it found its mark, knocking the fellow back with a thump against the wall. But he steamed in again, too soon, and collided with a punch that lifted him off his feet. All his breath left him as he reeled like a drunkard on the damp, mossy ground.

'Damn you,' he muttered, dizzy with pain, and another boot to his ribs took what air was left inside him. He lay breathless and in agony, and squirmed away from another vicious kick. But the weight of it sent his arm almost out of its socket. He tried to decide if he was capable of standing and knew in a flash he wasn't.

Raking in a deep breath, he braced himself and lowered his head. With a cry of desperation rather than anger, he threw himself sideways at the bugger's shins. The fall glued them together and they rolled, first Harry on top and then the other man. Over and over they went, in the filth and muck. Harry fought and cursed, and kicked when he had the chance, but soon he lost any feeling and all he could do was spit venom, and listen in shame to his wheezing breaths.

Release came, surprisingly, in the form of a police whistle. Harry lay there, watching the flight of his assailant as he sped down the alley and jumped aboard the wagon. As soon as it had disappeared, two navy-blue-clad legs filled his vision.

'You all right, son?' The policeman extended a hand. 'Come on, give us yer arm and I'll help yer up.'

Harry let himself be aided, but he quickly shook himself free and leaned stiffly against the wall. 'Reckon I owe you, mate,' he rasped to the young copper.

'Know them two, did yer? Right lot o' 'ooligans they looked like.'

Birdie was standing to one side of the policeman, now, and Harry saw the warning in her eyes. 'No, must've chanced their luck, thinking I had a few bob.' He gave a grim laugh. 'But I only got a hole in me pocket, see?' He pulled out the lining and added, 'I was taking a short cut after a bevvy at the Tall Ship. Well, to be honest, I probably supped one or two too many.'

'They must've followed yer. Seen the same trick, I have, up Mile End,' said the constable. 'The crafty buggers.'

Harry nodded approvingly. 'Yes, I 'spect so, Officer.'

'And this young lady? What you got to say for yourself, miss? It's a rough neighbourhood you're in 'ere.'

'I was visiting Ayle Street,' Birdie lied quickly, her glance catching Harry's eye. 'Lucky it was, Constable, that I saw you and your whistle saved this young man from further injury.'

'Lucky indeed for 'im,' the bobby nodded, 'but it's a shame you can't say who it was. Sure you can't put a moniker to the face?'

'Sorry, no,' said Harry with a painful shrug.

'Best keep to the main streets,' the constable told him, 'else you might not be so lucky next time.'

'Aye, that I will.'

'And as for you, miss . . .'

Harry limped off, unable to do anything else, but leave Birdie to her lecture. He would wait for her in the next street, and he turned at the corner, raising his hand as the bobby's back was turned. A second or two later he stopped to grip his knees, breathing in slowly and waiting for the air to return to his lungs.

'Harry!'

He heard her call and straightened, trying to disguise the

fact he was still winded. He hoped the lump on his chin wasn't as ugly as it felt.

'Oh, Harry,' she gasped, clutching his arm, 'just look at your poor face! It's all black and blue. And you've a lump on your jaw that's sure to swell more. Oh, the very devil, he was, but you gallantly fought him off.'

'I would've been brown bread but for you fetching the copper,' he replied, undergoing an immediate cure at her light touch. 'I don't mind admitting that I haven't had such tumble since my army days and find meself a bit out of practice.'

'You fought like a dervish,' she insisted, 'with you so light of frame and him such a big oaf. It was Erik, see? And the woman in the breeches. They were trying to trick me but I caught him out instantly. Frank promised me he'd never send the great eejit again.'

'I guessed who it was,' Harry admitted, 'and couldn't think of much else to say to the copper. Didn't want to drop Frank in it.'

'You said not a word out of place,' she breathed, and his heart gave a skip of delight at the lingering feel of her fingers. 'Oh, thank you, sweet Jesus, for this man's quick thinking. Where would I be if you hadn't come along? And so fast too. Harry, you were the wind itself.'

Though enjoying every moment of her gratitude, he thought it unwise to linger. As they walked he listened to her story again and fitted the pieces together well before they reached home. He was convinced that not only was Frank's freedom at stake but that now his life was in danger too.

Pat looked up accusingly from where he sat at the kitchen table, stuffing a lump of cheese in his mouth. 'Dad's gone down the Quarry,' he complained, as Birdie walked in. 'Said he'd not wait around any longer or he'd die of starvation. And all I could find in the larder was this . . .' His jaw fell open when he looked up to see Harry. 'Blooming heck, what's happened to you?'

'Shift your lazy self,' Birdie ordered at once, 'and pour some cold water in the bowl.'

Pat jumped to his feet, almost tripping over as he stared at Harry. 'Blimey, mate, what have you done?'

'Nothing.' Harry tried to grin as Birdie pushed him down on the chair that Pat had just vacated. 'It's just a scratch.'

'You've got a shiner,' Pat said admiringly, 'and a cheek as fat as a football.'

'Bet it's not spoiled me good looks,' Harry tried with a chuckle, but Birdie wagged a finger.

'Don't go laughing or it'll hurt all the more. Pat, where's that water?'

Soon she was applying the wet rag gently to Harry's wounds. Then she took a small bottle of witch hazel from the cupboard that stood by the Collis Browne's and the friars balsam.

'A dab of this will help,' she assured Harry, smoothing the sweet-smelling restorative over the bruising. 'Then perhaps my idle brother will find the strength to make us a cup of tea.'

Pat looked quite put out. 'I'm not idle! Seeing as there was no dinner ready—'

'And what about the broth on the stove? Were you and Dad expecting it to jump out of the pot and down your throats all by itself? If it wasn't for Harry that dinner would still be there in a week. I was on my way back from Flo's when I saw Erik, and he tried to carry me off – and he would have if Harry hadn't saved me.'

'Crikey!' Pat drew up a chair and sat down as Birdie gave an account of all that had happened.

'Did you really fight him off?' Pat asked Harry.

'It wasn't so much a fight, Pat, it was more of a dodge or two,' Harry said with a shrug.

'Oh, it wasn't like that at all,' Birdie scolded. 'Harry gave such a tackle that he brought us all down and rescued me, not caring a jot for the size of the great mauler. And it was just luck there was a copper in the next street and I got him to blow his whistle.'

'Just in time too,' agreed Harry with a nod. 'Or else the big ox would've punched all me lights out.'

'But they jumped on the cart,' continued Birdie, 'raced away, and left the bobby none the wiser.'

'If I'd been along with you,' Pat burst out, 'I'd have hung on to him while you gave him what for.'

'We'd have made mincemeat of him,' Harry agreed, his eyes twinkling under his bruises.

'Oh, if I hadn't been so full up with me own self and getting married an' all, I might have paid more attention to Frank and he'd never have got in with these ruffians,' Birdie sighed regretfully. 'But what did they want with me?'

'Must be a reason they need you,' Harry ventured. 'They had it planned, must have. And if Frank didn't turn up, it was because he couldn't.'

'You don't mean . . .?' Birdie gasped.

'I ain't suggesting they've harmed him, but your brother may have stopped short at something against his nature.'

'Like thieving or murdering,' Pat whispered. 'Or siding along with the Ruskies.'

'Oh, sweet Jesus!' cried Birdie.

'If only we knew *exactly* where Frank was,' Harry muttered.

'But I've got all those roads in my head,' Pat said eagerly. 'They might have taken away my sight, but I heard things and smelled them. Reckon I could find the way again.'

'No!' Birdie exclaimed. 'It's too dangerous.'

'I've got to do it for Frank.'

She looked at Harry and though he said nothing, she knew they were both thinking that Pat was their one chance of finding Frank.

Chapter 31

The next morning Flo called round.

'What are you doing over this way?' Birdie asked as she let her friend in.

'I heard from a neighbour about the fire in Poplar. I was worried about you. Are you all right?'

'Yes, but it's over between me and Don.'

'Because of a fire?'

'No. Come in and I'll tell you the story. Dad's just going out,' Birdie said as she led the way to the kitchen, 'so we can sit and talk with a cuppa.'

When they were seated at the table, Flo asked again, 'Is it true – the shop burned down?'

'Yes, but Aggie has started up business next door.'

Flo listened as Birdie told her the whole story, explaining Lydia's outburst and Aggie's manipulation, and finally her confrontation with Don. Flo's jaw dropped as Birdie explained that she had told Don there was no more to be said between them.

'Oh, it's just one of your spats,' said Flo dismissively. 'You wait and see. It'll be just like last time.'

'What do you mean, last time?' Birdie was rather disappointed that Flo didn't seem shocked at her walking out on Don.

'When you quarrelled over Frank.'

'Yes, but I never ended it then. This time I mean to. I'm

certain he's been unfaithful.'

Flo couldn't hide a giggle. 'You sound like an old married lady.'

'It ain't funny, Flo. Me chance to get married has really gone.'

'You make it sound like a bus you were waiting to catch. In that case, there's always another one stopping,' Flo smirked.

'I won't change my mind.'

'He'll be round with his smooth talking,' Flo said warningly. 'He always charms you, somehow. Even when you saw him with Lydia he sweet-talked you into believing he was innocent.'

'You seem to be suggesting we weren't happy,' Birdie objected.

'Birdie, if I'm to be honest, I don't think you ever was.'

Birdie stared at her friend. Could she be right? 'Oh, Flo, if what you say is true, have I wasted all those years?'

'You'll know, love, next time,' said Flo, sipping her tea.

'*If* there's a next time.'

'Don't be daft, there plenty more fish in the sea. Talking of wet fish, do you think Lydia would really leave the store? And would Don go with her?'

'I don't know,' Birdie said truthfully. 'And I don't care now. But it's poor little James I feel sorry for. He's really attached to Don.' Sometimes she felt as though Lydia and James had more of a right to Don than herself. If the war hadn't come along and Stephen was still alive, what would have happened? But the war had changed everything, leaving Lydia a widow and Don forced to leave his beloved railways to take Stephen's place at the store. Birdie sighed. 'It has to be said that Aggie rules the roost and has a hold on Don that I don't think even Lydia can break.'

'And as soon as Aggie discovered Lydia wanted her own way with the business,' continued Flo, nodding, 'the writing was on the wall for Lydia.'

'And it was all going on behind me back.'

'I should be angry if I was you,' said Flo fervently. 'You've got enough evidence from Lydia's lips, saying that if Casanova had any sense he'd go with her.'

Birdie stared down at her ringless finger. 'When I put that to Don he wondered where I'd got such an idea.'

'That's the kind of thing a guilty man would say.'

'How do you know that?'

Flo grinned. 'Because Reg says it every time he's home late and I ask him if he stopped for a drink, spending our hard-earned pennies. But when he kisses me, I know where the pennies have gone.'

'You don't seem very upset about that.'

'Because I ain't,' Flo shrugged. 'I'd rather him down the boozer once in a while than looking for excitement elsewhere.'

'You're lucky,' Birdie assured her, feeling a little better now. 'You've got the perfect marriage. I'm envious, don't you see? That's what I want, what you've got with Reg.'

'You can borrow him anytime, you're me mate,' chuckled Flo, then looking seriously at Birdie she added, 'You're no one's fool, Birdie Connor. And one day you'll meet someone who appreciates you.'

'Listen,' Birdie murmured, lowering her voice, 'there's something else I have to tell you.'

'Blimey, what is it?'

'It's just that yesterday, Harry and me—'

'You and Harry?' Flo gasped, clapping her hand over her mouth. 'Oh my God, I knew it!'

'No, you don't understand,' Birdie hesitated, but Flo looked on the point of explosion.

'You crafty moo! Keeping quiet all this time. Me and Reg always thought Harry was a good bloke. Didn't understand how you was so taken up with such a cold fish as Don. And you half had me believing that Harry was walking out some girl when it was *you* all along.' Flo threw her arms in the air. 'Well, all I can say is, I'm glad your wedding's off to old sober-sides and you've decided to have a fling. It's about time you had a bit of fun.'

'It's not what you think—' Birdie began again but Flo was laughing delightedly.

'All right, keep your hair on,' she grinned, sliding her arms around Birdie and hugging her. 'I forgive you for not telling me, even though I'm your best friend. I'd have done the same meself, come to think of it. No wonder you ain't heartbroken. You was in love with the right bloke all along.'

Birdie was squeezed half to death as Flo giggled, refusing to believe one word of protest she made. 'But, Flo, listen—'

Flo looked at the clock on the mantel and gasped. 'I've got to go now. Just look at the time! There's my shopping to do before the kids come home from their grandma's. And I promised them they could have their friends back for tea, so I'll just say goodbye to your dad and be on my way.'

She whirled her way out of the house and Birdie was left to wonder why it was that her friend had jumped so quickly to such a conclusion. What was Flo thinking of, believing that she and Harry were – well, *together*? She had tried to make it plain that they weren't, but Flo had been convinced. Birdie washed up the cups and looked out on the yard. Her cheeks went pink as she thought of what Flo had said. *You was in love with the right bloke all along.* But that was impossible. She didn't think of Harry in a romantic way . . . but why was she blushing? Anyway, Harry was already taken.

Harry knocked off early that evening. His crew, under Ned Shorter, could be relied upon in his absence to complete the digging of a new trench on the Blackwall site. He'd done his bit for the day, having been there since crack of dawn and marked out the land. Now it was a quarter to five and he'd arranged to meet Pat at the top of the Westferry Road at five o'clock. He'd borrowed a bicycle off Ned today, an old one but serviceable, and was pleased to save himself extra footwork. With what he had in mind, the scouting might prove considerable. Lucky the weather was holding out – no rain – and he stuffed his work-bag into the basket that hung by worn leather straps to the iron frame. Pulling on his rough jacket and sliding Ned's bicycle clips round his ankles, he pushed off, amused that he should be riding such an antiquated contraption.

But he soon forgot that he hadn't ridden a bike for years. The river breeze was refreshing but cold. The muscles in his calves and thighs rebelled at first, then relaxed as he got into rhythm. It was usually his arms and back that took the strain whilst digging. Bicycling was pure luxury, so much so, he wondered why he hadn't done it before. But he was a foot soldier in the army and earned himself the title of Lacky. It was Lacky, run here, or Lacky dodge there, and yesterday he was pleased that he still had his speed. That bugger Erik might have had an edge on the brawn, but his bulk had held him back.

As he steered himself through the evening traffic, Harry considered the route he was to take with Pat. They would begin in Stepney, as Pat would recall this easy enough, before being blindfolded. If they could find no clues there, they would press on to the Commercial Road. Then it would be a right turn to the river, easy enough on their bicycles, and Pat seemed certain yesterday he could guide them.

As soon as Harry saw Pat, he put down his boots and skidded to a halt.

'Do you call that a bicycle?' Pat grinned as he sat on his

own bike by the dock wall.

'Got to keep up with you, youngster.'

'Where did you find it, the British Museum?'

Harry laughed. 'It's solid enough.'

'Thought you were going to buy a horse and cart.'

'This will do for now. Did you tell your sister you'd be late?'

'Didn't say what we was up to. Don't want a girl tagging along.'

Harry hid his smile. 'We'll see first, how the land lies,' he agreed, 'and relay our findings to your sister. But now let's be off to Stepney.'

'No need,' Pat shrugged confidently. 'Let's go straight to Narrow Street.'

'Are you sure?' Harry was alarmed and thought the boy too eager. 'We'd be coming at Shadwell from an easterly direction.'

'I can do it,' said Pat dismissively. 'Easy as wink your eye.'

Harry paused, the noise of the horses and carts and motorized traffic creating such a din that he agreed, though his instinct was to start at Stepney.

Together they found Narrow Street. Here stood the lodging-houses for the workers of the river: the coal-heavers, the porters, the lascars, the seamen who frequented the areas of Wapping and Shadwell, a stone's throw from the gambling houses and vice dens of Limehouse.

Harry made certain to examine all directions, expecting almost that tall figure of yesterday to leap out. But this time he was ready. A sturdy length of lead pipe was in his bag, and he wouldn't hesitate to use it.

Pat was annoyed with himself. They had travelled miles in their search for Frank, from Narrow Street to Cable Street, and the shop he had been so certain of with its ice cream and tobacco smells and the lascars trotting past in their flimsy cotton pants and sandals. He knew the place whilst blindfolded, but with sight restored, he'd been at a loss as to how to continue.

In desperation they'd reversed to Wapping Wall, passed Tobacco Dock and ended up at the Dock Stairs. Still nothing had seemed familiar, and Harry had suggested they return to Narrow Street. Pat was in sweats of confusion and, worst of all, a yellowy mist was setting in. And now they had stopped, breathing hard and heavy, and he still had no idea where to go.

'Wait here,' Harry called across. 'We'll be going on no more adventures tonight, Pat. There will be a blanket of fog around us, soon. When you've got your breath, we'll make for home.'

As they paused, the water-laden air shifting like candle-smoke around their legs, Pat felt defeated. He couldn't even see the houses properly now. Not that he wanted to. For under those smoke-blackened roofs and behind the shuttered windows, were hovels. Shadwell was a pitiful place. In daylight they'd seen thin, ragged figures in doorways, with death and disease on their faces. Women and children, bruised and blackened, moving like ghosts under the cranes and hydraulic lifts of the docks. As dusk had fallen, a stretcher of sorts, carried by four hollow-faced men, had crossed their path. The body was still, bloated from the river and stinking. Harry had urged Pat past, but his legs had been shaking and still were.

'I'm sorry, Harry,' Pat said woefully. 'I've lost us.'

'We'll try again in the light,' Harry assured him.

'I thought I'd find it.'

'Let's be on our way,' Harry called to him as two figures swayed towards them in the mist. Their curses carried loudly in the air and Pat was on his saddle in a second and riding fast into the swirling, thickening veils.

But it seemed a lifetime before they found the highway

again. By the time they reached Poplar, Pat had lost heart as well as confidence. Without the light of a Tilley, they dismounted, and the strange fog, turning from yellow into pearly grey, clung to their skin and clothes.

'I dunno where I went wrong,' Pat admitted as they walked the lonely street. 'I was sure I knew the way to go.'

'We started in the wrong place,' Harry replied gently. 'Next time, we'll begin at Stepney.'

'But what if I still can't find the way?' Pat narrowed his eyes to search for the reassuring shape of the figure beside him. 'What do we do then? And what do I tell Birdie?'

For the next few paces Harry didn't reply. Then his voice came through the mist. 'We'll tell your sister what happened. It won't do to keep it from her.'

'She won't approve of us going without her.'

'She'll have to get a bike too if she wants to come.' Harry chuckled, but Pat was in no mood to joke.

'When's that going to be?'

'I can't say, Pat. I've got a big job on at work and left a mate there today to take my place.'

'But what about Frank?'

'Pat, I ain't got a crystal ball.'

Pat had a sinking feeling. He knew Harry was trying his best and wasn't even related to their family. He was just their lodger. But he'd become more than that. He felt like an older brother. Once more, Pat felt ashamed. He'd boasted he could find where they had Frank, thinking he knew the East End like the back of his hand. He was a messenger boy and a good one. He'd even got a promotion. The East End was his turf, his territory. He knew all the streets. But he had failed to find Frank today.

Chapter 32

Less than a week later, on the following Tuesday, there was a knock on the door. Birdie hurried to answer it, her heart beating fast. Every time there was a knock, she wondered if it was Don. She couldn't help it. Even though she'd walked out on the day of the fire, her pride had been hurt. Was Don so happy to be rid of her that he wouldn't try to win her back? Was he with Lydia, against Aggie's wishes? What had happened to the shop that Aggie intended to open? Her curiosity had almost overcome her unhappiness at times, and she had been tempted to go to Poplar just to see if the new shop had opened. But she'd been warned by Harry not to go out alone after what had happened with Erik.

Harry had confessed to going off with Pat to search for Frank. Then before she could get cross, he'd said she'd need a bicycle if she wanted to join them. That had made her smile instead!

The knock came again. 'I'm coming!' Birdie slid out the long pin that kept her hat in place and took off her hat. She almost fainted when she opened the door.

'Hello there,' Constable Rudge said meekly. 'I thought no one was in, so I knocked again, just in case.'

'What do you want?'

'It's to do with your father.'

'He ain't had an accident, has he?'

'Don't know,' the constable replied, trying to look over her shoulder. 'He was taken ill at the Quarry.'

Birdie felt her legs go weak. 'Was it one of his turns?'

'All I know is, he was taken by ambulance to the accident hospital at Poplar. We were informed and so here I am, doing me good deed for the day.'

'I'll go there now,' Birdie said, and was about to close the door, when the policeman stuck the tip of his boot inside.

'Er . . . don't suppose you've had any news of your—'

'You cheeky bugger!' Birdie exclaimed, her eyes bright with anger. 'That's all you've come for, ain't it, to find out about Frank? I thought you was minding your manners and almost believed you were human. Now take your foot out and clear off!' She slammed the door hard, hearing an 'Ouch' from outside. She wouldn't mind betting he'd come hoping to spot Frank. He certainly hadn't called out of the goodness of his heart. Well, what did she expect? Coppers were coppers, she fumed as she ran to the kitchen, trying to think what to do first.

What had happened at the Quarry? Who had been with Wilfred when he was taken ill? Was it a turn? She grabbed her hat again and left. Luckily a bus came along within minutes. She sat there clutching her bag tight, an ache of worry inside her as the bus neared the hospital. When she saw its tall chimneys rise in the sky opposite the East India Dock gate, she said a Hail Mary, remembering how a prayer was first on her mother's lips in times of trouble.

The blue-uniformed sister was firm, but reassuring, even though Wilfred looked a shadow of himself tucked under the white sheet of the hospital bed. There were other men around him in the ward, most of them looking into the distance with confused expressions, or asleep.

'This is a temporary bed as the hospital is primarily for accidents, Miss Connor,' the sister told her after Birdie had found the right ward. There were so many, all of them named after the shipping lines that sponsored them, like Cunard. She'd been given directions, but her panic had made her lose the way.

Together with the nurse, she stood at the doors looking

across to her father's bed. 'Was it one of his turns he had?' she asked anxiously.

'If you mean a seizure, we think so. The landlord of a public house called the Quarry found him. By the time your father arrived here, the worst was over. How long has he had this problem?'

'Not long.'

'And the cough?' The sister frowned. 'It seems very troublesome.'

'Yes, it's got worse. Even the Collis Browne's doesn't help as much.'

'The doctor will give him a thorough examination. You can sit with him for a few moments. Don't expect him to wake as he's had something to calm him.'

Birdie took a seat on a rough wooden chair squeezed by the bed. Her father suddenly looked so thin and small, yet she had only said goodbye to him this morning. If only she had made him eat breakfast. If only she hadn't gone out. But she couldn't have kept him under lock and key. It was dreadful to think of him outside the Quarry, collapsed and alone.

As he lay there, he coughed in his sleep. His chest rose and fell with difficulty. Birdie could see he was struggling to breathe. He looked so small, so vulnerable and she wanted to put her arms around him and hug him, but she knew that wouldn't be allowed. Instead, she bent close and whispered she loved him.

After a while, the sister tapped her on the shoulder. 'I must ask you to leave now. But before you go, I'd like to ask you a few questions. Come this way, please.'

Birdie followed the sister out of the ward. She felt in a daze, even though part of her had been expecting this day, in some shape or form. The Collis Browne's and castor oil and egg yolk had been of little use. Gradually the coughing had become more insistent.

'Sit down,' the sister told her, pointing to another wooden chair in a small office. The desk was piled high with notes of the patients and she could see her father's name on the front of one set of them.

'Now, can you tell me how long your father has had his cough?'

'Ever since he left work at the chemical factory years ago.'

'Oh,' said the sister darkly, writing it down. 'Is he under the care of a general practitioner?'

'Yes, Dr Tapper.'

'And what has he prescribed?'

'A restorative, he called it. A powder to mix with castor oil and the yoke of one egg'

Once again the sister frowned as she continued with her questions. Birdie answered as best she could but the smell of disinfectant and ether was making her feel sick. She had never liked hospitals, not since Bernadette had been taken to one and only baby Pat had survived. Now this one had claimed her father.

'I'm sorry, love, truly I am,' said the landlord of the Quarry, Bernie Hopper. 'He must've been waiting for his mates and I hadn't opened the doors. Sometimes I'm a bit late if we've had a busy night and the draymen ain't called.'

'Do you know what happened?' Birdie asked. She was standing at the back door of the Quarry, where the trap doors to the cellar next to the unused stables were open. The air was pungent with ale. Bernie wiped his hands on an old rag and stuffed it under one of his dirty braces. His shirt was full of stains, but he had a nice smile and had always been a good friend to her father.

'Nah. Someone was yelling and I stuck me head out and found him on the deck. He was blue in the face and his legs were going ten to the dozen in all directions. I got a bloke to help me hold him, make sure he didn't bang his head and we lifted him inside till the ambulance came.'

'It was a seizure, Bernie.'

'Ain't surprised. There was this froth coming from his mouth.'

'I should have kept him in.'

Bernie laughed shortly. 'You'd have had to tie him down. Don't mind saying that your dad is a stubborn old sod. What's the 'Ospital gonna do with 'im?'

'The sister didn't say. She's worried about his cough.'

'Reckon it's them bloody fags. He smokes like a chimney, one after the other. Told him he was choking himself but, course, he don't take no notice of no one. Give him me best when you see him.' Bernie took the rag from under his braces and swept the drip from his nose. 'This cold don't help, either.'

Birdie made her way home, thinking of her father in the hospital bed. There were so many ill people around him. He wasn't awake to see them, but when he recovered he wouldn't like it. Would the doctor be able to help him? How long would it be before he came home? Would the nurses see that he ate his meals?

Once home, Birdie went upstairs to Wilfred's room. The air was stuffy and smelled of roll-ups. She opened the sash window, which always creaked in protest. Her hands went over the patchwork quilt that she had made for his bed. Dark green and blues, his favourite colours, a Christmas present she'd made last year to brighten the sombre browns. He'd said it was too good to use and folded it away. Birdie had found it and put it over again. It was like a game they played, him wanting his way and she trying to get hers. If only she hadn't nagged him so much. She knew he was getting frailer and he feared the future. She felt very guilty. She had done nothing to help. Wilfred had been very upset when she'd told him about the registry office wedding. It had been a terrible disappointment to know that his only daughter, a good Catholic, intended to wed by licence.

Her father had been right. She had forsaken her values. Why had she been prepared to give them up? It was, she had believed, because she loved Don. But was it really the fear of being left on the shelf?

Birdie took a deep breath, fighting with the sob in her throat. She hadn't told Wilfred she had broken up with Don. But was the harm done already?

Pat took the news badly, especially when, the next day, Wilfred's condition deteriorated.

'He's been moved to the isolation hospital at New Cross,' they were told when they visited.

'Has he got something catching?' Birdie asked when they spoke to the doctor.

'We don't know,' he replied briskly. 'His cough is causing concern. Here, we treat accidents and are not equipped to give him the right treatment.'

'But New Cross is a long way.'

'I can't help you, I'm afraid. The nurse will give you your father's belongings.' The doctor strode off leaving the nurse to hand them a brown bag tied with string.

Birdie felt so angry. They were being treated as though Wilfred didn't matter. 'I'll take the bus tomorrow,' Birdie decided as they walked home.

'I'll come with you.'

'What about work?'

'Willie can run my messages. I'll cycle over and ask him tonight.'

'Will Willie do that?'

'I've done it for him before.'

Birdie didn't argue with this. People who had scarlet fever and typhus were sent to New Cross. It was said that many children never came home, and those that did were always weak and pasty-looking, just like those who had survived the flu outbreak. Was their father seriously ill? She wanted Pat with her.

'Frank's got to be told,' Pat said then. 'It's not fair he doesn't know. Oh, if only I'd been able to find the way and we'd been able to get him.'

'It's not your fault, love. Don't get down in the dumps. Being miserable won't help our dad. We've got to cheer him up.'

But that night she lay in bed and couldn't think of anything but Wilfred. Why had he been taken to the isolation hospital? What disease did he have? She had so many questions and there was no one to answer them.

The next day it was Harry who again came to the rescue.

'I'll take you on me cart,' he offered them as they were about to set out for the bus.

'Your cart?' Birdie was surprised. Although Harry had mentioned he'd like to buy a horse and cart, she hadn't thought he would as his job was only digging roads.

'Bought a nice apple and sauce from me pal who loaned me the pony and trap. Albert's only a plodder, a chestnut named after the old Prince. Very faithful, see, like himself was to the Queen.'

'Is he outside?' Pat asked eagerly.

'No. He's stabled at the smithy's off Manchester Road. It won't take us long to walk there.'

Birdie put on her hat and pushed a long pin through it. 'Well, just this once, Harry. We can't always be calling on you.' Ever since Flo had got the wrong end of the stick about her and Harry, she had felt embarrassed and guilty at all the help Harry gave them. He was very kind and a good friend, but there was nothing more to their friendship. After all, he had his own sweetheart.

So it was that Harry introduced them to Albert, a

powerful-looking chestnut with a dirty-brown mane, who had once been owned by the breweries. The old horse whinnied over the half-gate at the smithy and Harry led him out to the cart. When Albert was finally in harness, he helped Birdie up on the front, whilst Pat climbed in the back.

It was a long journey, and cold, but eventually they arrived at New Cross and the tall, forbidding-looking hospital building built of red-brick and stone.

The same strong disinfectant smell filled the main hall, and Birdie felt her stomach lurch as she enquired after her father.

'Mr Connor is being assessed,' said the woman who sat in a small office, a half-window to stare through. 'And for everyone's safety the ward is closed when a new patient arrives.'

'You mean we can't see him?'

'Not yet.'

'But what has he got?' Birdie was annoyed to think they had come all this way and were being now being prevented from a visit.

'As soon as we know, you'll be informed.' She slipped her glasses back on her long nose and shrugged. 'I'm sorry, but we have to be careful. This is an isolation hospital, you know, not like Poplar where it's mainly accidents.'

'So when can we see him?' Birdie was determined to get an answer.

'Try again tomorrow.'

'Try?' Birdie gasped, forgetting herself. 'Are you saying we might not be able to see him even then?'

The woman looked up, stony-faced. 'Unfortunately I can't see into the future. If I could, my job would be a lot easier.' With that she snapped the book in front of her shut, leaving Birdie open-mouthed.

★

As she sat on the front of the cart, with Albert's broad rump swaying in front of them, Birdie's anger was still simmering.

'Don't worry,' Harry told her, 'I'm sure it's for his own good. And probably everyone else's too.'

'Yes, but the cheek of that woman, talking as though I was daft.'

'We could've gone round the back,' shouted Pat from his seat in the rear. 'See if we could spot Dad and then at least we'd know he was all right.'

'He could be anywhere in that place. It was all corridors and long passages. No, we'll go again tomorrow, and I'll insist we see him.'

Birdie pulled up the collar of her coat as the cart rolled along. She was determined that, whatever anyone said, she would be at her father's side the next day.

Chapter 33

Later that evening, as they sat at the supper table, Harry said, 'I've read in the papers that in Russia the tide may be turning in favour of the Bolsheviks. Course, it may not be true but it's a new rumour.'

'What does that mean?' asked Pat.

'The Red Army is said to be defeating the White Army. on many fronts It's believed amongst a lot of people that the Whites have been betrayed by the British Government. Again, it's only hearsay – and propaganda has been a huge part of the Russian war – but if our friends Inga and Erik get wind of it, who knows what they'll get panicked into doing.'

'And what happens to Frank then?' Birdie asked anxiously.

Harry leaned forward, placing his arms on the table. 'I think tonight we should draw a map of the area from Stepney to Shadwell. Between you and me, Pat, we'll mark out a route between, which will help us get a clearer idea of where it might be likely that Frank is kept. We know for sure this place they're keeping him in must have a back yard for their cart and all the materials they have brought from Stepney. We also know it's not a waterfront building or warehouse. This limits the possibilities even more.'

'Are you planning on looking?' Pat asked eagerly.

Harry nodded slowly.

'If you can wait till Saturday, I'll come with you!'

'You'd better ask your sister.'

Birdie was silent. Could they find Frank before it was too late? Once again, they were relying on Harry to help them, though none of them knew if Frank was still alive. And even if he was, how could Harry hope to free him from these desperate people?

'There seems little we can do for Wilfred, but at least we can still search for Frank with the aim of rescuing him. Now we have Albert it will be easier.' Harry said quietly. 'Just two men with spades and shovels in their cart won't stand out. Pat can wear my old clobber, with a cap pulled down over his face, so there's no chance of him being recognized.'

'And what of me?' Birdie demanded, although it was only bravado. 'I don't want to be sitting here all on me own, wondering what's happened to you.' She knew Harry was right. She would only slow their progress.

'You'll need to visit your father.'

'Yes, but that don't stop me worrying about you two.'

'We'll be back before dark,' Harry assured her. 'And that's a promise.'

'You can say your prayers, ask Him upstairs to keep us safe,' Pat laughed, mischief in his eyes. 'You're good at them.'

Birdie smiled wistfully. 'Pat, you must keep right by Harry and you mustn't do anything daft.'

'You got me word, he'll be safe with me,' said Harry. 'We'll start off early and draw no attention to our activities.'

But Birdie couldn't stop thinking about their plans as she left them to draw the map. There was no guarantee they would find the street or the house, and even if they did, there was just one man and a boy against desperate, revolutionary people, used to fighting and trouble.

Her thoughts then turned to Wilfred. Was everything being done for him that could be? She felt so helpless. But she would find out tomorrow.

The next day, after Harry and Pat had left the house, Birdie caught the bus to New Cross. She was preparing for a battle with the authorities, but nothing would stop her seeing her father. So she was more than surprised to gain admittance to the wards, though from another, more approachable secretary.

'I'm afraid it has to be a short visit,' a nurse told Birdie as she was shown along a corridor with ornate arches.

'Did the doctor find out what's wrong with him?' Birdie asked for what felt like the hundredth time.

'Your father caught a cold,' said the nurse briskly, indicating a small room. 'So unfortunately we've not been able to complete our investigations as the doctor ordered complete rest. Now follow me and I'll give you some protective clothing to wear.' In the tiny room, which was very cold and smelled highly of disinfectant that seemed to come from a large white sink in one corner, she provided a white cape and mask. 'We ask visitors to wear this to prevent infection, and you mustn't touch your father or go near but sit on the benches provided, a safe distance away.'

Birdie felt very upset. Why were there all these rules? When at last she was shown to a side ward wearing the protective clothing, she found Wilfred lying on a long bed, wrapped in blankets.

'Dad, oh Dad!' Birdie gasped under her mask.

'Please sit down,' the nurse said quietly. 'Mr Connor has just had his medicine, so he may seem drowsy.'

Birdie sat on a hard wooden bench, which in itself made the visit uncomfortable and unnatural. The nurse was right, Birdie thought miserably. Wilfred seemed confused, not recognizing her, and it was all she could do not to rip off the mask and run to him.

But she knew she had to be strong for his sake. As she sat there in her strange cape and mask, Wilfred spoke ramblingly, oblivious of her presence. Her shoulders drooped. It was clear that whatever illness Wilfred had, it was not likely to go away quickly.

Saturday had arrived, and Harry hoped the cold day would remain clear and bright, but the tell-tale signs of mist were already threading the river air, as Albert pulled them along. Though Pat insisted he was certain of the way, Harry urged caution. He still hoped to find some tradesman or resident who might provide a much-needed clue to this foreign element. Any ammunition they could find against them might help in Frank's release – though Harry often found himself wondering if Frank had still survived.

Had their failure to capture Birdie resulted in Frank becoming a burden? It was easy to dispose of a corpse; bodies washed up from the river were often unrecognizable and untraceable. Perhaps Frank would never be heard of again. Yet, if by some miracle he still lived and was kept a prisoner, how could he be freed? Harry had no idea. But what was clear to him was the voice inside, urging him on to search for this man he didn't know, but who felt as familiar to him as a brother. A good man, he believed, but misled. A man who cared for his family, yet was parted from them. A soldier, like himself, who'd fought loyally, yet was labelled a deserter.

'This is it,' cried Pat beside him, jolting Harry from his thoughts. 'Look, Stepney Green, where Inga bashed the bruiser over his head.'

Harry pulled Albert to the side of the road, under the eaves of the tumbled dwellings. The air smelled of bread and bagels, of ripe fruit piled on the barrows of the coster-mongers as they competed with the cries of the gypsy women selling their lucky twists of heather.

'And you remember nothing more after they put you in the cart?' Harry asked.

'It was pitch-black under the blindfold. Like I said, I used my ears.'

Harry nodded thoughtfully. 'Well then, before we venture to Shadwell, we'll have a nose around.'

'Why waste time?' Pat demanded. 'They're not here now.'

'More haste, less speed,' Harry cautioned. 'Stepney is known for its unrest and politics. Many plans have been hatched here, Pat. Take that Russian sort, Peter the Painter. He was holed-up here in Sidney Street, him and his gang, causing a right rumpus with the law.' He turned and grinned. 'A plot you might well read of in your *Magnet*, son.'

Pat's eyes widened. 'But the gang were just burglars, shot clean through by the Scots Guards.'

'So it said in the newspapers,' Harry agreed cautiously. 'And the marksmen's bullets should have seen the end of the matter. But only two corpses were discovered. And the dead are never likely to spill the beans. Some believe the burgling was a story put out to cover the greater crimes of politics. The siege caused even Winston Churchill to pay

Sidney Street a visit. Now why should a top brass like him be bothered?'

'But that was before the war,' Pat dismissed. 'And another war isn't going to happen.'

'You think not?' Harry lifted the reins and slapped them gently. 'I wish I was as convinced. My time in the army taught me one thing. Each country is out for itself. The armistice has brought peace, but memories are short. And here, in England's great capital, there is as much greed for power as ever there was.'

'And you think our Frank is plum in the middle of all this?' Pat asked.

'Not by his own intention.' Harry urged Albert on, with the cold breeze starting to whistle around his ears. He felt uneasy, far more so than in Shadwell, where the drunks and harpies of sailor town lurked slothfully on the streets. But here, evil ran in strange guises. The dough trader on his pitch, ringing his brass bell, might transform into a foreign agent; a grinder at his wheel, pouring water over the spinning leather of his treadle, the ears and eyes of the government. A fishmonger, in his blue jersey, selling his fresh, shiny fish from his bucket, could well be in the pay of a union master.

Where were Inga and Erik in all this? What trail had they left? Who could provide a signpost? Harry examined the faces milling around them: the street traders, the gypsies, the butchers, the bakers, the tailors.

He felt a tug inside him, an instinct; it was no coincidence, he believed, that Pat was enticed here.

They had been moving in the direction of the Commercial Road, when Albert stopped, lowering his head to shake his mane and relieve his bowels.

A street urchin ran beside them. 'Can I 'ave your 'orse muck for me sack, mister?' he shouted up to Harry.

'You're welcome, son. But wait until we pass. The horse is new to me and may be skittish.'

But the boy paid no heed to the warning and darted out. The big horse tugged powerfully away, jolting every bone in Harry's body. 'Take the reins, Pat,' he shouted, jumping down to snatch the boy by his collar. 'Did you not hear my warning, young man?'

'Leg go of me, you bugger!' yelled the lad, and Harry, though annoyed, threw back his head and laughed.

'I admire your spirit,' he admitted, dangling the small body above the ground. 'But my horse could have bolted.'

'Put me down or else I'll kick yer.'

Harry laughed again. 'I'll let your collar go when you answer me this. We're on the lookout for a man and a woman, foreigners most like.'

' 'Ow should I know 'em? There's fa'sands of the bleeders round 'ere.'

'You might bring them to mind, when you see what I have in my pocket.'

The boy stopped squirming. 'How much?' he demanded, and Harry, seeing he had won the child's interest, slowly let go.

'Two bob, more than you'd earn in a month shovelling muck.'

'Give us the money then.'

Harry chuckled, sliding his hand in his pocket and jingling his change. 'I'm not that much of a fool, lad. Listen, the woman in question wears breeches and rides a covered wagon. Her companion sports a black beard and isn't the sort to tangle with. I'll give you a bob now for information and the other when I'm satisfied. An address will do. Or a name.'

'Dunno their monikers. But I seen 'em.'

'Where?'

'Round the corner. They 'ad a blackie's stablin'.'

'A blacksmith?' Harry nodded. 'Lead us there.'

'Give us the bob first.'

Harry dropped a shilling into the boy's palm. 'Remember, you'll be the loser, if you're deceiving me. This other shilling has your name on, but will stay in my pocket till I'm satisfied.' He looked sternly at the boy, then jumped back on the cart beside Pat.

'What was that about?' asked Pat.

Harry raised an eyebrow. 'Just keep your eyes glued to our guide.'

Pat did as he was instructed and Harry narrowed his eyes at the small, bobbing figure in front, who he knew at any moment might disappear and leave him to curse his stolen shilling and wasted words.

Chapter 34

'So where is this?' Harry asked the boy. They had been brought to a disused yard, where once there had been a stable. The wood of the stalls had been removed and the roof let in the light through its disintegrating beams. At the very end, a flight of worm-eaten stairs had led them downwards to a small room below. It was no more than a damp cellar alive with rats.

'It's where they was, gov, them foreigners. No one knew what they was doin' 'ere. But they upped and left one day without a word.'

'Did no one ask who they were?'

'You don't ask questions like that round 'ere, not if you want to go on breathin'.' The boy held out his hand. 'Give us me bob.'

Harry took out the shilling. 'But you recognized my description. They must be known to others, if they were known to you.'

'Mebe. But I keep what I knows to meself.' The boy licked his dirty lips. 'Now, let's see yer money, gov.'

Harry held the shilling out in his palm and the boy reached out. Harry snapped his fingers closed. 'Not before you tell me what they did here.'

'I ain't a bloomin' mind-reader, mister. This 'ad a roof and doors on then, but it's all been pinched.'

'When did they leave?'

'Dunno, just went.'

Harry closed the shilling into his fist. 'Not good enough, son.'

'Blimey, you want yer money's worth, don't yer?'

'Well? Was it weeks or months past?'

'It was cold, in winter.'

'And you've not seen or heard of them since?'

'Reckon they scarpered afore the Old Bill got on to 'em.'

Harry dropped the shilling and the boy fled. He looked around the dank, foul-smelling room and scratched the back of his neck. 'Well, what do you think, Pat? Was it them?'

'Don't reckon there's any mistake on that,' said Pat, kicking the wall with his boot. 'It's blooming ready to fall down.'

Harry frowned at the floor. 'Look!' He moved to the wall. 'Good grief, this part is false,' he said, breaking away the thin wood of a partition.

'Blimey!' Pat fell back, coughing in the cloud of dust.

Harry waved his arms, trying to clear the air and tear away the veils of sticky cobwebs that lay over a pile of sacking. He lifted it piece by raggedy piece. 'This is some kind of printing press,' he murmured as he blew the dust from the blackened rollers. 'There are still some papers in the machinery.'

'What do they say?' asked Pat.

Harry frowned, unable to decipher the language. 'Beats me, Pat, but it could be Russian.'

They peered at it together, then Harry nodded. 'I have an acquaintance who may be able to help us.'

'Are we going to Shadwell?'

'All in good time, Pat. All in good time.'

It was after dark when the kitchen door opened at the house in March Street, and Harry and Pat walked in. 'Sorry we're late,' Harry apologized. 'We've a lot to tell you.'

'Did you find Frank?' Birdie asked.

'No, but we got something else.' Pat couldn't wait to explain as he unwound his scarf, revealing two rosy cheeks and a red nose. 'We found this kid who led us to a cellar that had a false wall, see? And behind it was an old printing machine, and Harry reckons it was used by the gang who's got Frank.'

'Is this true?' Birdie looked at Harry.

He took a paper from his pocket. 'We found this.'

Birdie cast her eyes over the crumpled sheet. 'I can't read it. Do you know what it says?'

'A pal of mine had a gander. Whoever Frank is with, they ain't no angels of mercy, far from it. Fact is, this says they mean to overthrow the Russian gaffer, Lenin. He ain't your ordinary top brass, no, he's a tough nut and won't be best pleased if he gets wind of this.'

'But what can these Russians do in England? And why should they want Frank to do it?'

'I don't know their score,' Harry admitted. 'But Frank's a bloke on the run who the law has decreed is a deserter. And I'd say whatever goes down will be blamed on him.'

Birdie blinked in confusion. 'But he don't know anything about politics.'

'He doesn't need to. In fact, the less he knows the better.'

'You mean, they'll blame Frank for . . . for whatever it is that happens and make everyone think he's guilty?'

'Our Frank would never do anything bad,' Pat said heatedly. 'So that's why they came after you, Birdie. To make sure he does what they want.'

She stared at the sheet of strange writing. 'What do you think they have in mind?'

Harry shrugged uneasily. 'It will be something to get the attention of Whitehall, who ain't all that happy with the Commies, but have to keep shtoom, as we're rock-bottom skint after the war, and can't afford to oppose them. Holding the candle to the devil, you might say.'

'Harry, do you think Frank is . . . is still alive?' Birdie had to ask the question.

Harry gave it some thought, then nodded slowly. 'Yes, they'll not harm him, not until the moment comes when they can be sure he is no longer of use to them. But this indicates to me they are desperate people and will stop at nothing to achieve their aims. We must act quickly.'

'But the danger – I can't ask any more of you!'

'This is a personal matter now,' Harry replied firmly. 'I fought for my country before and I'm not standing by to see it brought down again by the likes of these scoundrels.'

Birdie could see by the look in Harry's eyes he would not back away from danger. Yet she now knew that the situation was even more dangerous than it had been before, and feared for Harry's life. But how would it ever be possible to get Frank out of this trouble?

After supper, Pat went to bed and Harry helped Birdie with the dishes.

'Did Pat behave today?' Birdie asked as she put on her apron.

'He was a great help,' Harry replied as he picked up the cloth. 'Even though we didn't get to Shadwell, he helped me to find the cellar and the printing machine.'

'Yes, but although we know now what this Inga and Erik are doing in England, they still have Frank and we are no closer to helping him.'

'I'll think of something,' said Harry.

'We always seem to depend on you.' Birdie began to wash the dishes. 'And you don't even know our brother.'

'I know his family, and that's good enough for me.'

Birdie smiled gratefully. She gazed through the kitchen window and thought of the night Frank had come here, dirty, freezing and frightened. His arrival had set off a train of events that had changed their lives completely. And now it was almost spring.

'I heard from someone in the corner shop that the Thornes have started up business again and Lydia has taken James and left.' She didn't know why she was telling Harry, but he always seemed ready to listen.

'So the widow has gone,' Harry murmured.

'It seems so.'

'Would you reconsider your engagement now?'

'After Lydia, how can I trust Don?'

'But you said he isn't with her.'

'Is that his choice or hers, though?' She threw away the dirty water and looked at Harry. 'What about you? You say so little about yourself. You do have someone special to care for, don't you?'

He put the plate down and frowned. 'Someone special?'

'Like the lady you hired the pony and trap for.'

He smiled, giving a soft chuckle. 'The only lady who rode in it, was you.'

'But I thought you were . . . that you . . .' She stopped,

blushing. How had she got herself into this embarrassing position? His dark eyes were so beautiful and rich with expression that her heart turned over and a peculiar feeling filled her. As though a powerful heat burned within her, spreading from the top of her head to the tip of her toes.

'If you want to know something about me,' he murmured, 'I can tell you that I consider March Street my home, the home I've never had and have always looked for. You and your family have been very kind to me.'

'We've done nothing special.'

'Birdie, I . . .' He stepped forward and took her hands. She felt the world was spinning, but pleasantly, taking her and Harry with it, in another direction. Her lips tingled in a way they'd never tingled before. Automatically she closed her eyes, as heat burst into her cheeks. Even the hair on her skin seemed to prickle. Then she knew, as he held her, that more than anything she wanted to be kissed. Kissed in a way she'd never been kissed before, in a way Don had never kissed her.

Just then a loud noise in the back lane made Harry pull away.

'W . . . what was that?' Birdie stammered, as he rushed to the back door and pulled it open. The cold air whistled around her as she stood alone in the kitchen wondering if it was the disturbance outside she could hear, or the blood pounding in her ears.

Harry's head was reeling as he ran towards Albert and the cart. Had he been tempted to kiss Birdie? The very thing he had promised himself he would never do. It could only put their friendship at risk. She wasn't his to kiss. He knew she was still in love with Don Thorne and that their unpredictable romance, far from ending, was likely to continue.

In the light of the lamp, he saw a group of kids around

Albert. The horse was stamping and shaking his head, but the kids only laughed and yelled more as they ran around the cart.

'Clear off, you little devils!' he yelled, scattering them in all directions. But one fell over and Harry pounced on him.

'It weren't me,' cried the child as he tried to squirm away from Harry's tight grasp.

'Were you with that lot?' Harry demanded angrily.

'No, I was just watchin'.'

'Do you know that a horse has feelings too? He doesn't appreciate being poked around, just the same as you wouldn't.'

'It wasn't me, honest,' cried the child, shivering under his thin coat. 'I'd never do nothin' to a horse. I want one meself when I grow up.'

Harry narrowed his eyes suspiciously. 'You do, do you?'

'Yeah, I was just talking to 'im when that lot came along.'

'What are you doing talking to a horse at this time of night?'

The child looked down at his scuffed boots. 'I was gonna run away. But it's too cold and me fingers are freezin'.'

Harry held back a smile. 'Where do you live?'

'Up Poplar.'

Harry shook his head disapprovingly. 'Your mum is probably sending out the law to look for you.'

The boy began to cry and Harry's heart softened. 'Oh, come on now, son, it ain't the end of the world. I'll take you home on the cart.'

'You mean you ain't going to belt me?'

'No. That's your dad's job, not mine.' Harry set the lad on the cart and, patting Albert's broad back, he checked the leathers and harness. No damage had been done. He looked up at the tiny, huddled figure. 'I'll be back in a minute. And don't think of bolting; you're in a mess as it is.'

He hurried back to the house and found Birdie still in the kitchen. 'It was just some tearaways having a go at Albert,' he said, trying hide his embarrassment as he looked at her.

'Is he all right?'

'Yes, but one of the kids says he wasn't with the bigger kids. Poor little blighter reckons he's run away from home and is regretting it. So I said I'll give him a ride back to his mum.'

She gave him an uncertain smile. 'That's nice of you, considering.'

' 'Night then, Birdie.'

'Good night, Harry.'

He closed the door and stood in the cold air. 'Damn and blast,' he muttered, feeling a prize fool. Should he have apologized? But he hadn't actually kissed her, though if those kids hadn't disturbed him, God alone knew what he might have done.

Harry jumped up beside the child and they set off for Poplar. Where were his brains these days? In his boots? But she had taken possession of his thoughts and as much as he tried, he couldn't get them back. At work, or drinking with his pals, or sitting in the airey with his feet up beside the fire after a long day's graft, his mind was always on her.

Chapter 35

By Sunday, Birdie hoped that Wilfred would at last be able to talk to them. She knew that Pat was very upset and it would be hard for him to sit still on the bench in the uncomfortable cape and mask. But they were to be disappointed when they arrived.

'Your father is still poorly,' the nurse told them. 'Please don't tire him.'

'Did the doctor make his tests?' asked Birdie hopefully.

'He's writing his report this week and when that is done, he will be happy to speak to you.'

They put on their white cloaks and masks, and were shown to the small room where Wilfred lay. He smiled at them and was helped to sit up by the nurse, but suddenly a bout of severe coughing made it impossible for him to speak. Then Birdie saw blood on the cloth the nurse held. She jumped to her feet and was about to rush over, when the doctor came in and, taking one glance at Wilfred, took Birdie's arm.

'I think it's best that you and your brother leave, Miss Connor,' he said quietly. They were quickly ushered out of the room and he drew them to one side. 'I am Dr Shaw and will be treating your father from now on.'

'Was it blood that Dad was spitting up?' Pat asked.

'Yes, I'm afraid it was.'

'That's serious, ain't it?'

The doctor nodded. 'I would like you to use the strong disinfectant to wash with before you go.'

'When can we see him again?'

'I must ask you to wait a few days, even a week until we speak again. With complete isolation and rest . . .' he shrugged. 'Perhaps next Sunday? I shall make it my business to be on duty and will tell the sister to show you straight to my office.'

'Thank you.' Birdie knew the doctor was being kind and she was grateful. But a week seemed a very long time.

'What good will a week do?' Pat asked angrily as they walked out.

'The doctor's right. In Dad's condition he could pick up any germs.' Though she didn't let it show to Pat, she was frightened. She would never forget the sight of Wilfred's heaving chest and the fear in his eyes as he clung to the nurse as that red stain appeared on the cloth.

That afternoon there was a heavy knock on the door. Birdie's heart jumped, as she wondered if it could be PC Rudge again. But when she opened it, Don was standing there. He pushed a bunch of flowers into her arms.

'These are for you, Brigid,' he said, bending to kiss her on the lips. 'I hope you like them.'

'But I—' she began, only to stop as he turned, gesturing to the delivery van that was parked, almost blocking the road.

'Today I have a surprise for you. I hope you're hungry.' He stepped past her and swept her coat from the peg. Raising his eyebrows under his immaculately parted hair, he added, 'Let me help you on with this, as we must fly. I even gave the van a good wash for the occasion.'

'Don, what are you doing? I'm not going with you.'

'Oh, please, my dear, just an hour of your time? Don't you think that we should finally make friends . . .?' He cleared his throat, looking sad. 'I can't tolerate the thought of us parting the way we did. And this is my way of making it up to you. Please indulge me just this once.'

'But I'm not dressed for going out.'

'You look most agreeable, as always. Now slip your coat on. The air still has a bite to it.'

Reluctantly, Birdie did as she was told. 'I must put these in water,' she told him, but he shook his head, holding her arm tightly. 'Later, my dear. I have something of far greater importance to take you to.'

With this, he took the flowers and placed them on the bottom stair. Then he whisked her out of the front door so fast, she was sitting inside the delivery van before she knew it!

*

'There now, Brigid,' said Aggie, cuffing the drip on her long nose with her cardigan sleeve. 'Just help yerself to more gravy if you want it. Or there's more spuds and veg outside if you ain't got enough.'

Birdie stared down at Aggie's Sunday roast set before her. If she had thought that Don was going to take her to a restaurant or somewhere special to eat, she had been sorely mistaken. She knew now that she should have refused and not been persuaded into coming. But the flowers and Don's flattery had taken her by surprise.

'I've got a nice fire going in your honour,' said Aggie, making herself comfortable beside Birdie. 'And no nutty slack that spits all the time. That's real coal, that is, straight off the coalman's cart.'

Birdie found it hard to believe that Aggie seemed to have taken up just where she had left off.

There was a distinct pungent smell ingrained in the walls and furniture that made Birdie want to cough. How could Don and Aggie choose to live here still? The fire downstairs had made its mark on the upper rooms, turning everything even browner and dirtier than before. She looked down at her plate spilling with thickly cut beef, rimmed by fat and dwarfed by a mountain of cauliflower.

'Yes, come along, eat up, Brigid,' said Don, who wore his Sunday-best suit. 'We need to put colour in your cheeks.' He glanced at Aggie. 'Don't we, Mother?'

'Yes, son,' agreed Aggie, tackling her own outsized portion with such eagerness that the gravy spilled over the edge of the plate. 'Now, Brigid, what do you think of me new store?'

No one had asked after her father or was concerned about her life. The Thornes were only interested in themselves. Don had brought her through the shop, proudly indicating the hastily erected shelves that bore every kind of jar and bottle, many of them singed, blackened and broken. Aggie hadn't thrown away anything that could be disguised, nor had she learned from the lessons of the past, as the smell of burning and rotting fruit was stronger than ever before. Birdie had no interest in it.

'A right tonic, ain't it?' Aggie went on. 'The Thornes won't be kept down for long. No, sir!'

'After we've eaten,' Don said, giving a little cough, 'you must see the rooms above, Brigid.'

'I've seen them.' Birdie wondered why neither of them appeared to remember she had been here the day after the fire.

'Ah, well, yes,' he nodded, 'but they are much improved now.'

'He's done them up for you two,' said Aggie giving her a wink. 'Somewhere you can be on yer own after yer wed.'

'But we aren't getting married,' Birdie insisted. 'Didn't Don tell you?'

'Oh, that was just another of your little tiffs,' replied Aggie with a shake of her head. 'Listen . . . if it's that sly wench you're jealous of, she won't be bothering him again.'

'I'm not jealous, not now,' Birdie said fiercely. 'And if Don wants to see Lydia and James, it has nothing to do with me.'

'*See* her?' Aggie repeated crossly. 'We won't ever be meeting again if I have my way! She only ran wailing and complaining to Mr Howells,' continued Aggie. 'And being a daft 'a'p'orth, he fell for her charms. Always thought he fancied her – couldn't keep his eyes off her at church. Lost his place reading the Bible any amount of times. All cow eyes, he was, but oh, no, this one here—' she tilted her head towards her son – 'he wouldn't listen when I warned him she had more than one iron in the fire.'

Birdie wanted to go. She knew she should never have come.

'Mother, it's time for afters,' said Don, red-faced and standing up.

'Deaf to my entreaties, he was,' Aggie chanted. 'So I don't suppose I'll be bothering to go out praying no more. Nor will the Church's representative be invited to this table again, expecting to be fed for free.'

'Please, Mother, this is not the time.'

'You know what she said to me after the fire?' Aggie's eyes became wild and fierce. 'Said I was a danger to life and limb, that I should be put away somewhere for me own good. The cheeky mare! But I know the real reason she wanted me ousted. It was the money she was after, through *him*.'

Birdie pushed herself from the table. 'I'm leaving now. Don, please take me home.'

'What about me rice pudding?' Aggie said, looking up in surprise.

'I'm not hungry.'

'Go on, girl, get it down you,' Aggie insisted. 'If you're going to work here again, you'll need building up.'

'Me? Work here?' Birdie looked at Don. 'Do you really think I would want to come back to this?'

'Mother, I haven't talked to Brigid about that yet.' Don took Birdie's arm. 'Please sit down. Come over here by the fire where it's warm.'

Birdie took her coat from the chair. 'Goodbye, Mrs Thorne. I don't expect we shall meet again. At least, I hope not.'

'What do you mean? You two are going to be wed just like you wanted. In a Roman church and all.'

'You didn't want a church wedding before your daughter-in-law went off with the Vicar,' Birdie said angrily. 'It was because of you that I told me poor dad – who, by the way, is in hospital – that I was going to be married by licence. I shall regret to me dying day that I ever went along with it and worsened his state of health. Now you change your mind to suit your own purposes, but I am still of the same opinion as I was when I last visited here, the day after the fire. I knew then you wanted me as nothing more than a skivvy. I just thank the Good Lord in heaven that my eyes were opened and you never made of me as unhappy a soul as your daughter-in-law is.'

Birdie swept out, leaving Aggie open-mouthed, her lips working and her face pale.

'Brigid!' Don caught up with her on the stairs, his eyes bulging from their sockets as he spluttered, 'I'm sorry . . . s . . . sorry. Mother is not very tactful.'

'For once I'll agree with you,' Birdie nodded, drawing herself up to her full height. 'She has no tact at all, not a shred. And I couldn't ever have been in me right mind to think I could tolerate her company. Now, for the last time, please drive me home.'

'If that's what you want.' He escorted her out to the delivery van but by the time they arrived at March Street, there had been very little conversation and plenty of clanking of gears.

'I love you, Brigid. No one else,' he protested when he turned off the engine.

'You have a very queer way of showing it.' Birdie lifted her chin. 'You and your mother thought I had nothing between my ears except air.'

He looked very embarrassed.

'It's over between us, Don. Please don't call again.' She climbed out and saw herself inside. But it was some time before she heard him drive off.

She looked at the flowers he had given her, still on the stairs. They were too beautiful to throw away so she stood them in a glass on the window sill. When had Don ever brought her such a gift before?

★

It was a very long week for Birdie. Each day there was news of the troubles in Russia, as the Bolshevik regime exerted its power over the people. Harry's appearance at the supper table was more frequent as he told them what he had read in the newspapers, though he was always mindful of Birdie's concern for Frank. When at last Sunday came, he offered to take them to New Cross. But Birdie shook her head.

'We'll catch the bus, Harry,' she told him. She knew that he would willingly give up his time, but he had his own life to lead.

'Harry would have driven us,' Pat complained as they sat on the bus.

'Yes, but as I said before, we can't always be asking favours.'

Pat was very quiet all the way. Birdie knew they were both anxious about the doctor's report. But when they arrived at the hospital the receptionist met them. 'Dr Shaw has been called to an emergency,' she said apologetically. 'He'll be back to see you, though I can't be certain what time. Why don't you wait in the room over there?'

Birdie thanked her, but said that she and Pat would wait outside in the fresh air. The smell of disinfectant and ether, combined with the stuffy air, made her feel ill.

'I don't like it here,' Pat insisted as they walked round the grounds that surrounded the impressive-looking red-brick building.

'Nor do I, but look at that.' They studied a large notice-board and read the information. There were many rules about preventing the spread of infection and, as if to terrify everyone more, there was a history of the hospital printed at the bottom. It was one of the successors of the old fever ships of the nineteenth century. 'A hundred years ago and our dad would have been put on one them fever ships.'

'What were they?'

'These big ships that were moored out in the river where people with contagious diseases were kept away from dry land.'

'I'd rather be on a ship than in there,' said Pat as they walked back to the hospital. 'At least you could sail off.'

Birdie sighed sadly. 'They weren't sailing ships, love. They were called the Death Ships. Because nearly everyone on them died.'

It was a depressing thought and Birdie was relieved to get back to the hospital, despite its smell.

'The doctor will see you now,' said the receptionist, and they were shown to his office on the first floor. Through the small window in the door she could see the doctor's bent head over an open book.

'Please sit down,' he said when they went in, indicating the hard, uncomfortable-looking chairs by his desk.

Birdie was surprised that he seemed to be in no rush as he closed the book and frowned. 'I'm sorry that I haven't been able to tell you much before. I can quite understand how worrying it must be for you, knowing your father has been transferred to a specialist hospital. But you see, the seizures have complicated the picture somewhat and we have to be absolutely certain before we begin treatment. However, my suspicions were confirmed when, last Sunday, as you saw, your father began to be very ill.'

'How sick is he?' Birdie asked, trying to prepare herself for the worst.

'I'm sorry to say that he has tuberculosis,' Dr Shaw said softly.

'Dad's got TB?' Pat burst out, and Birdie gasped.

'But how? Why? I mean, I make sure he eats well, that he don't get cold, that he's kept clean and—'

'The blame is not on you, Miss Connor,' the doctor answered carefully. 'I'm sure you've done your very best.'

'But TB is because people don't keep clean, ain't it? Or haven't enough to eat,' Pat asked, his voice shaky.

'Not necessarily,' said the doctor.

'I thought it was just his bad cough making him so poorly. From the chemicals in the factory.'

'In part that's true,' agreed Dr Shaw. 'My own feeling is, your father has been vulnerable since his health was affected earlier in his life by the fumes at the chemical factory. The environment would have had a detrimental effect on his lungs, weakening them and making them susceptible to tuberculosis.'

Birdie sat there, thinking how Wilfred had worked so hard, had always made certain his family were fed and clothed. Did he know the work was harming him yet still continued because he had to? As a child she remembered him hitting his chest with his fist, then lighting a roll-up. It was a natural thing to do and no one had taken any notice, not until this year when the turns had begun.

'Will he get well again?' Pat asked.

'A difficult question,' the doctor sighed, leaning back and folding his fingers together. 'If his treatment here is successful, he may go to convalesce in another hospital. We have to be most vigilant before releasing our patients. Now, there is something I must ask you.'

Birdie sat quietly, though inside she felt like it was all a dream and couldn't be happening. The doctor's gentle voice broke into her thoughts.

'Is there anyone else in the family with symptoms such as a cough, or fever, or lack of appetite or general malaise?'

'No,' Birdie said immediately. 'Only Dad's been ill. Pat and me are all right.'

'No children to consider?'

'Only my friend Flo's kids.'

'Do they come to the house often?'

'No, not much. But I see them at Mass on Sundays.'

281

'I see. Well, for just a few weeks I would suggest it was prudent not to see them whilst you are visiting your father. I must advise you, as I advise every family that has a member with a confirmed diagnosis, that tuberculosis is very infectious.'

'Does that mean any of us might have it?'

'No, not necessarily, but I would ask each member of the family to consult the doctor if any of these symptoms occur. By what you have told me, I am certain you are very clean in the house. But nevertheless, everywhere should be washed down with disinfectant. Dispose of any suspect garments and bedding, especially those belonging to your father. Wash your hands frequently and ask everyone else to do the same.'

'Can we see him today?'

'I'm afraid not. It's for the good of your father.'

'When, then?'

'Come at the end of next week.'

Birdie tried to take in all he had told her. How had Wilfred's cough turned into this terrible disease? As had happened to the victims of the flu epidemic, the TB had crept up on Wilfred and no one had guessed it, not even Dr Tapper. As the doctor seemed to have no more to say, they stood up.

'Thank you,' Birdie said.

'I'm sorry the news isn't better. But as I said, we shall do everything possible to restore your father to good health.'

Outside the hospital, Birdie pulled Pat against her. Very soon he let his grief out. Gently she stroked his hair. He was just a little boy to her, a mischievous imp who had never known a real mother. But she'd loved him like a mother would and for a few brief moments he let her comfort him.

As they walked to the bus stop they were silent. Pat seemed in a world of his own. The streets and houses, the horses, carts and trams, were familiar, but the world didn't seem the same after the news of the tuberculosis.

Birdie looked out for Harry that evening, but as time went on, she decided he was with his girl. On Monday she washed down the walls and surfaces with naptha disinfectant, just as she had done in the flu outbreak. She put Wilfred's things into a bag to dispose of, amongst them the things the hospital had returned to her. Clothes and bedding were hard to come by and it seemed such a waste. Even more so, the bedcover she had made. But the doctor had been very insistent and finally it went, along with the others.

'How is your father?' Harry asked when he came in that night for supper.

'He's got TB,' Pat blurted out in a choked voice as he slumped down at the table.

Harry sat down with a groan. 'I'm sorry to hear that.'

'He has to be kept away from germs,' Birdie said as she joined them. 'Dr Shaw told me to wash everything in disinfectant and throw away his old clothes because TB is infectious. I told him we were a clean house but he thinks Dad might have got it from the fumes from the factory that made his lungs weak.'

Pat blinked, his brown eyes still full of shock, like hers had been, when the doctor had broken the news. 'People die of TB, don't they? It's like the flu.'

'Yes, but they get better too,' said Harry encouragingly.

'The doctor was very kind,' Birdie added. 'Meanwhile we have to take care of ourselves. If any of us feels poorly or gets a cough, we must go to see Dr Tapper.'

'He's no use!' Pat burst out suddenly, pushing away his plate. 'He didn't do nothing for Dad.'

'Your father has been ailing for a long while,' said Harry reasonably. 'And the hospital will know what to do.'

Pat sniffed and Birdie's heart went out to him. He looked so unhappy.

They ate their meal without much talk. When they had finished it was Harry who spoke first. 'This is not the best time to say what I have to say. With the worry of your father, it's the last thing you'll be wanting to know. But the revolutionists in Russia who tried to kill Lenin, the Bolshevik leader, have failed. So the Whites are in crisis, begging the Allies to help them against the Red Army.'

'What does that mean?' Pat asked, suddenly alert.

'To drive home their point, the anti-Bolshevik underground movement here will try anything to damage Lenin's credibility, cause our government to poke their noses in where it's not wanted.'

'You mean Inga and her gang will do something *now*?' Birdie asked in a whisper. 'Something that affects Frank?'

Harry nodded. 'It's the perfect opportunity for them to use any device to blacken the Bolsheviks' reputation. I went to Shadwell early this morning and had a good look round. I've got a plan in me head now. The lads will help.'

'Your lads?' Birdie frowned.

Harry gave a casual shrug. 'The men who work for me. Tomorrow night, I'm intending to find Frank, and this time I will succeed.'

'What about me?' Pat asked, jumping up. 'You can't leave me out!'

'Sit down, lad,' Harry said quietly and glanced at Birdie. 'Your sister needs you after what happened at the hospital.'

'But I can't do anything for me dad,' Pat cried in distress. 'At least if I was with you, I'd feel I was helping. Frank is my brother and I know if I was to try again, I could find the way.'

Birdie caught hold of Pat's arm. 'Sit down, Pat. Let's talk this over.'

But he pulled away. 'You won't let me go. You'll say it's too dangerous.'

'Yes,' Birdie nodded, 'that's what I'll say, but let's hear Harry out and after he's spoken, I'll give me verdict.'

Pat sat down reluctantly.

'Tell us, Harry, what you plan,' Birdie said quietly.

'I've had a look at our map again. Then I took Ned and Lofty, my pals, to one side and told them I had a friend in trouble, an innocent friend accused wrongly of a crime and was hiding out with some unsavoury types. Now these two pals have known what it's like to be on the wrong side of the law for no good reason before I took them on to work for me. They fought for King and country but got a raw deal of it when injuries prevented them from fighting. I put it to them I was after rescuing this certain friend and it might be dangerous work. But even before I'd finished my story, they were with me, raring to go.'

'They must think the world of you, Harry.'

'I do of them. They're good blokes, but they've suffered trouble, like many a soul after the conflict.'

'But I know the way, at least, I think I do!' exclaimed Pat. 'You might be all night going round in circles. You'd stand a better chance with me.'

Harry looked at Birdie and she saw the unspoken truth in his eyes. What else could she do, but accept that this plan would fare much better with Pat? For a moment she felt tears close. She had been separated from Wilfred, and now Pat was to be put in danger. What was she to do? But the answer was clear, more clear than it had ever been, for this was their last chance of finding Frank, in the hope that he was still alive.

Chapter 36

It was a dull Tuesday morning and Birdie's thoughts were on what was to come that evening as she walked home from her trip to the market. Still wondering if she had been right to agree that Pat was to go with Harry, her attention was taken by Ma Jenkins, who, together with Vi and Annie Carter, stood gossiping in March Street. Ma Jenkins' large body was lost in the folds of a baggy winter's coat and her head was hidden under a misshapen hat.

'I've got a complaint to make,' she shouted boldly as Birdie passed, bolstered by the company of her two friends. 'There's a stink coming from your place, enough to make the eyes water. What's going on?'

'What stink?' Birdie grasped her basket tightly.

'You know very well.'

'What's wrong with disinfectant?' Birdie replied, shrugging. 'It's clean and wholesome.'

'Not in barge-loads, it ain't!' Ma Jenkins exclaimed angrily. 'The wind blows it over to me and all the 'ouses up the road. It can't be just the roaches, it's got to be something more. And I ain't seen your old man recently. What's up with him? He never missed a day trotting up the pub to meet his cronies.'

Birdie went scarlet. She was angry that Ma Jenkins should speak of her father in such a way, but if she admitted the TB, it would soon be all over the neighbourhood. Everyone would think they lived in squalor and disease. 'That's none of your business,' she answered shortly. 'As for the smell, I've had no other complaints.'

'That's because everyone's too scared to say. Frightened they'll get a punch in the eye.'

'That's ridiculous. I've never hit anyone in my life.'

'I mean that fancy man of yours,' Ma Jenkins retorted. 'Him going about threatening decent folk and spreading gossip about me and Charl—I mean, Mr Makepiece. We're just friends, there's no hanky-panky going on, like some I could mention.' She heaved in a quick breath. 'And another thing, that 'orse of his does its business right outside me front door. A pile of it there was, high as the bleedin' Alps.'

'Harry never stops the cart in March Street,' Birdie protested. 'He always leaves Albert in the back lane.'

'*Harry*, is it now?' Ma Jenkins sneered. 'What happened to the other poor sod? The one what had his shop burned down. Give him the elbow, did you, after that?'

Birdie had just said she'd never hit anyone, but she'd never felt more like hitting someone than now. 'Come here and say that again,' she called, taking a threatening step forward.

Ma Jenkins and her two friends jumped backwards. 'Don't worry, I wouldn't lower meself,' shouted the spiteful woman as they sheltered in their doorways. 'Everyone knows you've got somethin' rotten in your place. And whatever it is, I don't want to catch it. And believe me, nobody else in March Street does, either.'

The coven retreated and the two front doors slammed one after the other.

Birdie was quivering with anger. But was it true? Had the wind really blown the naptha into their houses? She felt the eyes and ears of March Street were looking at her as she opened her front door, but not even any of the Kirby kids or the Popeldos family were to be seen.

After she had let herself in, she thought about the accusations Ma Jenkins had made. Was it what everyone else thought too? It would shock the neighbourhood to discover there was TB in the street, yet another black mark against the Connors.

★

Later that day, when Harry came home from work, Birdie saw him stop Albert in the back lane. Two men jumped down from the back of the cart. One was a tall, well-built young man, the other was smaller and older with short-cropped hair.

'This is Ned, my foreman,' Harry said when they walked into the kitchen. 'And this is Lofty.'

The young man grinned down from his height, taller even than Harry. 'Nice to meet yer, missus.'

Ned held out his hand. 'I've heard a lot about you from the gov, Miss Connor.'

Birdie blushed as she shook his hand.

'Ned and Lofty are on overtime tonight,' Harry said simply.

'Don't worry,' said Ned, with a smile, 'we'll do our best for the gaffer here.'

'Would it be all right if we went in the parlour?' Harry asked.

'Course.' Birdie showed them through. 'I'll make the tea.'

She put on the kettle and listened to the low hum of voices. It had been strange to hear Harry called 'Gov' and 'gaffer'. It was clear the men liked and respected him. But had Harry told them the truth? That tonight they would be risking their safety for a man who was a convict and on the run from prison?

When Pat came in he couldn't wait to join them. Birdie busied herself making mugs of tea and slicing bread, covering the thick wedges with spoonfuls of dripping. If there was one thing she knew for sure about men, it was that they worked better on a full stomach.

At first, Harry thought he had struck lucky with the weather. The night was clear and bright, with not a hint of river mist. He drove the cart with Pat sitting up beside him, their heavy coat collars and caps pulled to their ears. Both Ned and Lofty had taken their places in the cart amongst the tools of their trade. The lead piping that Harry had taken before was belted tightly at his waist. After what had happened with Erik that day, he always kept it close. He felt that he had taken all the precautions possible to guard their safety. But if he could have changed anything about tonight it would have been to have kept Pat, who was unarmed, out of this. But it was only with his help that they had a chance of success.

Albert drew them steadily through the evening traffic, both four-legged and engine propelled, and the cold breeze marked the March evening with winter's chill. Harry took a right turn towards Stepney Green, recalling their last trip here and the luck they had had in finding the cellar. Would Lady Luck be with them again tonight? he wondered anxiously.

At the Green, he turned the cart and pulled Albert up. 'So, Pat, this is it,' he told the boy, their breath curling up wildly in the damp air. 'It's up to you now, lad.'

'I'll do it this time,' Pat answered, his eager eyes bright under the rim of his cap. 'I'm going to shut my eyes tight.'

Harry grinned, calling over his shoulder to his passengers, who returned his enquiry with a thumbs up.

At the Commercial Road, Harry waited for Pat's direction.

'Left, Harry, past the Roxy.'

Harry shook the reins above Albert's strong neck and they joined the main thrust of traffic.

'Can you see old Tickle Mary?' asked Pat worriedly.

'No, son, not yet.'

'He was here, I swear it.'

A little further along and to Harry's relief, a colourful figure dressed in gaudy rags, held out a battered top hat to the passers-by. 'Spot on, lad,' Harry commended. 'He's still bellowing out of tune and getting paid for it too.'

'I knew it!' cried Pat, opening his eyes as they passed.

'Now where?' Harry asked, his heart beginning to thump rapidly. It was from this point on that they must rely entirely on Pat's memory.

'It was a minute or two till we swung right to the river.'

Harry urged the horse into the traffic once more until Pat, with his eyes still closed, shouted, '*Here*, Harry. Turn now.'

Harry followed Pat's directions, but only to find that what he had feared most had come to pass: a thick yellow mist began to curl down the roofs and into the gutters.

'Look out for the shop,' Pat warned, unaware of the worsening conditions. 'It's close. I can smell the baccy the lascars use.'

Harry strained his eyes ahead and saw a glow. 'You've got it, Pat,' Harry acknowledged. 'But a fog's coming down. I can't see clearly.'

'Doesn't matter. I know where I am now. Take Albert southwards until I say.'

Harry clucked his tongue sharply to persuade the horse on. They had now left the highway behind and entered Wapping Lane. This was the turf of watermen and sailors, scurrying like ants under the cranes and derricks, with only the light of a tavern to warn of the dangers of the creeping black waters.

A wind picked up from the river and blew salt on Harry's lips. He licked them nervously, recognizing the stench of mud and fish that travelled on the air from the ancient drains. He would not like to do business here, not at all. The underground sewers had existed for centuries without maintenance, and the mean streets were hardly any safer; life was cheap here, disease brought in from all corners of the world.

But it was not any of this that concerned him tonight. It was finding Frank and facing those who had imprisoned him. And though the lead warmed his waist, he sincerely hoped that broad-shouldered Lofty and muscle-bound Ned were as proficient at wielding a spade as a weapon as they were at burrowing underground.

'Why have we stopped?' asked Pat.

'We must put on our Tilleys,' Harry told him, shouting to Ned and Lofty to light and hang the lanterns from the big iron cart-hooks.

'I've still got my eyes closed,' called Pat anxiously, 'but I want to open them.'

'Don't,' Harry instructed. 'You've brought us thus far and I trust you to take us the rest of the way.'

'Then take Albert slowly,' Pat nodded. 'I'm counting to the turn, see? Like I did in their wagon, between stops.'

Harry took a deep breath and shook the reins, narrowing his eyes into the fog, putting all his trust in Pat.

Ten minutes later, Harry creased his brow thoughtfully over the roughly sketched map they had made. In the pale light of the Tilley that Ned held, he pointed to a crossroads.

'By all accounts, this is where we are.'

'We turned right with the wagon, I'm certain,' said Pat.

'Keelhaul Street?' said Ned with a soft groan. 'A stinking slum in the light, but after dark, a hell.'

Harry nodded. 'I'll agree with you there, Ned.' He moved his finger an inch. 'There's a lane runs along the back. Now the fog has thinned a little,' he said folding the map into his pocket, 'I reckon Pat and me will take the rear whilst you and Lofty take Albert along the front.'

'You better watch yer step down there,' Ned warned, handing Harry the Tilley. 'Don't like the idea of you going it alone, gov.'

'You'll hear me if I shout,' Harry tried to assure him. 'And believe me, if I need assistance, I'll not be slow to call.'

They separated then, Ned and Larry rumbling into the swirling vapours on the cart and Harry taking Pat into the lane. The Tilley lit up the gloom and spilled over into the yards.

'Can you recognize anything, Pat?' Harry asked as they crept lightly along.

'I'm trying to remember.'

Harry knew the boy was afraid, and had cause to be. His hand went to his belt and the reassuring shape of the piping. 'There has to be room enough for stabling,' he whispered.

Pat shivered beside him. 'Wait a minute, what's that?'

In the darkness, the mist curled around them and the smell of decay hung heavily. Harry could see a yard wall and a light beyond it. There were raised voices and the sound of movement.

'Lower the Tilley, Pat,' he whispered as they crept closer. And, edging himself nearer, he gripped the top of the wet, mossy brick and eased himself up to gaze over.

'Christ Almighty,' Harry breathed. 'We've got them.'

'Is it our Frank? Is it him?' Pat asked excitedly.

'Damn this fog, I don't know if it's your brother. I was looking out for that red hair of his you told me about,' whispered Harry. 'But they have someone bound tight and, by the looks of it, intend to move him out. At a guess I would say they are loading cargo into the wagon with him.'

'It must be Frank!' exclaimed Pat. 'Let me see.'

'One minute, son, I want to count how many there are; be certain of what we are dealing with.' Through the shifting fog lit by the Tilleys hanging on and around the wagon, he could see a slight, boyish figure that must be Inga, and the tall man at her side was his previous adversary, Erik.

But there were two more, damn it! He growled angrily under his breath. Were there any inside the house? He should have brought more insurance tonight and now he regretted the mistake.

The question was, how was he to warn Ned and Lofty, without giving the game away?

Chapter 37

Birdie heard the knock but didn't want to open the door. What if it was Constable Rudge? What if Harry and Pat and the others arrived back as the policeman was standing there? But as she crept along the passage, she heard a familiar voice.

'Birdie, love, it's only me.'

She opened the door, relieved to see who it was. 'Mrs Belcher! What are you doing here?'

'Lady Annabelle sent me. Are you all right? We ain't seen you for weeks.'

'I'm all right.' She hesitated. She didn't want company, today of all days, as good-intentioned as the housekeeper was. 'It was very nice of Lady Annabelle to think of me.'

Mrs Belcher bustled her way in nevertheless. 'It was the fire, see? We read about it in the paper. They didn't report no casualties, but we knew you'd gone to help out there and wondered if you was all right.'

'Yes,' Birdie said hesitantly, 'I'm all right. But Don and me—'

'You ain't broken up, again?'

'This time it's for good.'

'Well, you two was always a bit up and down. And it's

not for me to say, but I always reckoned you deserved better. Couldn't see you grafting behind a counter, not with those lovely hands of yours. They're a gift, you know, you was born with a needle in them,' she smiled. 'And to be honest, there's a great big pile of alterations in me kitchen that need doing, and there's no one on this island will do them as good as you.'

Birdie was too polite to say that alterations were the last thing on her mind. She also didn't want to talk about Don as she knew that Mrs Belcher would be eager to know all the ins and outs.

'Don't worry, I'm not staying long,' Mrs Belcher said, easing Birdie's mind. 'Mr B is coming to fetch me after he finishes at work round the corner at the bakery in Manchester Road. But I've always time for a cuppa, love, if you're offering.'

Birdie knew that Mrs Belcher had come to find out why she hadn't turned up at the House. What was she going to tell her?

'Go and sit in the parlour, it's warm in there.'

Five minutes later, Birdie was sitting beside Mrs Belcher on the couch. The fire was blazing and they were drinking piping hot tea. 'It's a long time since I've been in this house,' Mrs Belcher said, looking round as she lowered her cup to her lap. 'It was when your mother was alive. We used to have the odd cup of tea together in my kitchen at the House and once or twice here when your father was at work and you kids were at school.'

'I didn't know that.'

'We were on good terms, Birdie. We saw eye to eye.' Mrs Belcher sighed heavily. 'And then she fell for the baby . . . your Pat. And she never came home again.' Mrs Belcher stared around once more, her eyes narrowing. 'But do you know, I can feel her presence here. Can you?'

'Sometimes I think I do,' Birdie nodded. 'But a feeling is

nothing like touching someone or seeing them in real life, is it?'

'No, that's true,' agreed Mrs Belcher thoughtfully. 'Though my mother's sister reads the teacups, you know. Aunt Jenny was a bit of a black sheep in our family as she married a handsome gypsy. Told me that I too had the gift of seeing, as she called it, but my mum soon knocked that idea out of my head when she packed me off into service. Said I needed to think practical and she was right, of course. When I started to work below stairs, the only reading of teacups I ever did was when I was scrubbing them.' Mrs Belcher laughed softly, then gave a long sigh. 'Still, as I've got older, I've realized Aunt Jenny wasn't so daft. I do get these odd feelings and I had one tonight when I walked in here.'

'Can you see anything that I can't?' Birdie asked hopefully. 'Is it really Mum who's here?'

'No, it's just a feeling I have.'

'I talk to Mum, when I'm on my own,' Birdie admitted.

'She would be very proud of you, ducks. She loved you and Frank dearly, and would, if she'd survived Pat's birth, have been overjoyed she'd had a son. Talking of which, is there any news on your Frank? They haven't found him yet, I take it, or it would have been in the papers?'

Birdie had always found Mrs Belcher to be very direct. And though Birdie didn't want to give away anything, she felt an honest answer was best. 'No, he's not been found.'

'No one's come forward to speak on his behalf?'

'Who would do that?' Birdie asked. 'Everyone believes he's a deserter.'

'Well, for what it's worth, me and Lady Annabelle believe different, my dear. Frank is a good lad and always was. He might have been a bit of a pushover where the ladies was concerned, and your mother was always a bit worried he'd get put on, if you know what I mean.' She crooked an eyebrow. 'He wouldn't be hiding out with an old flame, would he?'

Birdie felt herself go red. 'Mrs Belcher, I can't say.'

'Oh, so you do know where he is?'

'Please don't ask me that.' She didn't want to lie.

'I see.' The older woman gave a knowing smile. 'So it's like that, is it?'

'Please don't say anything to anyone!' Birdie begged.

'There's nothing to say.' The older woman reached out and took her hand. 'But would you take a piece of advice from an old friend?'

'I know you mean well, Mrs Belcher, but—'

'Listen, this is between us. Just you and me. I'll put it this way. If one of my sons was in trouble, as big and ugly as they are, I'd go to the ends of the earth to help them. Lawful or not, I'd do it. And I know it's the same with you.'

Birdie nodded. Those words were very true.

'Now, there may come a time when you need help – *real* help, I mean. Of a sort that most people like us couldn't get.' Mrs Belcher leaned forward and lowered her voice. 'Things can't always be done in the way you'd want 'em to be done, but there's others who'd do it. There's ways and means, see?'

Birdie was shocked to hear this, as Mrs Belcher had always seemed the height of properness.

'Anyway, remember what I said, won't you?' She looked Birdie in the eye and squeezed her hand. 'Just give me the nod.'

Birdie wanted to laugh and cry at the same time. Mrs Belcher's care and concern were very touching, but this suggestion, coming from such an upright and law-abiding citizen, sounded rather comical.

'Now, how is your dad and that cough of his?' Mrs Belcher asked. 'I expected to see him here tonight.'

Birdie swallowed hard as she tried to answer. 'He's very ill, Mrs Belcher.'

'Oh Lord, no!'

'Dad's in the isolation hospital at New Cross. That's why I haven't been to the House. He's got TB.'

'TB? Oh, you poor lass. I'm so sorry.'

Birdie couldn't say any more and Mrs Belcher reached out to fold her arms around her. 'You've had a basinful of it, ducks,' she murmured in her ear. 'Now I know why I feel that your mother is – well, let's just say, if she can help you, she will in her own way.'

Birdie quickly wiped away a tear. 'I think this is beyond even Mum.'

Mrs Belcher brought out a neatly ironed cotton square and blew her nose. 'Is there anything me or Mr B can do?'

'No. But thank you for asking.'

A knock came at the door and startled them. 'That'll be me other half,' sighed Mrs Belcher, standing up and pushing her hanky in her pocket. 'Now, I know you've a lot on your plate, but I would appreciate it if you could let me know how things stand. Meanwhile, I shall be thinking of you and your brothers, and hope you'll remember what I've said as regards Frank.'

The knock came again and Mrs Belcher rolled her eyes. 'He's hungry, that's what, and impatient to get home. Now stay here in the warm and I'll see myself out.'

After she'd gone, Birdie sat deep in thought. Mrs Belcher's visit had brought her comfort and had lifted her spirits. Was Bernadette really close by? Had she returned to her family in times of trouble? It was a question she had often thought about and she had talked it over with Flo once or twice. But there was nothing in the Catechism that said people returned to earth after they had died. Catholics were taught there was heaven and hell, with purgatory and limbo in between. But, as for revisiting this world . . .

Birdie gave a deep sigh. Whatever the truth, she felt better just thinking Bernadette was watching over them.

But as time ticked by, Birdie felt the pleasant feeling disappearing. What was happening to Harry and Pat and the others? Time was marching on. She got up and paced the floor, going from one room to another as her tummy tied in a knot.

When she looked out from the window, her heart sank. A thick, yellow-grey fog was creeping slowly along the cobbles and crawling up to the windows. This was the worst possible weather for any business down by the river.

Chapter 38

All the dogs in the neighbourhood seemed to start barking before Pat could warn Harry that someone was coming towards them. Wreathed in mist, the tall figure emerged silently from the shadows.

A cry came from Pat's lips, but too late as the blow landed on Harry's back and sent him sprawling to the ground. Pat saw the long, solid yard of wood rise again, about to swing down on Harry. But as it descended, Harry moved and only took a glancing blow.

It all happened so fast that Pat couldn't think what to do. If he yelled for Ned and Lofty, others would hear him too. Was this big man Erik? And if it was, what chance did they have against him?

Pat recoiled along the wall, feeling the wet, crumbling brickwork under his shaking fingers. He remembered the last time he was in a spot, amidst the demonstrators at Stepney. But this seemed worse. It was dark and foggy and the man's attack had come out of nowhere. Had he been watching them?

Harry tried to climb to his feet, but was knocked down again. Pat stood motionless. What *could* he do? Should he run and try to find Ned and Lofty? But he'd be too late.

Then he realized the Tilley was in his hand. He stepped forward, his heart beating violently in his chest at what he was about to do. Lifting the Tilley, he drew it back just as the man was about to bring the club down on Harry. The lantern hit him full square and oil spilled over. The Tilley clattered to the ground and rolled into the fog, leaving a bright orange flame trailing behind. Like magic, it spun a thin trail of fire back to the figure, coiling snakelike at his feet. The man kicked uselessly, trying to leap away from the rushing flames. But they licked upward, curling around his legs and clinging to his chest in an eerie orange glow. He flapped his arms in an effort to distance himself, but with each movement they ate up the cloth of his jacket. His screams grew wilder and more desperate as he fanned the heat into bright, dancing tongues around him.

Pat stared at the burning cone of fire and listened wretchedly to the pitiful cries. He had no intention of burning a man; his aim had been solely to save Harry. And as he stepped forward, intending to help in some way, a fresh vortex of fire leaped over its victim. With a scream that curdled Pat's blood, the staggering man fell away, falling and rolling into the fog.

'Pat!' a voice rasped in his ear and a strong pair of arms were pulling him back against the wall.

'I . . . I . . . I didn't mean it,' Pat howled, his eyes still glued to the blurred blob of fire. 'I've got to do something.'

'Let his pals help him,' Harry ordered breathlessly and, taking hold of his shoulders, Harry shook him hard. 'Listen, Pat, it was me or him.'

'But he's burning to death!'

'He was prepared to splatter my brains over the cobbles, lad. But you stepped in, thank the Good Lord.'

'I didn't think the oil would burn like that,' Pat whimpered, a sick feeling growing inside him. Had he burned a man to death this night?

'Your intention was not to roast him, Pat, but to help me. And from the shemozzle I can hear, they're dousing him with water. I'd not mark him down as a gonner just yet.'

Pat leaned against the wall, his heart beating so fast he could barely breathe. Then after a short while, Ned and Lofty's shouts could be heard. Harry let go of him and suddenly was leaping towards the yard. And somehow Pat found the strength to follow.

It was past midnight when Birdie opened the back door and gazed into the curtains of fog filling the yard. She had seen a faint light from the window and now a small group of men stumbled out of it. First came Pat and Lofty, and then Harry and Ned, with a figure slung between them.

'Pat, who's that?' She stepped towards her brother.

'It's Frank, we found him.'

Birdie put her hand to her mouth. She hadn't recognized his slumped form. Pat gently pushed her towards the house. 'Go in, Birdie. Don't let out the light. We mustn't be seen.'

'The buggers have done him over,' Harry told her as they stumbled in and Pat closed the door.

A thin, gaunt face with a long bloody streak over one eye, stared up at her. She managed to hold back the tears as she hugged him. He smelled terrible, much worse than he had under the arches.

'Frank, it's me, Birdie.'

His blue eyes stared out under their swollen lids. 'Hello, gel. Sorry, I . . .' His head sank down again.

Birdie nodded to the three men. 'Take him to the parlour and lay him on the couch. Pat, run upstairs for some blankets, whilst I tear up some sheets.' She knew she was speaking harshly, but she had to keep a cool head.

Harry, Ned and Lofty helped her to lift and undress Frank, after which she bathed and cleaned his wounds. He lay still and exhausted on the couch, his thin body lost under the folds of the warm blankets.

'Frank,' Harry said quietly as he sat at Frank's side, 'I'm Harry, your sister's lodger. And these are my mates.'

Frank's eyes tried to focus. 'I wondered who you was.'

'Do you feel up to telling us what happened?'

'Sh . . . she had me set up all along,' he stammered.

'Who? The woman in breeches?'

'Yeah, Inga.'

'A pretty face always was your weak spot, Frank.' Birdie smiled, touching his matted hair softly with her fingertips. 'What was she after?'

Frank gave a gurgle at the back of his throat. 'Tried to get me to drive the wagon up West. It was full of dynamite.'

Birdie gasped. 'Were they going to blow-up something?'

'Somethin' big, I think.'

'But you might have been blown-up too.'

'Yeah, that was the general idea.'

'From what I saw of them cutthroats,' growled Ned, as he pushed his hand over his dirty bald head, 'they would have done us in too, given half the chance.'

Frank lifted his hand to the piece of old sheet that Birdie had put round the wound near his eye. 'The bangs I've had on me head have done me brains in. And I didn't have many to start with.'

'You didn't . . . didn't kill anyone while you were away, did you?' Birdie felt compelled to ask.

Once more, Frank tried to smile. 'Course not.' His head sank back on the pillow. 'Where's Dad? He won't want me 'ere.'

Everyone was silent and Birdie looked at Harry.

'We'll talk more in the morning,' Harry assured him, patting his arm. 'Try to rest now.'

Frank closed his eyes and fell asleep.

'Leave him to kip,' Harry whispered, drawing Birdie out of the room.

When they were in the kitchen, she looked gratefully at Ned and Lofty.

'You saved our Frank tonight.'

'It was nothin', missus,' said Lofty, with a grin. 'All in a day's work.'

'Made a change from diggin' 'oles,' Ned told her cheerfully.

'Frank's very lucky.'

'Don't think he will be so trustin' of a female again.' Ned put his hand on Pat's shoulder. 'Those Ruskies soon buggered off when they saw what young Pat done.'

Birdie turned to stare at her brother. 'What did you do?'

'He saved my bacon, that's what,' said Harry with a grin, before Pat could answer. 'I was about to get hammered when Pat chucked the Tilley at one of them and gave Ned and Lofty time to arrive.'

'I never meant to hurt him,' said Pat miserably. 'I didn't think his jacket would catch fire like it did. It was awful, Birdie.'

'You did what was right,' Harry said, his face serious now. 'And seeing as we couldn't find him after, I'd say he got put out in time by his mates.'

Ned nodded firmly. 'You should have heard the ruckus they made dousing the fire. We was ready for a real ding–dong, but they was worried about their mate setting light to the wagon so they chucked water over him and there he was, still screaming like a banshee. Then they buggered off in all directions.'

'What happened to Inga?' Birdie asked.

'She jumped on the wagon and disappeared,' Harry said bitterly.

'But where would she go?'

Harry shrugged. 'God only knows.'

Ned took his cap from his pocket and pulled it over his head. 'We'd better be off now. Good luck, missus.'

Birdie smiled. 'Thank you.'

'Keep yer eye on Sleeping Beauty,' said Lofty with a wink.

Harry followed them to the door. 'I'll be back in the airey after I've stabled Albert.' He looked at Pat. 'You're in charge now, son. Make sure you draw the bolts tonight. And I'll be up to see you at first light.'

When they had gone, Pat drew the bolts on the door.

Birdie pulled him gently against her. 'Pat, I'm proud of you, love.'

'I was scared. I wanted to run away.'

'But you didn't.'

'I never meant to harm anyone. I only had the Tilley, so I chucked it.'

'I would have done the same thing.'

Pat looked at the door. 'What if the coppers come knocking?'

'Why should they? They know Frank's not here.'

'But he is now.'

She knew he was frightened and very upset about burning the man. 'Come along, stop fretting now. A good night's sleep and you'll be right as rain in the morning. We have our brother home again, and that's what matters.'

'I'll say good night to Frank.'

'Leave those filthy clothes on the landing and I'll give them a good wash tomorrow.'

He managed a smile as he left the kitchen and Birdie sat down at the kitchen table with a deep sigh. She drew her hands over her face tiredly. It was hard to believe that Frank was home again. What would he say when she told him their father was very ill? And was Pat right – would the police try calling again?

In the middle of the night, Birdie heard shouting. She rushed downstairs and into the parlour. Frank was sitting up, staring into the embers of the fire.

'Frank?' She pulled her dressing gown round her and sat beside him. 'What's the matter?'

'It's the nightmares. They never stop.'

'Nightmares of Inga?'

'No, the trenches.'

'The war is over now. You're home with your family.'

He looked around, his eyes vague. 'Am I?'

'This is March Street.'

'I can't stay here. They're looking for me. I'll put her in danger.'

'Who?' Birdie held his hot hand. 'Frank, the war has ended,' she told him again.

'Has it?' He looked at the door. 'But they might hurt her and she was only trying to help me.'

'Frank, you've got to stop thinking about Inga. Have you forgotten what she wanted you to do? Now lay back, you've got a fever.' She pushed him gently against the pillow and drew the blankets over him. She was frightened. He was becoming delirious and must have forgotten just what Inga was capable of.

She stared at his slight form, curled up under the blanket, and was overwhelmed with tenderness. He had suffered so much, yet was a good person at heart. If only they could prove his innocence, but it was months since the armistice had been called. If he ever did get to France, what hope had he of finding the people who could help him after all this time?

The thin morning light streamed through the parted curtains by the time Frank woke again.

'I need the lav, gel.' He tried to stand up but fell back again. Sweat was pouring from his face.

'Wait, I can't help you on me own. I'll get Pat and Harry.' She called out for Pat at the bottom of the stairs, then ran out of the front door to the airey. Harry answered her knock immediately. He was still dressed in the clothes he wore yesterday and his chin was covered in dark stubble.

'Are you going to work?' she asked hurriedly.

'Not yet. I was coming up to see Frank first.'

'He got a fever and needs the lav.'

Harry snatched his coat and followed her up to the house. Pat came running down the stairs, dragging on his trousers.

'What's up? Is it Frank?'

'Give me a hand, lad, will you?' said Harry, and they all returned to find Frank on the floor.

'Oh, Frank, I told you to wait,' wailed Birdie as Harry turned her brother gently over and slid his arm under his back. Birdie watched anxiously as Harry and Pat heaved Frank outside, his feet dragging on the floor as they half carried him along.

After ten minutes he was back on the couch and Birdie covered him with the blankets. 'Pat, you'd better be off to work.'

'I want to stay home with Frank.'

Birdie knew better than to argue this time. 'All right, just this once. But make yourself useful and light the fire. I'll make the porridge.'

But as much as she tried to make Frank eat, he wouldn't. He lay, exhausted after his efforts, the sweat pouring down his face under the bandage.

'Should I run for the doctor?' Pat asked.

'It's too dangerous to involve him,' Harry warned as he wiped Frank's cold, clammy skin with a cloth. 'Even Dr Tapper.'

'Then what do we do?'

Harry ran his fingers through his long, dark hair and frowned. 'We saw a lot of fever in the army brought on by infection. Mostly, it had to run its course until it left the poor blighter's body.'

'I hate her,' said Pat bitterly. 'I hope Inga blows herself up.'

'Come on now, Pat, love, that kind of talk won't do any good.' Birdie was glad he hadn't heard what Frank had said about Inga. Even though she had done such bad things to him, was he still under her spell?

They tried to clean each cut, but Birdie knew that dirt must have got in them in that dreadful slum. Left untreated, they had become open sores. Frank's bones stuck out everywhere. It was obvious they had starved and beaten him.

By the end of the morning, Harry was still at home. 'You'd better go,' she told him but he just smiled.

'Ned will look after things.'

All day they waited for an improvement but it never came. That night Harry took turns with Birdie to sit with Frank. In the early hours of Thursday morning, Birdie woke up in the chair, a blanket over her.

'Harry, you should have woken me.' She threw off the blanket and hurried over. 'Has the fever broken?'

'Not yet.'

'Harry, I know Frank is ill, but what am I to do about Dad? I told the doctor I'd see him today.'

Harry looked tired and had grown a dark beard. He gave her an encouraging smile. 'You go. I'll stay with Frank until you get back. And don't worry about Pat, I'll make certain he goes off to work today.'

Birdie wished she didn't have to ask this favour. But she had no choice. Frank moaned in his sleep and she felt very low. Why did all this have to happen when Wilfred was so ill?

Whilst on the bus Birdie thought about Harry's kindness. What would she have done without his help? If it wasn't for him, Frank may well be dead by now. She shuddered at the thought. Those violent people had hurt him and had never intended to help him. They had picked him out as vulnerable, a dispensible victim, and used him.

When the bus arrived at New Cross, Birdie hurried towards the daunting spectacle of the hospital's tall red-brick walls, her head down against the stiff March wind. Even from here she could smell the disinfectant on the breeze.

Once inside she waited in a very long queue at the desk. When at last she faced the secretary, she recognized her as the older woman whom she'd first spoken to. 'I've come to see Dr Shaw.'

'He's very busy.' As before, her tone was abrupt.

'If you remember, my father is Wilfred Connor and he has TB. Dr Shaw told me to come back today to see how he is.'

Showing no sign of recognition, the woman bustled down the long corridor towards the doctor's office. Did that mean she knew something about Wilfred? Was it more bad news?

But to Birdie's relief she soon came back with Dr Shaw at her side. His white coat flapped open as he took long strides and he looked very grave. She knew instantly something was wrong.

'Miss Connor, it's not good news, I'm afraid.'

'What do you mean?'

This time he didn't ask her into his office but drew her aside to the room that she had once been told she could wait in.

It was very cold in the sparsely furnished, high-ceilinged room, but the doctor sat beside her on one of the many chairs.

'He has suffered a stroke, an unfortunate setback, I'm afraid.'

Birdie felt sick. 'What does that mean?'

'Just as with the seizures, the stroke may be a result of the combined stress on his system and, due to his vulnerability, he isn't fighting the infection as we hoped he might.'

'Can I see him?'

The doctor sighed and nodded.

Birdie didn't argue and followed him to the room where she was asked to wash her hands in the strong disinfectant and was then given a cape and mask. When alone, she stood gazing down at the ghostly garb. She hated these clothes now. Would she even be able to get close to her father?

Chapter 39

Birdie walked into the small ward, each bed with curtains drawn around it. The nurse, also in a white gown and mask, beckoned her to follow. Birdie's heart pounded as the nurse drew back the curtains and gestured her in.

Under her mask, Birdie took a sharp breath, Her head

spun. Wilfred was lying on the bed, a mask over his face, and another nurse stood over him, removing it slowly.

'Dad, can you hear me?' Birdie asked in a muffled voice.

He made a strange sound and Birdie reached out for his hand but the nurse shook her head.

'I'm sorry I have to wear this,' she whispered and pointed to her mask. 'They make you wear them . . . otherwise I wouldn't be allowed to see you.'

There was a very tiny movement of his head and she smiled. 'Pat's at work today but he'll be with me next time. Please try to get better, won't you?'

She saw a small twitch on his lopsided mouth. Was it a smile?

'Dad, we miss you. Hurry up and come home again.'

He tried to say something but began to cough. Birdie jumped in panic. The nurse took her arm and gently guided her out as she listened to the awful sound of her father's coughing behind the now closed curtains.

'I'm very sorry you had to see him like that,' said the nurse as they stood in the small washroom and pulled off their masks. 'We weren't expecting you.'

'Dr Shaw said I could come in for a few minutes. But I . . .' Birdie turned away. There was a big lump in her throat and her lips were quivering. When she had seen a little trickle run from the side of her father's mouth and the nurse quickly wipe it away, she felt very sad. Wilfred was such an independent man and hated fuss. But ever since he'd been in hospital he had no control over his body and now was completely dependent on the nurses.

'You mustn't be discouraged,' said the nurse kindly. 'Many stroke patients recover and get back to normal in time.'

'Yes, but do many stroke patients who have TB get better?' she asked, and saw the nurse hesitate, her eyes flicking down.

'There is always hope,' said the nurse.

But Birdie wasn't listening. She was still remembering Wilfred's thin, pale face and the distressing sound of that terrible cough.

When Birdie got home, she hurried along to the kitchen.

'I'm sorry I'm late,' she apologized to Harry who stood by the sink.

'How is your dad?' Harry asked as he put down the dish he was drying.

'He's had a stroke.'

Harry went to her, reaching out to catch her arm. 'Sit down. Here . . .' he gently lowered her to the chair, 'tell me what happened.'

She sniffed and took out her handkerchief. 'Dr Shaw said it was because of the combined stress, of the TB and the seizures . . . His body had a setback.'

'Did you see him?'

'Yes, but he looked awful and had a mask on and then he started to cough and . . .' She put her hand to her mouth. 'Oh, Harry, it was awful.'

He took her hand and squeezed it. 'He's a fighter. He'll pull through.'

'Do you think so?' She sighed and then felt his warm fingers around hers. She asked quickly, 'How's Frank?'

'He's been asking for you.'

'Me? But he didn't seem to know me this morning.'

'He kept saying, "Where is she?" And unless he meant Inga, it must be you.'

'Did he say anything else?'

'Once or twice when he opened his eyes I said who I was. Told him about Shadwell and what happened again, as he don't seem to remember.'

'Harry, I'm worried,' she admitted, as she reluctantly drew her fingers away and stood up. 'Just before the fever took hold, he told me he had these nightmares. I asked him if they were about Inga and he said they were about the trenches. I told him the war was over and he was home safe, but all he said was he couldn't stay as they were looking for him. That he'd put her in danger and they'd hurt her. Kept on about how she'd just been trying to help him.'

'Reckon Inga got under his skin, meself.' He gave a thoughtful shake of his head. 'It's hard to believe, ain't it? Seeing as how she's a heartless bitch and a cold, calculating murderess.' Harry frowned. 'Are you going to tell him about your dad?'

'Not till he's better. But he'll have to know eventually.'

Birdie went into the parlour and sat beside her brother. How could Frank have been so beguiled that even in his fever he seemed to be obsessed with Inga? She reached out to clasp his hand. 'Frank, it's me, Birdie.'

'Be careful, they'll kill you if they find me,' he rambled, raising his head from the damp pillow. His eyes were haunted as he looked around, trying to see something that Birdie couldn't. His hand felt the same as her father's – long bones covered by fragile, stretched skin – only Frank was squeezing hers with great strength.

'Frank, please look at me. I'm not Inga, I'm your sister, Birdie. Inga hurt you, don't you remember?'

'She only tried to hide me.'

'You've got it all muddled. She did these terrible things to your poor body. You can't have forgotten that.'

He closed his eyes. 'I'll never forget her, no.'

Birdie felt very angry. This treacherous woman still held his mind captive. There was nothing she could do to help him.

'I can't make him see that she-devil for what she is,' Birdie whispered to Harry when he walked in.

'It's the fever talking. He don't mean what he says.'

'But what will happen when he recovers – *if* he does?

Will he still be under her spell?' Birdie fretted, but her anger melted away as she looked into Harry's dark eyes. What would she have done without her good friend to turn to? Even when things were at their worst, he found something to make her smile.

It was the next day, Friday, when at last, Frank's fever broke.

'Hello, gel,' he croaked, blinking his eyes as Birdie was bathing his wounds.

'Frank, do you recognize me?'

'Course I do.'

'Who am I?'

'You're me little skin and blister.' He gazed round the room. 'Blimey, what am I doing here?'

'Don't you remember?'

He frowned, trying to sit up, but he was too weak. 'I dunno. What are these?' He looked down at the sore, red cuts on his forearms.

'A woman called Inga did this to you. You've got them all over. She kept you a prisoner in Shadwell, until Pat and Harry, our lodger, and some of his friends came to free you.'

Frank sank back with a groan and nodded. 'Yeah, it's all coming back now.'

'Thank goodness for that.' Birdie rolled down the sleeves of his shirt and did up the buttons. 'You've had a fever and I was beginning to think you'd never come out of it.'

'You can't keep Frank Connor down for long.'

'I'm glad to see you haven't lost your sense of humour.'

He pushed his hand round his stubbly jaw. 'How long have I been here?'

'Harry brought you home on Tuesday and now it's Friday.'

He licked his parched lips. 'I'm starving.'

'There's a broth simmering on the stove. I hoped the smell would bring you round and it has.'

They both laughed. Then Birdie asked hesitantly, 'Frank, what are your true feelings towards Inga?'

'Why do you ask that, gel?'

'You've been saying she was only trying to help you.'

Frank looked down at the blanket and folded it over with his shaky hands. 'Must've been off me trolley. Don't take no notice.'

'You get carried away with a pretty face. And she seemed to have a hold over you.'

'That's all over now.' He looked up at her sadly.

'I hope so.' Birdie wanted to believe him, but could she? Once she had been able to see if he was telling her the truth, but now his eyes were distant, as if he was thinking of something far away. And although, whilst he'd been ill, she had cut away his long, dyed black hair and beard, leaving his true bright ginger to grow back, his face was so sunken and thin that it was hard to see the old Frank.

He caught her wrist as she stood up. 'What's Dad got to say about all this?'

She sat down again. 'Frank, Dad's in hospital. He's got TB. And then he had a stroke. He's not very well.'

'Christ Almighty!'

'But the doctor thinks he'll get better.'

'Poor sod.' Frank's lips trembled. 'So he don't know I'm here?'

'No.'

'I was hoping that distance had made the heart grow fonder and he might have forgiven me.'

'There's nothing to forgive you for. If Dad were to see you, though—'

'Do you really think he'd change his mind?' Frank asked, his eyes widening hopefully.

'We'll have to see. At the moment he's very sick.'

'Poor bugger. He always did have a rotten cough.'

'Frank, don't think about that, now. We've got to get you well.'

'Birdie?'

'What?'

'Thanks, gel.' He sniffed loudly. 'For believing in me.'

She smiled. 'I always have and always will.'

In the kitchen she dabbed her eyes with her apron hem. Then she pulled back her shoulders, took hold of the wooden spoon and turned the bubbling stew energetically.

That night, Pat burst in at the back door after work. The weather outside was cold and blustery. His nose and cheeks were red under his cap.

'How's Frank?' he demanded, as he tore off his coat. Birdie stopped him before he ran in. 'Don't go pestering your brother. He's coming round nicely.

'You mean the fever's gone?'

Birdie smiled. 'Yes, but he's still very weak. Listen, Pat, there's something I have to tell you.'

'What?'

'You know I went to see Dad yesterday . . .'

'Yeah, but you didn't say much. Just that they was looking after him all right.'

'I don't want to upset you or Frank. But seeing as Frank is better today, I had to tell him the truth. Our dad had a relapse, a stroke, that has set him back quite a bit.'

Pat stood still, his young face bewildered. 'A stroke! But he's got TB. People can't get both, can they?'

'Yes, in a way they are related. It's to do with the stress on the body, Dr Shaw said. Dad's very low, what with the seizures and everything.'

'Has he stopped spitting up blood?'

'I didn't see any.' She didn't want to say just how poorly

their father looked. Pat wanted hope. She couldn't take that away.

'That's a good sign then, isn't it?'

'Yes. Now go in and see Frank.'

He was going to ask more, but she pushed him gently into the passage. 'Go on, your brother is waiting to see you.'

Birdie heard his cry of delight when he saw Frank. And when Harry followed not ten minutes later, he, too, hurried to the parlour. As she went about her chores, she found herself imagining that Wilfred was in there too, reunited with his family, and the grievances of the past had all been forgotten. She would hold the picture in her mind of him looking well and happy again, and hope that wish came true.

'One day I was told to load these boxes that were bloody heavy,' Frank said hoarsely that night as they gathered together in the front room by the fire. 'They come off a Russian ship and, on the quiet, I had a gander inside. The moment I saw it, I knew it was explosives. Felt a right twelve-inch rule, didn't I? So I tried to make a break for it, but Erik, the bugger, caught me and shut me up in that pigsty. She came each day, trying to persuade me . . .' Frank swallowed hard and looked into the fire, 'but when I wouldn't play along, then came the rough stuff.'

'Oh, the devil-woman!' Birdie felt anger prickle every part of her body.

'Got to give it to her, though,' Frank said with a sigh, 'she had me on a piece of string up till then.'

'Did you know they tried to take Birdie?' Pat asked.

Frank looked shocked. 'No, I bloody didn't.'

'It was Harry that stopped them.'

'I owe you a lot, mate,' Frank replied, turning to Harry. 'And you didn't know who I was from Adam. And I couldn't believe my eyes when I saw you lot running into the yard, your mates with their shovels flyin' everywhere and that big bastard on fire, screaming at the top of his voice. I thought I was seeing things. But then you and Pat was dragging me down from the wagon and I thought, blimey, my prayers have been answered!'

'But alas,' Harry muttered, 'we were too late to stop her.'

'She can handle that wagon as good as any bloke,' Frank nodded, his face dark and drawn.

Birdie knew that although no one said it aloud, they were all wondering what or who she would harm next.

'What do we do now?' Pat asked. 'What if the law comes round?'

Harry sat forward, his elbows resting heavily on his knees. 'As soon as you feel up to it, Frank, you could come down to the airey. They wouldn't look there. They've searched the place thoroughly already and they know I only rent the rooms.'

'You sure, mate?' Frank asked. 'What if they catch you helping me?'

'I'll take that chance.'

'I won't stay long. I've got to get across the Channel.'

Birdie looked at Harry. Did he think, too, that Frank's idea was just a pipe dream? How would he ever do that without being caught?

'Frank, you have to get better, first.'

'Yeah, I know. And there's something else I want to do.'

'What?'

He rested his head back on the pillow and sighed. 'Before I leave, I've got to see Dad and tell him my side of the story. I've got to . . . somehow, I've got to . . .' Frank's head dropped to one side and a loud snore rippled through the room.

Birdie gently pulled the cover over him, and Pat and Harry quietly left the room, closing the door softly behind them.

In the glow of the fire, she returned to sit in Wilfred's chair, watching over her brother as, for the first time since his rescue, he slept peacefully. The sharp lines of his face reflected the anguish he had suffered. If only their father would forgive him! But in her heart she knew that it was as unlikely to happen as was Frank's dream of being a free man again.

Chapter 40

The next day, Frank got up and dressed. 'Me stomach feels like it's not seen food for years,' he said as he hungrily ate the last of the bread in the cupboard.

'I must do some shopping at the market,' Birdie murmured, reflecting that it was now possible, with Frank being on the mend, that he could eat her out of house and home.

'You go, gel. But I've got no money to give you.'

'Don't worry, I've got some of Lady Annabelle's money left. She paid me for her party frock, one that she's going to wear at Easter. But I've yet to deliver it.'

'Don't mind me, Birdie. I'll make meself at home.'

Birdie smiled. 'It's just like the old days.'

'Yer, I could get used to this.'

Birdie felt sad. How Frank must have missed his home. Even now, his future was in jeopardy. Could he really clear his name? He was in limbo and they both knew it.

'Don't answer the door when I'm gone,' Birdie instructed as she put on her coat. 'Or go outside. Ma Jenkins is always on the lookout.'

Frank laughed. 'She ain't changed, then. Always was an old gasbag.'

Though Birdie didn't really want to leave Frank alone, she also wanted to deliver Lady Annabelle's frock, the final adjustments now neatly done. It was an opportunity she might not get again before Easter. Placing the frock over her arm under a clean cloth and bidding Frank goodbye, she set off for Hailing House.

'Come in, love,' Mrs Belcher greeted her when Birdie arrived, her cheeks glowing red with the brisk walk. 'Is the dress ready?'

'Yes.' Birdie placed it over the chair, lifting the cloth and arranging the folds.

'Oh,' gasped Mrs Belcher. 'Lady Annabelle'll turn a few heads in that. I'll go and call her.'

'Is she here?' Birdie asked in surprise as she warmed her hands by the stove.

'There's a lot going on, love, at this time of year,' Mrs Belcher reminded her. 'We've got the council nurse coming to look at the poor blighters who attend the soup kitchens. They've got to be deloused, or else the walls of the House will be running alive with vermin. Then the ladies are kitting out all the homeless with new clothes after the winter. We'll have to burn most of the cast-offs, mind, and, as I told you, there's a pile of stuff over there from the Sally Army for you to work on.'

Birdie admired the ladies so much. Easter was the beginning of a very busy year for the charity. After the long winter, the poor and homeless who had survived the winter were the first to be put under the council's scrutiny.

'I'll just go and let her know you're here.'

When Lady Annabelle appeared, she pulled Birdie into a warm embrace. 'I'm so glad to see you. What, no Harry?'

'He's at work.' Birdie blushed. 'And anyway, he's got other things to do.'

Lady Annabelle grinned but made no reply as they all

sat in the big, friendly kitchen and Mrs Belcher served tea. 'Now, is that my frock?'

'Yes, it's all done.' Birdie removed the cloth again.

'Oh!' There were gasps all round. Lady Annabelle put it against her.

'Yes, that's looks better,' Birdie nodded, very pleased to see the hem was straight and the little pleat made just the right shape.

Lady Annabelle hugged it to her. 'Thank you so much. I can't wait to wear it.'

'I hope it's a wonderful party.'

Lady Annabelle smiled as she sat down. 'Now tell me what's happened in your life,' she insisted, as Mrs Belcher lowered the hot scones to the table. 'After reading about the shop fire in Poplar I asked Mrs Belcher to call on you. I hope you don't mind?'

'No, it was very nice of you, Lady Annabelle.'

'She assured me you were in the best of health, but that your father has been taken ill?'

'Yes, he's in the isolation hospital at New Cross. The doctor found out he had TB. And since I saw Mrs Belcher, he's had a stroke too.'

'Oh, I'm so sorry.'

'They're doing all they can for him.'

'Poor soul,' Mrs Belcher commiserated. 'Can he speak, ducks?' The housekeeper sighed heavily as she buttered the scones and set a pot of jam beside them.

'He was trying to, though he began to cough.' Birdie glanced at the big wooden clock on the wall. Time was ticking by. Although it was nice to be sitting here, enjoying tea and scones with Lady Annabelle and Mrs Belcher, she was thinking of Frank. Was he safe to be left alone?

Lady Annabelle looked concerned, her big grey eyes creasing at the corners as she frowned. 'I was very sorry to read of the fire. But very relieved when Mrs Belcher told me you had not been involved.'

'I don't think me future is in the shop,' Birdie announced. 'Don and me have decided to part.'

Lady Annabelle discreetly touched the corners of her mouth with her white napkin. 'Well, as you can see by the amount of work we have put aside, over there – 'she pointed to two large bags stowed by the hearth – 'there is enough to keep those clever fingers of yours active for simply ages. And if you are happy to take what's there, and since we haven't the assistance of that very nice young man who brought you last time –' she gave a mischievous smile – 'then James, our chauffeur, will take you home.' She added very quickly, 'Birdie, may I tell all my friends who made this lovely dress?'

Again Birdie blushed.

'I hope you haven't forgotten the suggestion I made,' Lady Annabelle said before she could answer. 'I would be very pleased to bring one or two of them round to you, to discuss the matter.'

Birdie's thoughts flew to Frank. She couldn't have anyone come to the house, not whilst he was there. 'I'm afraid I can't at the moment . . . er . . . with Dad so ill and needing visits.'

'Of course, but perhaps when he's recovered.'

Birdie was about to leave when Lady Annabelle took her arm. 'What news, if any, of Francis?'

Birdie gazed into the young woman's gentle, refined eyes. How could she even begin to explain what had happened?

'Not a thing in the paper,' interrupted Mrs Belcher, and when Birdie looked at her she caught a little twitch of her eye.

'Well, keep up your spirits, Birdie,' Lady Annabelle said kindly. 'Now, I shall find James and have him take you home. Again, thank you for such a beautiful creation.' She smiled, adjusting her fine, soft woollen sleeves of the expensive jacket she wore. Leaning forward, she kissed Birdie's cheek.

'She's very fond of you, ducks,' Mrs Belcher remarked when they were alone.

'And I'm fond of her.' Birdie felt the familiar guilt weighing her down. Lady Annabelle was always so kind and caring. What would she say if she knew the truth?

Mrs Belcher opened the back door. 'It's chilly but spring is on the way. Now, I've some nice fresh vegetables in this bag and a chicken that I was going to roast for the ladies, but they decided they are going to eat up West tonight. Lady Annabelle told me to take it home and make use of it, but I've already got a nice bit of beef for tomorrow. Now let's get those bags aboard.'

When at last Birdie was ready to leave, Mrs Belcher hugged her. 'Don't forget what I said when I came round, ducks, will you? There's ways and means, remember?'

Birdie looked into her eyes. What was she trying to say? But all too soon, James, in his smart uniform was waiting with the car door open, and the moment passed.

That night, Birdie cooked the chicken for supper. It had tasted delicious with Mrs Belcher's fresh vegetables. And there was enough to see them through to next week, if she did a little bubble and squeak. Frank was very thin, but he ate all he was given. As they enjoyed the meal, Birdie wondered if he would speak more about Inga. Last night he had woken and called out. Birdie never heard him say Inga's name, but he was trying to warn someone. She still wasn't convinced this woman was out of his thoughts.

Harry and Pat scoured the newspapers afterwards, hoping to read an article that would shed light on Inga and Erik's activities. Eventually Harry read out, 'Last night, close to number ten Downing Street, the peace was broken by an explosion. One policeman was injured and a man's remains were found in the debris of the horseless wagon. Evidence found at the scene suggests this is the work of a disparate Russian group, protesting against the withdrawal of Allied forces from Russia.'

'They pretended they was my friends,' Frank nodded slowly. 'But I know they only wanted someone to blame for their crimes.'

'What happened to Erik that night?' Birdie asked curiously.

'No one saw him,' Pat answered after a while. 'They all scarpered.'

'Could it be Erik they found?'

Once again, everyone looked at Frank. He was the only one who knew Inga well enough to know if she would kill one of her own for the sake of their cause.

But if Frank guessed the answer to that, Birdie decided, he wasn't about to say. And she was beginning to believe that Inga's hold on him was still just as strong as ever. She had come to the conclusion that he had fallen for the Russian woman in a big way. Perhaps she had told him that she was in love with him and convinced him they had a life together. Even though Frank now knew this to be false, his broken heart found it hard to accept the truth.

'It might be safer if Frank moves down in the airey with me without delay,' said Harry, breaking into Birdie's thoughts. 'Just until we decide what to do.' He glanced at Birdie. 'If that copper comes round again, you'd be able to open the door without any worry. Or if anyone calls, you can carry on as normal. Otherwise you'll be jumping at every knock.'

Birdie looked at her brother. 'What do you think, Frank?'

'I reckon that's best,' he nodded. 'I don't want no trouble for you, Birdie, or Pat.'

'I can come down and see you after work,' said Pat eagerly.

Frank grinned. 'I'll be a man of leisure for a while.'

Birdie knew he was trying to make the best of things – they all were. But he had only just come home and she didn't want him to leave so soon.

Much later that evening, Birdie stood beside Frank and Harry. Her heart squeezed tightly. She was saying goodbye to her brother once more. Though Harry had promised to look after him, she felt as though the family was being divided again.

'Pat's downstairs waiting to welcome him,' Harry reassured her as he picked up the bag of Frank's few possessions. 'We'll go out the back alley and nip round to the airey steps. I'll go first and give Frank the all clear. But it's Saturday and we've waited for the pubs to turn out. We ain't gonna be spotted at this time of night.'

Birdie looked at her brother. His close-cropped ginger hair was hidden under a peaked cloth cap. Underneath, his honey-coloured eyebrows grew bushy over his long, fair lashes. It was decided that he should wear Wilfred's heavy tweed coat buttoned securely across his chest and heavy boots so that he would look like every other working man on the island. His blue eyes were big and childlike in their dark sockets and his shoulders were hunched, as though he was carrying the weight of the world.

'Now, Harry will be coming in for his dinner, as usual,' she reminded him briskly in an attempt to disguise her dismay. 'And I'll be putting a good solid meal in the bag, to bring down to you each night.'

'Thanks, gel.'

'And Pat will be calling in every day when it's dark,' she added. 'I'll come down meself when I get the chance.'

'I'm gonna miss seeing you each morning and getting me porridge cooked.'

'You'll have to cook it yourself now. We've been lucky so far, that bobby ain't called again,' she encouraged him, 'but we don't want to push our luck.'

'You're right there, gel,' he nodded obediently.

'Well, good night, then, love.' She went on her toes and he put his arms around her like a child.

'Don't worry about me, I'm on the mend,' he mumbled. 'Another week or two and I'll be fighting fit.'

'I'd expect nothing less of my big brother.'

But as Harry led the way out into the yard and Frank trod slowly after him, shoulders hunched against the cold, Birdie knew that he was only half the man he used to be. Once he had been her older, stronger, wiser brother, with his life before him, his teasing blue eyes and cheeky smile winning all the girls' hearts. But now his brave spirit had been broken by the injustice of war and that woman, Inga.

Would he ever be the same man again, Birdie reflected sadly, the kindest of souls who had looked after her and Pat through thick and thin? Her laughing, devil-may-care brother, who never let a day pass without a smile.

Chapter 41

The next morning there was a loud banging at the door. Birdie looked through the letterbox and saw a pair of eyes looking straight into hers. She gave a sigh of relief.

'Let me in, you lemon!'

Birdie opened the door to a tall woman with fashionable frizzy blonde hair trapped under a blue cloche hat.

'Flo! Oh, Flo!' Birdie gasped as she was squeezed tight. 'I didn't think it was you.'

'I thought you was hiding from me.'

'No, I thought it was the law. Where's the kids?'

'With Reg. Well, are you going to invite me in?'

'Course.'

Flo took off her hat and coat and they made their way to the kitchen. Birdie put the kettle on and turned to find Flo already seated at the table. 'I had to come over. You wrote that letter saying about your dad and the TB and to keep the kids away. But I can't wait any longer. I want to see you. So I thought to meself, sod the TB, I'm going to see me mate.'

'I don't think you could catch anything now.'

'Then why haven't you called round?'

'Flo, Dad's had a stroke.' Birdie sank down on a chair beside her.

'Oh Gawd! How did he get that as well as the TB?'

'The doctor said it might be the strain of everything. He can't speak very well and his cough is still bad. Each time I go, I have to wear a cape and mask, and poor Dad don't even know what day of the year it is.'

'When will he come home?'

'I don't know. But we miss him.'

'Course you do, it's only natural.'

The kettle boiled and Birdie made the tea. When she sat down again, Flo was looking at her critically. 'So how is the new romance going?'

'What?'

'You and Harry, of course.'

Birdie blushed. 'We're just good friends.'

'But I thought you said—'

'No, it's a long story.'

'Go on then, tell me.'

'I'd rather hear about Reg and the girls.'

'They miss you and don't understand why you don't come round.'

'I had to be sure I didn't infect you.'

Flo gave an impatient sigh. 'Listen, you've not gone back to old sober-sides again, have you, and don't want to tell me?'

Birdie laughed. 'If you mean Don, no, we are well and truly over. Not that he gave up completely. He came round and took me to Sunday dinner with Aggie. Flo, it was then I saw it all through different eyes and knew it would have been a terrible mistake to marry into the Thornes.'

'I could have told you that. In fact I did several times, but you wouldn't listen.'

'I had my mind set on marriage, you see.'

'All I can say is, you had a lucky escape. And if you don't mind me saying something else, you want to look after yourself a bit more. Don't let yourself go.' Flo wrinkled her powdered nose thoughtfully. 'You look different to me, though I can't put a finger on what it is. Your hair is all over the place. You used to be so particular once.'

Birdie couldn't help laughing again. 'Trust you to notice.'

'Do you like me new waves?' Flo touched her bubbly blonde curls.

'They're just the job.'

'I got meself a few hours' cleaning at the school. One of the other mums suggested we went up West for a Marcel. Well, couldn't miss an opportunity like that, of course. And whilst I was up there, I bought meself this hat.'

'It suits you.'

'And this coat.'

Birdie nodded at the fashionable deep blue coat that Flo wore.

'So you see, you've been missing out on a lot. If you'd come round sooner, you could have come up with us.'

Birdie smiled. She realized this was a clumsy effort to make her jealous and her smile soon turned into a chuckle.

'What are you laughing at?' Flo asked indignantly.

'Nothing. It's just like the old days, that's all. Seeing you and hearing a bit of good, old-fashioned, down-to-earth normal talk that makes you feel like a woman again.'

Flo grinned too. 'You don't get that with blokes, do you?'

'No, you get a lot of other things, though.'

'Like what?' Flo's eyebrow shot up.

Birdie sighed heavily. A whole lifetime seemed to have shot by since she'd last seen her friend. Could she tell Flo all that had happened? It would be nice to share this heavy weight that had followed her around for so long.

'Well, I was nearly kidnapped.'

'What!' Flo almost choked on her tea. 'Who would want to kidnap you?'

'A very nasty woman, who pretended to befriend Frank so that she had someone to blame for blowing up a wagon near Downing Street.'

Flo stared at Birdie open-mouthed. 'Brigid Connor, have you gone daft?'

Birdie smiled. 'No, and you might have trouble believing me, but if you like, I'll tell you what's been going on. But you must promise not to say a word, not even to Reg. All right?'

'I don't tell him nothing anyway,' shrugged Flo. 'So that won't be difficult.'

'After leaving Aggie's that day I went round to dinner, I just couldn't go home. So I caught a tram to Aldgate.'

'What did you do there?'

'Nothing. I ran out of money and had to walk home. I was even going to call on you and pour out me troubles . . .'

'You should have. Nothing like this ever happens to me,' Flo giggled.

'It really began with Frank's escape.' Birdie told Flo

everything, from that moment to the meeting at the pitiful slum in Shadwell and his rescue, finally ending with Frank's return to March Street and his hideaway down in the airey.

'So he's here? Downstairs?' screeched Flo.

'Yes, but you mustn't tell a soul.'

'Blimey, no wonder you didn't want to let me in.'

'I thought it was the police.'

'What's going to happen now? What's Frank going to do?' Flo burst out. 'And what about your dad and what's he gonna say when—'

'Flo, I can't answer your questions. I don't know meself.'

Flo reached over and grasped her hands. 'Listen, if you want any help, just say. Me and Reg ain't much, but we're your mates. Frank can even come and live with us, if it's safer.'

It was then that Birdie's resolution failed and she burst into tears. Flo was so kind and meant what she said. 'Thanks,' was all Birdie could mumble as Flo hugged her tight.

'Go on, dry your tears. Now, you and me are going back to see Reg and the girls. They've missed you.'

'What about the TB?'

'Bugger that. A bit of fresh air will do you good.'

'I was going to see Dad.'

'Can't you go tomorrow?'

Birdie nodded. She felt very down, but Flo's company was cheering and she longed to see the girls. And perhaps the fresh air would help. And with luck, tomorrow Dr Shaw would be on duty and she could speak to him.

It was late on Sunday night that Harry noticed Frank was becoming irritable. The scar on his head and his cuts were healing and his general health had improved. But whilst he had been occupying himself as best he could, the strain of the empty hours were showing in his restless behaviour.

After Frank had eaten the supper that Birdie had sent down in the shopping basket, they sat and talked, mostly about the army, in front of the roaring fire. 'I've been reading your books, Harry,' Frank said, nodding to the shelves.

'Any one in particular?' Harry sat himself by the fire, pulling off his working boots and easing his back.

'Yeah, it's this.' Frank selected a large, leather-bound atlas and returned to his chair. 'I've been looking at where me battalion was holed up. It was Arras.'

Harry studied the map and nodded. 'Arras took a pounding.' He frowned at Frank. 'You were there?'

Frank nodded slowly. 'We was with the Canadians, about the pluckiest buggers I ever met. There was traps everywhere, trenches full of bodies. Sometimes we were standing on 'em. There had been snow . . .' Frank's eyes moved into the distance. 'They looked like they was covered in sheets, till our boots marked them and the blood mingled with the mud. We didn't care. We were just fighting for our lives. They were dead. Gorn for ever. There was sod all we could do for 'em. It went on like this for days, the bitter wind howling so loud we couldn't hear the tanks, rolling into the wire and taking down the bodies stuck to 'em. We found where the Huns had built their lines. Our guns was frozen to our hands, but we pressed forward, into their machine guns rattling bullets like rain. It was then we all got separated.'

He swallowed, passing his hand over his face then drawing his fingers down his shirt. 'I found meself alone and some of them poor Frenchies ran out. This old bloke stumbled forward by this tractor and some of his mates tried to follow. I shouted, "Take cover, you silly bugger, we ain't saved you yet."'

Harry felt all the memories tumble back as Frank spoke. For he too had seen men die so cruelly that, until he heard Frank's words, he had locked the sight away.

'Then I saw this Hun appear,' Frank continued as if to himself. 'He was on his own, like me. He was gonna shoot 'em all, these poor defenceless bastards.' Frank cleared his throat with an effort. 'So I ran at him and stuffed me bayonet through his back. Not once or twice, but I kept on going, again and again. And then I got this bang on me head and I fell down on top of him. I looked him right in his dead eyes. He was only a kid, just a kid. I thought, I'll see this youngster that I've just sliced up. I'm gonna meet him at heaven's gate.' Frank looked up slowly. 'It's all come back, see? I was so ashamed of meself I must have blocked it out.'

Harry sat in silence, until he brought himself to say softly, 'It was war, Frank. You did what you had to do.'

'I killed others, see, but at a distance. I never looked in their eyes.'

'Frank, did you tell your CO this when you was returned to your unit?'

'Nah, you're the only one I've told. See, I never give that Hun a chance.'

'You killed him, yes, but you saved those others.'

'Didn't occur to me that the army would think I'd done a bunk. That's why I gotta get to France. Go back to this place, try and turn somethin' up.'

'Yes, but how?'

'I'm gonna stow away.'

'You're what?' Harry stared at the haunted-eyed, sallow-faced man, bearing a halo of ginger-red hair. He had come to like and admire this person, who went about the airey quietly and cleanly, and who had gradually revealed his thoughts on the hell he had endured.

'That's me plan.'

'Frank, we'll talk about this again.'

'You think I'm off me rocker, don't you?'

'No. But it's early days yet.'

Frank collapsed back and closed his eyes. 'I've spent a lot of time thinking. And now I just have to do it.'

Chapter 42

On Monday, Birdie slipped out early to the corner shop just to buy a few provisions, in case she didn't have time when she came home from the hospital. But on her return, she saw Ma Jenkins, her arms folded over her bosom and a paisley turban wrapped round her head. She was talking to Vi and Annie Carter, who, when they glimpsed Birdie, stepped quickly inside. Only Ma Jenkins remained, a defiant glare on her face and her small, spiteful eyes trained on Birdie as she approached. Then, as Birdie drew level, her attention was taken by a blue uniform that appeared to be standing inside her house.

Her heart leaped as she saw Pat, his face pale and anxious as he stood in the passage. Constable Rudge, his hands clasped behind his back, rocked back and forth, a smug smile on his face as Birdie hurried towards them.

'What's going on?' she demanded, trying to hide the fear that was quickly filling her. 'Why are you home?'

'I took the day off. I wasn't feeling well. Then this lot comes hammering at the door.' Pat stopped abruptly as the policeman's gaze fell accusingly on him.

'The lad was about to tell you that your little game is over.'

Birdie stood still, trying to quell her panic. 'I don't know what you're talking about.'

'They took Harry,' Pat burst out.

'Harry?' Birdie glanced down the airey steps where she saw another policeman stationed. 'But why?'

'He's an accomplice to a crime, ain't he?' PC Rudge boomed.

'What crime?' Birdie stood beside Pat. 'What are you talking about?'

'Aiding and abetting a criminal, that's what.'

'They're after Frank,' Pat said in a shaken voice. 'Three of them arrived in this big motor vehicle. A copper in ordinary clothes, and them two. They searched all over, then went down to the airey.' He lifted his shoulders and looked into her eyes as if to warn her, before saying, 'I couldn't do nothing, Birdie.'

Birdie felt fear and anger rise inside her. Pat hadn't said they found Frank. So where was he? And how did the law know he was here?

'A nice man like Harry Chambers,' Birdie accused angrily, 'you should be ashamed of yourselves. He wouldn't harm a fly. Now, if you're finished turning me house upside down, you can get out.' Birdie stuck her hands on her hips. The policeman hesitated but only for a moment.

'Good riddance to bad rubbish,' she called after him.

'I couldn't stop them,' Pat said in a rush, his eyes wide and frightened. 'I just got home and there was all this thumping at the door.'

'But where's Frank?' Birdie breathed softly. She still felt they were being listened to.

'Don't know.'

She put her finger to her lips. 'Let's see if they're gone.'

They stood together at the window in the parlour. The two policemen were talking outside and strode across to Ma Jenkins. She unfolded her arms and wagged a finger fiercely.

'I'll bet it was her,' Birdie breathed angrily. 'She's pointing to the airey.'

'She must have seen Frank and told them,' Pat murmured.

'But when?'

'When he left, I suppose.'

'But why did he leave?'

Birdie sank down on a chair. 'Oh, Frank, what have you gone and done? They're sure to find you now.'

Pat sat beside her. 'They might not. He might be on his way to France by now.'

'But why didn't he tell us?' Birdie looked fearful. 'You don't think he would . . . No he wouldn't!'

'What?' Pat looked alarmed.

'Could he have gone to find *her*?'

'Who?'

'Inga, of course.'

Pat shook his head. 'He doesn't know where she is. Anyway, our Frank's not that daft.'

'Not daft, but perhaps possessed,' Birdie whispered sadly. 'He might know where he can find her and was afraid to tell us, so strong is the hold she has over him.'

'So what do we do?' Pat said dejectedly.

Birdie watched the two policemen leave Ma Jenkins and walk along March Street. 'The only thing we can do. Carry on as normal.'

'What about Harry?'

'I'll think what to do later.'

Pat looked unhappy. 'Sorry I didn't go to work, but I wanted to see Dad. I just said I wasn't well in front of the copper.'

'Oh, Pat, I can't blame you for that.' She patted his shoulder and with a deep sigh, gathered up her things. She knew Pat wanted to do something to help Harry, but she couldn't think of a plan. She hoped that by the time they got to the hospital, at least one of her prayers would have been answered and Wilfred would be making a recovery.

Harry sat in the empty room fitted only with a grimy wooden table and two chairs. A smell of stale tobacco and sweat hung to the smoke-stained walls and badly varnished dark wood. Opposite him sat a thin, hawk-eyed police-man, who went by the name of Detective Inspector Puxley, who had, for the past three hours, been grilling him, asking him the same questions over and over again.

'So you deny any knowledge of Francis Connor, or his whereabouts?' persisted the copper aggressively.

Harry shrugged. 'You've got me name, rank and serial number. What more do you want?'

'So,' sneered the copper, thrusting back his lank, greasy hair and lighting a cigarette, 'we've got a smart arse here, have we?' He blew the smoke across the table into Harry's face. 'Do you know you could go down for this?'

'For what? I've done nothing wrong.'

'You expect me to believe that?'

'It's the truth.'

The Inspector leaned an elbow on the dirty table. 'Connor was seen at your place. We've got an eye witness.'

'So you keep telling me.'

'Then why not co-operate, chum? You don't want any part of this, not really. You tell us you're just the lodger – nothing to do with the Connors – so what do you owe them, other than the rent?'

'You're right,' Harry nodded casually. 'I pay my dues and keep to meself. That's how I like it.'

'Not according to some,' smirked the policeman. 'You put yourself about a bit with the woman of the house.'

'Ah,' said Harry, nodding slowly. 'You've been rabbiting to the old gasbag across the road.'

'She knows the Connors well, so I'm informed.'

Harry laughed. 'And that's why you're up the Amazon without a paddle, mate, listening to the likes of her.'

The detective made a sucking noise and spat tobacco from the side of his mouth. 'Oh, so it's going to be like that is it?' he grimaced spitefully. 'Well, by the time you face the old beak, sonny boy, that smile will have left your face.'

Harry knew he was being threatened, but the one thing in his favour was that he truly didn't know where Frank was. He hadn't seen him leave and as far as he knew, no one had spotted Frank move down to the airey, or the police would have nicked him sooner. There was no evidence in the airey to connect him to Frank, just a comb and packet of Woodbines and a cutthroat, and they could be any bloke's. The coppers were up a blind alley.

'He's been with you, ain't he?' the detective probed again.

'Who?'

'You know bloody well who. That old girl described him down to a T, red hair and all.'

'So what does that prove?'

'That he was there in your gaff, you cocky devil.'

'He could've been sitting on me steps.' Harry smirked. 'In fact, I'd say that is the long and short of it. He come calling, found no one above and parked himself for a breather, hoping to escape the long arm of the law. Course, he didn't reckon on old eagle-eyes across the road.'

The policeman pushed his cigarette butt into an already over-flowing brown-stained ashtray. 'You're not helping yourself by being smart.'

'Didn't know I was. Never had any brains, me.' Harry disliked intensely this arrogant, ferret-faced charmer and was certain that the detective couldn't pin anything on him, not unless Frank spilled the beans when and if they caught him. And under normal circumstances, however, Harry was certain that Frank was no snitch. But these were not normal times for Frank, and there was something amiss with him running off like he had.

'Sad case, ain't you?' muttered the policeman, standing up and prodding Harry hard in the shoulder. 'We shall see what a bit of solitary does for them missing brains of yours. We'll find that shit-scared deserter, you know. It's on the cards. He's making mistakes, and when he makes the next one, we'll grab him and he's gonna sing like the proverbial canary, taking you down with him as he goes.'

Harry felt another prod and another, and knew it would go on like this, as he gritted his teeth and prepared for a long night ahead of him. Or, if the copper had his way, a lot longer.

Chapter 43

'Miss Connor has never spoken about another member of the family.' The nurse stared up at Frank, her slim eyebrows knitted together.

'I've been at sea. I ain't seen me dad for ages.'

'Your sister isn't visiting with you?'

'No. Come on me own today. I just got a few things to say to me dad, private, like, before I go back to me ship.'

The nurse looked unimpressed. 'You may not be acquainted with our rules. They are very strict and we only allow close family to visit our sickest patients. Even then, there is procedure to be followed.'

'If you say so, missus.'

She looked him up and down and he wished he'd shaved that morning. But the urge to see his father had over-whelmed him so suddenly that he'd just thrown on his coat and cap and walked up the airey steps, as though he did it every day of the week. Perhaps it had been a bit of a mistake after all the trouble everyone had taken, but he'd managed the walk to New Cross without being spotted.

No copper had stopped him and he'd seen a few. But he'd just walked on; he was going to see Dad and it was as though everything else, like getting to France and proving his innocence, suddenly seemed far away. All his concerns were lost in the burning desire he'd had to see Wilfred. And now he was here and it would only be a minute before he saw the old man again.

'I'll just report to Sister. I will need her permission.'

'I can't stay long,' he replied uneasily. 'It's that boat, see? I gotta catch it soon.'

'I'll do my best,' the nurse replied, giving him a long frown as she departed.

Frank stood alone in the corridor, intensely aware of the urgency inside him. It was a sort of pull, low down in his gut, like an invisible cord that ran between him and his father. It felt like it had wound out to its fullest extent ever since France, and now there was only one way to go, and that was to reel himself back in, holding tight until he looked Dad square in the face.

Frank blinked his eyes to clear them. Peace floated around him like a milky sea. He hadn't felt like this in a long while, not since he was a kid and there was only him and Birdie, and the smell of the docks all around them as they roamed on the foreshore by the barges.

'Mum, if you're listening, it's your boy, Frank here,' he said out loud, smiling into the distance. 'I reckon me and Dad have got a lot of catching up to do. I only hope he believes what I've got to say. But I'd regard it as a favour if you'd give me the right words to say, put 'em in me head like, so our dad and me can make up and we can be the family that we were once, when you was here.' Frank braced his shoulders and cleared his throat roughly.

The room had a wicker chair in it that looked like a bed, positioned by a tall window that overlooked a garden.

Under his mask Frank took a deep breath at the sight of the frail figure half lying, half sitting there. He walked slowly forward, not expecting the sharp jab of emotion that deepened into an intense pain in his ribs as he sat down on the wooden bench provided. Everything in the room was a dull white. The walls, the doors, the cape he had on, and the old man's face. It wasn't like a real face, it was like marble, sculptured and smooth, and the two eyes in it were like marbles, dark and brown and staring at him. Right at him. Beneath, a lop-sided mouth was wet with spittle. Frank swallowed hard.

'Dad, it's me, Frank.'

There was no reply, well, not much anyway. A croak perhaps. But Frank knew that his father was listening. He didn't know how, but he knew it.

'I suppose it's me that's gotta talk and it's about time I did, ain't it?' He laughed unnaturally, the echo going round the room. The nurse had gone out, leaving them alone briefly and Frank pulled the bench closer. 'Can't make meself understood in this.' He tore the mask away. 'That's better.'

Wilfred moved fractionally, though Frank couldn't see quite how as he was wrapped round in hospital blankets. 'Dad, we ain't got much time, so I'll spit it all out best I can. They never give me chance to tell you, see? But I bloody didn't desert, I swear I didn't, and that's what I've come to tell you.'

Frank saw the movement in his father's fingers and before he could stop himself, though he'd been warned not to go near, he was at his father's side. Leaning over him he whispered, 'I'm sorry I mucked everything up. I never meant to. I never ran away. I did something else I wasn't proud of, see? I killed someone, a Hun, just a kid really, like so many of them and our lot, were. I'd killed before, must've done, but I never done it in no one's back and this kid, not much older than our Pat, was the one that played on my mind.'

Wilfred exerted a little pressure on his fingers and for one exultant moment, Frank thought he saw the tilt of a smile. It was all wobbly and wet, but it was the light in the eyes that meant the most, the light that meant his dad was pulling on that cord too and they were almost joined again. 'I never deserted, Dad. I was wounded and that's what kept me from joining me company. I wouldn't disgrace you. I love you, Dad.'

Frank slid his arms gently round the frail body. He knew that when he was old, he, too, would look like this. He felt the separation between them but also the closeness; he knew then what life was about, and death too. And everything in between, that seemed to have no meaning, but was in fact, the very knuckle of existence. Like love and forgiveness and hope. He bent down and put his lips to his father's cheek.

The next moment he looked into Wilfred's eyes and heard a cough catch in his throat. He watched helplessly as the old man's chest swelled upward in a choked gasp. Frank was about to shout for the nurse, but Wilfred's fingers tightened around his and stayed so tight that Frank knew this moment was just for them. It was a moment he'd waited for, for so long and he was hardly able to believe it had finally come.

By the time Birdie and Pat had changed buses and arrived at New Cross, it was the middle of the afternoon.

'How is our dad?' Birdie asked hopefully as she found a nurse she recognized coming out of the ward. 'Is he any better?'

'Have you seen Sister?'

'No. Why?'

'I think you had better speak to her.'

'Perhaps Dad is better now,' said Pat when they were left alone in the long corridor.

'Yes,' Birdie nodded. 'Oh, Pat, I do hope this is good news.'

But when the sister walked towards them, Birdie felt the strength seep from her legs. 'What is it?' she asked, looking into the sister's sad gaze.

'I'm very sorry, very sorry indeed, Miss Connor.'

Birdie stared at the woman, who took her arm and led her and Pat to a seat in her small room. Birdie sank on the chair. Her legs seemed to have no life in them.

'Your father passed away peacefully just after one o'clock today.'

Pat let out a choked moan. 'It can't be true – it can't!'

The sister looked at Pat sympathetically. 'I am truly sorry.'

'What happened?' Birdie asked in a flat voice.

'He wasn't alone. In fact it was remarkable that your brother came when he did.'

Birdie looked up, a sob in her throat. 'My brother?'

'Yes, Mr Connor, who has been at sea. He was with your father when he died.'

'But . . . but . . .' Birdie looked at Pat, then at the frowning woman. 'Our Frank was here, in this hospital, with our dad, do you mean?'

'Yes. You haven't seen him?'

'No.'

The sister sighed and folded her hands in her lap. 'He did impress on us that he had very little time.'

'Did . . . did Dad recognize him?' Birdie could barely breathe in her distress. Was this why Frank had left the airey? Had he come to see Dad? It wasn't Inga that he had been thinking of at all, it was their father.

'Yes, your brother thought so,' the sister nodded. 'I assume they were close but separated by your brother's profession?'

Birdie glanced quickly at Pat's stricken face. She knew that they had to go along with whatever Frank had told the hospital.

'If there is any comfort I can give you, it was that he was not alone when he died.'

Birdie's eyes filled with tears.

'I'll leave you for now.' The sister stood up. 'Dr Shaw is on his rounds and will make out the death certificate but you will have to wait.'

'Did my brother say anything?' Birdie whispered forlornly.

'No, only what I've told you.'

'He left no message for us?'

'Not to my knowledge.'

When they were alone, she looked at Pat. 'Frank was with Dad when he went. We should be happy for them both.'

'But we weren't there,' Pat whispered tearfully. 'I ain't ever gonna see me dad again.'

'One day you'll take the good from this. Our Frank and our father were reconciled.'

'There's never any good comes from dying,' Pat shouted and jumped angrily to his feet. He brushed his face with his sleeve.

'Pat, Dad will always be with us, like Mum is. They're together now and happy again.'

'That may be true for you, but it's not for me.'

Pat ran from the room. Birdie sat, trying to think, to reason with her grief and her shock and find some consolation in the fact that, with Frank beside him, Wilfred hadn't left this world on his own. But in her heart, there was doubt. Why hadn't they been able to say their goodbyes too?

Chapter 44

On a wet and grey April morning, two days later, just as Birdie was about to leave the house, the back door opened and a tall, tousle-haired figure stood there.

'Harry! Oh, you must think me terrible not trying to help you! But I thought it best, for your sake. If they knew we was friends—'

He put up his hand as he closed the door quickly. 'Never mind that, Birdie. There's something I have to tell you.' The lines of tiredness showed at his eyes and round his mouth as he came close. 'You'd better sit down.'

'It ain't Pat, is it?'

'Frank's given himself up.'

The feeling came back that she had had at the hospital, and she sank down on a chair, her mouth falling open. 'Why did he do that?'

'The copper that gave me a right ear-bashing at the nick just told me that I was free to go as they'd pulled in Frank. He turned up at Poplar nick on Monday. They can't have got anything out of him, though, or else I wouldn't be here.'

'Frank gave himself up on Monday?' Birdie repeated. 'On the day Dad died?'

Harry stared at her. 'Christ, Birdie, you mean your dad's passed away?'

She nodded, unable to reply.

'I'm sorry,' Harry said in bewilderment. 'I didn't think that was on the cards.'

'Me and Pat went to see him and was told that Frank was with him when he died.'

'Frank?' Harry shook his head slowly. 'You think the reason he left here was to go and see your dad?'

'I feel so guilty. I thought it was to do with Inga.' Her voice faltered. 'When all the time, it was Dad he was thinking about.'

Harry let out a long sigh, his brow creased in a frown under his dark hair. 'Blimey, he never said a word to me.'

'I hope they made up, like Frank always wanted.' She smiled. Though Pat had said nothing good came from death, in this case, perhaps something had.

Harry put out his hand and gently touched her arm. 'You can be sure that Frank did his best. It shows the mettle of the man that he threw everything aside to make peace with your dad. You can't speak higher of a bloke than that.'

Birdie knew that was true. Frank's concern had not been for himself but with Wilfred. She had trusted Frank all along, but even she was struggling to recognize the fact that Frank had thrown away his chance of escape to put affairs of the heart and conscience first. What more proof could anyone want that Frank was no coward?

It was the week before Easter and the Requiem Mass was held for Wilfred in a church filled with those eager to pay their last respects. Birdie was dressed in a sombre black coat and felt hat that had been brought out of mothballs for the occasion, and Pat, in his Sunday suit, stood next to Harry, ready to support the coffin on their shoulders. At the sight of this and the bunches of violets that she and Pat had picked in the graveyard where Wilfred was to be buried, it was difficult to hold back the tears.

Outside the church, she thanked those who had attended: Wilfred's friends from the Quarry and Bernie Hopper, the landlord, Mr and Mrs Mason and Willie, even Amelia Popeldos and Mrs Kirby, who seemed to have forgotten their indifference to an old neighbour. It was Ned Shorter and Lofty, who had not known her father, who touched her by their presence and genuine concern.

There was also Mrs Belcher, and Flo and Reg and the girls, who all held her close for a brief moment, murmuring precious words of comfort. There were others too, figures from Wilfred's past and factory days. Though Birdie was grateful so many had come, she was relieved when at last the ordeal was over and finally Lady Annabelle arrived to take her and Pat in the chauffeur-driven car to Kensal Green, where Wilfred would be buried beside Bernadette, in the Catholic cemetery.

But it wasn't until Birdie stood at the graveside that she gave way. As Pat felt her tremble, he took her hand and clutched it as the simple coffin was lowered gently into the gaping hole beside their mother's grave, and Father Flynn completed the burial service. When the dirt had been sprinkled on the coffin, Pat dropped in a sprig of purple heather, their mother's favourite flower.

'I'm taking meself off for a breath of fresh air,' Harry stepped forward to say quietly. 'Lady Annabelle's waiting for you in the car.'

'Thank you, Harry.' She watched him walk away, his tall figure weaving slowly between the headstones. She knew he wanted to collect his thoughts.

'Do you really think Mum and Dad are together now?' Pat asked as Birdie slipped her arm through his.

'Yes, course I do.'

'But all that's left is just a lot of earth over Dad to say he ever was alive.' He shuddered. 'I'd rather be a sailor and get ditched at sea.'

Birdie smiled understandingly. 'Our mum paid for the plot before you was born, love. She didn't have much money to spare, but Catholics are particular about where they end up. You and me should be grateful that we didn't have to witness our dad going in a pauper's grave.'

An April breeze swept across the churchyard as if in answer, ruffling the tangled weeds and brown grass. Birdie knew that it would be a long time before either of them came here again. She brought flowers to Bernadette's grave once a year, on her mother's birthday. But she never felt Bernadette was there. She was closer when she looked at the picture on the mantel. It would be at home they would find comfort in the memories of the happy lives they had led as a family.

As Birdie was about to follow Pat into the waiting vehicle, a hand grasped her shoulder.

'I was very sorry to hear the sad news,' Don said as he stood breathlessly beside her. He wore a long, smart, dark coat with a black velvet trim and black tie, as though he too had been one of the mourners. 'I would have got here sooner, but I was detained at the store. I do hope you will allow me to place this on your father's grave as a tribute from Mother and me.' He raised a large and imposing wreath made of expensive laurels.

Birdie was surprised to see him but all the same she nodded politely. 'Dad's buried over there, beside Mum.'

'We were truly shocked to hear the news,' he went on, seeming not to want to leave. 'Brigid, I know this isn't the time or place, but I still think of you and hope that one day we might be together.' Without warning he bent and kissed her cheek, whispering again how much she meant to him.

Why had he come here today, she wondered. He hadn't cared about Wilfred in life, so why in death? All the same, emotion filled her and without a word more, she climbed into Lady Annabelle's car.

'Is Harry home yet?' Birdie asked as Pat walked into the kitchen later that afternoon and placed the last empty plate on the draining board.

'No. Must have needed some air.'

Birdie looked down at the few triangles of curled bread that hadn't been eaten, the remains of the wake she had prepared for those who decided to call by. There wasn't much left for Harry, but she had kept a thick slice of ham and cold pickles for him, under the muslin in the larder.

The first through the door had been Mrs Kirby and Amelia Popeldos, who had sat in the parlour with their glasses of port wine, all grievances of the past apparently forgotten. Bernie Hopper had provided the ale and port wine, and Flo and the kids had just said goodbye as Reg had to get back to work. Willie's mum and dad had accompanied them, and Lady Annabelle had been driven home by James, leaving Mrs Belcher to remain behind and help Birdie with the clearing up.

'Just pile those last plates here, ducks,' Mrs Belcher told Birdie as she stood at the sink. 'We'll soon have them washed.'

Just then Pat raced into the kitchen. He slid off his tie and pulled open the top buttons of his collar. 'Now I've done my bit, can I get changed and go out with Willie?'

'No, it wouldn't look right,' Birdie told him, only to draw an immediate protest.

'Listen to your sister, lad,' Mrs Belcher called firmly as she scrubbed the dishes. 'Tomorrow will be here soon enough, and you'll be out on your bicycle again, delivering your messages.'

Birdie saw Pat turn sulkily away, flashes of red on his cheeks. She gave a long sigh as he slouched out of the kitchen.

'Take no notice, he's at that age,' Mrs Belcher smiled as they stood together at the sink.

'I wish Frank was here.'

'Where is he love, back in Wandsworth?'

Birdie shrugged. 'No one will tell us. I went up to Poplar police station where Frank had turned himself in. But they claimed they wasn't allowed to tell me anything.' Birdie dried the plates slowly. 'Mrs Belcher, I have to admit, I'm frightened. Will they ever let us see our brother again?'

'They've got to. They can't just lock him up and throw away the key.'

'It ain't right, I know, yet what can one person like me do against the authorities?'

'I told you, there are ways and means.'

'It's too late for that sort of thing.'

Mrs Belcher turned round and lowered her voice. 'It's never too late to make a stand for justice. You've seen those suffragette ladies, haven't you, with their banners, and undergoing those dreadful hunger strikes in prison?'

'But how can I do that? I can't see me marching up to London and knocking on the Prime Minister's door to tell him about Frank. Although I would, if I thought it'd do any good.'

Mrs Belcher picked up the towel and, after drying her hands, looked Birdie steadily in the eye. 'Are you willing to take me into your confidence and tell me the truth, the whole truth about Frank? And I mean by that, all that's happened that you haven't told me, and probably not told another soul in case you should make it worse for Frank?'

Birdie stared at this surprising, elderly rosy-cheeked woman, who stood with her head tilted to one side. 'How do you know that?' gasped Birdie.

'Because I know *you*, love. I know your family and the strong bond between you all. You'd face the devil himself if it was for the benefit of each other.'

Birdie sank down on a chair. 'Oh, Mrs Belcher, you wouldn't believe the half of it. When I think back meself, I wonder if it all really happened.'

Mrs Belcher bustled to the kitchen door and closed it. Then she peered out of the kitchen window. 'No one about, so come on, ducks, out with it, while we still have the chance.'

That night, Birdie sat alone in the parlour. Pat had gone to bed and Harry hadn't come home for his supper. She stared at Wilfred's empty chair and wondered if she had done right to reveal her secrets to Mrs Belcher? The story had seemed incredible, even to Birdie's ears: Frank's visit to the house after his escape, their meeting under the arches the next day and his involvement with the Russians. Mrs Belcher's eyebrows had risen as she'd listened, and she'd muttered encouraging sounds at the tale of Harry, Pat, Ned and Lofty and their assault on Shadwell. But when Birdie had finally come to the end, explaining Frank's determination to see their father in hospital, Mrs Belcher had said in a firm voice, 'Very well, dear, thank you for trusting me.'

After yet another cup of tea, Mrs Belcher had left with the promise she would soon be in touch and in the meantime Birdie was not to worry.

But as Birdie stared at Wilfred's empty chair, it was not worry for Frank or even Pat that tugged at her heart and caused a great, aching space inside her. It was, she knew, a deep longing to see and touch the father that she had left behind her in that cold and unwelcoming place of last goodbyes.

Harry sat himself down at a quiet table in the Nag's Head. He'd downed a couple of sterling good ales, but as he pondered over the day, the alcohol did nothing to cloud the memory of Birdie and the shopkeeper, standing beside Lady Annabelle's car. Harry had skulked by a clump of leafless trees and watched, listening to the shovelling of dirt, with his heart dropping to his boots as Birdie had been taken in an embrace and, to his everlasting dismay, not seemed to resist.

Then he'd seen the car drive off and when it was out of sight, Don Thorne had shouted to the groundsman, who had made his way over to take the wreath he had been holding. Harry had then watched the smartly dressed man, who was obviously in too much of a hurry to pay his respects at the graveside, climb into a motor car parked just outside the gates. It wasn't as big or flash as Lady Annabelle's but was impressive enough. And it was then the fierce pains of jealousy had beset Harry, crawling under his ribcage and into the muscles of his heart, which truly felt gripped by a vice.

Harry passed his finger round the rim of his froth-stained glass and shook the dark liquid. Throughout Frank's disappearance and Wilfred's illness he'd indulged in the thought – the hope – that he could provide the Connors with something they did not have: true friendship that came only infrequently in life. But having achieved this goal, his own feelings had strayed far beyond friendship. And it was as he had witnessed Don Thorne once more re-enter Birdie's life that Harry knew for certain: his feelings of deep strength could never be returned.

He took a long gulp from his glass, then got up and left, to wander around in the damp, early evening, finally making his way down to the park, where he had once sat with her. And when he had first allowed himself to think that it was possible for a man like him to have a family and a home.

A few days later, Birdie and Pat had just finished supper, but Harry's place at the table was unoccupied. Both she and Pat had made a brave attempt to enjoy the thinly sliced meat, roast potatoes and vegetables that had been cooking slowly on the stove, but even the custard that was poured thickly over the bread pudding was proving a challenge.

'Harry wouldn't miss this,' Pat decided as he spooned the hot pudding carefully into his mouth. 'I reckon he's got a girl.'

Birdie frowned at her brother. 'But we thought that before, yet he told me he didn't have one.'

'Why else would he miss his grub? And he's not been home much since the funeral.'

Birdie nodded. 'Perhaps you're right.'

'It don't seem like home,' sighed Pat, managing to finish the last mouthful. 'Not without Dad and Harry.'

'We can sit by the fire and play dominoes.'

'I've something to tell you first.'

'What is it?'

Pat twisted his spoon in the bowl. 'Mr Marchment called me in to his office last night. He told me the Steamship Company had asked him for a reference of my abilities.'

'Why would they do that?'

'Don't you remember, I applied for a job with them? The purser had said he would have taken me and Willie on but the company was selling to another operator.'

Birdie shook her head. 'I thought it was just one of your adventures you wanted to go on.'

Pat looked down at the table again. 'Mr Marchment said he put in a good word for me and I've got a test very soon.' He added hurriedly, 'Mind, it won't be much, I expect, just baker's scullion or something. And if you said you were against it, well, I shouldn't bother.'

Birdie stared at her brother. 'Is it what you want?'

'I can't deliver messages for ever. I'm growing out of my tunic.' He looked into her concerned gaze. 'But with Dad not being here, I'd understand if you was against it.'

Birdie saw the disappointment in his eyes. 'Pat, I won't be the one to hold you back.' She reached out and put her hand over his. 'This is your life, your chance to do as you want. Nothing must stand in your way.'

Pat's face brightened. 'I'll come home between trips.'

'I'd be cross if you didn't.' She smiled. 'Mum and Dad would be so proud of you.'

Pat sniffed and once more lowered his head.

'But as there's only me to wish you success, love, come here and give me a hug.'

They embraced and Pat mumbled, 'Birdie, you're the best sister anyone ever had.'

She pressed him to her, against the ache that filled her chest. It wasn't the best news she had ever had, but she was filled with happiness for Pat. 'This is your dream coming true,' she whispered, wondering how many years would pass before the Connors were all to be reunited.

Chapter 45

It was on a late April evening when Birdie ran into the street, ready to stop Harry as he came home from work. She hadn't seen much of him since the funeral but she had received a letter that morning that had made her jump and scream aloud for joy.

He strode towards her and waved, his work-bag slung over his shoulder and his collar turned up against the biting cold.

'Harry!' She ran up to him and clutched his sleeve. 'I've some wonderful news!'

He smiled, his dark eyes shining out of his weather-beaten face. 'Pat beat you to it. He told me yesterday that he was successfully tested for the steamer job and starts next Monday.'

'Yes, I know that, and it is wonderful, but this is even better.' She waved the envelope in his face. 'Even Pat doesn't know this yet, as the postman only delivered it this morning after he'd gone. I must show you.'

'Me boots are filthy.'

'It doesn't matter.' She pulled him into the house, where he stamped on the mat and dropped his bag on the floor, careful not to let any mud go onto the boards.

'Don't stand there. Come in by the fire.'

'No, I won't thanks. I've, er . . . got to nip out again.'

Birdie frowned, her excitement dying. 'Harry, what's the matter? We ain't seen nothing of you since Dad's funeral.'

'I'm just a bit pressed for time.'

'If you don't come right in this moment, Harry Chambers,' she threatened him, 'then you'll be missing out on the best news it's possible to have, better even than a field of shamrocks from the Emerald Isle.' She laughed, her heart feeling so light, she could hardly say the words.

'Well, put like that . . .' He followed her in, going to the fire and warming his cold hands. 'That's a good blaze you've got going. Just like the ones Wilfred—' He stopped and gave a click of his tongue. 'Sorry, I keep forgetting.'

'So do I,' she said quietly.

He smiled. 'Go on then. What was you going to tell me?'

Birdie pushed the long, slim envelope towards him. She had kept it close to her all day, reading it over and over again ever since the postman had slipped it through the letterbox. There was a seal on the back, of red and gold wax, indented with the sender's initials, HW.

'Blimey, that looks posh.'

'Read it, Harry.'

'Not with me filthy fingers. You do the honours.'

She drew out the smooth, buff-coloured paper and held it out so they could both see the professionally scripted words. 'It's from a firm of solicitors called Hethrington Wright,' she said, trying to contain her excitement. 'Their offices – can you believe? – are in Westminster, and Lady Annabelle's country address is written at the top too. It's

Mr Hethrington himself who has written this.' She cleared her throat, giving Harry a nervous smile before she began.

'Dear Miss Connor,
  I am writing to tell you that Lady Annabelle Hailing has engaged our services, in respect of your brother Mr Francis Connor, who at present is detained at Her Majesty's convenience for an unspecified period. Lady Annabelle has provided us with comprehensive details of Mr Connor's (unjust) dismissal from his regiment and subsequent term of imprisonment, leading to his escape from custody in November of last year. This evidence has been brought to light by a team of private investigators who have been deployed to the regions of France where your brother served between the years of 1915 and 1917. These new, incontrovertible facts we believe, will be pertinent to an appeal, which, if necessary, shall be taken to the High Court for review . . .'

Birdie stopped, drawing her finger gently under her eye. She could not believe yet that Lady Annabelle had done all this for them.

'Is it true, Harry? Am I dreaming it?' she whispered. 'Is Mr Hethrington going to help Frank?'

Wiping his hands on his jacket, Harry reached out for the letter. Silently he studied it and Birdie's heart beat fast as she waited. At last Harry nodded, lifting his gaze to hers. 'Looks like they're trying to get Frank off the hook.'

'Do you really think so?'

'It sounds that way.'

'Mrs Belcher said there were ways and means. But I didn't think she meant this. I thought she was talking about something a bit underhand, not at all legal like this.'

'That's what a bit of clout does for you,' Harry smiled,

returning the letter to Birdie. 'Frank's in with a chance now.'

'I daren't hope too much.'

'They must have searched all of bloody north France.'

'More than Frank could have done on his own.'

Harry scratched his head. 'It's that word they used, the long one, what was it?'

'In-con-trovertible,' Birdie said without hesitation. 'I've read it over so many times, I can say it.'

Harry shrugged. 'What does it mean?'

'I went up to Pat's room and looked in his dictionary. It means, it can't be proved false.'

'Blimey, that's a turn up for the books.'

'Oh, Harry,' she gasped, 'I asked Mum to help us and I believe she did.'

'You could be right there.'

She wanted to put her arms around him and hug him, but now there was an awkwardness between them, a distance that seemed to have happened since Wilfred had died. 'You've been a true friend, Harry,' she said gratefully instead.

She saw the light in his eyes fade as he softly replied. 'I'll always be your friend, Birdie.' He looked away. 'Even from across the other side of the world.'

'The other side of the world?'

'You know we was talking once – about the places we'd like to see? Well, I've made up my mind that as soon as you and Pat was all right, like – and now I know you are, with Frank's troubles likely to be sorted – I'm going to scratch that itch before I grow old and grey.' He gave an uneasy laugh. 'See, I've made enough on the drains to take meself off to the one special place—'

'That mountain that looks like a table?' she whispered slowly, 'where a person can see all of Africa and smell the perfumes of heaven itself.'

'Blimey, you remembered.'

'Yes, every word.'

The silence lingered in the room, his words drifting around them, creating as they had done before, a picture that Birdie knew herself she would never have the chance to see.

'Ned and Lofty are gonna take Albert and the cart on,' Harry continued, 'till I let 'em know what me plans are. But I reckon it's time for a change as I've not had me heart in the job recently.' He paused and added hurriedly, 'Owing to me wanderlust, an' all.'

Birdie turned to the fire, her heart heavy once again.

He took her arm gently. 'We'll stay good pals, won't we? I'll send postcards, cross me heart. You can put 'em up on yer mantel and remember me now and again.'

Birdie gazed into the fire, which, before Harry had told her he was leaving, she had thought of as the symbol of her hope for a new family life. One that she had wanted to share with him, believing that they would come to know each other fully as time went on. And one day perhaps, become more than just good friends.

But now she knew it was all a dream that could never be. One gift had been given to her today and one had been taken away.

Chapter 46

July 1919

Two weeks had passed since Frank had been granted his freedom after an appeal, when Birdie's spirits had been high one day and low the next. With Pat away on the steamship, she had been very lonely. And though Harry had promised to write, only two postcards had arrived. They were very beautiful – of a lush, green land with a sea so blue surrounding it that Birdie knew it was a heaven no man would want to leave. Like Harry had said once, a place where you could smell all the perfumes of heaven. He had got work in the mines and intended to try to make it his home, he had written.

But these last few weeks of waiting for news from Mr Hethrington had eclipsed everything else in her life. When would Frank come home, she wondered.

The answer had come yesterday when Lady Annabelle had called round and given her the news that James was to bring Frank here this very morning.

Birdie smiled at the wonderful memory. She had temporarily forgotten Lady Annabelle was from a well-to-do family and had thrown her arms around her in a warm embrace. In delight, Lady Annabelle had teased her, saying that now Birdie must return the favour by making lots of wonderful dresses for her friends.

Birdie had agreed without hesitation. She would have agreed to anything in that precious, unbelievable moment.

Now Birdie stood waiting, the door open wide and all of summer rushing in. Dressed in her floral frock, with her shining brown hair waved gently around her ears, her heart pounded as she looked along March Street. Lady Annabelle had told her mysteriously, that Frank was to be accompanied by two other people. Birdie wondered who they could be. Were they the private detectives who had secured the vital evidence? Or perhaps representatives from the court? But wasn't Frank done with all that now? He was a free man. She had said it over and over again in her mind. Frank was free and proved innocent!

Ma Jenkins' curtains were twitching across the road and Birdie smiled, knowing the small, sunken eyes of the mischief-maker of March Street were watching her every move. But today Birdie felt nothing but happiness that even Ma Jenkins could not dispel.

A car turned the corner and Birdie thought she might faint with delight. The big black shiny vehicle drew slowly along the road as if James was driving royalty along Pall Mall.

Birdie's head was held high and her heart full of pride. Slowly each door in the street opened: the Kirbys, Edna Legg and Marjorie Coombs, the Popeldos family, even the Carter sisters, with all the kids tumbling out to see Frank Connor returning home.

When James stepped out of the car, he gave a brief salute, lightly touching his flat peaked-cap. Birdie blushed. She knew he was doing this for all to see. Then he opened the rear door and a young woman stepped out. Her long fair hair tumbled to her shoulders, partly covering her anxious eyes. Behind her appeared the tall figure of Frank, who wore a light-coloured jacket and open-necked shirt. In his arms was a small, red-headed child with laughing blue eyes, a mirror image of Frank himself. And Birdie's heart leaped as the happy trio walked towards her.

Epilogue

Cape Town, South Africa, September 1920

Warmed by the burning African sun, Harry stood in the long queue waiting to board the *Kensington Castle*. Above him the lower deck of the stately mail ship was already crowded with passengers. Anxiously, he patted his cream linen jacket pocket, unconsciously confirming the presence of Birdie's letter, arrived at his rooms in Johannesburg just a month previously.

Harry glanced up at the clear blue sky and thought of the day he had arrived in Cape Town sixteen months ago. Then, he had been welcomed by a thick, impenetrable mist that had descended over the harbour, forcing the captain of the steamship to ferry the passengers by launch to land. It was a week until Harry had managed to see clearly the flat-topped mountain that he had read about so often in his books. The climb to its lower ridge had been every part as breathtaking as he'd dreamed it would be. Here, he'd breathed in the salt of the sea mingling with the lush scents of the land, and found it was not Africa that filled his heart; instead it was a longing for the woman he had left behind in Blighty.

After that he'd tried to lose himself in the big country, from Port Elizabeth and East London and Durban, to the mining town of Jo'burg. Here, the hard life had suited him best; toiling daily in the bowels of the earth and by night, facing the cold rasping winds that blew clouds of dust along every gravel road and pathway. He'd even welcomed the deafening roar of the mine batteries that pounded ceaselessly, and the gruelling shifts that turned out every white man as black as his brother. He'd posted a couple of cards back home, but he'd had no word back, until that morning when he'd received Birdie's letter.

The queue began to move upward and Harry lifted his travelling bag. He went slowly, savouring the experience of leaving African soil. The noise of the big red and black funnel above him joined with the shouts and cries of the porters who scurried between the passengers.

When at last Harry stood on deck, no longer buffeted by the choking winds of a mining town, but caressed by the warm summer breeze of the Cape, he gazed back at the land that had provided him with such good fortune. He had tasted the magic of Africa, and he admired the majesty of the mountain, as flat as any pancake and a sight to behold in the dazzling sunshine. But now it was time to go home.

'Goodbye, Africa,' he whispered, narrowing his eyes at the spectacular scene. Then, unable to resist the urge to read Birdie's letter again, he drew it slowly from his pocket.

'My Dearest Harry,

Thank you for your wonderful postcards and the photographs of South Africa. I should have written sooner, but I thought it wasn't fair to say all that is in my heart, not after you wanting for so long to take that adventure you dreamed of.

Now more than a year has passed and there is much to tell you. I'll begin with Frank, his wife Françoise, and their young son, Frank Junior. He is just the image of his father, with red hair and Frank's sunny smile. The family have settled well at March Street and you may ask how they (the family) fetched up here, so I'll begin.

After your departure, it was Mr Hethrington (whose letter you read) and acting on Lady Annabelle's instructions, who arranged passage for Françoise, Frank Junior, and his grandfather, Pierre, from Arras to testify on behalf of our brother. How all this came about was that Pierre is the farmer that hid Frank when he was injured. He saw Frank shoot a Hun in defence of his friends and Frank being injured in the head after. Mr Hethrington, in possession of this information, asked him and his daughter, Françoise, to be witnesses at Frank's appeal and so they agreed.

It turns out that whilst recovering our Frank was swept away by the charms of the angel of mercy (Françoise) who nursed him back to health. Would you believe that little Frank Junior is the result? At Frank's trial the old beak made some crack about his war wound not being that disabling. This, as you can imagine, is a tale that Frank loves to repeat! But, at the end of it all, justice was served and it was proved that Frank was no deserter but a hero, who returned to the front line just as soon as he was physically able. Lady Annabelle paid every penny of Frank's defence and pulled a few strings into the bargain. That was what Mrs Belcher was hinting at all the time, and me, I was blind to it!

And as for that cheating shopkeeper I once was daft enough to moon over, Lydia gave him his marching orders and married the vicar, Mr Howells. I can imagine they will live a very Christian and God-fearing life, giving James a good home at last. But Aggie, so it's said, has never recovered from the shock. The new store I hear, has gone down the pan, and God forgive me, I can't be sorry for the Thornes, not one jot!

Oh, and there is Pat, who is still sailing with the steamers, but lives for the day when he'll see you again. He has grown up now, a fine figure of a young man, mature in many ways, which are, not least, down to you, his best friend.

So now, that's my happy story, that is to say, very nearly happy. For Harry, life has not been the same without you. The empty airey reminds me daily of our loss – my loss. You saw us through such ups and downs that it seems downright unjust you're not here to share in our joy. Each morning, after praying to Mum and Dad (who I know are happy together now) I look at my black cat broach and think of you. But I would rather have you here, with us all, where I could see and touch the object of my great affection.

So if it is at all possible you feel the same too, I beg of you, Harry, to consider returning home. Your home, March Street, as it will always be.

With love it is that I end this letter. True love, Harry, not just the deep like of a friend.

Yours, as I will always be,

Birdie Connor

PS. We heard no more about the Russians. P'raps they blew themselves up? Frank insists he was never put under a spell by the woman, just that he had his head turned by the breeches and those dark eyes that she kept dazzling him with, and that in the end it was the pure and sweet face of Françoise and his son that returned him to sanity! Have you heard that that fearsome man Lenin is in charge of all Russia now? Frank says the Whites have had their chips.

One more thing, Flo and Reg and the girls send their love and hope to see you again and hear all your tales. And another development – with Frank home and the toast of the neighbourhood, Ma Jenkins don't even look out of her window and her head sinks deep into her hat when she ventures forth!

And, by the way, I got your address from the cards you wrote and hope this letter finds you safely.

And now I'm finished at last, your Birdie.

As the vessel drew slowly out of harbour, Harry reflected that a good and loyal woman had finally been the saving of Frank. Leaning over the polished guardrail, Harry smiled ruefully. For it wasn't the mountain of his dreams he was seeing under the flawless turquoise sky, but the face of his own good woman, Birdie Connor, whom he had never ceased to love.